Praise for Thomas Fleming's *Remember the Morning*

"In *Remember the Morning* Tom Fleming lays the foundation to a classic historical series, a saga that fires the imagination and stays with you for a long time after you read it. This is an important book, but also a delightful read, as the pages seem to turn of their own accord."

—Margaret Truman

"What a stunning book—two dramatic and powerful women, radically different yet bound together by love, heritage, experience, circumstance, in a blazing tale that plumbs morality as brilliantly as it illuminates a crucial part of the American past. A tour de force."

—David Nevin,
New York Times bestselling author of *1812*

"Tom Fleming has created an inspiring tale, a *Gone With the Wind* set in pre-Revolutionary America!"
—Jack Anderson, Pulitzer Prize–winning columnist

"The historical details that run through the saga are marvelous and fascinating. That the central characters are strong women who are anything but victims, resonates with the 1990s, particularly to women readers."

—Sybil Downing, author of
Ladies of the Goldfield Stock Exchange

"*Remember the Morning* is a wonderful American panorama! I read it with admiration and delight. Thomas Fleming brings the Colonial period of our country's history to full life—this is a learned, passionate, and completely absorbing novel."

—Max Byrd, author of the bestseller *Jefferson*

REMEMBER

the

MORNING

Thomas Fleming

FORGE®

A TOM DOHERTY ASSOCIATES BOOK
NEW YORK

To Alice and Gary

This is a work of fiction. All the characters and events portrayed in this book are either products of the author's imagination or are used fictitiously.

REMEMBER THE MORNING

A Forge Book
Published by Tom Doherty Associates, Inc.
175 Fifth Avenue
New York, NY 10010

Forge® is a registered trademark of Tom Doherty Associates, Inc.

ISBN: 0-812-50849-1
Library of Congress Card Catalog Number: 97-16643

First edition: September 1997
First mass market edition: September 1998

Printed in the United States of America

0 9 8 7 6 5 4 3 2 1

We are lost in the heart of time!
What peace to be so lost!
But we must go on.

JANET LEWIS
CORA'S SONG
FROM THE OPERA
THE LAST OF THE MOHICANS

PROLOGUE

✺
ONE

WHAT A STRANGE CREATURE MEMORY is. Half a thing of dreams, half raw pulsing flesh. Half an enemy, half a friend. The enemy lurks like an Iroquois in the forest of the past to ambush the unwary wanderer. As she writhes in his grip, her lips feel the caress of kisses—and terror turns inexplicably into love.

I am writing this in my Louis Seize parlor looking out on the broad waters of the Hackensack River. Surrounding me is the furniture of wealth: robin's-egg-blue Queen Anne armchairs and couches, a lofty Sheraton secretary, a rose-red Aubusson rug. Opposite the window is a dignified portrait of me in middle age by my younger son, one of the best painters in America. The resolute mouth, the cold defiant eyes, win my reluctant approval—until memory hurls imprecations at them—and silvery soprano voices fill the room with a song.

> *Ter roorches, ter roorches*
> *She Mameche bucleche, broche*
> *Ter roorches, ter roorches*
> *As me mither le waffles she boxes*
> *De butter la door de groches*
> *Ter roorches, ter roorches*
> *She Mameche buckle che boo.*

I am back fifty years watching five-year-old Catalyntie Van Vorst sing that song. Beside me sits my favorite playmate, Clara, whose gleaming black hair is a lovely counterpoint to her creamy brown African skin. On the other side of the mahogany table looms a big grey-haired man with a hooked red nose and ruddy cheeks and a balloon of a belly bulging against his green waistcoat. He is my grandfather, Cornelius Van Vorst. He is singing the song too, beating time in the air with his long-stemmed clay pipe.

The song mixes English, Dutch, French, and Irish in its paeon of praise to *ter roorches*—hot waffles. What echoes of unfathomable love are in those silly buoyant rhymes! Love wound like an enigma into the facts, the faces, the tongues of history. *Ter roorches* was a New York song, redolent of the nations mingling on the noisy twisting streets of the little city at the tip of the island the Indians called Manahatta.

Now, fifty years later, in the next room I can hear my husband and my older son discussing the latest news from London. *Taxation. Taxation without representation.* The indignant words swirl through the house. The upheaval that I foresaw long ago, the revolution for which my Dutch blood has hungered for decades, is beginning. The arrogant men in London would continue to misjudge and misrule the Americans in the name of an idiot king and their own immeasurable greed.

I will play no part in this upheaval, nor will my husband, even though he might try. Revolutions are the property of the young. Already knowing how it will end, I can barely summon interest in the process. I prefer the company of memory, my half enemy, half friend.

Pettikin.

How cruel memory is—and how wonderful. To compress a lifetime of love into a single word. Was the whole secret of the story in that word? Could an old man's love be unwound like a silver thread to stretch from this expensive room down the shining river to the tumultuous streets of New York and up the mighty Hudson to the silent forests and surging rivers of the virgin continent? Could that strand of love cleanse fifty years of wars and revolts, regrets and betrayals? Can it exorcise so much spilled blood, so much torment?

Clara's dusky voice whispered in my throbbing heart. *Perhaps it's time. You have my permission to speak for me. But I warn you, no one will believe it. God's purposes are too obscure for human hearts. Do you have the courage to tell the whole truth—especially about yourself?*

For a moment I was almost ready to surrender my role as memory's scribe. But I still possessed some of the flintiness of that cold-eyed woman on the wall. Memory also remained a creature with stony eyes and nerves of brass. The story began again, as insistent, as irresistible, as the river. I heard Cornelius Van Vorst's husky baritone teaching me about the onrush of the world's most ineluctable mystery, memory's wry collaborator, time.

Believe it not, Pettikin, when I was your age singing ter roorches to my dear mamma, there were barely a hundred houses on Manhattan. Now we have nine hundred in the city alone. There were scarcely a thousand people on the whole island. Now we have nine thousand in the city alone. Three hundred ships a year sail from our docks. Little did I think I would roam the five seas and see so much of the world when I sang ter roorches on our farm in Bloomingdale. Who knows what you may do or see in your day?

"AHHHHHHHHH! AHHHHHHH!"

The scream leaps from memory to smash through fifty years. Its blare annihilates Grandfather's voice and the town of Hackensack and the river of the same name, the peaceful fields of New Jersey, the winding streets of New York. It is 1721 again and I am five years old, staring sleepily at Clara. In the flickering candlelight my playmate clutched her mother's long cotton nightgown, which seemed doubly white against her black skin. My own mother stood in the doorway, a frown on her severe earnest face.

"What is it, sweet?" asked Clara's mother, Myrtle. "What's wrong?"

"I saw an Indian," Clara sobbed. "I saw an Indian hurting you. I saw Indians hurting everyone. Master, Mistress, Catalyntie. Everyone!"

"It was only a dream, sweetness," Myrtle said in her soft dark voice.

"No, it was real. It will happen! I don't want to go to the Mohawk country," Clara sobbed.

"There's nothing to worry about, Clara," I assured her with serene confidence. "The Mohawk Indians are Grandfather's friends."

Clara sobbed and trembled until her mother gave her warm milk and honey and hummed her to sleep with a lullaby. I watched, a little envious. I almost wished I would have a bad dream so I could have some warm milk and my mother's arms around me.

None of us, adults or children, gave a moment's thought to the possibility that Clara's dream might come true.

TWO

GODDAMN. GODDAMN-GODDAMN-GODDAMN! GODDAMN!

The curses flew from the lips of the captain of the broad-beamed sloop my father, Hendryk Van Vorst, had hired to carry us up the Hudson River the next morning with our furniture and barrels full of meat and vegetables and boxes full of trade goods. The captain was scolding his crew for not loading the ship fast enough to catch the incoming tide.

"Do you want to take a year and a bloody day to get to Albany?" he roared. He was a chunky red-bearded man with a wooden stump where his right leg had been until it was torn off by a French cannonball a long time ago. He was one of Grandfather's best friends.

Finally Grandfather swept me up on his big chest and kissed me three times for luck. He kissed Clara and my brother Peter and my sister Eva too. He gave my mother a briefer kiss and hugged my father. "God be with you, son," he said. "I hope to visit you in six months' time."

"We'll have a feast worthy of the burghers of Amsterdam," my father said. "We'll turn you into a *boer*, Father."

Although I spoke English most of the time, I knew *boer* meant farmer and *burgher* meant city dweller in Dutch. My father and grandfather had been joking about *boers* and *burghers* for weeks.

"I may convert for the chance to see my Pettikin every day," Grandfather said, sweeping me up for another kiss.

The captain began goddamning his crew again because they were not casting off the lines fast enough. Out onto the broad rippling river the sloop glided. The Africans whom Grandfather had bought to work the land in the Mohawk Valley were in another sloop behind us under the stern eye of Clara's father, Joshua, who was almost as big and fat as Grandfather. With more goddamns from the captain, the sloop's crew raised a wide dirty white mainsail and we began cruising up the river, faster and faster with a brisk wind and a favorable tide until New York was only a few church steeples in the distance.

Eva cried and Peter looked like he might cry too. For the first time I felt sad about leaving New York. I realized I would not see Grandfather for six months. That sounded like a long time to go without hot waffles.

Pettikin. The word whispered loving reassurance in my mind. Peter and Eva got out their arithmetic books and began working on lessons Father assigned them. Mother let Clara and me go out on deck and play at being *boers*. We chattered to our dolls about planting vegetables and picking apples and riding ponies. We watched the scenery along the river slide past. Great high cliffs at first and then big rounded mountains covered with thousands of green trees. Other sloops passed us and called out greetings.

We ate in the cabin with the captain while Father talked about how happy and healthy we were all going to be in the Mohawk country, where the air was pure and the water was clean. Never again would we have to worry about yellow fever and smallpox, those terrible diseases that killed so many people in New York. We were also going to get rich, trading with the Indians. Grandfather had dealt fairly with the Mohawks. He had given them cloth and guns and jewelry worth a thousand English pounds for their land. In return their chiefs had promised Father a rich share of the trade in beaver skins and other furs. They were sure the Van Vorsts would not cheat them like the merchants in Albany.

I did not especially care whether we got rich. But I loved to hear Father talk about it. He looked so strong and brave and handsome when he described how the Van Vorsts would soon be more powerful than the Livingstons and the Van Rensselaers and the other great landowners living along the Hudson River. *Patroons*, the Dutch called them. The Van Vorsts might even make the English bow down to them as they did to Governor Peter Stuyvesant when the Dutch owned New York City and it was called *Der Colonie Nieu Netherlander*.

After five days and nights we reached Albany, where almost everyone spoke Dutch and some houses were as big and fine as Grandfather's house in New York. Nearly all the Albany houses had heavy wooden stoops with seats at their doors. The main street was very wide and led up a hill to a fort. We stayed overnight at an inn with huge fireplaces and a dining room where everyone ate at long tables. We children all slept in one bed and Peter and Eva complained about bugs biting them. In the morning we went to the First Church on Pearl Street and heard a tall thin minister with a face like an axhead preach in Dutch about the importance of obeying God.

During the night our furniture and food had been hauled from the sloops to six big wagons, each pulled by two horses. For most of the day we jolted over a rough road to the town of Schenectady, on the Mohawk River. There the wagoners transferred the goods to flat-bottomed boats called bateaux. Each one had six long oars, pulled by white men with dirty faces and soiled leather coats and breeches. They rowed us up the Mohawk River, past grassy meadows and tall thick trees, until nightfall. We slept in the open around a great fire, while wolves howled in the forest around us. Clara and I were frightened but Father showed us his gun and said he would shoot any wolf that tried to hurt us.

Late the following afternoon we reached a bend in the river and saw our house. It looked like a fortress in a fairy tale, two stories high, made of fat grey stones. It was surrounded by a meadow a hundred times as big as New York's Bowling Green. Giant trees stood silently on three sides. Inside, the rooms were twice as big as the ones in our New York house.

While Mother and Father and Myrtle talked about where to put the furniture and trade goods the men were unloading from the bateaux, we children began exploring our new home. Peter and Eva dashed upstairs to the second floor. Clara and I ran down a hall to the kitchen, a dark cavern at the back of the house.

Braving the shadows, we tiptoed across the stone floor

and peered into the empty fireplace and oven beside it. Soon a fire would be lit and porridge would be bubbling and bread rising. Maybe hot waffles would sizzle on Myrtle's black iron griddle.

Suddenly Clara was screaming and pointing at the window. An Indian was peering through the glass at us. He had streaks of red and yellow and blue paint on his face and brass rings that dangled from his ears and nose.

I had often seen Indians at Grandfather's house. In Dutch they were called *Die Wilden*. They came down the river to visit Grandfather. When he was a young man he had lived in their country, trading with them. I was used to their scanty clothes and strange haircuts with the sides shaved and a narrow ridge of black hair standing up straight in the middle. Grandfather's visitors had sat me on their knees and let me play with the beads and chains they wore around their necks.

But this Indian was not one of Grandfather's friends. He glared at us as if we had done something bad. Raising a big black stick with a round head on the end of it, he smashed out all the glass in the window and jumped into the kitchen. His body cast an oily gleam in the half light. It was streaked with the same red, yellow, and blue as his face. From his mouth burst the most terrifying sound I had ever heard—a howl that repeated itself again and again. Outside it was answered by other howls followed by the smash of more glass.

Pettikin. Somehow the word no longer protected me. I joined Clara in a scream of terror. The Indian had gotten out of Clara's dream. He was going to hurt us.

Pounding footsteps in the hall. Father rushed into the kitchen, his face chalky white, his mouth twisted. "What do you think you're doing?" he shouted. "Get out of my house!"

The Indian hurtled across the room, his club raised, the worst howl yet bursting from his mouth. Father ducked to one side and the club smashed into the wall.

But in his other hand the Indian had a hatchet. The shining steel edge sank into Father's head and he fell against the wall with an awful cry.

"FATHER!" I screamed but it did not stop the Indian. His hatchet flashed through the dim air again and my father fell to the floor, his yellow hair stained with blood, his eyes bulging with dread.

The Indian drew a knife from his shell-encrusted belt and grabbed Father's long hair. Grunting, howling, he cut off the hair and part of the top of Father's head and raised the whole thing in the air to admire it. Blood dripped from the scalp onto Father's face.

"FATHER!" I screamed again. Even now, fifty years, eighteen thousand nights and days later, I cannot hear that word without pain. I flung myself on top of dying Hendryk Van Vorst, frantically trying to clutch his life in my small arms.

The Indian tore me away and hoisted me on his hip like a sack of corn. I squirmed, clawed, spit at him, but I could not break his grip.

Pettikin. The word was slipping and sliding into mockery, horror. In the next room Mother lay on the floor already scalped, blood pouring from a gaping cut in her throat. Clara's mother, Myrtle, was lying beside her and another Indian was cutting off her black hair. Clara was screaming and kicking and hitting the Indian.

Impervious to her rage, the Indian picked up Clara and smiled at her, as if she were a pretty toy he had discovered in the white man's house. When Clara tried to hit him, he laughed and said something to the other Indians, who laughed too, their white teeth flashing in their paint-streaked faces. The sound swirled through the house like the crash of drums.

Outside, Peter and Eva were sobbing and wailing. The Indians had tied leather ropes around their necks as if they were dogs. They did the same thing to me and Clara. Down on the riverbank, other Indians were fighting Joshua and the Africans and the white men who had brought us to this terrible place. They killed everyone except a few white men who jumped into one of the bateaux and escaped downstream.

Clara and I screamed and screamed and finally clung to each other, our eyes closed, trying to escape into darkness, blankness.

When we opened our eyes again the Indians had dragged the furniture from the bateaux to the house and shoved it through the front door and windows and set everything on fire. Flames began crackling and roaring inside the house; smoke gushed from the smashed windows.

"FATHER!" I screamed one last time. For the next eighteen thousand days and nights of my life I would never speak that word again.

Seizing the leather ropes around our necks, the Indians trotted into the forest. In minutes we went from sunlight to shadow. The great trees loomed around us, their leaves so thick the blue sky was lost. Looking back, I saw tongues of fire leaping from the windows of the house, making it look as if it were full of devils. Mother had told me that devils breathed fire from their mouths and noses and eyes. I wondered if the Indians were devils and were taking us to hell.

Clara and I and Peter and Eva had to run to keep up with the Indians. If we fell down we were dragged along the ground until we managed to scramble to our feet again. Soon our hands and elbows and knees and feet were cut and bleeding. No one seemed to care.

Pettikin? I could not understand why Grandfather's friends, the Mohawks, did not help us. Why did these Indians hate us? Were Father and Mother and Joshua and Myrtle killed because they had broken God's law?

When we finally stopped for the night, the Indians flung themselves on the ground and slept. No one lit a fire or had anything to eat. A cold wind swept through the gloomy forest, rustling the leaves of the great trees. Somewhere an owl hooted, a wolf howled. Clara and I clung together, whimpering and trembling.

I wondered if what had happened in the house was a bad dream, like Clara's. Maybe I would wake up soon and Mother would give me warm milk and honey and I would forget the whole thing. I wanted to forget it. I wanted to stop feeling cold and numb and afraid. I wanted to be happy again.

Pettikin. The word no longer meant anything. Memory had become an enemy.

BOOK

ONE

ONE

TWELVE YEARS LATER, IN THE village of Shining Creek on the shore of Lake Ontario, the girl who once had been Catalyntie Van Vorst slept in the longhouse of the Turtle Clan of the Seneca tribe of the Iroquois. I no longer remembered my white name. I was She-Is-Alert, daughter of Early-Day, granddaughter of She-Shakes-The-Trees. (I am translating the Seneca names, which are almost unpronounceable for white people's tongues.) You who will read this story in the distant future may wonder how I could forget my white name and the way my parents died beneath the hatchets of Seneca warriors in that terrible moment on the Mohawk River. Few people understand how pain and sorrow affect a child's soul.

Grief not only makes memory a child's enemy. It awakens in her soul a hunger for love and a desperate desire to escape the shadowy ghosts that loom in dreams and darkness. A grieving child turns to love like a plant to the spring sun, not only for nourishment but for the healing balm of forgetfulness.

I found love in abundance in the village of Shining Creek. Having recently lost a child to sickness, my Seneca mother's heart was full to bursting with love that she yearned to bestow on someone. I became her favorite child—in fact the favorite child of everyone in the longhouse of the Turtle Clan. They were fascinated by my white skin, my blond hair. Other mothers gave me toys. The warriors let me play with their dice and marveled at how often I threw winning numbers. They said I would bring them good luck.

Beyond the longhouse lay the glistening lake and the winding creek from which the village drew its name. With the other children, I swam in the lake and wandered the nearby forest in the spring and summer and fall. I learned to identify the calls of the birds and chased brilliant butterflies around the cornfield as my mother sowed and hoed our golden crop. As the seasons turned and the great trees shed their leaves and budded and shed again at the end of another summer, a contentment that transcended understanding grew in my soul.

When the snows of winter whirled out of the north, my mother and grandmother wrapped me in bearskin against the cold and told me ancient tales about famous warriors and the women they had loved. They told me that someday I would marry a mighty warrior whose deeds would make me and my children proud and happy. Memory, that enemy who inflicted pain, dwindled slowly to a tiny whisper and finally vanished in my new Seneca self.

For years I accepted my mother's assurance that my white parents had died of sickness while journeying through the country of the Senecas and the Master of Life, the being who presided over the world, had sent a hunting party to discover me before I starved to death. How many times did I lift my eyes heavenward and thank the Master of Life for granting me the privilege of becoming a member of the Seneca tribe of the great league of the Iroquois!

Only in the last year, as I passed from girlhood to womanhood, did I begin to realize that my white skin and blond hair made me different from the other young women in the village—different in a way that hurt and wounded, and stirred vague fragments of memory in my soul. On this particular morning of my twelfth year as a Seneca, I was having a dream that reflected these feelings. I dreamed I was presiding over a great feast. Many warriors were there, and many women. I was serving them venison and trout, corn cakes and squash. They saluted me with shouts and chants.

I awoke and lay quietly, thinking of the dream. So much food! But in my waking belly, hunger prowled. Yesterday I had eaten nothing but a few mouthfuls of parched corn. The day before I had eaten nothing at all.

My mother's hand shook my shoulder. "Wake up," she said. "We have something to eat. Your friend Nothing-But-Flowers has left us a bushel of corn."

With a cry of joy, I flung aside my bearskin blanket. It was not the first time Nothing-But-Flowers had saved us from starvation. As my mother combed out my long blond hair and tied it in two plaits down my back, I told her about my dream. My mother excitedly summoned Grandmother to interpret it for us.

Grandmother's wrinkled face glowed with delight. "It can only mean one thing—a marriage! She-Is-Alert will soon find a husband."

My mother struggled to believe Grandmother. She was famous for her skill in understanding dreams. Only the village shaman[1] had greater powers. But my mother had begun to think her white daughter would never find a husband. The young warriors called me the Moon Woman. They said it would be like marrying a ghost. In the dark my white skin and yellow hair would make their flesh freeze. What if I had white children? What good would they be in a night attack? They would have to stain their bodies with the juice of whole baskets of berries each time they went to war.

Grandmother insisted her understanding of the dream was correct. "Before the next snow, She-Is-Alert will meet the warrior she will marry! Perhaps he will be a visitor from another tribe. Many warriors want to join

---

[1] *Medicine man or priest who presided at religious ceremonies, healed the sick, helped mourn the dead.*

the Iroquois, who rule the land from the shores of this mighty lake south to the great ocean.''

Grandmother was always boasting of the power and greatness of the Iroquois. They were *On-gweh On-weh*—''real people.'' Everyone else was a poor imitation. Her pride in the Iroquois was her consolation as she faced old age with only her daughter and adopted granddaughter alive. Her husband and her two sons were dead, the husband killed in war with the Ottawas long ago, the sons in a white man's plague, called measles, when they visited the French fort at the great falls of the Niagara River.

I understood everything that passed between my mother and grandmother, both the spoken and the unspoken parts. I too had begun to think I would never find a husband in the village. My white skin and yellow hair were not the only problems. My grandmother and mother belonged to one of the lesser families in the Turtle Clan. They did not have the power to appoint and dismiss chiefs and sachems, like the matron of the clan. They were not consulted on great decisions of peace or war, of joining the French or the English.

Next year, if I lacked a husband, I would probably become a hunting woman. That was a hard fate. Hunting women went into the winter woods with the warriors who traveled west to trap beaver and otter to sell to the English and French. A hunting woman cooked meals and dressed the skins and let the trappers take her when they felt the need for a woman. If she bore a child, she would never know who was the father. A hunting woman's life was full of cold and sadness.

I tried to put this evil thought out of my mind and waited patiently while my mother cooked the corn and pounded it into cakes. Then all the members of the other families in the longhouse were summoned to the feast. Fortunately there were no warriors—they were out hunting for the game that often mysteriously disappeared at this time of year, after the snows melted but before the first flowers of spring appeared. Even without the warriors, the basket of corn became only a single small cake for each person in the Turtle Clan. But it tasted wonderful. I hurried from the longhouse to thank my friend Nothing-But-Flowers.

It was a beautiful day. The sun glistened from a blue sky on the wide waters of Lake Ontario. Several young women were trying to organize a game of double ball—a sure sign that spring was on its way. My long legs and angular frame made me very good at this game, in which young women chased two deerskin pouches stuffed with feathers tied to a stick up and down the village street. It was a female version of lacrosse, the warlike game the young warriors played with ferocious frenzy.

In double ball, each woman was armed with a stick that enabled her to whip the pouches twenty or thirty paces toward the goal. I loved to score goals. I had won many pairs of mooseskin moccasins and leggings as prizes. Unfortunately, my pugnacious style of play did not endear me to the other young women of the village.

I found Nothing-But-Flowers sitting in front of the longhouse of the Bear Clan, her grandmother plaiting her gleaming black hair. Nothing-But-Flowers had painted several streaks of vermilion on her creamy brown face. Yes, she was my former playmate, Clara, but I had forgotten that name too. I asked her why she had painted her face. Nothing-But-Flowers explained that she had dreamed she would meet her husband today. I thanked her for the corn and decided not to mention my poor dream. Nothing-But-Flowers's dream was so much better.

Instead of desperately inspecting the whole village for a possible husband, Nothing-But-Flowers was allowing *orenda*, the spirit that pervaded all things, to search out the future for her. Everyone agreed that Nothing-But-Flowers's personal *orenda* was very powerful. Her mother and grandmother had seen it the day they adopted her. That was why they had given her a name that predicted she would become a woman with both a beautiful body and a beautiful spirit.

A tall thin young woman named Big Claws sidled up to us. She was one of the worst gossips in the village. "Why don't you loan Moon Woman some vermilion?" she said. "She'd paint her whole face with it and maybe her cunt too but it wouldn't do her any good. Do you know what Running Wolf called her after they went into the woods? Dead Otter."

"Ho!" All the other young women laughed and whirled their ball sticks over their heads. Even Nothing-But-Flowers's grandmother laughed—although usually she was very dignified. As the matron of the Bear Clan, she was the most powerful woman in the village.

I felt so ashamed I wished I could die. Running Wolf was the fourth young man who had taken me into the woods without proposing marriage. He had not been cruel to me. But after he emptied his seed into me he had not been tender. He had spent the rest of the time boasting about what a great warrior he would become when war came.

I often thought about dying, especially during the starving times. My white brother and sister had died in the first starving time after we came to the village. Their Seneca mothers had not liked them very much—especially my brother, who refused to go hunting in the woods when it was cold. His mother had decided he would never become a warrior and stopped giving him food during the starving time.

Nothing-But-Flowers became angry at Big Claws for insulting her friend. "You should talk about not getting a husband. You know what the young men call you? Barking Stick."

Everyone laughed even harder and Big Claws slunk away like a wounded snake. Not for the first time, my heart flooded with gratitude to Nothing-But-Flowers. Everything about her was beautiful, from her spirit to her body, which was small and perfectly shaped, with curving legs and full breasts and slender arms. Yet she always treated me, with my sharp nose and thin lips and white skin, as her equal, her friend. Obnoxious pride seemed foreign to her soul.

Before I could thank her for routing Big Claws, a great clamor began at the other end of the village. Young boys came running from all directions, shouting "Ho, ho!" Dogs barked fiercely. Babies, frightened by the noise, began to howl. In a moment through the crowd burst the young warrior Bold Antelope. He had a buck deer slung over his shoulders. He carried it as carelessly as if it were stuffed with feathers. He flung the dead animal at Nothing-But-Flowers's feet and said: "See what I've brought you and your honorable mother and grandmother? I killed it with a single shot at a hundred paces."

There was, in fact, only one wound in the animal, a bloody patch behind its ear. Nothing-But-Flowers's eyes glowed with admiration. Everyone knew Bold Antelope loved her and hoped to marry her. He was from a lesser family of the Wolf Clan. To marry Nothing-But-Flowers would be a great thing for him. He would join the noblest family in the village. But he could only do it by proving himself a future chief, a pine tree around whom warriors would rally.

Nothing-But-Flowers's grandmother asked if the village's other warriors had found game. "Yes!" Bold Antelope said. "So much that their canoes are almost sinking with the loads they are carrying. I took this buck and went ashore to help keep my canoe afloat. They will be here before the sun begins to fall in the sky."

"Ho!" The young women shouted and danced with joy. The starving time was over! When the warriors returned, we would have a feast. There would be many trips to the woods for lovers. There would be marriages before summer began. There would be babies after the next snows.

"I also brought this gift for you and your honorable grandmother," Bold Antelope said.

From a deerskin pack on his shoulder he drew a scalp, dried and stretched on a hoop, the edges painted red. The hair was golden yellow. "It is a Frenchman's scalp," Bold Antelope said. "We found him and his friends hunting on our lands. When we ordered them to go they threatened us. We opened fire and I killed this one with a bullet in the heart. The rest ran away."

"That was not a wise thing to do!" Nothing-But-Flowers's grandmother said. "At this very moment there is a great council in the land of the Mohawks, trying to make peace between the French and the English and the Iroquois and the Seven Nations of Canada."

"There will never be peace between the white men and us, no matter how many presents they give us," Bold Antelope said.

"That is not for you to decide. That is for the sachems, who will weigh the matter carefully," Nothing-But-Flowers's grandmother said. "You are too young to remember other wars when the French and the Hurons attacked us and drove the Senecas from the shore of the lake. Our warriors had to flee like children to the protection of the Mohawks. The French are as strong as the English up here on the lakes. We must tread carefully between them."

I barely listened to this exchange, although I was usually fascinated by the stories the village's grandmothers told about the old wars of the Iroquois against the French and the Indian nations of Canada. I could not take my eyes off the yellow scalp. It seemed to be turning the inside of my head into a swamp in which thoughts sank like footsteps and snakes rose to twine themselves around the unwary traveler.

The sun whirled in the sky, its rim as red as the edges of the Frenchman's scalp. Was it hunger returning? Surely I could live for a whole day on a delicious corn cake. My friend Nothing-But-Flowers's hand seized my arm. "Let's go for a walk along the lake. Maybe we'll see the warriors returning. We can swim out to greet them."

"You must swim with no one but me!" Bold Antelope said.

"I'm not married to you yet," Nothing-But-Flowers said. "I'll swim with anyone I please."

I heard the spoken and the unspoken parts of this exchange. I knew my friend Nothing-But-Flowers wanted to get me away from the scalp. Perhaps she wanted to get away from it herself. When we were small, we were both afraid of scalps. We would cry and hide our faces when the warriors displayed them in the long-houses.

I also knew Nothing-But-Flowers was not yet sure she loved Bold Antelope. He was still very young and lacked the dignity of Nothing-But-Flowers's father, Hanging Belt, the village's greatest war chief. There were many other young men courting Nothing-But-Flowers. She had no need to throw herself at Bold Antelope.

We walked quickly away from the village, our arms around each other. I had told Nothing-But-Flowers about the swamp that appeared in my head at certain times. Nothing-But-Flowers had told me it belonged to the Evil Brother of the Master of Life, the great God who brought spring and fruitfulness to the world. The Evil Brother was trying to suck me back into the unhappy winters of our girlhood, just as each year he tried to prevent the Master of Life from bringing us the spring. The Evil Brother lived in the cold dark past and he wanted others to join him there.

I listened carefully to Nothing-But-Flowers, as always. I respected the strength of her *orenda*. But her words did not stop the swamp from filling my head. In the gloom ghostly white faces appeared, names drifted vaguely, hissing like snakes. *Vorrrrst*, whispered one. *Vorrrst*. On the branch of a dead tree, an evil crow croaked *Van. Van. Van.* A woodpecker went *Cat Cat Cat.* I knew it had something to do with how I came to the Senecas. But I could not remember any of it. There was only this swamp in my head and a terrible fear in my heart.

I walked along the shore of the lake, my heart almost bursting with gratitude for Nothing-But-Flowers's friendship. Everyone was sure that someday she would take her grandmother's place as the matron of the Bear Clan. She would become the most powerful woman in the village. She would rule the clan's longhouse and their corn and squash fields. Even if I never found a husband, as Nothing-But-Flowers's friend I would always be sure of having food to eat, a warm place to sleep.

"Here come the warriors," Nothing-But-Flowers said. "Let's swim out to meet them."

The canoes came toward us swift as birds on the lake's surface, six warriors in each one, bending forward to take a mighty stroke in unison. Quickly we kicked off our moccasins and stripped off our deerskin leggings and wool dresses and plunged into the water. It was very cold but it felt wonderful on my skin. It was our first swim of the spring. Soon we would swim every day until the snow came.

"We have heard about your good fortune!" Nothing-But-Flowers called as the canoes approached. "My friend She-Is-Alert and I come to congratulate you."

Nothing-But-Flowers's father, Hanging Belt, was in the lead canoe. "Good, good!" he called.

The warriors stopped paddling and drifted toward us, contented smiles on their faces. "Look at these two juicy fish," shouted one of the young men.

"I know where I'd like to hook them," another young warrior called.

Hanging Belt became uneasy. "Does your grandmother know you are behaving this way?" he said. The last thing he wanted was Nothing-But-Flowers's grandmother angry at him. Even a great chief, with twenty-three scalps on his war belt, could not afford to lose the favor of the matron of his clan. She could "knock off his horns" any time she chose.

"Grandmother saw nothing wrong with it," Nothing-But-Flowers said. Her grandmother seldom found fault with anything she did but Hanging Belt was still uneasy.

"Why do you have paint on your face?" another young man asked Nothing-But-Flowers.

She told him about her dream and he immediately became serious. A half dozen young men became serious. All of them had been secretly hoping to win Nothing-But-Flowers's heart and they realized they could no longer hesitate.

As always, I heard the spoken and the unspoken part of what was said. Nothing-But-Flowers was telling the warriors if any of them hoped to win her heart, a friend would have to consider marrying She-Is-Alert. It was the perfect time to suggest such an idea. There would be a great feast and everyone's heart would be light. A young warrior might decide it would be worth marrying the Moon Woman if it earned him the favor of the Bear Clan's favorite daughter.

We swam back to shore and watched the canoes resume their journey to the village. Nothing-But-Flowers looked knowingly at me and we burst out laughing. The swamp had disappeared from my head. I felt free and happy. I loved the way the lake's water gleamed on Nothing-But-Flowers's brown skin. I looked forward to the feast and the games we would soon be playing. Perhaps I would win another set of moccasins at double ball. Perhaps I would have a husband before the next dawn.

Back in the village the excitement continued. People lugged carcasses of deer to the longhouses to be skinned. Older women were building fires. Dogs barked furiously. Little children ran in all directions. The warriors sat in front of the longhouses telling the boys and young women how they had made their kills.

Just as the first odor of roasting meat began to drift through the village, there was a cry of recognition from the south. Into the center of the village strode Black Eagle, the sachem of the Bear Clan, escorted by two Mohawk warriors. A tall commanding old man, Black Eagle had been chosen to represent the Senecas at the Great Council in the Mohawks' country.

"Brothers and Sisters!" Black Eagle said. "I bring news from the Great Council. The hatchet has been buried forever between the French and the English and between the Iroquois and the Seven Nations of Canada. A treaty has been signed and many presents have been received. Our English father has commanded us to make no more war on the French. We have agreed to let the Seven Nations hunt in peace. Our brothers, the Mohawks, have promised in our name that the people of this village, under pain of the severest punishment, would never again make war on the English. I have consented to this agreement as well, in the name of all our warriors. To prove our good faith, I have promised to return the children we have adopted to their English relatives."

A terrible wail burst from the longhouse of the Turtle Clan. From the house hurtled my mother and grandmother, tears streaming down their faces. Another wail burst from the longhouse of the Bear Clan. Nothing-But-Flowers's mother and grandmother rushed into the circle of men and women around the sachem.

"How can you kill us this way?" my mother cried.

"She is my only living child. I depended on her to care for me in my old age."

"Yes," cried Nothing-But-Flowers's grandmother. "How can you kill us this way? How can you take away the most beautiful daughter of our clan? How can you take away the bride of a young man who is certain to become a great chief?"

"What have the English done for us, here in our northern land?" my grandmother cried. "They give all their presents to the Mohawks. The French give us more presents year in year out than the English."

The Mohawk warriors listened to this uproar with stern faces. They could not remain silent in the teeth of this challenge to the league of the Iroquois, which had held the six nations together in brotherhood and friendship for so many hundreds of moons.

"Brothers and sisters!" one of the Mohawks said. "We come here to assure you that the Covenant Chain is still strong, the Pine Tree, the sign of our great league, still stands. Your sachem Black Eagle speaks the truth. We also speak the truth. The Mohawks receive no presents they do not share equally with the other nations of the league. This peace will be a good thing for all the nations of red men. All the tribes of Canada have also agreed to return their captives. We are returning many captives to the French. Let there be no more complaints. The thing must be done!"

The swamp was back in my whirling head. *Vorrrst* hissed the snakes. *Van Van Van* croaked the crows. Fear crawled like a spider around my heart. The Evil Brother was dragging me back into the dark past. He was dragging Nothing-But-Flowers too, in spite of her *orenda*.

Into the circle around the sachem sprang Bold Antelope. He had his hatchet in his hand. A war cry burst from his lips. "You will never return Nothing-But-Flowers to the English alive!" he said. "I was only a boy when Hanging Belt brought her here. I loved her beauty even then. I will not allow an Englishman to enjoy her!''

"We have pledged our honor," Black Eagle said. "If you violate it, you will become an outcast, roaming the woods in the winter, begging for a home with distant people who have never heard of the Iroquois."

"Hah!" Bold Antelope shouted defiantly and flung his hatchet into the soft earth. The edge sank deep into the ground. Nothing-But-Flowers began to weep. She was afraid Bold Antelope would kill her. The swamp heaved and sucked in my head. My thoughts sank deeper and deeper into it, while the snakes hissed *Vorrrsst*. Why was the Evil Brother pursuing us?

Two

THAT NIGHT, IN THE LONGHOUSE of the Turtle Clan and the longhouse of the Bear Clan, although there was plenty to eat, there was no joy, no dancing. Instead everyone sang songs of the dead. Our mothers and grandmothers wrapped themselves in black shawls and wailed for their daughters. Flying Crow, the village shaman, wore the false face that frightened away the evil spirits who always sought to capture a dead person's soul. He brandished his rattles, he howled defiance of the Evil Brother and his devils. Everyone mourned She-Is-Alert and Nothing-But-Flowers as if our souls had left our bodies. Was there any difference? They would never see us again. We would spend the rest of our lives with white people.

The next morning the sachem Black Eagle chose four warriors to escort us to the great council. Bold Antelope insisted on joining them. ''When I am with Nothing-But-Flowers my heart is like a hawk in the sky over the lake,'' he said. ''Without her I will live in the mud like the turtle. I want to be at her side as long as possible.''

As he spoke, his hand grasped the handle of his hatchet. I saw the fear on Nothing-But-Flowers's face and knew what she was thinking. Bold Antelope would kill her in sight of the English, to defy them. He hated white men. In the last war, the French had captured his father and given him to the Ottawas for torture. He lived three terrible days before he died.

Black Eagle had been a friend of Bold Antelope's father. He consented to let him join the escort and we began the journey along the shore of the lake to the mouth of a swift river with many rapids which took us south to the lake of the Oneidas.[1] After crossing that body of water, the warriors lugged the canoes along a trail to the river of the Mohawks. We paddled east down that stream past a half dozen Mohawk castles, with their high wooden walls. At night we slept in grassy meadows beside the river.

Throughout the journey Bold Antelope did not say a word to Nothing-But-Flowers or to me. But there was death in his eyes. Why could not Black Eagle see it? Not for the first time, I concluded warriors and even sachems did not see very much. They were too preoccupied with their own glory. Only women saw things beneath the surface of words and gestures.

Finally we reached the falls of the Mohawk at the village of Schenectady and journeyed east on foot at a rapid pace. The Mohawks told us we would soon see the great council. In a little while we came over a low hill and looked down on a broad meadow. It was a beautiful spring morning. The grass in the meadow seemed as green as midsummer. There was not a cloud in the

[1]*Another tribe in the Iroquois confederation.*

blue sky. In the middle of the meadow were many Indian wigwams and cloth shelters Black Eagle said the white men called tents. Smoke was rising from many cooking fires. Between the tents a crowd of white warriors in red coats stood in a long line. Above them on a pole flew a red flag with a white cross in the middle. Black Eagle said it was the flag of the King of England.

A swarm of spiders crawled around my heart, webbing it with fear. What was going to happen to me and Nothing-But-Flowers? How could we ever be happy among white people? We were Senecas. We had been named by our mothers and adopted into the tribe forever. How many times had my grandmother told me white people had no honor, they had no regard for the truth? They were cowardly warriors who hid under beds like children when Indians attacked their houses. Again and again my mother had told me even though my skin was white, my heart was red, my blood was red, I was a Seneca.

Black Eagle led us into the Indian side of the camp and one of the Mohawks went in search of the white leaders. The other Mohawk went into a wigwam and came out with a jug of rum. He poured it into a cup and gave it to Black Eagle, Bold Antelope, and the other Senecas. They drank it greedily.

"You see the Mohawks share the white man's presents with their brothers the Senecas," the Mohawk said.

I was horrified. Nothing-But-Flowers's grandmother had persuaded our village council to refuse all gifts of rum. Many moons ago, when my fruitful blood first ran from my body, an English trader had brought a barrel of rum to our village. The warriors had drunk it and sold him all the beaver skins they had trapped in the winter for a few pounds of gunpowder and lead and some paltry strips of cheap cloth. They let the Englishman rob them. Then the warriors started quarreling. Before the spree was over, four of them were dead and many others badly wounded.

I watched Bold Antelope demand another drink from the jug. His eyes acquired a ghostly shine, like moonlight behind a cloud. Soon he would be ready to violate the honor of the Senecas.

Nothing-But-Flowers was paralyzed with dread. She was preparing to sing her death song. Before I could think of what to do, the other Mohawk returned and said the white men were ready to receive the captives. We were led into the field where the warriors with red coats stood in a row, with guns on their shoulders. A short stoop-shouldered white man with a mournful mouth and sad eyes stood beside a taller, thinner white man with hair growing out of his chin. I disliked both of them on sight. They looked as if their souls had shrunken to the size of pumpkin seeds. They were soon joined by another man, who walked with the strut of a turkey. He gazed at us with proud despising eyes. The other two men deferred to him. They called him "Judge."

Beside the older men stood two younger men. One had corn-yellow hair, the other black. The yellow-hair was a giant, with wide shoulders and long arms. He had the face of a well-fed bear. The black-haired man had the face of a hungry fox. He wore clothes far more beautiful than the giant's—gleaming green breeches and white stockings, a waistcoat of bright yellow and a coat of brilliant blue. Although I did not especially like his crafty expression, I was pleased by the way he gazed at me with desire in his eyes. His clothes, which must have cost the skins of a thousand beavers, meant he was a man of power and wealth.

Black Eagle made a speech, declaring that he was delivering these two captives to prove his village would honor the pledge the Senecas had made to remain faithful to their father, the King of England. The thin man with the hair on his chin stared at me. He asked a question and Black Eagle told him my Seneca name. The man asked him another question. Black Eagle asked me if I remembered my white name.

Cat Cat Cat went the woodpecker in the swamp. *Van Van Van* croaked the crow. I shook my head. I did not remember having a white name. "Tell him we wish to remain with our brothers and sisters of the Seneca," I said.

Black Eagle told the white men what I said. The stoop-shouldered man looked at me with friendship in his sad eyes. I saw something else in the thin white man's eyes. An angry shine that made me wonder if I had offended him. The stoop-shouldered man said something to the thin man. He still hesitated. Then he leaned toward me and said. "Cat-a-lyntie?"

The earth shook beneath my feet. The young giant's yellow hair seemed to be filling the whole sky with evil light. "Cat-a-lyntie?" the thin man said again.

"Van . . . Vorst?" said the man they called Judge.

The swamp in my head was spewing up a red mist. Invisible fingers seemed to grip my throat, choking me. I could not breathe. "I am She-Is-Alert," I gasped. "I wish to go home to my village."

They turned to Nothing-But-Flowers and asked her name. The thin man paused and read from a paper in his hand. "Clar-a?" he said.

Nothing-But-Flowers stood very still for a long time. Then she nodded her head. She remembered her old name! All these years, she had never revealed this to me.

The thin man pointed to me and said again: "Cat-a-lyntie?"

Nothing-But-Flowers nodded again. She remembered my name too. It was astonishing. Was it because of her powerful *orenda*? She was able to live in the past without fear of the Evil Brother?

The three older white men conferred. From a box at

their feet they drew a long belt of white wampum.[2] Judge gave it to the Mohawk, who handed it to Black Eagle with a speech, saying this was a payment for the two women to prove the King of England's desire for peace and his approval of their decision to surrender such beautiful maidens. The king understood they were losing many fine warriors with the loss of these women. He hoped the wampum would enable them to buy wives from other tribes to replace them.

It was over. We belonged to the white men now. Where was Bold Antelope? I found him in the crowd, the ghostly shine still in his eyes. Nothing-But-Flowers was far from safe. I desperately wanted to tell this to someone. But I did not speak a word of the white man's language.

We were handed over to the yellow-haired giant and his foxy-faced friend. Delegations from other villages were bringing more captives to be redeemed with wampum belts. The two young men tried to talk to us. They spoke very slowly but the words meant nothing. I kept looking for Bold Antelope. Glancing over my shoulder I saw him about ten paces behind us.

He was going to sink his hatchet into Nothing-But-Flowers's flesh as he had sunk it into the soft earth in our village street. Out of the swamp in my head came a face, a flash of yellow hair. I almost remembered but a false face leaped between me and the evil thing. Bold Antelope was drawing closer to us. He was only six paces away now. His hand was on the handle of his hatchet.

We reached a tent and the yellow-haired giant gestured for us to go inside. It was empty, except for big boxes full of clothes. They gestured to the boxes and made signs to tell us to take off our Indian clothes and

---

[2]*Small cylindrical beads made from polished shells. It was used as money by the Iroquois, and as gifts. White wampum signified peace.*

put on white clothes. The foxy-faced man said something to the giant about "watching." The giant struck the fox on the arm and pulled him out of the tent.

Outside the back of the tent, a shadow appeared. It was a man with a ridge of hair in the Indian fashion: Bold Antelope. His knife slit an opening in the canvas and he stepped inside. "Come with me," he said to Nothing-But-Flowers. "We will go away together. We will find another home in a distant tribe."

"No!" I cried. "He's going to kill you. When he gets you in the forest he'll kill you."

"Shut up!" Bold Antelope snarled and struck me in the face with the back of his hand, knocking me to the muddy floor of the tent.

"Don't hurt her," Nothing-But-Flowers said. "I'll go with you. I loved you above all the others. But I wasn't sure you were worthy of the Bear Clan. There were many who spoke against you. They said you were rash and lacked true honor."

"Her?" Bold Antelope said, glaring at me. I could see he wanted to kill me to keep the secret of Nothing-But-Flowers's fate.

"No. She never spoke against you."

"Do not break that rule," Bold Antelope said to me. "If you want to keep your breath in your body."

He seized Nothing-But-Flowers by the arm and dragged her through the opening he had cut in the back of the tent. I ran into the street, frantically searching for the yellow-haired giant. There were many rows of tents. I finally found him in the last row, joking with his foxy friend and a third man, who was short and ugly and had a hump on his back. He looked like Hah-doo-wee, the evil spirit who had been tamed by the Master of Life and agreed to help human beings.

I ran up to them and made the sign language for hatchet. I placed my right elbow in the palm of my right hand and made a chopping stroke. I made the sign for knife by placing my left hand in front of my mouth and slicing between it with my right hand. I drew my finger across my throat.

"Clar-a!" I said, pointing toward the tent.

The hunchback said something to the giant and the three men ran back to the empty tent. The giant burst through the slit at the back. In the distance, Bold Antelope and Nothing-But-Flowers were on the edge of the forest. "Stop!" the giant shouted and ran after them as swiftly as I had ever seen a Seneca warrior run. His foxy-faced friend hung back. He had no desire to fight Bold Antelope. The hunchback ran after the giant but he could not keep his pace.

"Stop!" shouted the giant again and Bold Antelope turned. For a moment I wondered if I had made a terrible mistake. Would it have been better to let Bold Antelope and Nothing-But-Flowers go? Maybe he had been telling the truth when he said he would take her to a distant tribe.

Bold Antelope had his musket in his right hand. His left hand held Nothing-But-Flowers's arm. He let her go, dropped to one knee and fired a shot at the running giant. As his gun flashed the giant dodged to one side and the bullet missed him. Bold Antelope sprang to his feet and drew his hatchet. The giant did not stop his headlong rush. At six paces he leaped through the air and crashed into Bold Antelope before he could swing the hatchet.

The gleaming weapon flew out of Bold Antelope's hand. He drew his knife and tried to stab the giant but the white man caught the downward thrust and held it against Bold Antelope's full weight. With a mighty shout he flung Bold Antelope on his back and pressed the knife against his throat. Bold Antelope, facing death, released the knife. The giant flung it into the woods. He flung the hatchet after it and smashed Bold Antelope's musket against a tree.

Totally defeated, Bold Antelope fled into the forest. I

ran up to Nothing-But-Flowers and covered her face with kisses. I turned and kissed the giant too. He was a true warrior. Maybe white people were not as lacking in bravery as my Seneca grandmother claimed.

Into my head flashed my grandmother's prophecy that I would meet my husband before the snow fell. Was this the man? He smiled at me in a very interesting way. But he also smiled at Nothing-But-Flowers—and she was smiling at him. With a sinking heart, I realized Nothing-But-Flowers might fall in love with this yellow-haired warrior too. I could never compete with her beauty—even if I wanted to try. I owed Nothing-But-Flowers too much to steal a husband from her.

"Cat-a-lyntie?" the giant said.

I nodded shyly. I could accept my white name now.

"Clar-a?" the giant said.

Clara nodded too—not shyly. She was never shy. She let the giant take her hand. He took my hand too and we walked back toward the white tents together. Above us the sky was a blue dome ablaze with sunlight. The hunchback danced around us, laughing and shouting and slapping the giant on the back. None of us knew we were enjoying one of our last moments of pure happiness.

THREE

"Mal-colm."

"Rob-ert."

"A-dam."

Laboriously, we learned the names of our new friends. Mal-colm was the bear. Rob-ert was the fox. A-dam was the little man with the hump on his back. Every time I looked at Mal-colm's thick blond hair, I felt a tremor of desire. I imagined myself alone with him in the woods, taking him inside me, while that wonderful hair swirled above me, full of sunlight. I tried to speak to him with my eyes, but he did not understand my looks any more than he knew my Seneca language.

I wondered why the fox seemed so sure of himself, even though he was no warrior. Why was he richer and more powerful than the bear? I wanted the bear to be immensely powerful in the white world. I wanted a powerful husband who was also a great warrior! That would make up for all the insults the Moon Woman had borne as a lowly member of the Turtle Clan.

Warily, while I struggled to pronounce their names and the names of other things they were busy teaching us—shoe, foot, hand, mouth, pistol—I stole a look at Clara. Was she attracted to Mal-colm? It was hard to tell. Clara always withheld that part of herself when she was with a man. She did not have to beg for attention, like the Moon Woman.

The three men returned us to the clothing tent with fresh instructions to outfit ourselves. We found the dresses with their long skirts and pleats and ruffled sleeves, the heavy petticoats and bonnets, the strangest assortment of nonsense we had ever seen. How did white women live in such clothes? We both chose white petticoats and red shoes and ignored the rest of the stuff.

When we emerged from the tent, Mal-colm, Rob-ert, and A-dam doubled over in laughter. Soon we were surrounded by two dozen grinning white men who said things to each other that produced bursts of guttural laughter. The voices had the same hot crackle I had heard when young warriors joked about sticking a pretty girl. I smiled and joined in the laughter, delighted to have so many men desiring me. But Clara became furious and dragged me back into the tent.

"Can't you see they're laughing at us?" she said.

In a few minutes a white woman with a dirty face and even dirtier clothes came into the tent. With her was the older white man with the tuft of a beard on his chin. He spoke harshly to the white woman and she helped us put on dresses over the petticoats. She made no attempt to match anything. Clara got a blue skirt and a bright green blouse. My skirt was green and my blouse brown.

Trailing in the mud, the skirts soon grew sodden and tripped us. Rob-ert showed us how to hike the hems high enough to walk freely and we finally made some progress toward a tent where we were served ham and venison and bread and butter and hot bitter tea. We consumed everything in quantities that astonished our hosts, who had no idea we had eaten nothing but a few mouthfuls of parched corn for three days, in the style of Indians on a journey.

At noon there was a final parade. The company of red-coated soldiers fired a cannon and several volleys of musketry while the Indians watched with expressionless faces. I saw the whites were trying to impress the Indians with the power of the British nation. The cannon was a terrible creature. Clara and I put our hands over our ears each time it roared and spewed a round iron ball into the woods, where it smashed down tall trees.

On that warlike note, the great peace council broke up and the Indians vanished into the forest. Within an hour, the wind shifted and a cold rain began to fall. The beautiful morning became an ugly grey afternoon. With rain whipping our backs, the negotiators and soldiers and redeemed captives trudged south to the Hudson River. The white leaders rode on horses, the red-coated soldiers and ex-captives walked.

Pausing only to bolt down some cold food, we reached the river as night fell. A half dozen sloops were waiting for us. The sight of the ships, with their white sails flapping like ghosts in the darkness, stirred the swamp in my head again. *Cat cat cat* went the wood-pecker, *van van van* croaked the crow. Then another word, which erased these other sounds like the cannon's roar: *Pettikin*. What did it mean? I wondered dazedly.

I wanted to ask Clara, but aboard our sloop, the bearded man forced a smile to his thin lips and introduced himself as Joh-annes. He added that other name, *Van Vorst*, and another word in Seneca, which his thin smile seemed to belie: *uncle*. He directed me to a cabin on deck. Clara casually followed me. Joh-annes seized her arm and roughly thrust her back on deck. I was baffled. Why was I being given a dry cabin while Clara was forced to sleep on the deck in the rain? To my relief, Mal-colm, took off his cloak and wrapped it around Clara.

Weary from the march, I stripped off my wet clothes and huddled under a blanket in one of the cabin's narrow bunks. There were five women redeemed from other villages in the remaining bunks. All of them were as unhappy about their return to the white world as I was. One of them repeatedly cried out the name of a warrior she loved. The youngest, who was about twelve, sobbed for her Indian mother. An older woman wept for a sick child she had left behind her.

In the morning, in the sloop's main cabin, Clara rejoined us and we were fed gruel and cider and some stale bread. Uncle Johannes Van Vorst gazed at us with a strange mixture of fear and dislike. The stoop-shouldered man's eyes continued to speak pity and the judge's eyes retained their haughty disapproval. Only the fox seemed to regard me with enthusiasm. He used a word whose sound I liked, even though I did not understand it: *beautiful*.

My uncle replied with words that made some men laugh in the hot crackly way that meant desire. That did not bother me particularly but I was troubled by one strange word my uncle used: *whore*. I had no idea what it meant but I did not like its sound. Now I know he was saying that he was worried about us because Indian women—in his opinion—were all whores. I turned to Clara, hoping she understood what they were saying and could reply for both of us.

But Clara was angry about other matters. She told the white men she was a member of the noblest family of the Bear Clan of the Senecas and had decided to go back to her village. She did not like the way the white men were treating her. The captain of the sloop, who knew some Seneca, translated her words.

Johannes Van Vorst and the judge gazed at Clara with contempt. I was amazed. I had never seen any man gaze at Nothing-But-Flowers that way. Then Johannes spoke so slowly, I was able to remember all the words. "Tell her she's a slave. We own her."

The closest the captain could come to slave was the Indian word for captive. There were no slaves among the Seneca. Clara and I exchanged baffled glances. The captain did not know enough of our language to explain slavery to us. The yellow-haired giant looked sad as he gazed at Clara and said something the captain did not translate. "She'll have to learn the hard way."

In four days we were in New York. We were totally bewildered by the brawling confusion of the docks, the shouts and curses of cartmen clogging the narrow streets. Even more astonishing were the hundreds and hundreds of houses. It was a thousand times bigger than our Seneca village. How could anyone live in such a place, surrounded by strangers who might be enemies?

Clara and I were taken to Johannes Van Vorst's redbrick mansion on Broad Street. The place left us breathless. Every inch of the wooden floor gleamed and white tiles glistened on the stairways. Thick yellow curtains framed the shining windows and tables glowed with polish. The upholstered chairs had yellow and blue cushions on them. Rugs decorated with brilliant pictures of ships and cities covered the floors. To young women used to the rough simplicity of a Seneca longhouse, the place was a wonderland.

A tall thin black man with a mournful face emerged from a door that led to the cellar. Uncle Johannes pointed to Clara and spoke curtly to him. "Yes, Master," the black man said and seized Clara by the arm and led her down a flight of dim stairs. Before I could protest this separation, a woman hurried into the room wearing a beautiful blue dress with a great hoop skirt. The hoop was so wide she had to come in the door sideways.

The woman gazed in amazement at me, tears leaping from her eyes. "My God!" she cried and rushed across the room to kiss me, no easy task in a hoop skirt. Her small thin-lipped face and expressive blue eyes stirred a fragment of memory in my head. Where had I seen her before?

I was introduced to Uncle Johannes's wife, Gertrude. She wiped fresh tears from her eyes with a small handkerchief and smiled tenderly at me. Aunt Gertrude had large eyes and almost no chin. Her face resembled the face of a cat. Her hair was piled on top of her head in a great tower of curls, decorated by many ribbons.

Johannes said something harsh to Aunt Gertrude. Her tender smile vanished. The words "father" and "will" were repeated many times. I sensed unhappiness in their voices. As they talked, two women around my age crowded through the door in beribboned green dresses which also swayed around them on hoops. Their hair was also piled high on their heads in thick curls. One had her mother's cat face. The other resembled her father, down to his hard mouth and narrow eyes. Their mother spoke excitedly to them. They gazed at me in amazement.

The young women were named Anna and Esther. "Cousins," Mrs. Van Vorst said, with another smile. I did not know what the word meant. At an order from Aunt Gertrude, Anna and Esther led me upstairs. In a room with a canopied bed that was almost as large as an Indian cabin, they stripped off my peace council costume and washed my dirty hands and feet and face—which left me baffled. When people were adopted into the Seneca tribe, they were taken into the lake and washed from head to foot to cleanse them of their old identities. Were the Van Vorsts only adopting my hands and feet and face? I would soon learn that the hands and feet and face were the only parts of their bodies New Yorkers washed from New Year's to New Year's.

While they washed me, my cousins talked about me in the same nasty voice and with the same mean expression I often saw on the faces of Big Claws and my other enemies in the village of Shining Creek. From the drawer of a great chest the sisters seized a device made of bone and steel and tried to strap it around my body. They were simply obeying their mother. Fashionable young ladies wore corsets from the age of ten. But I had never seen or heard of such a strange garment. I reacted with violent alarm. They were going to torture me!

I spied a nail file on a dressing table. Bursting out of the corset before my cousins got a single strap buckled, I seized the file and retreated snarling to a corner of the room. The Misses Van Vorst ran screaming downstairs and the house erupted into chaos. Gertrude Van Vorst sallied into the room and retreated crying to her husband for help. The rattled Johannes rushed upstairs armed with a pistol.

At that moment the rumble of a coach filled the street. Gertrude Van Vorst reappeared in the bedroom doorway crying that word ''father'' again.

Everyone froze. Johannes and Gertrude gazed at each other with anxiety in their eyes. Then a deep voice rumbled up the stairs. ''Pettikin!'' the man boomed. ''My darling Pettikin!''

The word crashed through my terrified soul like a cannon shot. I remembered! The swamp filled my head with cold mud but I walked above it as if it were firm earth. I suddenly remembered so much. Trembling, I pulled on my soiled traveling dress and ran to the head of the stairs. At the bottom stood a fat red-faced old man with a great hooked nose. Leaning on two canes, he gazed up the stairs at me, a smile illuminating his face.

"Pettikin!" Cornelius Van Vorst said—and added in Seneca, learned from his years as a fur trader. "I am the grandfather of your dreams. Come down and embrace me."

I flung myself into his arms. In the doorway to the street stood the sad-eyed stoop-shouldered man from the peace council and the yellow-haired giant, Malcolm, smiling cheerfully. I realized they were father and son— and had brought the news of my return to my grandfather.

Johannes and Gertrude Van Vorst watched the tender scene with thinly disguised disapproval. They barely managed to smile and nod as Cornelius, playing interpreter, introduced them to me as my uncle and aunt.

"Oh, Grandfather," I said in Seneca. "I remember the terrible thing that happened."

For a moment the swamp sucked at me again. "You really are my grandfather. You're not the Evil Brother?"

"No, no, Pettikin," Cornelius said. "You'll never have to fear the Evil Brother again."

I did not believe that assurance but this huge old man's arms around me seemed protection enough for the time being. I was able to tell him the story of my parents' death without trembling or weeping. I told it without hate or remorse, as part of the war that had raged through the forests and over the lakes for all the years of my life.

Released from the swampy clutch of memory, I felt lighter than air. But I was dismayed to see I had shifted the burden to my grandfather's aged shoulders. Cornelius Van Vorst slumped in a chair and berated himself for sending his son and his wife and children into the wilderness. His face grew mottled, his breath came in ratchety gasps.

Johannes said something to the old man that troubled him. The word "will" was mentioned several times. Cornelius gazed at his surviving son in a heavy mournful way. I recognized the same discouraged look my Seneca mother had often cast on her white daughter. She loved me but there was always the wish that I were different, more attractive and popular. Cornelius wished his son was a better man.

I watched my grandfather struggle to overcome the regret that was engulfing him. "Well, at least I have the consolation of seeing this beautiful creature before I die," he said in Seneca, gazing fondly at me.

Gertrude Van Vorst said something harsh to Cornelius. I saw that my grandfather disliked his daughter-in-law. I watched as she began lecturing him in a sharp voice. Now I know she was warning him that I was a savage who would need constant watching and discipline if there was to be any hope of civilizing me.

"Is she telling you that I tried to stab my cousins with that little knife?" I said in Seneca. "I thought they were going to torture me with the strange metal thing they tried to strap on me."

"I understand, my darling," Cornelius said. "You will come home with me now—I'll explain it all later."

"What about my friend Clara?" I asked as Cornelius led me to the door. "They've treated her very badly. I don't know why. Can she come to your house with us?"

Cornelius asked his son Johannes a sharp question. His reply included that baffling word "slave." He gestured to the basement door to explain where Clara had gone.

Cornelius shook his head angrily and pointed to me.

After several tense exchanges between the father and son, Johannes summoned Clara from the basement. Gertrude Van Vorst made one more attempt to protest her release.

"She will live with us!" Cornelius thundered. It was another sentence I found easy to remember, although I did not understand it at the time.

Clara and I departed with the old man, followed by the yellow-haired giant and his father, who continued to gaze sadly at us. Johannes and Gertrude Van Vorst said nothing, but their eyes were livid with dislike or fear—perhaps both. Why?

FOUR

"SLAVE?" CLARA AND I SAID, almost in unison. "I still don't understand."

Grandfather had tried to explain slavery to us a half dozen times. He finally decided only seeing was believing. On our second day in his house, he bundled Clara and me into his coach and we rumbled to the East River docks. There we watched black men emerge from the hold of a ship. Many of them were strong-looking young warriors—except for the lack of flesh on their bodies. Their bones were almost visible beneath their skin. They resembled Senecas during a bad starving time. Grandfather explained the ship had captured them in a place called Africa and carried them across the Great Ocean to New York.

One by one the black men were led to a platform in the center of the dock, where many white men clustered. Another white man stood on the platform and pointed to each black man and made a speech to the crowd. The white men in the crowd shouted back to the man on the platform and eventually the black man was handed over to one of them, when he gave the man on the platform a certain number of gold and silver coins. The buyer marched the black man to a carriage or a wagon and rode away.

"They buy them exactly as you buy a dress or a horse or a plow," Grandfather said. "They own them in the same way."

"Did her father buy me?" Clara said, looking at me for the first time with unfriendly eyes.

"No. He bought your mother and your father from me. But under the law, you too became his property. When Catalyntie's father and mother died, under the law you became her property."

"What kind of law is that?" Clara cried.

"A bad law, my dear girl. But a law nonetheless. A law that men enforce with guns and whips and penalties."

"Then I must do Catalyntie's bidding forever?" Clara said. "She has become my mother and father?"

"The stupid law means nothing to me," I said. "I'll never order you to do anything. I love you. I'll always love you."

"As soon as it can be arranged, I hope we can free you," Grandfather said. "It can't be done immediately. You must learn some trade, so you can support yourself. Otherwise you'll starve. White men don't share their food and clothing like Senecas."

"Why should I believe you?" Clara said. "Maybe it would be better if I ran away now. There is a warrior in Shining Creek who loves me and wants to marry me."

"Your father Joshua was my brother," Grandfather said. "Together we went into the wilderness, long before you were born. We brought back the furs that began the

New Netherlands Trading Company.'' The old man's voice grew thick with sorrow. ''He was a great warrior, as brave as any Seneca. I promised him one day his children would be free.''

Tears poured down Clara's cheeks. She clung to Cornelius Van Vorst. Her *orenda* told her he had a truthful heart. ''You shall be my father now,'' she said.

She embraced me too. ''You will always be my sister,'' she said.

''Always,'' I said.

If either of us knew how much pain those words would cost us, would we have refused to speak them? Probably not.

Looking out the windows of Grandfather's house that evening, we saw two women standing on the corner wearing brightly colored clothes. Whenever a man walked by, they raised small tin lanterns to their faces, which were covered with red and white paint. We asked what they were doing.

''They're whores,'' Grandfather said. ''They're trying to sell their love to those men.''

I remembered Uncle Johannes using the word on the sloop. Neither Clara nor I could grasp the idea of a woman selling herself for money. ''Without hope or interest in a husband?'' I said.

''Whores don't marry,'' Grandfather said. ''They're considered bad women by respectable people. But I've known a few in my time who were as good in their own way as any Christian in the pews of our best churches.''

''Why are they considered bad women?'' Clara asked. ''If they haven't married, they can't be unfaithful to their husbands. Did they refuse to work in the cornfields? Did they neglect their children?''

With a groan of exasperation, Grandfather called for his coach. Together we rumbled to a winding road called Pearl Street, which ran along the river on the eastern side of the city. On corners in the twilight stood dozens of these women with red and white paint on their faces. Grandfather said they took a different man into their beds each night for a silver Spanish dollar—perhaps two dollars if the woman was pretty. Clara and I could only exchange bewildered, appalled looks.

So much to learn, so much to understand! Grandfather hired Harman Bogardus, a young Dutch divinity student with thin shanks, a solemn mouth, and cheerful eyes to help Clara and me shed our Indian identities. From the start, at my insistence, he treated us with complete equality. Clara had no interest in learning Dutch, however, while I spent extra hours struggling with that tongue as well as English. I also showed a surprising proficiency in arithmetic. Within a few weeks, I could look at a column of numbers and add them at a glance.

At first we learned with a certain reluctance, determined to compare Seneca knowledge with white knowledge. That changed when Bogardus showed us a map. We had never seen one of these wondrous things, which enabled a man or woman to look down on the world with God's eyes. Clara was especially fascinated. For her a map was a magical thing. She ran her finger along the wide line of the Hudson and followed it north to the Mohawk, retracing our journey from the shore of Lake Ontario. The lake was a great eye with our Seneca village a tiny dot on its lid.

The map convinced us that white power was greater and wiser than Indian power. Somehow, the whites had entered the mind of the Master of Life and brought his knowledge down to earth and printed it on paper.

But white politics, which the map was supposed to introduce, proved to be almost as difficult for us to understand as prostitution and slavery. When Bogardus said the province of New York was owned by the King of England, we asked to see a picture of him. We were astonished to discover he was a fat old man in a grey wig.

"Was he a great warrior when he was young?" Clara asked. "Has he many scalps on his war belt?"

Bogardus shook his head.

"How did he become king?"

"His father was king before him. The crown belongs to him by divine right. It's God's will."

I could see Bogardus did not believe a word of this.

"Has the king ever come to America to claim his power over us?" Clara asked. "Has he led war parties against our enemies, the French and the Ottawas?"

Bogardus shook his head.

"Why do we owe him any allegiance?" I asked.

"He's the father of the country," Bogardus said. "His navy, his army, his judges and governors, keep order here and in the other provinces of his empire, just as a father governs a family."

"A mother can govern a family far better than a father," I said, speaking from my Seneca heritage.

I thought even less of the king when my grandfather told us how a British fleet had seized New York from the Netherlands in 1664, when he was a boy of fourteen. "That was nothing but thievery!" I said.

Grandfather explained that the two countries had been at war, which permitted such conquests. "Perhaps there'll be another war and the Dutch will take it back," Clara said.

Grandfather shook his head. "Our power has declined while England's never ceases to grow. Their merchants rule the trade of North America. If a man is Dutch or any other nationality, he must be careful not to offend them. They can ruin his business overnight."

"They're tyrants, like the ancient Romans," I said. We had just finished reading about these people in a history book Harman Bogardus gave us.

Grandfather laughed and lit his pipe. "A good comparison," he said. "The English talk more about liberty.

They claim to be very proud of it. But they never had to fight for it the way the Dutch fought the Spanish.''

He told us about the series of wars the Dutch had fought in Europe for almost a hundred years to drive the Spanish out of their country. ''The Dutch are the real lovers of liberty. Never forget that.''

The next day, I pursued another branch of this conversation. ''What is a merchant?'' I asked Grandfather.

''A man or woman who buys goods in one place and sells them in another place for a profit.''

''There are women merchants?''

''It's always been a tradition among the Dutch. My mother kept the books and managed our store on Pearl Street while my father was away on trading voyages. She made more money from the store than he ever did from his voyages and loaned it out at interest. No one got higher rates.''

I found the idea of interest on money especially fascinating. ''If it's well sown and watched, money will grow like corn or squash,'' Grandfather said. ''It can be as fruitful as an apple tree or a cornfield.''

''A Seneca woman is trained to do such things well,'' I said. ''But if I become a merchant, I'll never bow down to the English!''

''If I become one, I'll never bow down to white people!'' Clara said.

Grandfather looked alarmed. He threw his big arms around us. ''Let me tell you both the secret of making your way in the world. You have to bow down now and then to those who are richer and more powerful. But you must never bow down in your heart. That's the great thing to avoid.''

Clara disagreed with this advice. ''I can never be false to what my heart speaks,'' she said.

''The world will break your heart, my dear, if you try to live that way.''

I heard sorrow in Grandfather's voice. Did he know

that the world would probably break Clara's heart, no matter what she did? Perhaps that was why he did not press the argument. Instead he returned to describing the merchant's life. He said it was full of risks and anxiety. A merchant had to be prepared to make long dangerous journeys in search of new goods to sell; he had to fight rivals for a share of the market.

"That's why I sent your father into the Mohawk country," he said to me. "To fight the Albany merchants for a fair share of the fur trade. They were on their way to creating a monopoly of it—always a bad thing in business. Now that I know from you the full story of what happened, I think the Senecas who raided the house that day were sent on purpose by men who were ready to commit murder to protect their profits."

"A Seneca would never kill for hire!" Clara said.

"White men from Albany told them lies that persuaded them to do it for honor," Cornelius said. "If my health improves, I hope we can journey to your village next summer and speak to warriors who were in that war party. Perhaps we can find out the names of these Albany murderers and bring them to justice."

Murder for profit. The words burned themselves into my heart, leaving ugly scars. I lay awake nights for a week, remembering the terrible day in the house on the Mohawk, grateful to Grandfather for removing the blame from the Senecas, hungering for revenge against the faceless merchants of Albany.

Harman Bogardus had even more trouble explaining the Christian religion to us than he had had describing the British empire. As soon as we could read, he gave us the New Testament. We found Jesus a very confusing figure.

"Sometimes he talks like a warrior, sometimes like a sachem," I said. "Which was he?"

"He was neither. We believe he was the Son of God," Bogardus said. "The Great Spirit, the being Indians call the Manitou, the God above all gods, inhabited his flesh during his time on earth.''

''We're all sons and daughters of the Manitou,'' Clara said. ''Many times he enters our flesh and speaks with our tongues.''

''No, no,'' Bogardus said. ''Only once in history has this happened. Without faith in Jesus as the only true Son of God, there is no salvation. If you lack faith in Him, you'll go to hell.''

The cheer vanished from Bogardus's eyes. He meant every word of this pronouncement. Both greatly upset, Clara and I asked Grandfather what he thought of Jesus. He shut the doors to the parlor and made us promise we would never repeat what he was going to tell us. With great uneasiness he confessed he did not think Jesus was a god. He was a good man, a kind man, a wise man, who was betrayed by his enemies and died a painful death.

''There are many in this city who would blacken my name if I admitted this in public,'' Grandfather said. ''Profit by my example and go to church now and then and pretend to believe what they preach from the pulpit. In your heart believe what you please.''

I decided I did not believe in Jesus. I was not even sure I accepted a Manitou who permitted my parents to be murdered so brutally in front of my eyes. Clara, on the other hand, admired Jesus deeply, the more she read about him. She decided he was one of those rare spirits through whom the Master of Life spoke profound truths. She was especially moved by the passage in Luke where Jesus proclaimed the heart of his teaching.

> *But I say unto you which hear, Love your enemies, do good to them that hate you, bless them that curse you, pray for them that despitefully use you. To him that smiteth thee on the one cheek, offer also the other; and from him that taketh away thy cloke, withhold not thy coat also. Give to everyone*

*that asketh thee; and of him that taketh away thy
goods ask them not again. And as ye would that
men should do to you, do ye also them likewise.*

I could not begin to comprehend such advice.
Jesus was telling us to forgive hatred and forgo revenge,
to let people steal from you—and if they merely asked,
to give them your property! Clara saw the beauty and
power of it instantly. We did not have time to argue
about it because neither she nor I could understand
Schoolmaster Bogardus's attempts to explain his next
topic—the war between the Protestant and Catholic re-
ligions.

Both faiths believed in Jesus, but Catholics thought
their leader, the pope, who lived in Italy, was the only
person able to speak in Jesus's name, while Protestants
believed Jesus spoke directly to each person who pro-
fessed faith in him. If that was not confusing enough,
there was also a political side to the quarrel.

"The King of England does more than keep order in
his empire," Bogardus said. "He's the great defender
of the Protestant religion against the pope of Rome."

"As Senecas, we shall be neutral in this quarrel,"
Clara said, with a smile.

"No one can be neutral. You'll be hated by both
sides," Bogardus said.

We ignored this prophetic remark and groaned in protest when he made us study the history of the "Glorious
Revolution" of 1688, in which English Protestants had
hurled the Catholic king, James II, off the throne and
replaced him with a Protestant. The Stuarts, father and
son, had fled to France, where they began plotting to
regain their power. France and Spain recognized James's
son, James Edward Stuart, as the true King of England.

"As long as the Jacobites[1] wait in France, the Prot-

[1]From the Latin word for James, Jacobus.

estant King of England sits uneasily on his throne," my grandfather said.

"It's all so complicated!" I complained. Already I was more interested in talking about business and a merchant's life than history and politics.

"History is always complicated. That's why it's important to understand it," Grandfather said. "Otherwise it explodes in your face with no warning."

To make his point, he invited two of his closest friends, Nathan Franks and William Laurens, to dinner to tell us how history had changed their lives. Franks was a small, lean man with the shrewd eyes of a sachem. He was Jewish. He told us his family had lived in Spain for many centuries, where they had prospered as merchants. But some Spaniards began preaching hatred against the Jews because they were not Christians. In 1492, the King of Spain expelled all the Jews from the kingdom. They became men and women without a country, wandering the world in search of refuge.

"For us, New York is an earthly paradise," Franks told us. "No one preaches hatred here."

"Only against Catholics. But that's politics," my grandfather said, gazing fondly at his old friend.

William Laurens was a French Protestant. A swarthy man with a gold tooth, he told us about another explosion of religious hatred which drove his family from France. In 1572, on St. Bartholomew's Day, the French Catholics launched a general massacre of all Protestants. Before it ended, over six-hundred thousand people died and the country was convulsed by civil war. Tens of thousands of French Protestants fled France to settle in England and the American colonies.

"I begin to think the world is a terrible place," I said. "The Evil Brother seems at work everywhere, sowing hatred and war."

"That's as good an explanation as any," Grandfather said.

"I believe that in America, as it grows, we will see an end to such hatreds," Nathan Franks said. "They are rooted in envy and greed more than anything else. Here, there will be abundance for all."

"Let us drink to that noble vision," William Laurens said.

The three old men raised their glasses to an America that existed only in their hopes. Clara and I would soon discover the real America was still far from their benevolent dreams.

FIVE

IN ABOUT THREE MONTHS, WHEN we could express ourselves in English, Grandfather summoned Madame Mercereau, New York's best dressmaker, to outfit us. A tiny woman who talked rapidly in a heavy French accent, she tempted us with a half dozen fashion dolls wearing the latest Paris and London styles. We were dazzled by the profusion, the detail, the luxury of the dresses, with their rococo shell motifs, combined with flowers, feathers, ribbon bowknots, and every imaginable curve and curl. The range of fabrics—silks, satins, woolens of a dozen different textures—was equally incredible to us. Told we would have to tolerate corsets to wear them, we capitulated instantly.

Grandfather gave us each an allowance of fifty pounds—two hundred and fifty Spanish dollars—to spend on our clothes.[1] We both bought expensive dresses that dismayed the old man, who had urged us to

---

[1] *The equivalent of about $5,000 in late-twentieth-century money.*

be frugal and sensible. "These could only be worn at the King's Birthday Ball," he said.

He mournfully added that there was very little chance of Clara being invited to such a ball. "In that case I won't go either!" I said.

Grandfather paid for the gowns and gave Madame Mercereau another fifty pounds for some everyday dresses. We paraded around the house in our ball gowns, learning to maneuver the hoops through doorways, curtsying to each other, posing in front of mirrors, reveling in our womanhood. The full-length mirrors in Grandfather's house had almost as much influence as the maps in changing our Seneca identities. A mirror made us aware of ourselves in a new way. We saw ourselves in our beautiful gowns and felt reborn. We could believe we had become new women.

Looking in the mirror, with rouge and lipstick on my white face and my hair crimped in the latest style, I convinced myself I was almost as attractive as Clara. I was a head taller, and my breasts were not as luxurious, but I had a long, graceful neck and a passable face. My nose was either sharp or fine, depending on your generosity, but my eyes were a bold blue. I told myself I was like a piece of fine filigreed ivory, while Clara's beauty was a dark glowing opal. Men might love both kinds of women.

For almost six months, we lived in our unreal world of learning and luxury. Our meals were prepared by Grandfather's aging Negro cook, Shirley, and her husband, Peter. In the evenings we were entertained by musicians and singers Grandfather invited to perform the latest scores from London. He was particularly fond of George Frideric Handel, who was King George's court musician. Clara found the music thrilling. She could not hear enough of it. I listened to it, but my mind traveled up the Hudson to Albany and imagined agonizing deaths for my parents' murderers.

On other nights Grandfather entertained us with the story of his life. It was full of narrow escapes from death in the northern forests and on the sea. Listening to him, I concluded that the hidden power who ruled the world had decreed long ago who would die and who would live to grow old.

Almost as astonishing were the bitter disappointments Grandfather had known in his long life. "There was another Catalyntie, for whom you're named, Pettikin," he told me. "She was my first wife. We were married less than a year when I took her with me on a voyage to Holland. In the English Channel we were struck by a great storm. A wave rolled over the entire ship, flinging her on her beam ends. My darling wife was swept from our cabin into the sea."

His voice grew so choked, his breathing so labored, we were alarmed. "I found another good woman to love. But nothing can replace the love that awakens the heart. Hold fast to that love if you can, dear girls. Though life often seems determined to fling difficulties in your path."

Dark thoughts, deep thoughts. But we were too young to value them. As we mastered the customs and language of New York, we grew more and more impatient to join the world that was swirling past our windows each day. On a sunny Sunday afternoon in October, while Grandfather was taking a nap, we each put on one of our expensive gowns and strolled down Broad Street arm in arm, as we had often walked along the shore of Lake Ontario.

On the green lawn known as the Bowling Green, beside the looming walls of Fort George at the tip of Manhattan Island, we gazed in astonishment at the swarms of people promenading in brightly colored silks and satins, the men flourishing canes, the women parasols. Was everyone in New York as rich as Cornelius Van Vorst?

Suddenly a sharp voice cried, "This won't do!"

It was my aunt, Gertrude Van Vorst. She was dressed in the highest style, a silk kerchief over her lace-edged cap, a taffeta cloak with wide ruching at the waist, elbow sleeves with deep cuffs—and an enormous hoop. With her was her glowering husband, Johannes, and the man everyone had called "Judge" at the peace council. He flourished a gold-headed cane and gazed at us as if we were poisonous snakes.

"This won't be tolerated in New York," Aunt Gertrude shrilled, pointing to Clara. "That Negar should walk ten steps behind you, her head meekly bowed, as befits a servant! You must never allow so much as a finger to touch her in public. Where did she get this dress? It must have cost twenty or thirty pounds! Do you want us all to have our throats cut some dark night? I shall speak to your grandfather about this, straightaway!"

"Aunt," I said in somewhat halting English. "I'm sure Grandfather will tell you what I tell you now. It's none of your business."

"It's the business of every white person in New York, as you will soon discover," Uncle Johannes said. "Don't you agree, Judge Horsmanden?"

"I certainly do," said Horsmanden. "In my opinion, the Common Council should pass a law to be enforced under a penalty of thirty lashes for each offense, forbidding such displays. Nothing but firm unwavering authority can control these people."

He glared at Clara as he said this. A dozen other women—and several men—were staring at us with the same angry disapproval on their faces. Flustered, I withdrew my arm from Clara's—and saw for the first time—but not, alas, for the last—pain and reproach gather in my Seneca sister's brown eyes.

The Van Vorsts and Judge Horsmanden proceeded on their way. In the crowd of hostile spectators I saw a familiar face: the blond giant who had rescued Clara from Bold Antelope. Malcolm Stapleton—I had made a point of learning his full name—sauntered over to us, accompanied by his hunchbacked friend, Adam Duycinck.

"Is what my aunt and uncle tell me true?" I asked. "I can't treat Clara as my friend in public?"

"It might be better to walk a few paces apart," Malcolm said. "But side by side is all right. I don't make Duycinck here walk behind me. Though he's so ugly I probably should."

"If I did, it would be only to plant my foot up your backside," Duycinck said.

I liked the little hunchback; he talked like an Indian. "What's wrong with me putting my arm around Clara?" I asked.

"People want to keep the Africans in their places," Malcolm said. "They're worried about an insurrection. I think it's all stuff."

"Why do you bring them here if you fear them so?" I asked.

Malcolm shrugged. "A lot of people say it's a mistake. But the mechanics and the farmers need the labor. White men don't come to New York much since our trade dropped away these past five years."

He fell in step beside us. Duycinck walked a few paces behind us, bawling, "Is this far enough, Master?"

"Is he a slave?" I asked.

"He's an indentured servant. That means he's signed a contract to work for my parents for a certain number of years in order to pay off the cost of his passage across the Atlantic."

"Why was he unable to pay for it?"

"He was a convict. The British accused his mother of being a witch. They burned her at the stake and deported him. Now he wants revenge on every Englishman under the sun."

"That's not true," Duycinck howled. "I'm perfectly

willing to let all the Englishmen on the islands of Bermuda, Jamaica, and Barbados die in their own good time—of sunstroke. It's the rest I want to kill.''

I hesitated, confused. ''Aren't you English?''

''He's American,'' Duycinck bawled. ''Though the booby can barely admit it. He'd rather kiss English asses until they pretend he's one of them.''

American. It was the first time I had heard the word. It made perfect sense. This continent was called North America. Why not call the people born on it Americans? It was silly to call them English. England was three thousand miles away.

Malcolm did not seem to like being called American. He raised a fist which could demolish the hunchback with a blow. Duycinck danced away, pretending to cringe.

''Miss Van Vorst!''

Strolling toward us in a brilliant blue coat, green silk waistcoat, and snowy white breeches was Rob-ert of the foxy face. ''How lovely you look,'' he said. He gave me a sweeping bow and kissed my hand. I had learned his full name too: Robert Foster Nicolls.

I felt my face grow hot. The man was attractive. By now I had learned that his father was the royal governor of the province. Mr. Nicolls knew how to compliment a woman. Malcolm Stapleton seemed to have none of his graces. He did not even talk in the same liquid voice.

''I've been wondering what happened to you and your pretty little Negar,'' Nicolls said, smiling at Clara. ''How quaint of you to dress her in such high style.''

''Clara is my friend,'' I said. ''We don't regard her as a slave. My grandfather intends to free her as soon as possible.''

''A noble sentiment,'' Nicolls said. ''Worthy of a lover of liberty. May I call on you, now that you have mastered our language so well?''

''Of course,'' I said, immensely flattered.

In the middle distance, I glimpsed Malcolm Stapleton gazing on us with a glum expression on his face. Did he wish that he was charming me in Nicolls's suave style?

Back at Grandfather's house, we found a fuming Cornelius Van Vorst saying good-bye to Aunt Gertrude and Uncle Johannes and their friend Judge Horsmanden. "The notions these people are acquiring. Aping British attitudes," he roared, as soon as the door closed. "We Dutch have never treated our Africans as lower beings. We eat with them at our tables. We consider them part of our families."

As his anger mounted, the dark red color flooded into Grandfather's cheeks again. His breath came in short heavy gasps. He collapsed into a wide-bottomed armchair and pulled on his grey side-whiskers. "But I fear you'd better follow your aunt's advice," he said to me. "Twenty years ago, in the year 1712, the blacks attempted to revolt and seize the town. They killed twenty-eight white men. One of them was your Aunt Gertrude's father. Ever since, many people live in fear of another insurrection. You must accept the fact that you and Clara are of different races and act accordingly in public."

"What a hateful idea!" I said.

"To get safely through the world, you must often wear a false face," Grandfather said.

"False faces are evil!" Clara said. "Only shamans, people with special powers, can wear them and keep their hearts pure."

"You must try to discover that power in your own heart," Grandfather said.

"How do you keep your heart pure?" I asked.

"By loving people," he said. "Love cleanses the heart of the world's filth and shame and sorrow."

"I met a man today who loves me," I said. "I sensed it from the moment he first looked at me."

"Who is he?" my grandfather said, alarm in his voice.

"Mr. Nicolls, the royal governor's son."

"My dear, that fellow—"

A choking sound erupted from Grandfather's throat. The purple color crowded into his cheeks until they were almost black. With a groan he toppled from his chair, striking his head on the claw foot of a nearby couch.

"The doctor," he whispered. "Dr. Hopper."

I sent our butler Peter rushing into the street to find Dr. Hopper. His wife Shirley, Clara, and I tried to lift Grandfather onto the couch but he was much too heavy. We put a pillow under his bleeding head and Shirley gave him some brandy. The liquor seemed to revive him briefly, but he soon sank into a dazed torpor.

A tall, dry-lipped man with a withered neck, Dr. Hopper was almost as old as Grandfather. He ordered Clara to summon the coachman and with the help of two husky Africans recruited from the street, they carried the old man upstairs to his bed. He vomited up black blood, which Dr. Hopper said was a very bad sign.

"We must bleed him immediately," he said.

Opening a vein in Grandfather's arm, the doctor extracted an astonishing amount of thick dark blood. Clara and I watched, wondering what good this sort of treatment could possibly do. The Seneca's false faces, the chants and spells to banish the Evil Brother, seemed a better way to challenge death.

Nevertheless, the bleeding revived the old man. He recovered from his daze and reached out for my hand. "Stay with me, Pettikin," he murmured.

I sat on the bed holding his big rough hand throughout the night. Clara made him as comfortable as possible, bathing his forehead with cold water, giving him brandy mixed with eau-de-vie, at Dr. Hopper's suggestion.

Grandfather's mind wandered. At times he talked to the other Catalyntie. "Oh Pet, Pet," he whispered. "If

I could have you in my arms again I'd live like the poorest sailor on Dock Street. Are you waiting for me on the far shore? That's my only prayer.''

He returned to the present and smiled at me. ''Petti-kin,'' he murmured. ''You've come back to me. Doesn't that prove God is good? Don't blame Him for the terror and grief of this world. He's doing the best he can with His mercy. He gives us just enough to trust in His good-ness. None of us deserve more.''

''You deserve all the mercy in this world and beyond it!'' I cried.

''Yes,'' Clara said. ''You have nothing to fear. The room is full of good spirits. I can feel them pressing around us, their arms open to you, saying come, come.''

The reassurance seemed to give the old man strength. He spoke to me in a calm clear voice. ''My will leaves you everything I own. It's not a great deal of money. When I retired from business, I gave most of my wealth to Johannes and his family. I thought you were dead. Much will depend on the price they can get for this house and my Long Island estate. I've urged Johannes to add to it the value of the Mohawk lands, which are rightfully yours, as well as a share of the New Nether-lands Trading Company. Whatever you get, be careful with it. Go into business in a small way at first. Open a store. Never risk everything on a single investment. If you need to borrow money, go to Nathan Franks. Don't worry about him being a Jew. He's an honest man.''

Tears trickled down his cheeks. ''I had hoped I could stand behind you and protect you for a while. But you must make your own way. It will be difficult at first but don't lose heart. Remember who you are—a Van Vorst. We triumph over our mistakes. Always look to the fu-ture, foresee it—and you'll grow rich.''

He closed his eyes and struggled for breath. ''That's not the whole of life. I hope you'll find a husband who loves you and gives you healthy children. A loving family is the only real source of happiness in this world. But sign nothing that limits control of your money. Remember you're Dutch, which means you value liberty above all things.''

Love. The dying old man was flooding the room, the house, the whole city with his love. ''Always believe, no matter where I go or what I become, if I can reach out and protect you, I'll do it,'' he said. ''Now I must begin my voyage. Hold my hand until I cast off.''

Tears streaming, I pressed his hand to my lips, then clutched it to my breasts. Grandfather closed his eyes and his breathing grew slower and slower. Then came a last shuddering sigh and his big head fell to one side on the pillow. Clara reached over and closed his eyes.

''Let us sing a death song for him,'' Clara said. ''To make sure his spirit is not assailed by the Evil Brother.''

We began wailing the chants we had heard since girlhood in our longhouses on the shore of Lake Ontario. The songs were full of magic phrases that had protected the souls of warriors for hundreds of years. Again and again we repeated them, our young hearts swelling with a near frenzy of love and sorrow.

''What the devil is this? Stop that infernal racket!''

Johannes Van Vorst stood in the doorway of the bedroom. With him was his frowning wife and a tall solemn man in black, who looked equally angry about our Indian behavior.

''Can't we pray for his spirit?'' I said.

''That's precisely what we've come to do—with the Reverend Van Dam,'' Gertrude Van Vorst said. ''Christian prayers, not heathen howling from the bowels of Great Satan.''

''Kneel down,'' Johannes Van Vorst said. Clara and I obeyed him, though we found the idea of kneeling to pray absurd. How could the Manitou respect someone who crawled to him like a dog?

Crowding into the room behind them came the Van

Vorsts' daughters and a half dozen strangers, all men around my uncle's age. They knelt and the Reverend Van Dam called on God to forgive Cornelius Van Vorst for his sins as he approached the seat of divine judgment.

"What are you talking about?" I said. "What sins has this man committed?"

"Be quiet! No one has the slightest interest in your opinion," Uncle Johannes said.

The Reverend Van Dam departed after another ten minutes of morose pleas for mercy on the soul of Cornelius Van Vorst. Uncle Johannes rose to his feet and began doing business. "Under the terms of my father's will, this house and his Long Island property are left in trust to my niece," he said. "As the executor of the estate, I'm prepared to take bids on them at my office tomorrow morning. Be good enough to let your friends know about it. I wish to convert the estate into cash as soon as possible."

The men murmured their assent and followed the Reverend Van Dam into the night. "Why must you sell the house?" I asked. "Clara and I would prefer to live here. I plan to open a store on Pearl Street with whatever money Grandfather left me."

"Under the laws of the province of New York, eighteen-year-old girls cannot inherit land or money," Johannes said. "Much less open stores. The best thing to do is convert everything into cash and invest it in the New Netherlands Trading Company. That way your money will grow and when you reach the age of twenty-one you'll inherit twice as much as you have now."

"I'd rather loan it out at interest," I said.

"It's a good thing you have a wise uncle," Gertrude Van Vorst said. "Otherwise you'd be penniless within a year. Pack your things. You're moving to our house in the morning and don't argue about it."

"What about Clara?" I said. Clara was standing to one side, fear of these people all too visible on her face.

"She'll have plenty to do—in our laundry room," Aunt Gertrude said.

"Is this what my grandfather intended in his will?" I asked Uncle Johannes.

"Yes," he said. "It's all being done in strict accordance with the law."

"Is that what is known as a clever lie?" I said.

Gertrude Van Vorst slapped me in the face with the flat of her hand. "You will learn to control your Indian mouth, young woman. You will learn a great many things in my house. Now get upstairs and pack."

I rubbed my burning cheek. "Come, Clara," I said, "We'll pack our things together."

Johannes shoved Clara back against the wall. "There's nothing she needs to pack. We'll sell her finery at auction tomorrow, with the house."

I heard Grandfather saying the way might be hard for me. Already it was harder than he had foreseen. How much harder would it be for Clara? "You're still my sister," I said. "You'll always be my sister, no matter what they do."

"How can you say such a thing!" Gertrude Van Vorst cried. "I'm beginning to think you're possessed by the devil."

BOOK

TWO

ONE

So BEGAN OUR SOJOURN IN the Van Vorst household. Clara was consigned to the servant quarters in the basement. Her bedroom was windowless, airless, more like a cave or a prison cell. I was given a comfortable room upstairs. We saw each other daily but it was dangerous for us to speak. Clara was threatened with a whipping if she said a word to me. I was told I would be locked in my room without food for the rest of the day. I slipped her a note, urging her to have patience. I would do my best to extricate us from this nightmare.

That proved far from simple. Each day I was sent to a school with my two Van Vorst cousins, where young women were taught to read French, dance minuets, and serve tea—the three accomplishments a wealthy young New York female was expected to acquire before marriage. The school was run by a fat bustling Englishwoman named Madame Ardsley, who also devoted a good deal of time to scouring any and all traces of a New York accent from our vocabularies. New Yorkers were inclined to say "tree" instead of three and "dem" instead of them—a tribute to the numbers of Dutch in the city. We were all required to talk through our noses like highborn Englishwomen.

Clara, meanwhile, was toiling as a washerwoman below stairs, under the eyes of Fat Alice, the African who ran the house, along with her somewhat feckless husband, Thin Tom. Fat Alice and her daughter, Hester, who was her mother's size, regarded Clara with undisguised dislike. My grandfather's cook, Shirley, had told them about our comfortable life in his house and they had also heard about our stroll to the Bowling Green in our London-style gowns.

Fat Alice called Clara "the Princess" and gave her all the dirtiest jobs in the house—emptying the chamber pots each morning, scrubbing the floors, doing the heaps of wash that Aunt Gertrude, a fanatic about cleanliness like all Dutch *vrouws*,[1] required each week. While Clara labored, she was subjected to a running chorus of abuse. "What was you doin' for old Cornelius?" Fat Alice would ask. "He was too old to fuck. You do Indian dances with nothin' but candlelight on your pretty little chocolate ass?"

"I did nothing. He was kind and good," Clara said.

"How come he sired a son of a bitch like Master Johannes?" Fat Alice said.

"Why don't you ask Mrs. Van Vorst that question?" Clara said.

"You watch your tongue, girl. Or you'll get de whippin' of your life," Fat Alice said.

Her daughter Hester overheard this exchange and told Aunt Gertrude that Clara called her husband a son of a bitch. Clara was locked in her basement room and deprived of dinner.

I could see that the situation was building toward an explosion. On Saturday afternoon, I went off to the Bowling Green and found Malcolm Stapleton talking to a broad-chested freckle-faced young man in a stylish blue coat and yellow waistcoat. He was introduced as Guert Cuyler.

"My God!" Mr. Cuyler exclaimed. "You're far more lovely than this tongue-tied lout said you were. I'm honored to meet you, Miss Van Vorst."

"Guert's a direct descendant of Peter Stuyvesant," Malcolm said, winking at me. "He thinks you should

[1]Housewives.

have nothing to do with Robert Nicolls. If you fall in love with him, he'll consider it treason."

"I'm afraid I have a much more serious matter to discuss with you, Mr. Stapleton," I said. I described Clara's unhappy life in the Van Vorst household—and my own unpleasant one. I begged him to ask his father or someone else for help.

"I'll talk to my father," Malcolm promised. "I'm not sure what he can do. He's involved in business with your uncle—"

"I'm studying law in my father's office. I'll speak to him," Guert said.

"I have no money to pay a lawyer," I said.

"There will be nothing to pay," he said.

As they walked me back to my uncle's house on Broad Street, Thin Tom came running toward us. "Help!" he cried. "Get a constable. The Indian Negar's going to kill my mistress!"

We raced to the house, followed by a considerable crowd. Fat Alice and her daughter were screaming around the entrance hall and parlor. "What's happened?" I asked.

"Your friend Clara's got a carvin' knife in her hand. She's gonna kill my sweet momma!" Hester howled.

"What did you do to her, you fat bitch?" I screamed at Alice.

"She said she wouldn't do der wash widdout somethin' to eat," Fat Alice said. "I called my mistress who come down to de basement with a cat[2] in her hand. Dat Indian grabbed a knife and chased her upstairs and me and Hester wid her."

Aunt Gertrude came downstairs with the cat still in her hand. She was blowing like a racehorse. She had obviously run all the way to the roof. "That creature

---

[2]Cat-o'-nine-tails—a whip.

will be punished at the public whipping post or my name is not Gertrude Van Vorst!'' she cried.

"Wouldn't it have been simpler to give her something to eat?'' I said.

In a passion, she raised the whip to lash me but Malcolm Stapleton caught her hand. "Calm down, Mrs. Van Vorst,'' he said.

"I will not calm down! Who invited you into my house?''

"Your niece here.''

"She's not entitled to such privileges.''

At this point Clara emerged from the basement with no sign of a knife in her hand. Almost simultaneously, Thin Tom appeared at the street door with a squat middle-aged man who wore a shoemaker's leather apron around his thick waist.

"Constable[3] Warner, I want this creature taken before a magistrate!'' Aunt Gertrude said. "She's threatened us with murder for no reason.''

"She threatened to whip me with that cat-o'-nine-tails. Isn't that a reason?'' Clara said.

"Madam Van Vorst,'' Warner said. "I've got a business to run. It's not a constable's part to keep peace among quarreling females.''

"You're paid out of the public purse, sir!'' Gertrude Van Vorst cried. "I insist you take her to the jail and bring her before a magistrate in the morning. She's a danger to every person in this house. Only a public whipping will change her ways.''

"Did you mean what you said about murdering?'' Warner asked Clara.

"I meant every word. I'll kill anyone who tries to whip me,'' she said.

"Goddamn all,'' Warner roared. He seized Clara by

[3]At this time New York had no daytime police force. Law was enforced by part-time constables.

the arm and dragged her into the street. Pushing and prodding her ahead of him, he hurried her to a big stone building on the corner of Wall and Nassau streets, which she soon learned was New York's City Hall. In front of it was a set of stocks, in which two disconsolate-looking whores sat, their arms and legs pinned in the holes, while a crowd of boys hurled jeers in their painted faces. Beside the stocks was a bright red post with manacles dangling from it.

"There's where they're going to cure you of murdering talk tomorrow," Constable Warner said. "I wouldn't be surprised if you get twenty or thirty lashes."

Downstairs in City Hall's gloomy basement, a stumpy man wearing a dirty grey wig was eating a plate of oysters. He had crossed eyes, which struck fear into Clara's soul. Was it a sign that he was in the service of the Evil Brother?

"What's this, more thievery?" he asked Warner.

"Nothing of the sort, Sheriff," Warner growled. "The piece belongs to Her High Mightiness Van Vorst. Says she wants to murder the lot of them. I was tempted to tell her to go to it."

The cross-eyed man stood up and stretched. A dozen heavy keys clanked at his waist. "Old Staats is sitting tomorrow," he said. "He'll take good care of her. They killed one of his sons in 1712."

He unlocked a heavy door and waved Clara along a narrow foul-smelling corridor, illuminated only by a single small window at the end of it. Halfway down, he unlocked another heavy door and shoved her into a cell that stank of piss and shit. A bucket, half full of the stuff, had obviously gone unemptied for a week. In the light from a dirty window Clara saw the floor was covered with a horde of roaches and other crawling creatures. There was neither a bed nor a chair. She would have to share the dirt-crusted floor with the insects.

"You got any money?" the sheriff asked.

"No."

"You better find some if you want to eat anything."[4]

He slammed the door and clumped back down the corridor to finish his oysters. Out of the silence a voice spoke from a cell on the other side of the corridor: "What's your name, beautiful?"

"Clara."

"Caesar over here. I'll get you somethin' to eat. What do you like? Oysters? Roast potatoes? Clams?"

"I don't care."

"You got to change that way of thinkin', beautiful. You can make a man give you just about anything you want if you set your mind to it."

Clara was too miserable to reply. She huddled against the wall by the cell door, her head bowed on her knees. Perhaps death was better than this sort of life. If they beat her at the whipping post she would murder someone, preferably Gertrude Van Vorst, and let them hang her.

The cell door swung open. "Caesar says you can have some of his dinner," the jailer said. "You want to risk it?"

Clara did not know why she should fear Caesar. She crossed the corridor to find herself facing a husky young African. He was as tall as a Seneca warrior, with a flashing smile and bold carefree eyes. He gave the jailer some gold coins and bowed Clara into his cell, which had a cot, blankets, and a chair and table. The floor was relatively clean and his slop bucket was empty.

On the table was a big plate of roasted clams, some ale, and plates of roasted potatoes and vegetables. Caesar grandly waved Clara to a seat. She was too disconsolate to eat much but Caesar did not let her gloom discourage him from enjoying a hearty meal. While he ate, he persuaded her to tell him why she was in jail. She described

---

[4]*Prisoners in eighteenth-century jails had to pay for decent food.*

her persecution by Gertrude Van Vorst, Fat Alice, and her lying daughter, Hester.

"Fat Alice's mad at the world because she's so damn ugly she couldn't get no one but that walkin' skeleton, Thin Tom, to fuck her," Caesar said. "She used to parade after me but I told her I'd rather do it with a sheep."

"Do all the people of color hate me?" Clara said.

"Of course not. But they can't stop talkin' about you."

"Why are you in jail?"

Caesar grinned. "If I told you that, you might blab it to the judge and Caesar would be dancin' at the end of a rope the next day. Let's just say they don't like the way I get my hands on ready money."

"What will they do to you?"

"Depends on the magistrate I draw. I might get forty or fifty lashes or maybe just a warnin'. I usually get a warnin' because my master, old Johnny Vraack, can't run his bakery without me. He'd starve without Caesar. So he puts in a plea to the magistrate not to damage his property. Since it's all just talk and suspicion anyway, if the magistrate's Dutch, he goes along. The Dutch hate English law and love to thumb their noses at it."

"What if you get an English magistrate?"

"He may decide to inflict some damage, just to be on the safe side. But I been lashed before. It's just another debit in Caesar's book."

"Debit?"

"A debt. A debt of honor." Caesar drained the last of the ale and smiled mysteriously. He was a little drunk. "Someday Caesar's goin' to rule this town. I wasn't named Caesar for no reason. It's the name of a great general from long long ago, a man who was more powerful than this Jesus the whites are always talkin' about. General Caesar hung Jesus from a cross, that's how powerful he was."

Caesar leaned across the table, his voice low, his eyes hooded. "There's goin' to be another war. The French and the Spanish are goin' to attack New York from outside. Caesar will have an army inside. We'll help them win the battle. We'll pay back every one of the debits the whites owe us."

Caesar leaped from the table and bounded around the cell, swinging an imaginary sword, slashing the shadows along the walls of the cell, spearing the empty ale bottle. "What a day that will be, beautiful. What a day—and what a night. We'll burn their houses. It's easy to do. You take a hot coal from the fireplace and carry it upstairs in a tin cup and stick it under the eaves. Four or five hours later, there's a blaze! The whole town will burn. The whites will come screamin' into the streets— where we'll be waitin' for them."

He lunged, parried, slashed. Finally, breathless and sweaty, he bowed before her and declared: "Then we'll make you the Queen of New York. Caesar's wife."

Was this man inspired or was he simply drunk? Before her grandmother banned rum from Shining Creek, the warriors often drank too much and made boastful speeches about killing all the whites in the world. But in the morning they were much quieter and more sensible. They listened mournfully to the sachem, Black Eagle, who had been to Quebec and New York and told them the white men were as numerous as the leaves on the trees and it would be impossible to kill them all.

Suddenly Caesar was leaning over her, a warm male smell coming from his black flesh. "Now, beautiful, it's time to pay for your dinner."

"You know I have no money."

"There's another way a pretty girl can pay."

"I'm not a whore," Clara said.

Caesar's smile only grew wider. "All women are whores and all men are thieves," he said. "Eventually you'll sell your love to someone. Why not start with me, the prince of thieves?''

Clara shook her head. Caesar tried to pull her to her feet for a rough kiss. She sank her teeth into his shoulder and he let go with a howl of pain. She was sure she was going to get a beating but Caesar only rubbed his wound and glowered.

''You're lucky you belong to Van Vorst,'' Caesar said. ''If it was anyone else, I'd spoil your pretty face for you. But he's the sort who'd sue my master for damage to his property. If I ever cost Old Vraack real money, he'd let me hang the next time they caught me.''

''I want to go back to the other cell,'' Clara said.

''Oh no. We're goin' to spend the night together. Maybe by mornin' we'll be friends.''

Clara crouched in a corner of the cell and Caesar talked about Africa. His father had been a great chief and he had led their tribe into battle against an enemy tribe on the other side of a tremendous river, ten times as wide as the Hudson. They had lost the battle and the enemy had crossed the river with his father's body and seized their village. They had cooked his father over a bed of coals and eaten him in tribute to his bravery. They had let him eat some of his father's flesh.

None of this surprised Clara. She had seen the Senecas eat the flesh of captive warriors after they had died bravely at the torture stake. It was the way warriors tried to steal the courage of their enemies. But Caesar's story carried at its heart a different kind of pain. He told her of the long march to the shore of the ocean, where his mother and brothers and sisters and everyone else in his village were sold to white men on ships that brought them to America.

Clara asked him if Africa was like America. ''No,'' Caesar said. ''Africa's warm. No one freezes in the winter in Africa the way people do in New York. Every year poor people freeze to death here when they run out of wood.''

Caesar talked on about the wonders, the beauties, of Africa. The great river never thickened into ice. There was no snow in Africa, no north wind that whipped cold rain and colder sleet into a man's face. The animals were beautiful. The horses had black and white stripes and there were animals even bigger than horses, with floppy ears and great long noses and teeth as long as swords. Africa was a loving mother and America was a harsh pitiless father.

''No one steals in Africa, no one lies and cheats. Women don't sell their love for money. Men don't own slaves and live off their labor. Everyone shares in the bounty of the land, the fish of the great river, the game of the forest.''

''I begin to think even if you become a king in America, you'll still long for Africa,'' Clara said.

''I'll build a royal ship, a ship big enough for my whole army, and sail back to Africa. We'll go up the great river to my old village and start a new tribe.''

Caesar was back to boasting again. Clara had watched her grandmother listen to bragging warriors and silently calculate how much truth there was in their oratory. Her calculation of Caesar's truth was low. But there was something else loose in Caesar's words—a sadness that Clara began to share for the first time. It was part of the new truth, the new self she was slowly discovering. She too was an exile in this white world.

What else did she sense, as Caesar prowled the dark cell, imagining himself as king of New York? Danger. There was danger and blood and death in Caesar's words. Clara did not know how or where or when the danger would erupt, but she sensed it like heat from a flame. Caesar was like a spark blown into a dry forest, igniting a blaze that consumed everything and everyone, trees, animals, humans.

But the sadness slowly overwhelmed the danger as Caesar grew weary of the sound of his own voice. "Come on, my beautiful one. Make Caesar happy for a little while," he whispered. "Let him make you happy. There's so little happiness in this miserable world. Let's make some here in the dark."

As Caesar's hands prowled her body, Clara found it more and more difficult to refuse him. Intertwined with the sadness and the smell of danger was a mad angry hope that connected to something deep inside her. She let him carry her to the cot and kiss her until the smell of desire oozed from his flesh and the blind wish to be filled, to be held, throbbed in her belly.

What came next was not happiness. In these moments, her grandmother had taught her that spirits should touch, the whole world should sigh and sing like a summer wind in leafy trees. Wherever Caesar's spirit dwelt, it did not speak to her. Had slavery destroyed it? Was he only a talking machine that stole and baked and schemed? Would it be different, would there be joy and music, if she and Caesar were free?

☀

TWO

CLARA WAS TWINED IN CAESAR'S arms when the sheriff awoke them with guffaws and leers. She felt ashamed and vowed she would never surrender that way again, especially when Caesar strutted and winked while the sheriff mocked her with stuff about Caesar having every black woman in New York thanks to his clever mouth and big cock.

Suddenly the sheriff was no longer friendly. He

clapped manacles on Caesar's wrists and ankles and tied Clara's hands behind her back and ordered them ahead of him to the courtroom. On a high seat in a room lined with dark wood sat a gloomy-eyed old man in a black robe, with a long white wig that fell to his shoulders on both sides of his head. Behind him on the wall hung a portrait of King George II. This was "old Staats"— Judge Walter Van Staats, the man who liked to punish blacks. On a bench in the center of the courtroom sat Mrs. Van Vorst and Fat Alice and her daughter Hester.

Caesar was tried first. The sheriff reported he had been spotted by the constables of the Night Watch[1] at the foot of Dock Street with a bag over his shoulder. The Watch gave chase and Caesar threw the bag into the harbor. The Watch was convinced it was stolen goods that Caesar was on his way to sell to sailors on nearby ships. The judge told Caesar this was his third arrest this year on the same charge, suspicion of theft. What was his explanation this time?

Caesar said the bag contained various things he had won at cards with his friends. He did not want the Watch to get it because some of the items might have gotten the friends in trouble. He swore none of them were stolen—they had all been given to his friends for being good servants. He also said he was angry at the Watch for persecuting him.

From a bench in the rear of the courtroom tottered John Vraack, Caesar's master, a bent old man who pleaded with the judge to be lenient with Caesar. He needed him to run his bakery. His health no longer permitted him to do heavy work. Without Caesar, he and his wife would have to go out of business. They could not afford to buy another slave.

Judge Van Staats swore if Caesar was arrested again, he would hang, even if John Vraack and his wife starved

---

[1] New York's part-time police force.

and half of New York went without bread. Caesar pi-
ously vowed to stop gambling and attend to his work.
He said he would go to church every Sunday and ask
God for help. Grumbling and snarling, Judge Van Staats
dismissed the charges.

It was Clara's turn. The sheriff had said very little
against Caesar. He had stated the facts of his case in a
bored monotone. With Clara he became furiously indignant. He described her threats and called her a savage
who needed to be taught that Indian ways were not white
ways and New Yorkers would not tolerate threats of
murder and mayhem.

"I agree with every word you say!" the judge rumbled. "Summon the witnesses."

Gertrude Van Vorst and Fat Alice testified to Clara's
threatening them with the knife. She was sure she was
on her way to the whipping post when the doors at the
back of the courtroom swung open and Malcolm Stapleton and his friend Robert Foster Nicolls hurried up
the aisle. With them was the hunchback, Adam Duycinck, and a third man, followed by her Seneca sister,
Catalyntie Van Vorst.

I had spent the intervening hours quarreling violently
with my aunt and uncle and beseeching Malcolm Stapleton and Guert Cuyler to save Clara from the whipping
post. Guert could not prevail upon his father to take the
case. Nor could Malcolm persuade his father. No estab-
lished lawyer wanted to defend an African who had
threatened a white woman with a knife. Guert decided
to plead it himself, even though he was far from a thorough lawyer.[2] When Robert Nicolls heard about my distress, he volunteered to join us as a friendly witness.

[2]*There were no law schools. Lawyers studied in the offices of other
lawyers.*

"Your Honor," said Guert, "I would like to represent the defendant in this matter."

"On what grounds? She's not your property," Judge Van Staats said.

"She's the property in fact if not in law of Miss Van Vorst here, the granddaughter of your late lamented good friend, Cornelius Van Vorst," Guert said. "He was also among my grandfather's dearest friends. Miss Van Vorst is not yet old enough to inherit her estate. But I think she has a right, in the law, to protest the abuse of a slave that belongs to her, just as she might protest if her uncle, the executor of the estate, began damaging or otherwise maltreating a house which was left to her."

"How dare you, sir?" Gertrude Van Vorst cried. "How dare you accuse my husband of such a thing?"

"For the moment we're only accusing *you* of maltreating this girl, madam," Guert said.

"What about the right of the community to protect itself against the creature's violence? Am I supposed to let her return to the house she's threatened with murder?" Judge Van Staats said.

"If it please the court," Guert said. "I would suggest an order from Your Honor to place the wench in the custody of my friend, Malcolm Stapleton here, and his father. They'll negotiate a fair price with the Van Vorsts for the loss of her services."

At this point, Robert Nicolls stepped forward and gave an eloquent defense of Clara's character. "I saw this young woman when she was exchanged at the great peace council last year," he said. "She did not display a hint of violence or resentment in her demeanor."

"I'm inclined to order her sold to the West Indies at a fair market value and the money to be placed in Miss Van Vorst's estate!" Judge Van Staats roared.

"Your late lamented good friend, Cornelius Van Vorst, when he drew his will, urged that this young woman be treated with kindness and forbearance, out of a debt of gratitude he owed her father for saving his life in the northern woods,'' Guert Cuyler said.

The repetition of Cornelius Van Vorst's name had a marvelously soothing effect on the old judge. He rumbled and grumbled about Clara still being a danger to the peace of the city but he was no longer threatening her with punishment. ''If it would satisfy Your Honor,'' Malcolm said, ''she can be sent to my family's house in New Jersey. My mother is in need of a servant out there.''

''Done,'' the judge said, whacking the bench with his gavel. ''In the name of the best friend of my life. For no one else would I hesitate to mete justice to one of these black vermin. They murdered my son, you know. Every time I see one of them on the street I can taste the bile of that memory in my throat.''

''They murdered my father!'' Gertrude Van Vorst cried.

Black vermin. The words struck Clara like a lash across the face. Was this what white men thought of them?

Them. Who was she talking about? She was a Seneca. She was not one of these Africans.

Dazedly, Clara let me embrace her and lead her from the courtroom, while Gertrude Van Vorst raged at us. Guert Cuyler struggled to play the peacemaker. He obviously had misgivings about offending the Van Vorsts. It was a good indication of how rich my uncle had become.

''I took the case at Miss Van Vorst's request, madam,'' Cuyler said. ''My father drew Cornelius Van Vorst's last will. We consider her our client.''

''The whole matter is an unfortunate misunderstanding,'' Robert Nicolls said. ''I'm sure you never intended to mistreat her, madam. It's hard for us civilized folk to appreciate the way Indians act and react. You should think of her that way, madam—and consider yourself well rid of her. I'm sure, when you have time to reflect on it, you'll agree with me.''

"You may have a point, sir," Aunt Gertrude said, soothed by Nicolls's ingratiating manner.

My admiration for—not to mention my gratitude to—this self-assured young men quintupled. It mingled with my satisfaction at extricating Clara from the Van Vorst household. I could only hope she would be happier with the Stapletons, even though she was still a slave.

We escorted Clara to a boat waiting at a Hudson River dock. "The sooner you're out of Aunt Gertrude's reach, the better," I said. "Mr. Stapleton's assured me you'll be treated with perfect kindness and respect. We can exchange letters and perhaps I can visit you, if I can persuade my uncle to lend me the money for the trip. As soon as I inherit my estate I'll free you."

We reached the dock as I said these last words. The rage they created in Clara's eyes made me wonder if our love had ended. I had blundered from the white world back into our Seneca past. Even if I freed her from slavery, the gift was poisoned. How could she accept as a gift the liberty every Seneca inherited at birth?

"Forgive me!" I cried.

"There's nothing to forgive," Clara said.

In that moment, Clara donned an invisible false face. She no longer cared about the teachings of Jesus. She did not even care whether her words and acts created good or evil. She saw her soul, fleeing through the moonless forest to be devoured by demons and devils, all of them white. Somehow she would outwit them.

THREE

THE STAPLETON MANOR HOUSE STOOD on a broad meadow, a few miles from the falls of the Passaic River. Beyond it stretched fields of green corn and wheat and orchards full of flowering apple and pear trees. The fieldstone mansion looked huge, compared to the size of the houses Clara had seen in New York. It was four stories high, with a central hall that separated it into two massive wings. There were six matching windows on each floor—proof of the builder's wealth or arrogance or both. The cost of heating such a house had to be stupendous. On the red tile roof a half dozen chimneys poked red brick snouts into the sky.

Around the mansion were red barns, a fieldstone carriage house, and at least two dozen smaller wooden huts, which she would soon learn were slave quarters. "Does this village have a name?" Clara asked.

"Happenstance Hall," Adam Duycinck said.

"Hampden Hall," Malcolm Stapleton said. He was holding the reins of the two-horse team that was pulling their springless wagon, in which crude seats had been fastened by a country carpenter.

"After some bloody English hero," Duycinck said.

"He was a real hero, you stupid Dutch bastard," Malcolm said. "John Hampden defied the Stuart kings and their corrupt ways. My grandfather, Hugh Stapleton, served in his regiment in the civil war. He was with him when he died at Chalgrove Field."

"You can't get an idea into this fellow's noodle that

isn't connected to a battle," Duycinck said to Clara. "All he thinks about is war."

"What's wrong with that?" Clara asked. Among the Senecas, men thought of little else except the exploits of the great warriors they hoped to match.

"You can get yourself killed in a war," Duycinck said.

"What difference does that make, as long as you die with your honor unbroken?" Clara said.

"Listen to that, Duycinck!" Malcolm Stapleton said. "From the mouth of a slave girl."

"I'm not a slave," Clara said. "I'm a Seneca. A daughter of the Bear Clan!"

Startled, Malcolm looked over his shoulder. Was he seeing her for the first time? Words from her Seneca mother leaped into Clara's mind. *There are people who look and see nothing. Trust only those who look hard and see truly.* This young man was learning to look hard. Should she trust him?

No, it was impossible. He was white. With him, as with the others, even Catalyntie, she would always wear a false face. But she soon saw the value of having Malcolm Stapleton's good opinion. In the lofty entrance hall, they met the mistress of the mansion, whom Malcolm introduced almost rudely as "my stepmother."

A tall, and fair-skinned woman, Georgianna Stapleton faced the world with the hauteur of a queen. Her hair was a glistening auburn, strewn with darker shades. She was wearing a green riding outfit and green hat with a black raven's feather in it. "Who is this beautiful creature?" she asked, with the hard eyes of a woman who does not tolerate rivals.

Malcolm explained who Clara was and why she was here. "We have no need of another house servant," Mrs. Stapleton said. "She'll have to go into the fields."

"She's too educated for that," Malcolm said. "She can read and write. Father thinks she can help Jamey with his lessons. She can also help Adam with his accounts.''

"Lessons!" Mrs. Stapleton said. "I fear scholarship will be as lost on Jamey as it was on you. I will never understand how an intelligent man like your father sired two such boobies.''

Malcolm flushed and struggled to control his anger. Mrs. Stapleton went blithely on: "What does Adam need with an assistant, unless she knows how to turn red ink into black?''

"She's turned black blood into red, madam," Duycinck said with his leering smile. "Her mother was killed by the Indians and she was adopted by them. She considers herself a Seneca.''

In a more confiding voice, he added: "They say her mother had powers. She may be able to change our luck.''

"That would be a novelty," Mrs. Stapleton said. "I'm off to the Alexanders for a fortnight. We'll decide what to do with Clara when I return. If she wants to try teaching Jamey in the meantime, good luck to her.''

"As for you," she said, poking her riding crop into Duycinck's protruding stomach. "If there's a Negro born with a twisted back in nine months, I will personally persuade Governor Nicolls to deport you to the West Indies. I'll color you black first to make sure you go directly into the sugarcane fields.''

"Madam, that would be Satan at work, not poor pathetic Adam," Duycinck whined.

"You were born a scoundrel and you'll die one," she said. She seemed more amused than angry. "We're entertaining the governor and his entourage on my return. Make sure the kitchen, the bedrooms, the public rooms, are ready to receive them. I've written out the menus for the dinners.''

"All will be attended to exactly as you wish, madam," Duycinck said.

"You may kiss me good-bye, Stepson."

Georgianna Stapleton turned her head, permitting Malcolm to kiss her rouged cheek, and strolled past him onto the sunny lawn, where an African in a red coat was soothing a skittish white horse. Malcolm glared sullenly after her. The encounter had annihilated his good cheer.

"If there's any trouble in this neighborhood, it'll be between her legs, not mine," Duycinck muttered.

"Shut your filthy mouth," Malcolm snarled.

"I don't know what you people are talking about," Clara said, concealing her disgust behind the false face of a timid bewildered girl. Duycinck's remark was not much different from jokes she had heard in the longhouse of the Bear Clan since she was a child. Her performance was designed to win Malcolm Stapleton's sympathy.

Malcolm watched his stepmother canter down the curving drive, followed by the red-coated groom on a smaller horse. "Mrs. Stapleton rules my father and the rest of us like a Russian czarina," he said. "My father loves her extravagantly. He built this great pile for her—going monstrously into debt—but as far as I can see she loves no one but herself."

A big black man named Samson lugged Clara's trunk up the stairs to her room on the top floor. "How long have you lived here?" Clara asked him.

He shook his head angrily, as if he disapproved of her question. Duycinck, who had followed them upstairs, explained: "He's just off a ship from Africa. He doesn't know a word of English."

He spoke rapidly to Samson in a language Clara did not understand, though the sound of it stirred a tremor in her flesh. Had she heard similar words from her parents as a child? Samson retreated down the hall and Clara asked Duycinck the name of the language. The hunchback shrugged. "I picked it up from the blacks on the ship that brought me here," he said.

Suddenly his arm was around Clara's waist. "I'll be glad to teach it to you between midnight and dawn," he said. "My back may be crooked but there's other parts of me that can stand as straight as a pine tree with a little encouragement."

"Why should I be so generous?" Clara said.

"I can help you with Madame Stapleton. No one else can tease her into a decent humor when she goes on her rampages. Malcolm flees to the woods, his father to New York City."

"Why does she rampage—as you call it?"

"She regrets leaving England. She considers the Stapletons—and everyone else in America—beneath her. Her father was a London merchant who went bankrupt after presenting her at court and otherwise raising her to live like a princess. She had to take the best offer she could get."

"Was the first Mrs. Stapleton as beautiful?"

"Pretty enough. Scottish. It's where Malcolm gets his name and his warrior blood. She died giving birth to Malcolm's brother, Jamey. Malcolm gets drunk on the anniversary of her going, every year. Can you imagine a soldier with such a heart? It's fitter for a woman."

"Soldiers never let their hearts trouble them?"

"They must never admit the pain to their mind's eye. A soldier's heart must be as tight and tough as a drum, and he marches to its martial beat, no matter what sort of vapors rumble inside it!"

The little Dutchman swelled his chest like a screech owl as he declaimed this fustian. "You too have a warrior's heart?" Clara asked.

"Haven't I just told you I'm a man?" Duycinck cried.

"I'm glad you'll be able to bear the pain of what I must tell you. I'm not interested in your proposal. I can only give myself to a man I love."

This was another false face, Clara told herself, even if the words were true. She watched with amusement as

Duycinck deflated like a frog in a kettle. "You'll soon find you need me," the hunchback said.

"If so, I hope I'll discover a friend generous enough to help me without any expectation of a reward," Clara said.

Muttering, Duycinck withdrew and Clara unpacked the half dozen everyday dresses and petticoats Catalyntie had hastily given her. As she finished hanging the clothes in a dusty wardrobe, Malcolm Stapleton appeared in the doorway, an unhappy expression on his face. "You must never cross my stepmother. Her good humor can vanish in a flash. She can persuade my father to do anything."

"Is your father pleased with her when she behaves that way?"

"He stopped being pleased with her a long time ago," Malcolm said. "Except when she deigns to comfort him in bed."

"Why doesn't he find another woman to live with?"

"Because marriage is for life," Malcolm said.

"What a foolish idea," Clara said. "Among the Senecas people often have two or three husbands. My grandmother had four."

"That's easy for them. They're heathens," Malcolm said. "We have to bear witness before God."

"We too bear witness before God about important things," Clara said. "Everyone does."

He gave her that hard look again. But this time his eyes were cold. She sensed a darkness in his soul, born of a disappointment that was profound. It was a strange spirit for such a young man. Clara had only seen it in old men who had failed to win greatness as warriors.

"Do you plan to become a soldier?" she asked.

"It's what I want to be," Malcolm said. "But I'm as like to do it as I am to fly to the moon. My father's determined to pound me into a lawyer, whether I like it or not."

"Is that so bad? Lawyers grow rich, don't they?"

"I hate the whereases and whereifs—I'm no good at it—but I hate it first and last."

Clara heard real pain in this young giant's voice. He was almost as shackled by his father's will as she was by the arbitrary laws of the slave trade.

"A Seneca believes if something is truly your heart's desire, you must seek it, no matter what it costs you," Clara said.

Her head did not reach Malcolm Stapleton's shoulder. But she spoke to him with such calm authority, he forgot the color of her skin, her status as a slave. Clara's *orenda* was at work here, shaping both their lives.

"I applied for a commission in one of the king's regiments," Malcolm said. "The answer came back from London only last week—there's no room for someone from an insignificant colony like New York."

"You must never think of yourself that way," Clara said. "No man with a low opinion of himself can lead men in battle. New York is not insignificant. New York is part of America. When you place a map of America over England, it becomes a little island, no bigger than a mudbank in Lake Ontario. Duycinck is right, when he calls you American. You and I and Catalyntie—all those who were born here—are Americans."

There was skepticism in Malcolm's smile. She could see he did not really agree with her. But he honored her good intentions. "I'll try to remember that," he said.

Malcolm led Clara downstairs to the kitchen, where he introduced her to Bertha, a black woman who was almost as big as Fat Alice, but had a much more cheerful disposition. "This manor would fall apart without Bertha," Malcolm said. "She keeps us all happy with the best cooking in the colony."

"Oh, go on, since you been a tot barely up to my knee you ate everythin' I put in front of you. Would've eaten grass or dirt, I swear, if I put a little gravy on it,'' Bertha said. ''Never seen a boy with such an appetite.''

She examined Clara with shrewd humorous eyes that evoked memories of her Seneca grandmother. ''I already heard all about you from the Dutchman,'' she said, meaning Duycinck. ''What a high and mighty lady you is, with your head full of readin' and writin'.''

''That doesn't mean I'm afraid of hard work,'' Clara said. ''I'll be glad to help you here whenever you need it.''

''I got all the help I need,'' Bertha said, gesturing to two younger black women, who were stirring and mixing at the other end of the big sunny kitchen. Clara saw that Bertha, while not an enemy, declined to become a friend. Even the color of her skin seemed to separate Clara from Bertha's people. Theirs was so intensely black, light seemed to vanish into it. Clara's creamy tan was almost white in comparison. Yet she was one of them, she reminded herself bitterly. The word *slave* united them.

She wondered if she would ever have a friend in this black and white world, except Catalyntie. She was miles and miles away, on the other side of the Hudson River. For a moment Clara felt overwhelmed by a desolating loneliness.

Was flight the answer? The forest loomed not more than a mile or two beyond the Stapletons' tilled fields. Perhaps she should flee back to her Seneca family now, before she became alien to them. But something dire, a wedge of darkness containing the voice of the Evil Brother, told her that a fatal separation had already occurred. The knowledge of maps, of white ways and white gods, of black ways and black dreams, had already separated her from the people she loved.

Later in the day she met Jamey Stapleton, Malcolm's seven-year-old brother. He was a plump lazy boy, with round red cheeks and hair so blond it was almost white.

He gazed at Clara with astonishment when Malcolm said she would teach him arithmetic and reading. Duycinck, who was supposed to be doing the job, had given up in disgust.

"How's that possible?" Jamey sneered. "She don't look like she knows enough to sling a hoe."

"I know how to do that too," Clara said. "I've hoed enough corn to make you as fat as Bertha. But that isn't hard to learn. Can you add this column?" She scribbled a dozen numbers on a sheet of paper. Jamey looked at them with dismay. Clara swiftly added the figures and said he would begin learning how to do that tomorrow morning.

That night, Clara lay in her bed, listening to the distant sounds of the forest. The call of an owl, the howl of a wolf, the murmur of insects. She thought of Bold Antelope, tormented by his love for her and the disgrace of his defeat in combat with Malcolm Stapleton. Could she love a man who had failed as a warrior before her eyes? It was almost impossible for a daughter of the Bear Clan. Here too an eternal separation had occurred.

A muffled cry, the thud of feet in the third floor hall startled her. She rushed to her bedroom door and saw Malcolm Stapleton's huge figure in the semidarkness. He was stumbling up and down the hall, his arms outstretched, groaning like a man in agony. Duycinck rushed up to Clara, who had a candle in her hand. "He's at it again!" he hissed. "He's been doing this since his mother died. Once he climbed out on the roof and almost killed himself."

"Don't wake him," Clara said. "He must finish his dream."

There had been several sleepwalkers in her Seneca village. They were all men and their dreams as they walked often turned out to be crucial revelations of their *ondinnonk*—their secret desires. Clara and Duycinck tried to guide Malcolm back to his bedroom but he violently resisted their touch, snarling and swinging his huge fists at them.

Only Duycinck's voice calmed him. The little Dutchman capered around him in the candlelit darkness, crying: "It's all right, Malcolm, it's all right."

Something in the dream released a flood of tears. "No, no," Malcolm sobbed, falling to his knees. He seemed to be holding someone in his arms. "Clara!" he sobbed. He allowed them to lead him back to his bedroom, head bowed, like a captive.

In the morning, Clara asked Malcolm to describe his dream. "I was in an Indian village. Someone was being tortured at the stake. I realized it was me. But I didn't feel anything. I was watching it like a spectator—or a ghost. You were there too. Someone had hurt you. You seemed to be bleeding. I heard your voice telling me something—but I couldn't make out the words."

This was not a dream of *ondinnonk* but of *utgo*, of the evil fate that ruled so much of the world. At times it invaded the minds of certain people and gave them a glimpse of the future. The vision was not always true. Sometimes the Evil Brother used false *utgo* to harass and frighten people. But Clara sensed this dream was true—it would become real in the vast undefined future. It made her wonder if her life was intertwined with this young giant—perhaps unto death.

FOUR

IN NEW YORK, MY LIFE with the Van Vorsts became less acrimonious without Clara around as a source of contention. Aunt Gertrude, claiming to know best, absolutely forbade me to write to her. When Clara wrote to me, Aunt Gertrude must have confiscated her letters. I never saw one. I won't say I forgot Clara. But she receded from my mind as the social world of wealthy Manhattan absorbed me.

Aunt Gertrude realized I was going to be a permanent part of her household and sat me down for a motherly lecture. She warned me against Dutch stubbornness and clinging to old ways, traits she feared I had picked up from my sojourn with my grandfather. She told me the philosophy that guided her and her husband.

Simply put it was: The English ruled the world and only fools were refusing to join them. That was why her daughters were going to Madame Ardsley's school. That was why her husband slogged into Indian country as the royal governor's representative to help pacify the Iroquois and the Canadian tribes. English styles, English books, English songs, English plays, English customs, English furniture, were the future, the Dutch version of all these things the discarded past.

Who was I to dispute Aunt Gertrude? Partly because I was touched by her maternal concern, I did my best to follow her advice. I paid attention at Madame Ardsley's school and was soon able to persuade my aunt I was ready to graduate by demonstrating that I could read French passably, dance a minuet, and serve tea. Aunt Gertrude, never one to miss a chance to save money, agreed. My days instantly became more pleasant.

I spent the morning cleaning my room, arranging my clothes and supposedly reading the Bible for an hour (which I never did) and after dinner[1] set out to visit friends such as the Frankses, the Laurenses, or the Cuylers. These survivors of my grandfather's generation had large families who welcomed me into their houses. Laurens had two agreeable granddaughters my age, Rebecca

---

[1] *A midday meal; there was no such thing as lunch.*

and Anne, and the Frankses' grandson, Jacob, was a clever young man, full of jokes and good humor. Guert Cuyler was always glad to see me.

Accompanying me was my favorite companion, a greyhound named Walpole that I had rescued from a visiting ship's captain who had grown tired of the dog. That Walpole was named after the prime minister of England meant little to me. I had no idea that naming a dog after a politician was a way of showing one's contempt for the man. I liked Walpole because he was a sweet obedient creature—and in several portraits of highborn Englishwomen I had seen in books, they were accompanied by such dogs.

Evenings were spent at supper parties in various wealthy homes or at assembly balls in one of the better taverns. Some evenings we entertained ourselves with minuets and country dances. Other times we performed a play, such as Joseph Addison's *Cato*, a tale of old Rome, in which a noble hero dies for liberty. Other evenings were devoted to winning or losing at whist, a card game which had recently emerged from the servants' quarters to absorb the *ton*. Whatever the entertainment, at eleven o'clock servants brought in a feast of cold pheasant, quail, salmon and wines from France and Germany, and the merriment often continued well past midnight.

At first, I felt overmatched by the other young women at these parties. They had played together since babyhood—and they seemed to know exactly what to say to the young men who swarmed around us, full of teasing jokes and amorous looks. I reverted to the Moon Woman, convinced of my inability to attract or interest a man. My cousin Esther soon informed me that the young men called me "the ice queen"—a tribute to my apparent coldness.

Gradually, I began to notice more than a few similarities between my old life at Shining Creek and my new life in New York. Among the young women of my age, the conversation was almost entirely devoted to the same topic: men. Every New York maiden was looking for a husband at least as anxiously as the young Seneca women of Shining Creek. But there was one very large difference. It was all talk. There were no experimental visits to the woods, no reports on a male's skills or inclinations as a lover. Instead, through both sexes—but especially the women—swirled a veritable maelstrom of suppressed desire, which led to violent outbursts of anger and envy.

Not a few of these eruptions of spite were directed at me, when Robert Nicolls began paying special attentions to me. As the royal governor's son, he was New York's equivalent of the Prince of Wales and the natural social leader of our generation. Unintimidated by my reserve, he insisted on making me his partner in at least half the dances. When we performed *Cato*, he assigned me the role of Marcia, the hero's virtuous daughter, and himself the part of Juba, a brave Numidian prince who is hopelessly in love with her. Although I knew it was all make-believe, my heart beat with more than ordinary vigor when Robert/Juba declaimed his adoration unto death. At whist, when my luck faltered, he often sat beside me, helping me play my hand.

At the end of the night, we sometimes sent our coaches home empty and strolled back to our houses by moonlight or torchlight. Two or three soldiers from the fort carried the burning brands—and guaranteed our safety. The streets of New York, thick with drunken sailors and indentured servants and slaves relieved from obedience for a few hours, were by no means safe. In these postmidnight rambles, Robert was invariably my escort. Guert Cuyler or Jacob Franks occasionally vied for the post, but Robert was always there to wave them off.

Aunt Gertrude's older daughter, Esther Van Vorst, reported Robert Nicolls's attentions to her mother, who evinced grave alarm at the dinner table. Mr. Nicolls's reputation was less than praiseworthy. There were rumors of him "ruining" the daughters of at least two prominent families.

I was baffled by this idea. "What did he do?" I asked.

"He . . . he . . . deflowered them," Aunt Gertrude stammered. "They surrendered a woman's most precious possession, their virginity, to him—only to discover his plighted word meant nothing."

"You mean he stuck them?" I said incredulously. This hardly seemed worthy of the word *ruin*. As a Seneca, I had no great respect for virginity. Aunt Gertrude's emotion seemed wildly out of proportion to me.

Esther and Anna, who were facing me across the dinner table, emitted small cries of horror. "Stuck them?" Aunt Gertrude said. It was her turn to be incredulous.

"Rogered them," I said. "Is that the right word in English? Or is it *fuck*?"

More squeals of horror from Anna and Esther. "Catalyntie Van Vorst! Leave my table. Leave it this instant!" gasped Aunt Gertrude. "Go to your room!"

"Aunt, I don't understand. What's so wonderful about virginity in a grown woman? Doesn't it mean she's too ugly to attract a man?"

"Did you hear your aunt? Go to your room," roared Johannes Van Vorst.

I retreated in confusion. Several hours later, Aunt Gertrude visited me. Still distraught, she lectured me about my language. "Respectable women simply do not use such words," she said. "Where did you hear them?"

I had overheard them from Aunt Gertrude's household servants, Fat Alice and her daughter, Hester. But I did not want to get them into trouble. "People say them on the street."

"Only the lower sort. Let me ask you something far more important. Are you a virgin?"

"No," I said.

Aunt Gertrude all but reeled in horror. "When . . . where . . . did you . . . forfeit it?" she said.

"Several warriors of my village took me into the woods. But no one was willing to marry me."

Instead of the sympathy I thought I deserved, Aunt Gertrude's reaction was more horror. "You must *never* tell that to a living soul in New York."

"Why not?"

"You will never get a husband."

Anxiety swirled through my flesh. Was I doomed to be the Moon Woman wherever I went? Aunt Gertrude left me to my reflections, which were not very positive. This fanatic concern with virginity made no sense to me. I was too young to understand the consequences and the cost of raising a bastard child in the white world, where each family must pay its own way.

A more loving woman would have kept my confession to herself. Perhaps that was too much to expect of Aunt Gertrude and her daughters after my dinner table conversation. I would soon discover there were other reasons, revolving around that word "will," to make the Van Vorsts feel less than friendly to me. At any rate, Aunt Gertrude told her husband and her daughters of my unvirginal condition—and it was soon all over New York.

"Is it true—you're not a virgin?" Sophia Fowler, daughter of New York's wealthiest distiller, asked me one day as we sat out a dance at an assembly ball. Sophia was a small, tremendously proud girl with the face—and shape—of a mouse. Her gowns were by far the most expensive in our set, covered with alençon lace, Chinese silk bows, and other costly fripperies.

"Is it true you are?" I replied, throwing several listeners into fits of laughter.

Among the men, the news seemed to ignite a certain earthiness in their manner. They were no longer put off by my ice queen demeanor. On the contrary, several boldly suggested a visit to the woods, where they would show me they could make love like an Indian. Only Guert Cuyler, out of Dutch loyalty, perhaps, continued to treat me with the utmost respect. I was unmoved by his kindness. I was only concerned about one thing: how Robert Nicolls felt about the news of my condition.

By now it was summer. Robert invited a dozen or so couples aboard the royal governor's yacht for a cruise up the East River through a treacherous passage called Hell Gate to Long Island Sound. In an hour or so we debarked at a place called Oyster Bay on Long Island, where we spent the morning playing croquet, bowling on an exquisite green, and strolling the grounds of a handsome country estate.

At a midafternoon picnic on the grass, Robert sat beside me and said: "Don't you recognize this place?"

I shook my head. I had never been on Long Island in my life. "It belonged to your grandfather. Sophia Fowler's father bought it from your estate and gave it to my father for a country house."

"Really?" I said, gazing with renewed interest at the handsome shingled house, the groves of fruit trees and the well-tilled fields beyond them. Grandfather had talked several times of taking me and Clara out here for a visit. I instantly wondered what the Fowlers had paid for it.

"Do you realize what a fascinating creature you are?" Nicolls said.

I felt warmth rush through my body. "Perhaps no one has ever told me," I said.

"I sense you're not a saint," he said. "So many American women are drenched in ridiculous piety. You were raised as a child of nature—with all that idea implies."

"It doesn't trouble you?" I said.

"That you're not a virgin? Not in the least. I'm not

one either. I deplore the hypocrisy of permitting one sex liberty and binding the other to slavish obedience to supposedly divine commandments."

"You don't believe in God?"

"Let me say I have grave doubts about His existence."

"Exactly my state of mind."

"How alike we are," he said, taking my hand.

Again, warmth, desire, flooded my flesh. But I was sensible enough to realize it would be foolish to capitulate immediately. "My aunt tells me your plighted troth means nothing," I said. My tone was light, implying I did not believe Aunt Gertrude.

"Your aunt knows nothing of the heart. That's why she has two simpering idiots for daughters."

This more or less coincided with my opinion of Anna and Esther. I began to see Robert Nicolls as more than a potential lover. He was an ally in this strange white world, where respectability was such a strict religion.

But I still could not stop thinking about Grandfather's estate. "How much did Mr. Fowler pay for this place?" I asked him.

"I have no idea," he said. "Money bores me."

In my bemused state, this sounded brave—even vaguely heroic. Perhaps it meant he had so much money, he never had to think about it.

That afternoon, as we voyaged back to New York in the sunset, Robert led me to the prow of the royal yacht and slid his arm around my waist. "Where can we arrange to meet?" he said.

"For what?"

"To explore our hearts. They're so much alike. It would be a shame to part without them touching."

"If we were in the village of Shining Creek, and you were a warrior named Racing Deer or Sleeping Fox, I would know exactly what to suggest. But we're living in New York. You know what you must say first."

"Don't you want my heart to compel the words from my throat? That would be far more likely to happen in the midst of our exploration. Whatever the result, it will all be done in perfect secrecy and safety to your reputation."

His lips nuzzled my neck. "Secrecy is the true womb of love," he said.

I saw the dimension of the siege that was about to begin. If I were a betting woman—outside the trifling sums I risked at whist—I would not have laid a very heavy amount on my ability to withstand his weaponry.

"Where is your friend Stapleton these days?" I asked, trying to change the subject. "From what I hear, you and he were inseparable in times past, prowling the midnight streets in search of Cyprians."[2]

Robert replied with a shrug. "He's become a mystic, communing with the woods and waters of New Jersey."

That night, at the Van Vorst supper table, I asked my uncle how much he had gotten from Fowler for my grandfather's Long Island estate. "Good value, I assure you," he said, in an irritated voice.

"How *much*," I said, as politely as I could.

"It's none of your concern, I assure you!" he said.

"If it isn't my concern, whose is it?"

"Mine—and mine alone, as your estate's executor. The law gives me the exclusive right to deal with such matters. I haven't time to explain real estate values to a moonstruck girl."

"Moonstruck?"

"Or sunstruck," Aunt Gertrude said. "Esther tells me you retreated to the prow of the governor's yacht and permitted his son to take liberties with your person."

---

[2]*This was a polite name for whores. They were supposed worshippers of Aphrodite, the goddess of love, whose cult was celebrated on the island of Cyprus with wild orgies in ancient times.*

"I did no such thing!" I said. "He put his arm around my waist—that was all."

"Others thought as he bowed his head above your breasts he was doing a good deal more."

"Damn you for a gossiping bitch!" I said to Esther.

"That is enough of your foul talk!" cried Aunt Gertrude. "I begin to believe you're beyond redemption."

"If you and your daughters are saved, madam," I said, "I will happily forgo sharing such a salvation."

"*Go* to your room!"

Once more I found myself alone and hungry in my bedroom. I began to see myself as marooned in this house by these pious schemers as Clara in her enslavement in New Jersey. The conviction that my uncle was planning to cheat me of my inheritance grew powerfully in my mind. What better way to outmaneuver him than to win the support of the most powerful man in the province, the royal governor, through his son? Bitterly, I thought—even if Robert Nicolls loved and abandoned me, he might at least feel compelled to win me justice before a court of law. I would soon learn to my sorrow that passion and money are a poisonous mixture.

FIVE

AT HAMPDEN HALL, CLARA'S DAYS settled into a placid routine. She spent the morning trying to teach Jamey Stapleton how to read and figure. It was slow work. The boy could not grasp the simplest addition and subtraction remained a mystery to him. He saw no point to any of it. "A soldier doesn't need to know bloody arithmetic," he said. "That's what I'm going to be. A soldier!" Obviously he had been talking to his older brother.

Malcolm Stapleton spent the morning hours on horseback, riding across the huge manor with Luther, the African overseer, to inspect outlying farms. In the afternoon he studied—or pretended to study—his father's lawbooks. Most of the time he gazed longingly out the window at the sun-drenched countryside.

Occasionally, Clara helped Duycinck bring his master's financial ledgers up to date. She swiftly learned George Stapleton was a wealthy man—with very little money. He owned thousands of acres of land in New York and New Jersey. He sold timber from the forests and wheat from his farms and charged fees for his services as a lawyer. But his profits were devoured by the need to pay huge amounts of interest to men in England who had loaned him the money to build Hampden Hall. Each year he fell deeper and deeper into debt.

"All these great Americans live the same way, owing more than they make in a twelvemonth," Duycinck said. "No wonder they worship Mother England. She owns them, lock and stock."

The thud of hooves, the rattle of carriage wheels on the circular drive announced a demonstration of Duycinck's wry remark. From a pearl grey carriage descended Georgianna Stapleton in a fawn-colored traveling dress, followed by her husband, George Stapleton, and a fat red-faced man whom Duycinck identified as Henry Nicolls, the royal governor of New York and New Jersey.[1] He looked to be as much a warrior as his fat old master, King George. With them was the haughty man called "Judge" at the peace council—the same man who had denounced Clara on her Sunday visit to the Bowling Green—Daniel Horsmanden.

Behind these primary guests came a half dozen other

---

[1] New Jersey did not become a separate colony until 1738.

carriages and several wagons full of baggage. From the carriages stepped a dozen ladies in similar traveling dresses, without hoops, and gentlemen wearing long coats to protect their clothes from the dust of the road. Everyone sipped iced tea while the Stapletons, including Malcolm, circulated among them, chatting and laughing.

Inside Hampden Hall, the African house servants had shed their shabby everyday clothes and were wearing dark red livery. The house gleamed from days of scrubbing and dusting and polishing under Duycinck's nervous direction. Although Clara had no uniform, the little Dutchman shoved her into the ranks of the servants marshaled by the main staircase as the governor and his entourage entered the house. Everyone bowed and said in unison: ''Good morning, Your Excellency!'' The great man rewarded them with a smile. Clara had helped Duycinck rehearse this performance for most of the previous day.

That night, a five-piece orchestra, imported from New York, filled Hampden Hall with music. Clara watched the assembled ladies and gentlemen parade down the center of the west wing ballroom beneath two huge candlelit chandeliers. Georgianna Stapleton led the way on Governor Nicolls's arm; behind them strode George Stapleton escorting another lady. The women were wearing satin and velvet gowns woven with pearls and brocade; their faces were as painted as any warrior's but the red, the white, the inky black on their eyelashes, created beauty, not terror. The men were no less splendid in waistcoats and breeches of a half dozen brilliant colors. The musicians struck up a sonorous minuet and the dance began.

For Clara it was dreamlike, a pomp she had never imagined. It gave the white world a new aura of power and mystery. What was the purpose of all the stately bowing and prancing and circling, the delicate touching of hands with the barest of smiles? Was it a magic ritual that reinforced their power? She watched from the sidelines, offering punch and champagne to the guests as they rested from their exertions.

When Judge Horsmanden took a glass from her, he paused to study her intently. "Are you the Van Vorst slave? The one who caused such trouble?" he asked. "The Seneca from the peace council?"

Clara declined to answer him. "A good thing you didn't come before me," Horsmanden said. "You would have gotten a hundred and fifty lashes."

At midnight the guests proceeded to the dining room for a feast. Red wine and white wine flowed, and a dozen courses, from cold salmon to clear soup to chicken pies to great chunks of roast beef and pork, were tasted but seldom consumed. Toasts were drunk to the king and queen, First Minister Walpole, Governor Nicolls, and a dozen other personages and topics, such as "Death and Destruction" to France and Spain. As Clara removed plates and poured wine, she felt Daniel Horsmanden's eyes on her. He was sitting next to Georgianna Stapleton and several times she overheard him talking about her.

"Much too beautiful to . . ."

"Such flowers should be plucked before they . . ."

Mrs. Stapleton laughed in a throaty, somehow ominous way. At the end of the night, she and most of the ladies and gentlemen were quite drunk. George Stapleton was among the drunkest. Malcolm and Duycinck half carried him from the dining table to his bedroom. Mrs. Stapleton watched him depart with the enigmatic smile she reserved for almost everything—and beckoned Clara to her side.

"Let the others finish the housekeeping," she said. "Judge Horsmanden will be waiting for you in his room on the second floor. The third door from the stairs on the right."

"What does he want?" Clara said.

"What do you think, booby?" Mrs. Stapleton said, as a flushed Governor Nicolls staggered across the dining room to slide his arm around her waist. "He's very attracted to you."

"Are you talking about me?" the governor said, with a smile so twisted it looked like a Seneca false face.

Perhaps all these whites wore false faces of their own clever making, Clara thought. Perhaps that was why they never worried about telling the truth to each other.

"Your attractions are less visible, Henry dear," Mrs. Stapleton said. "But no less *potent*."

The governor laughed in a grunting way and pressed her against him. "Go. Now!" Mrs. Stapleton said to Clara.

At Horsmanden's door, an inner voice told Clara not to knock. But she heard Duycinck and Malcolm warning her never to cross Georgianna Stapleton. Clara knocked. Horsmanden flung open the door. He had a glass of wine in his hand, although his slack mouth suggested he was in no need of it. He was wearing a long red velvet night coat.

"Ah, the Princess of Sheba," he said, slurring his words.

"What is it you wish, sir?"

A candelabra filled the room with flickering light and shadow. In the center of the tan Turkish carpet was a huge bed, hung with green drapes, creating a cavern of darkness. Clara was suddenly certain that if she entered that cavern, she would disappear forever.

Horsmanden drained his wineglass. "Don't you understand what Mrs. Stapleton said? She owns you. Take off your clothes and get into that bed."

"You'll have to kill me first."

His hand whirled out of the shadows to smash her in the face. The blow flung Clara against the door. She groped for the handle, screaming with pain and terror.

Horsmanden seized a fistful of her hair and dragged her toward the bed.

"Judge Horsmanden! Your . . . Your Honor. What are you doing?" Malcolm Stapleton said. He stood in the doorway, a candle in his hand.

"Your mother sent me this bitch with her compliments—"

"Let her go."

"What?"

"I said let her go."

"Well well well. I didn't know you were in the business of giving orders to your elders."

"My stepmother doesn't own this woman. She has no right or authority to dispose of her to anyone."

Malcolm lifted Clara to her feet and led her into the hall. "Go to bed, quick," he said.

Muffled cries and shouts of laughter echoed from other bedrooms. The Stapletons' guests were all enjoying themselves. Clara fled upstairs to her room and spent the rest of the night dreading the sunrise. The guests assembled for a late breakfast, as sedate and decorous as they had seemed while dancing minuets last night. No one paid the slightest attention to her except Daniel Horsmanden, who confined himself to surly stares—and Malcolm Stapleton, whose gaze was far more anxious.

At the end of the meal, Horsmanden spent several minutes talking to Georgianna Stapleton in a low voice before she left the dining room. Upstairs, Mrs. Stapleton summoned Clara to her bedroom as she dressed for an afternoon of fox hunting. "You've insulted the governor's closest friend," she said. "Your value to this family has declined to the vanishing point."

An hour later, in the kitchen, Duycinck caught Clara's wrist and whispered: "Why the devil didn't you listen to me? It's only a matter of time before she'll have the master sell you to the West Indies to keep her in humor and give your friend Catalyntie money and an apology.

Meanwhile you'll be working in the sugarcane fields under a sun that's hotter than the devil's breath.''

For the next three days, the Stapletons, the governor, and their friends drank and ate in the same royal style. They fox hunted and shot grouse and other game birds in the woods, and whiled away the evening hours at cards. George Stapleton seemed to make a point of getting drunk early each night, giving the governor unimpeded access to his wife. Judge Horsmanden ignored Clara, devoting most of his time to dallying with a pretty redhead from another New Jersey manor.

Early in the morning of the fourth day, as the guests were preparing to depart, Georgianna Stapleton summoned Clara to her room and told her to pack her trunk. ''We're selling you to Judge Horsmanden,'' she said. ''Perhaps you'll learn to be more complaisant, once you're his property.''

Weeping, Clara fled to Malcolm and begged him to help her. ''You won't be sold,'' Malcolm said.

He strode down the hall to his stepmother's room. Clara hovered near the door, listening to the angry voices. ''Madam,'' Malcolm said, ''I seldom try to challenge your power over my father. But in this matter I will. Let me remind you, considering my father's declining health, as the first-born son in a few years' time I'll be the owner of this estate. I'll be in a position to do you much good—or ill.''

''Don't be so sure of what you'll be in a few years,'' Georgianna Stapleton said.

''This land was bought with my mother's fortune!'' Malcolm shouted.

''Piffle. You're talking piffle as usual. But if you prefer this girl to your chance to study with the one man in New York who could teach you English law, so be it. I'll indulge you.''

''Simply tell him she's not for sale!''

''I'll tell him you forbade me.''

The stricken look on Malcolm's face as he emerged from the room told Clara he felt the price he had just paid to protect her might have been too high. Clara was swept by gratitude—and pity. He reminded her of warriors like Bold Antelope when they tried to argue with her grandmother or one of the tribe's wily old sachems. A warrior was a simple creature, unable to win a war of words.

For a day Malcolm avoided Clara, spending all his time out of doors. She resumed teaching Jamey Stapleton, who seemed to have receded from the slight progress he had made in their first two weeks and stared at the figures on the page as if they were evil spirits. Mrs. Stapleton intruded to check his progress and pronounced Clara a failure as a tutor—as well as a woman of pleasure.

She gazed at Clara with her diminished, diminishing smile. "You don't realize what an opportunity you failed to grasp, my dear," she said. "Once a woman beds a man, he becomes remarkably complaisant. You could have been a free woman, with money enough to live in comfort, in a year's time."

Clara wrote *WHORE* on a piece of foolscap and asked Jamey if he could read it. "Whore?" he said. "That's what Bertha calls you, Stepmother."

Georgianna slapped him in the face. "Tell Bertha she'll get fifty lashes if I hear of her saying such a thing again," she said.

She whirled on Clara. "I will have you sold to the West Indies by next spring, or I'll go there myself."

The next day, Malcolm invited Clara to join him for a horseback ride. She said he would have to teach her how to control a horse. By noon she was confidently managing a big roan stallion named Trumpeter. They cantered off to the Passaic River to admire the turbulent stream as it plunged over its series of falls. Clara told Malcolm of a much greater falls in the country of the

Senecas, on the Niagara River. The water fell hundreds of feet with a roar that could be heard for miles.

Malcolm talked passionately of his desire to see such a wonder. He yearned to roam the continent, the whole world, and sample its marvels. That was another reason why he wanted to become a soldier. The British Empire fought its wars in Europe, Africa, the West Indies, distant India.

Subsiding, Malcolm stared past her at the white water cascading over rocks and shallows. For a moment Clara pitied him again. She saw how miserable he had been since boyhood, raised by a woman who did not love him, with his father absent most of the time pursuing profits in New York City. That vision somehow made it easier for her to lean toward him and say: "I had a dream last night. We were in the forest together. Your lips were on my mouth."

He gazed at her with eyes full of pain. "I've had the same dream, five nights running."

"Perhaps it's time for us both to fulfill our heart's desire."

For a moment Clara wondered if she were committing an evil act, lying to this love-starved boy/man, using the ancient wisdom of *ondinnonk* to deceive him. She told herself it was only half a lie. She pitied him as much as she needed him for protection against his stepmother. Her false face love would be a gift that could only do him good. It might even bring him happiness.

The day was Indian summer at its most glorious. That term, with its subtext of terror and beauty, was unknown to Clara.[2] She only knew sunlight streamed from a cloudless sky. Trees were thick with chattering birds as Malcolm led her north toward the forest, first at a canter, then at a gallop, until the road became little more than

---

[2]*On the frontier, Indian summer days often brought war parties for a final raid before the onset of winter.*

a footpath. They dismounted and Malcolm led the horses along the banks of a gurgling creek until they reached a small circular lake surrounded by steep granite cliffs. It glistened in the sunlight like a promise of happiness.

Calmly, carelessly, Clara stripped off her clothes and walked to the edge of the cliff and dove into the shining water. It was shockingly cold, but she did not make a sound. Malcolm dove too and swam toward her. They met in the center and his hands explored her body while her dark hair streamed around them, like the strands of a magical net.

For a moment Clara felt like a being with the ability to cast spells, command evil spirits. She was swept by a terrible, nameless foreboding. Wrong, whispered her grandmother's voice. She was using good medicine for a false purpose. There was only one way to redeem the evil before it became a curse. She had to cast aside her false face and let her heart speak, no matter what the color of this boy/man's skin.

It was impossible. The vow she had made when she said farewell to Catalyntie barred that path, like an armed warrior with his war paint gleaming on his maddened face. Her heart still shriveled and slunk like a wounded wolf into a dark icy cave. All Clara could do, as Malcolm's tongue explored her mouth and his hands glided down her body, was summon a promise to try to love him someday, somehow. She could only hope, she could only pray to her Seneca gods to protect her as Malcolm carried her out of the lake's shallows onto a grassy shore opposite the cliffs.

The first time was swift and almost angry, like the coupling of animals in the spring. But the second time was slower, richer, closer to a dream of happiness—and the third time was almost happiness itself. Lifted into sweet bewilderment, Clara looked down on their joined bodies and asked if such a transformation was possible without the blessing of some powerful spirit. Finally the question dissolved into mystery, the indescribable dimensions of love.

Yes, Clara thought, yes. False love could be transformed into true love. The false face could be banished, her heart could speak to this man without a double tongue. Not now perhaps, but surely in a year's time. Perhaps even in a month. Or a day. The Evil Brother could not challenge this unique *orenda* they were creating around and within themselves with their lips and hands and thighs.

Let us leave them there, sheathed in the happiness of flesh and sun and shining water, immune for a little while to the future that was stalking toward them in the forest with the inexorable stride of a hunter on the track of his prey.

SIX

AT THE VAN VORST HOUSE on Broad Street, all was bustle and confusion. My cousin Esther called frantically for a curling iron. Her sister Anna wailed about a wrinkle in her gown. Aunt Gertrude flew up and down the stairs like a witch on a broomstick, screeching orders to the servants. We were on our way to the King's Birthday Ball at the governor's mansion in Fort George. I sat in my room, fingering a note from Robert Foster Nicolls.

The note contained only a single word: *Tonight?* Beside that tantalizing proposal lay two playing cards, the queen and king of hearts.

Tonight would undoubtedly be an ideal time to begin the secret exploration of our matching hearts. The city was in a frenzy of merrymaking. The male half of the population was already drunk. They had begun cele-brating at noon, when a parade of red-coated soldiers from the fort, followed by a troop of young gentlemen on horseback, followed by members of the governor's council and then by Uncle Johannes and other members of the provincial legislature, paraded through the streets to City Hall. Militia, their muskets at the ready, lined the route while from every window cheers poured down. The males devoted the rest of the afternoon to what Robert Nicolls called "patriotic eating" at various taverns, offering innumerable toasts to the fat old king, the governor, First Minister Walpole, and other notables.

At six, as the sun declined beyond Hudson's River, the city came aglow with a thousand candles in house windows. In the Van Vorst coach, we clattered over to the Broadway and down that cobblestoned road to the turnstile that gave us entry to the lawns and finally the gates of Fort George.

Over our vast hooped ball gowns we females all wore ample silk aprons in a variety of vivid colors—the garment was part of full dress at the English court. Around our shoulders flowed a purple or blue cardinal[1] with an enormous hood, which made a woman look like a ship in full sail. Uncle Johannes was no less splendid in a royal blue coat, a yellow waistcoat, and green silk breeches. On his bewigged head sat a gold-trimmed cocked hat.

Above us on the darkened ramparts, one of the governor's African slaves sawed English airs on his fiddle. As we entered, the melancholy tune he began playing sent words flowing through my mind. I was suddenly at a supper party at the Cuylers and Robert Nicolls was singing them, picking the melody on a lute in his lap.

[1] A large cloak.

Oh mistress mine, where art thou roaming?
Oh stay and hear; your true love's coming,
  That can sing both high and low:
Trip no further, pretty sweeting;
Journeys end in lovers meeting,
  Every wise man's son doth know.

It was an old song from a Shakespeare play. But it spoke powerfully to our present concerns. I thought of all the poems Robert had sent me. He had introduced me to the literature, the language of love—a topic that Harman Bogardus eschewed. *Tonight?* The word all but sang in my mind.

A moment later, Robert greeted us at the door to the governor's mansion. We passed from the late October chill to the warmth and cheer of a wainscoted salon, with two huge fireplaces blazing at either end. "The Van Vorsts en masse!" Robert said. "A mass shot through with beauty. What gifts you bring to our revels, madam."

He kissed Aunt Gertrude's hand, making her visibly palpitate. He paid the same attention to Anna and Esther and finally to me, and offered Aunt Gertrude his arm. We proceeded down the room, Aunt Gertrude nodding and smiling to the elite of New York, glorying in the attention of our local prince. Uncle Johannes smoothly detached himself to shake the hand of the most powerful member of the governor's council, a frowning swarthy man named Oliver Delancey.

"You received my note?" Robert murmured, as we ended our promenade beside the rear fireplace, where a half dozen musicians were playing country dances on oboes and trumpets.

"Yes," I said.

"What saith the queen of hearts?" he asked, with a foxy smile.

"The queen's heart says yes, her head says no. Aunt Gertrude is watching."

"There are ways to circumvent that obstacle," Robert said.

A waiter passed with a tray of mulled wine. Robert seized a glass and from beneath his shirt sleeve procured a small packet of powder, which he slipped into the drink. "You must try this canary,[2] madam," he said, handing the glass to Aunt Gertrude, whose back was turned to us as she gazed out at some dancers who had begun a minuet. "It's Portugal's best."

"Thank you, Mr. Nicolls," Aunt Gertrude said, and sipped it greedily.

Robert led me out on the dance floor. "Have you poisoned her?" I asked, almost ready to believe the worst. Robert's pleas had been rising to something like a crescendo lately.

"No, no. She'll soon grow so drowsy she'll ask to be taken home."

Gazing down on us as we danced were huge portraits of rotund George II in his royal robes beside his equally fleshy wife, Queen Caroline. There was, of course, no portrait of the king's mistress, Henrietta Howard, the Countess of Suffolk. But Robert Nicolls had told me about George's notorious infidelity in salacious detail. He added similar drolleries about First Minister Walpole and virtually every other member of the cabinet. The message was clear: If great folks paid no attention to the sixth commandment on Moses's slab, why should lesser mortals?

As we bowed and postured to the stately measures of the minuet, Robert murmured, "Do you know how much I love you?"

"I have some idea—if your heart resembles mine," I said.

[2]Wine from the Canary Islands.

By now, I was profoundly attracted to this man. The calculation that had entered into my early thoughts of him had long since vanished. His polished manners, his ready wit, his status as the governor's son, made him seem infinitely superior to every other young man in New York. He had been pursuing me with a passion worthy of the knights of earlier centuries, who willingly enslaved themselves to their lady's love. He swore—and gossip seemed to confirm it—that he had reformed his character to prove himself deserving of my affection. He no longer roamed the midnight streets with friends like Malcolm Stapleton in search of Cyprians. He devoted himself to searching old books for poems that praised my beauty—and sent them to me in his handwriting. I found myself compared to Philip Sidney's Stella, Christopher Marlowe's Hero, Henry Constable's Diana.

"I thought—tonight—if your answer is still no—I might leave this country forever. I'm not sure I can survive in the same city with you so close—and yet beyond my reach."

Desire warred with prudence in my heart. "I feel the same melancholy," I said. "But there is a way—a simple way for you to resolve the matter."

"There's an even simpler way for you to resolve it."

As he passed me down the line of dancers in the later stage of the minuet, I suddenly found myself facing Malcolm Stapleton. I was as startled as if he had been an apparition from the dead. "Has patriotism lured you from the wilds of New Jersey?" I asked.

"In a way," he said.

"How is my friend Clara?"

"I think she's happy. As happy as she can hope to be in her present condition."

"Tell her I haven't forgotten my promise. She won't be a slave a single day after I pass the age of twenty-one."

"And you, Miss Van Vorst. Are you happy?"

Suddenly I wanted to cry out the truth: *No.* How could I be happy when I dreamed night after night of pressing my lips to Robert Foster Nicolls's supple mouth? I remembered the morning I had met this huge young man—and the way I had desired him. How had I been tricked out of that simple wish into this game of erotic hide-and-seek?

Instead of the truth, I gave him a polite answer. "I'm much happier than I expected to be. Please give Clara my love."

More dances, country gavottes, which set the pulses pounding, then a feast of wild boar, wild turkey, enlivened by glasses of Negus.[3] Robert talked wryly of his friend Stapleton. "I think he's more than a little fond of your friend Clara," he said. "I wouldn't be surprised if she reciprocates. Would you approve of such a match?"

"It's none of my business, don't you think?" I said.

"I suppose so. Shall we go up on the ramparts for the fireworks?"

I flung on my cardinal, a good thing because the night had grown quite cold. No one else followed us into the dangerous air.[4] We quickly crossed the inner ground of the fort and mounted the battlements. The moon had risen, flooding the river and the far shore with golden light. Below us, a woman began to sing an old song:

> *Never love unless you can*
> *Bear with all the faults of man.*

A dozen red rockets with blazing tails soared into the sky and exploded into a million fragments of green and yellow and blue light. Others whirled into

---

[3] *A drink of hot water, wine, and lemon juice, sweetened and spiced. Named for Col. Francis Negus, its creator.*
[4] *It was almost an eighteenth-century article of faith that night air was unhealthy.*

fiery girandoles,[5] or exploded into brilliant flowers and stars. On the ramparts, the artillery regiment added the throaty roar of their guns to the tumult.

The whole chaotic wondrous sight seemed to express—and simultaneously release—the turmoil in my wild heart. Below us we could hear cries of wonder and admiration as the dancers in the salon threw open the windows to enjoy the spectacle. Could Clara, across the river in New Jersey, see the bursts of blazing incandescence? Did they signify a violent desire for Malcolm Stapleton in her heart? I had no chance to ponder such questions.

Out of sight of the people at the windows, Robert's hand sought my breast, his lips pressed my mouth. "I have a carriage waiting," he whispered.

Within minutes we were rumbling up Broadway's cobblestones past the still-illuminated windows of the houses fronting it into the darkened fields beyond City Hall. We kissed and kissed and kissed. The journey was one perpetual embrace. I lost all sense of distance and time. Eventually we stopped and I could hear the coachman trying to soothe his snorting half-blown horses.

Someone carrying a lantern opened the door and addressed Robert. "The room is ready, my lord. I hope it meets your expectations."

"It had better, if you hope to be paid," Robert said. "Avert your eyes from this lady's face."

The man, who was as huge as Malcolm Stapleton, turned his head away. Robert bundled the hood of the cardinal around my face until all but my eyes was concealed. We followed the man down a winding path to a country inn. Revelers were toasting the king in the taproom. He led us around to the back of the building, where an open stairway mounted to the second floor. Soon we were in a warm room with a fine fire flickering

[5]*Circles of fire.*

in the grate. Beside the bed were tumblers of mulled wine and a bottle of brandy.

Through a side window, we could glimpse the fireworks still exploding over the river. Beyond them the fields and woods of New Jersey lay dark and still. Robert handed me the mulled wine, which I hardly needed. I downed it in one reckless swallow.

Wait, whispered the voice of She-Is-Alert, of the analytic, restless head. *You have one last chance to extract a promise from him.*

But the Moon Woman answered: *Never will you know a love like this unless you seize it.*

"Do you love me as much as I love you?" I asked. My voice sounded forlorn in my ears.

"I hope so," he said. "I know this much. There's no other woman like you."

"Tell me why that's so."

"The way you walk, talk, dance, hold your head— it's as if affectation was impossible for you. Sincerity is as natural to you as rain and snow and sunlight is to the earth."

I saw he had constructed a mythical Catalyntie from his notions of Indian ways and my refusal to apologize for my lost virginity. But I believed every word of it because I loved him. At least, I believed enough of it to let me think I could correct it later and still retain his love. For his sake I would be sincere, I would try to be as natural, as simple, as a rain shower.

"I want to love you as a mistress and as a wife," I said. "As full of ardor as the most wanton Cyprian in New York and as devoted as one who has sworn her vows before a sacred altar."

"I hope we can and will do first one and then the other," he said.

He finished his wine and began to undress me. As he discarded the corset with a satisfying *clunk* and reached my chemise, he reached over and pinched out the candle.

"No," I said. "Light it again. I want to see you. I want to see everything."

It was my first discovery that white New Yorkers made love in the dark, apparently convinced it was sinful or at least shameful to see each other naked. At first Robert was reluctant to light the candle again and remove his clothes. Was it because his expensive costume was a kind of protection, a reassurance of his rank?

I was less than thrilled by the body he finally revealed. Used as I was to the muscular torsos of Seneca braves, I was disappointed by his sunken chest, his flabby arms. Robert was a city creature, born and raised in London. But his rump was full and what dangled—or, to be more exact, rose—between his legs bid fair to more than compensate for the other deficiencies. Besides, I told myself it was his spirit, his wit, his good taste in music and poetry, that I loved.

"You need have no fear of a bastard," he said. "I've brought armor."

I did not know what he was talking about until he showed me the soft shiny tube he deftly drew down his member, like a stocking on a leg or a glove on a finger.[6] His concern only deepened the sweetness of my feeling for him. I opened my arms, crying: "I want to love you forever!"

He began in haste, with a wild gavotte. It was over so soon, the music had barely started; my blood had scarcely begun to stir. But the second time was different, closer to a minuet, tender and slow at first, giving love a chance to swell like a bursting bud in spring. By the third time, he was murmuring adoration. "You—are—the—most—amazing—creature," he said, punctuating

---

[6]*Contraceptives at this time were usually made of sheep gut or sometimes of fish skin. Manufactured by wholesalers in England, they were available in apothecary shops.*

each word with a stroke. "You—actually—enjoy—this. I never—knew—such a thing—was possible!"

"Why shouldn't I enjoy it," I said, when he lay exhausted in my arms at last. "The Manitou made our bodies for pleasure as well as toil."

"All praise to the Manitou," he said. "I shall worship him henceforth."

Downstairs, a grandfather's clock bonged the hour. "We must get back to the fort before midnight," Robert said. "Let's hope my potion worked on Aunt Gertrude."

"What's our excuse if it failed?" I said, struggling into my corset with his assistance.

"We dallied on the parapet until we almost froze. Only your kisses kept us warm."

"Won't that bring on a storm of censure?"

"To admit half the truth is usually far more effective than a lie."

It was an aphorism I vowed to remember. "What now?" I said, as I huddled against him in the cold carriage.

"We continue the exploration of our hearts."

"What did you discover about my heart tonight?"

"It's one of the rarest in this wide world."

"Would you like to know what I discovered about yours?"

"Of course."

"You fear me. For no reason."

"Fear you? Why in the world would I do that?"

"I don't know. You seem to think I have the power to hurt you."

"You do."

"We both have that power," I said. "I hope we never use it. Isn't it possible to go on from happiness to greater happiness? Do all lovers quarrel in the end, as the poets seem to say?"

"I don't know. This is the first time I've ever been in love," Robert said.

My heart leaped at those words, remembering Grand-father's words about first love. *"Moi aussi,"* I said, us-ing one of the few fragments of French I had acquired at Madame Ardsley's.

I began to murmur my favorite English poem.

> *"Come live with me and be my love,*
> *And we will all the pleasures prove*
> *That valleys, groves, hills, and fields,*
> *Woods, or steepy mountain yields."*

He answered me in a voice that was, I thought, a trifle hesitant.

> *"And we will sit upon the rocks,*
> *Seeing the shepherds feed their flocks*
> *By shallow rivers to whose falls*
> *Melodious birds sing madrigals."*

So we returned from our first tryst, believing in poetry, hoping it would not turn into prose.

Back at Fort George, the party was just beginning to break up. We managed to get inside the gate and, hug-ging the shadows, skirt the governor's house and mount the parapets again. After five minutes of lingering kisses, we descended the steps to discover my cousin Esther looking distraught.

"Catalyntie," she cried. "Where in the world have you been? Mother was taken ill. My sister took her home and Father went with them."

"Robert and I were on the parapet watching the fireworks," I said.

"They ended a half hour ago," Esther said in her nosy way.

"We were communing with the stars thereafter," Robert said. "If there is any blame to be attached to it,

I take full responsibility. I wouldn't let your cousin return until she surrendered a kiss.''

Esther, who was half in love with Robert Nicolls like almost every other young woman in New York, shot me a look of consummate envy. I saw how right Robert was: Secrecy would redouble the pleasures of our liaison.

☀

SEVEN

I MUST ALSO REMEMBER FOR Clara what her love for Malcolm Stapleton was like before it became a nightmare. Memory must summon the trembling flesh, the animate blood in the pounding heart, the swelling sweetness of desire in the plangent soul. In some ways their love was a nightmare from the first, a dream stalked by the Evil Brother. But Clara chose to ignore what lurked in the shadows.

At first she saw her body as a tribe, a dancing, singing people who were too powerful, too satisfied to wage war. She adopted this great white stranger into the mysteries, the rituals, of her flesh, weaving around him the singing embrace of the Master of Life, the joy of those who have visited the world's heart and found it good. She was a counselor, a sachem, a shaman with the power to bless all things.

For those first weeks, love was transcendent, as absolute and infallible as a new religion. They worshiped it while the woods turned crimson and gold and saffron all around them and huge flocks of birds twittered in the trees or darkened the sky with thrumming wings as they prepared to flee the coming cold. From the center of the lake they watched deer gambol on its edge, images of innocence, and saw themselves mirrored in their fearful eyes, their ecstatic human opposites, forever fearless and unquenchably proud.

Yes, ultimately it was pride that betrayed them, a mad irreverent pride that escaped its cage to roar defiance at the sober sensible world of money and laws and rules of conduct. Clara was too proud of her body, her beauty, too proud of the way she had possessed this huge male, with his fumbling stunted spirit, to see the dangers all around them as the woods grew bare. She tried to dismiss the sense of sin that tormented Malcolm. It was an idea she simply did not understand. She begged him to open his soul to the presence of the Manitou as he spoke in their bodies. It was an idea he simply did not understand.

Gradually, she saw they worshipped different gods. Her god was far more Indian than white. He dueled the Evil Brother for power in this world, but in the shadow world beyond death he ruled with perfect peace and benevolence. He urged the practice of happiness, of generosity to all things living, he rewarded courage and magnanimity and taught indifference to pain and sorrow. In his deepest heart he was a joyous god, but he expected his followers to obey his precepts without extravagant display.

Malcolm's god was angry. He warned his followers of the awful punishments that awaited them in the world beyond death. In this world his voice was entirely absorbed by the word *father*. He was a commanding, a demanding, a joyless god, whose central word was duty and whose other face was law. Failure to obey him was a sin and the punishment for sin was eternal damnation in a hell of fiery torment—another idea Clara could not comprehend.

When Malcolm told her how sin turned the soul black, she laughed at him. ''What's wrong with black? Bears are black. Their coats are the warmest in the forest. The night is black but the moon fills it with golden light. Don't be afraid of blackness, darkness. We have the power to make it glow with the happiness in our hearts.''

Sin was an empty word to her. Especially the so-called sins of the flesh. But she would learn, oh how painfully she would learn that there was such a thing as sin, she would eventually see how it deformed the soul, made it as ugly as Duycinck's body. For now she struggled to free Malcolm from the grip of God the Father, his father as the voice of God. She urged him to find his own path, to walk down it unafraid with her beside him.

''You can't let your father live your life for you. You must seize it and make it your own life,'' she whispered in the darkness before dawn in Malcolm's bed.

Snow whipped through the woods now. Winter had fastened its grip on the fields and rivers. Almost as soon as Clara spoke these combative words, quarrels raged. Malcolm struggled to take Clara's advice and extricate himself from his father's grasp. George Stapleton was adamant. His older son would study law under Judge Daniel Horsmanden in New York. He had spent five hundred pounds repairing the breach between them over his penchant for Clara. His friend Governor Nicolls had promised to appoint Malcolm to the Chancery Court the moment Horsmanden gave his approval. The salary was a thousand pounds a year. Malcolm would never have to sit on a case. For a hundred pounds he could hire an assistant to do all the work. All he would have to do is sign a few documents once or twice a month.

That was how a man got ahead in the British Empire, George Stapleton shouted. He found a place for himself, with a salary paid by the king or the province. Look at the newspaper publisher, Ben Franklin of Pennsylvania. He had made his son William the clerk of the assembly, a job that put him in constant touch with the governor and every important man in Philadelphia. Compare that certainty of a prosperous future to a soldier's life.

"A soldier spends nine-tenths of his days getting drunk in miserable garrison towns or isolated forts, exposed to the pox[1] and the clap[2] from local whores—and when a war comes his chances of glory are as likely to end with a bullet in the belly as a commendation from his general. The pay is miserable, the rewards dubious. Who but a fool becomes a soldier—unless he has a great lord or the king himself behind him to push his career?"

"It's what I want to *be*, Father," Malcolm said, his big head drooping.

"It's what you'll never *be* as long as I'm alive!" George Stapleton shouted.

Georgianna Stapleton watched these scenes with her enigmatic smile intact. Did she know from the start who was the source of Malcolm's defiance? Had she extracted the truth from Adam Duycinck, who lived in terror of her ruthless temper? Perhaps. The little hunchback muttered warnings to Malcolm, advice to Clara. There were ways to prevent a child. His mother had taught him these arcane mysteries and he tried to share them. A patch of wool, dampened with a sticky substance like honey, inserted with care, could work wonders. But Clara ignored him, convinced she was under the protection of the Master of Life.

Georgianna did not need Adam to find out what was happening. The hunchback was by no means the only servant who knew about Clara and Malcolm. In a great house, gossip about the lords and masters is as pervasive as mold and mildew. It is more likely that Georgianna was merely biding her time, waiting for the inevitable event to happen in Clara's body.

In the spasmodic moments when Clara thought about a child, she saw it as a decisive statement of Malcolm's love for her, a way to bind him to her in a new, con-

---

[1]*Syphilis.*

[2]*Gonorrhea.*

clusive way. How this would work in a practical sense never entered her mind. Living in Hampden Hall, she half imagined she was in another longhouse, where children became part of the clan, a welcome addition to the supply of warriors or future mothers of warriors. Calculation of a more practical sort was not in her nature.

If Malcolm thought about a child, he thrust the possibility aside as something too complicated, too portentous to contemplate. Like most warriors, who blunder through life with their fearful combination of naivete and loyalty and blind confidence in their destiny, he too was no calculator. Fortune has always favored the calculators, the politicians of this world, and always will. One envies them until one peers into their stunted hearts.

In December Clara realized that the blood which flowed from her womb every month in the nights of the full moon had ceased. In January the child spoke in Clara's body with a blinding nausea that sent her fleeing from the mere sight of food. In February she told Malcolm, who clung to her and vowed that he would protect her and the baby.

In April, Georgianna Stapleton told her husband about Clara's interesting condition. She asked him if he was ready to start a colony of mulattoes here in the wilds of New Jersey. She told him Clara was the source of Malcolm's stubborn refusal to study law in New York. She revealed that with Duycinck's help, Malcolm was still sending letters to London, attempting to obtain a commission in the British army.

"I will have no chocolate bastards on my property!"

George Stapleton's furious words thundered against the beamed ceiling of Hampden Hall's library. Malcolm and Clara stood before him like condemned criminals. It was the voice of the white God incarnate, condemning their sin. Clara was inclined to be defiant. What could they do to her? She had proof that Malcolm was her lover, proof in her belly. But Malcolm did not join her defiance. He hung his head like a penitent. Clara saw with a sinking heart the power of the father-God, the ugly idea of sin as disobedience, dishonor, disgrace.

George Stapleton raged at his son's stupidity. Was he planning to marry this woman? If so, he was instantly disinherited. They would have to live in the forest with the Indians. No one else would tolerate a public mingling of the races. Even if he merely planned to raise his chocolate bastard here at Hampden Hall, he was equally stupid. Every slave would hate the creature. He would hate his father if he remained a slave. If he freed him, did he want him walking the streets of New York with Stapleton as his last name?

"Cato Stapleton. Can you imagine it?" George Stapleton roared. "Can you hear every respectable family in the city having a laugh on us every time they heard it?"

Fear clutched at Clara's throat. Were they going to kill her? How else could they destroy the child? The Manitou had breathed life into her womb. How could they prevent the child from entering the world? She got her answer from Georgianna Stapleton.

"I'll fetch Duycinck."

Before Clara could speak, she was dragged upstairs by house Africans and flung on a bed, stripped naked and her arms and legs tied to the posts. Malcolm followed them, calling: "What are you going to do to her?" until his father ordered him to his room. Helpless, Clara watched Adam Duycinck reel into the room, propelled by Georgianna Stapleton's arm. He carried a sack that rattled as if it were full of coins.

"There she is. Get to work on her," Georgianna said.

"Madam—it's against nature," Duycinck said. "She could die. It's what they hung my mother for doing in England. The witchcraft stuff was court nonsense. She killed babies. I knew she would hang for it someday. I told her so. I told her my humped back was no excuse.

She hated God for my back, madam, and she murdered with that hate in her heart—''

"Do you want to live here in comfort—or sweat out your days aboard a king's man of war?" Georgianna said. "I'll have the governor deport you tomorrow for whatever charge comes readily to mind. They put the incorrigibles into the fleet, you know."

Duycinck's face twisted into the mask of the Evil Brother. "All right. Get her some whiskey first."

"She doesn't deserve any whiskey."

"Get her some whiskey, madam! Or I'll let you perform this murder!"

Mrs. Stapleton ordered one of Bertha's daughters to bring up a bottle of brandy. She handed it to Duycinck. "Get to work," she said, and slammed the door.

"Didn't I tell you never to cross her?" Duycinck whined, gulping a tumbler of the brandy. He refilled the glass and put it to Clara's lips. She turned her head away. "Take it!" Duycinck said. "It's the only help I can give you."

Clara whirled her head against the tumbler, spilling most of the brandy on the bed. "Stupid bitch!" Duycinck said. He poured himself another tumbler and drank it down.

"Mother," Duycinck said. "Wherever your damned soul lives, ask God or Great Satan to have mercy on poor Adam."

From the sack he drew a half dozen grisly instruments and laid them on the bed. There were knives and scissors with ragged edges to their blades and long narrow bars with sharpened points. Ripping pieces from the pillowcase, he made a gag and thrust it into Clara's mouth, and bound it with another strip of cloth. He drank another tumbler of brandy and mumbled drunkenly: "If you'd lain with old Adam, this never would have happened."

What came next, as Adam began probing for the child

in Clara's womb, is better forgotten. But that would be a crime against history and Clara, against the lost soul that bled into oblivion between her legs. It would be a crime against the pain that lurched madly through her mind and body like a captured bear against his cage. It would be a crime against the mystery of women's fate and men's laws. It would be surrender to time's spider, who weaves years around us until we cease to struggle in their languid grip. Memory is as weak, as treacherous, as poor Adam, performing murder in a drunken haze to save himself from damnation in this world.

No no no. Better forgotten but never forgotten, the two ideas must live side by side, locked in irreconcilable conflict, like a husband and wife who hate each other forever. Eventually the murder ended, as all murders must, the blood-soaked sheets were flung into the wash, the mangled corpse was buried in a nameless grave at midnight. Clara, the victim's only mourner, was left alone to weep away the darkness.

Duycinck hovered over her, executioner turned nurse. He forced brandy down her throat, he gave her medicines that he hoped would banish fever and infection. But both these servants of the Evil Brother ravaged Clara. For a week she writhed and sweated while nightmares stalked the room. She saw Malcolm's innocent face, a mask of contorted grief, and screamed curses at him until the mask shattered and he fled to New York for drunken solace with the city's whores.

Drifting along the edge of eternity, Clara received the gift of second sight. She saw Georgianna Stapleton hovering above the bed, her face a whitened skull. It was the face of the demon who inhabited her rosy beauty, her flushed cheeks, her glowing red hair. Long ago, she had made a pact with the Evil Brother; she was one of his creatures, ready to commit any act that multiplied the power of his reign.

She saw George Stapleton's sorrowing double, a

hunchbacked parody of the expostulating attorney, forever bent under some mysterious burden, perhaps the loss of his Scottish bride, Malcolm's mother. Whatever tormented him, his eyes were crossed with secret rage at the Master of Life. She saw Adam Duycinck's spiritual self, a tall straight-backed warrior, a man without illusions, cursing his humpbacked reality. She saw herself, an empty shell of a woman with a barren womb, forever childless, thanks to the fever and Duycinck's vile medicines and viler surgical instruments.

Ultimately she stood on the precipice above an immense river, watching it plunge into a foaming, thundering, spray-engulfed gorge. Behind her in the forest peered Malcolm and Bold Antelope and her Seneca grandmother, waiting for her to leap into eternity. Each of them wanted her to vanish for a different reason. Malcolm to escape the guilt of his sin, Bold Antelope to banish the shame of his defeat, her Seneca grandmother to know she had escaped the white world with her *orenda* unblemished, to await her in eternity.

Clara swayed there, wondering why she did not leap. Duycinck watched her, gulping brandy, alternately crying "Jump" and begging her to live, to forgive him, to love him in some impossible world beyond the stars. None of them cared, Clara thought. None of them cared for Clara beyond her meaning to their hungry souls. She would jump. She would vanish into the roaring oblivion of eternity.

"No!"

Catalyntie's arms were around her, dragging her back from the precipice. Catalyntie, her Seneca sister, who loved Clara without qualifications, reasons, demands, laws, explanations. How could she be here? Was it her real self or a spiritual shadow, lured on the wind by the distant sound of her pain?

EIGHT

IF WINTER WAS CLARA'S UNDOING, spring—and She-Is-Alert's calculating brain—were mine. Winter, far from being the season of my discontent, was the icy zenith of my happiness. In New York, when the snow began to fall—and that first winter saw the streets and roads and fields heaped with it—young people bring sleighs out of their family barns and hitch them to teams of fast horses. Off they go on parties of pleasure into the shrouded countryside.

Sleighing is one of the world's most exhilarating sports. You zoom along the roads, two or four to a sleigh, beneath great bearskin rugs, feet encased in fur-lined boots, hands in furry mittens. Best of all, no member of the older generation, prey to ague and chilblains, has the slightest inclination to join the party.

I have since been told that no other country in the world allows its young women the freedom Americans permit their daughters. I am inclined to agree with this observation. Whether other couples took advantage of it, I can only wonder. But for Robert Nicolls and me, winter was heaven-sent. In his wondrous sleigh, pulled by two of the finest Arabian horses in the province, we hurtled across the frozen Hudson to the town of Hoboken, we zoomed up Manhattan Island to the little community near Kings Bridge on its northern tip and sometimes ventured into the county of Westchester.

On all these trips, Robert saw to it that a tavern was alerted along the way for a pause that included a warm room and mugs of hot flip[1] beside the bed. How we basked in our secret when we returned to New York that night for a decorous dinner party at the Cuylers or the Franks or the Van Vorsts. Aunt Gertrude patently suspected the worst but she could prove nothing. My sense of triumph multiplied my conviction that I was binding Robert to me with ever-deepening love.

He heaped presents on me. Baskets of flowers from the greenhouses of the Long Island estate, a second greyhound to keep Walpole company, a golden locket on my birthday[2] with a miniature painting of him inside it. On New Year's Day he insisted I stand beside him and greet the hundreds of guests who swarmed to shake his and the governor's hands. He was treating me as if I were virtually a member of the family.

The governor himself was scrupulously polite to me. He was twenty or thirty pounds heavier than his son, with a pot belly and dewlaps that drooped like a turkey's wattle, but he had the same sunny good nature and foxy smile. His eyes were far more cunning, however. I sensed he was a man who was always looking for the main chance. A widower, he seemed fond of a half dozen different ladies, but I made no effort to learn anything of his private life. I had no idea, for instance, of his liaison with Mrs. Stapleton.

Robert and I continued to enjoy our blissful winter trysts until spring winds weakened the ice in the rivers and thawing temperatures turned the roads to gumbo. Sleighs were hauled into barns to be polished and oiled for six months of hibernation. We were effectively trapped in New York, which made a rendezvous far more difficult. Even the little country tavern where we

---

[1] *A drink that mixed rum, brandy, milk, and beaten eggs, stirred by a hot poker.*
[2] *December 21.*

met that first night was beyond our reach, on the far side of a river of mud.

All in all, I felt nature had timed the descent of spring perfectly to suit my hopes. When you are in love, it is so easy to believe the world is revolving around your throbbing heart. I sat in my room, gazing at the miniature of Robert in my locket, reading a letter in which he mixed poems and paeans to my beauty. At the close he wrote: *Remember those words that I once told you I could only speak when my heart impelled them from my throat? I think I hear them blowing on the April wind that fills my room with the promise of summer.*

In that moment, I thought I was the equal, even the superior, of every diplomat in the world. Horatio Walpole, the first minister's brother, who was renowned for his ability to manipulate the French, acknowledged my supremacy. The Moon Woman was no more. She had been annihilated by She-Is-Alert's agile brain and knowing heart. I wrote a spirited reply: *I'm sure Aunt Gertrude and Uncle Johannes would be happy to entertain almost any offer to take me off their hands!*

How little I knew of how the white world worked. At Shining Creek, when a warrior claimed a young woman as a wife and the matron of the clan gave her approval, the bridegroom simply took her to his longhouse, leaving behind appropriate presents—some wampum or a haunch of venison or a swatch of good cloth. In New York, I soon discovered, a marriage was more like the negotiation of a treaty of commerce between rival tribes or nations.

"Robert Nicolls has asked for your hand," my uncle said to me one evening at supper. "Are you agreeable?"

"Yes. I love him," I said.

My cousin Esther looked as if she were going to choke on the oyster she had on her fork. Her hard-eyed sister Anna, who had no hopes for such a catch, gazed at me with something close to admiration.

"He will have to take you as you are," Johannes said. "It will be a nice test of his devotion."

"What do you mean?"

"Your estate will be your dowry. I can add nothing to it. I have two daughters of my own to marry."

"My dowry?" I knew about such things. Princesses brought dowries to princes and kings, but I never realized they were integral to the weddings of lesser mortals.

It so happened that the day of this conversation was the anniversary of my grandfather's death. "What is my estate worth, Uncle Johannes?" I asked.

"That depends on the value of New Netherlands Trading Company stock," he said.

"And what does that depend on?"

"The profits we have made in the previous year."

"What percentage of the stock can I expect to own?"

"Computed against the money we made from the sale of your grandfather's assets—about one percent."

"One percent!" I cried. "How much did you receive from the sale of the houses—and the Mohawk lands— are they sold too?"

"They are. I received fair market value for all," he snapped.

"I would like to know an exact figure," I said.

"Don't be impertinent, young woman," Uncle Johannes said. "I can arrange for you to get nothing at all. And no court of law could ever challenge me."

The next day, the Governor called on Uncle Johannes. His Excellency greeted me with an affectionate kiss. Then the two men adjourned to the parlor to discuss my fate. I never felt so powerless—and so dreadful. Not even the memories of my sobbing childhood journey from the bloodstained banks of the Mohawk to Shining Creek compared to it. The anguish seemed redoubled by my undoubted adulthood. I was a grown woman—but I was being treated like a child.

No, I thought. More like a piece of merchandise. Or

a slave. How odd it was—and how prophetic—that I would feel kinship with Clara at this moment. I suddenly yearned for her presence. I desperately needed someone who was a true friend.

After a half hour's conversation, His Excellency the Governor departed without giving me another kiss. I found this ominous. If the negotiation had been successful, wouldn't he have welcomed me into the family? I dressed for a supper party at the Cuylers with a foreboding-laden heart.

In the spacious parlor and dining room of the Cuyler mansion on Pearl Street a merry party was in progress. Robert was dancing a gavotte with pert Elizabeth Cuyler, Guert's sister, as I arrived. He saw me across the room and his face acquired a stricken expression—like a man who had learned bad news and had been trying to forget it until he saw someone with whom he must share it.

I watched while he finished the dance and let him bring me a glass of punch. "My dearest love," he murmured. "We must have a talk."

"Where?"

"Let us go up on the roof."

The Cuyler house, like the mansions of many merchants, had a walk on the roof from which they could watch the lower harbor for their ships. It was in some ways a poor choice, because it inevitably reminded me of the night last fall when I had capitulated on the battlements of the fort.

"My father told me the most stunning news," Robert said, in a wavering voice. "Your estate is worth less than two thousand pounds.[3] Your uncle flatly refuses to supplement it for your dowry. My father says anything less than thirty thousand pounds[4] is out of the question."

[3]About $200,000 in late-twentieth-century dollars.
[4]About $3,000,000 in modern dollars.

"Then we must marry for love," I said. "The poets seem to think it's a fine idea."

"Most poets die poor," Robert said. "My father has no great sum at his command. Don't you notice how eagerly he snaps up every present that's offered to him? If I'm to make my way in the world, I must marry a decent fortune."

"Robert, together we can overcome this, this monstrous injustice. With your father's help, we can force my uncle to admit I'm entitled to half the worth of the New Netherlands Trading Company. I'm my father's only living heir! I foresaw this problem a year ago—"

"Did you?" he said. "You knew it—and never so much as hinted it to me? You let me continue to this nice point, where I must prove myself a scoundrel or a fool?"

"Foresaw is perhaps too strong a word," I said. "I had only a passing insinuation."

"You used foresaw. It's much too late to withdraw it. Much too late for a great many things! Do you seriously think my father is going to challenge the honesty of a man who has given him one of the finest estates on Long Island?"

"I thought you said George Fowler gave it to him."

"It was sold to Fowler for a pittance, to make it legal. In return, your uncle received the contract to carry all the new recruits and supplies for the garrison of the fort for the next five years."

He turned his back on me and gazed out at the dark river. "I almost wish you'd never broached such a topic. I would rather go to my grave thinking you truly loved me and I was a coward who abandoned you for money than believe—as I now think I must—that you never saw me as more than a cat's-paw to your own avarice."

"You can't believe that," I said. "Not after the nights we've spent together. How can you speak of avarice—

when I'm only trying to win what's rightfully my own property! If anyone has avarice in his heart—it's you!''

"Not avarice. Simply the desire of a reasonable man to see the world as it is. To cope with it. Your condemnation of me only suggests the ugly motive that lay like a canker at the heart of our love.''

"Let's forget that. Let's go back to damning you as a coward. I find that far more satisfying. That is what you are. A pusillanimous mercenary coward!''

It was unbelievable. We had gone from lovers to loathers in fifteen minutes. For a wild moment I wondered what he would do or say if I flung myself off this roofwalk to smash my skull against Pearl Street's cobblestones. Would that prove I was sincere—that I truly loved him?

She-Is-Alert's cold cutting snarl rescued me. *Once and for all, when will you trust only my voice in your head? When will you stop listening to your brainless heart?* Through thick welling tears I said: "I will repeat it one more time, although the words all but choke me— I truly loved you. I think you truly loved me.''

"I did!'' he said. "Now the mere sight of you will be enough to poison my digestion for a week. I've told my father I wish to return to England. I hope to be at sea a week hence.''

"*Bon voyage,*'' I said. "That's French for good riddance.''

That night, back in my room, I copied the opening stanzas of Sir Walter Raleigh's "The Nymph's Reply to the Shepherd'' out of a book of poems which Robert had given me.

If all the world and love were young,
And truth in every shepherd's tongue,
These pretty pleasures might me move
To live with thee, and be thy love.

The flowers do fade, and wanton fields
To wayward winter reckoning yields;
A honey tongue, a heart of gall,
Is fancy's spring, but sorrow's fall.

I gave Thin Tom two pence to take this sweet farewell to Fort George, addressed to: *The Hon. Robert Foster Nicolls, Esq.* After this gesture of defiance, I relapsed into total misery. For days I lay in my room weeping. My woe was hardly lessened by the knowledge that my cousin Esther was spreading the story of my rejection all around New York. I had no doubt the flinthearted *vrouws* and burghers of the older generation would find no fault with Johannes Van Vorst for his parsimony. Thirty thousand pounds was far beyond the dowry of most New York maidens—and why should he part with it for someone who had no maidenhood worth mentioning?

When I finally emerged from my room, I found my situation was even worse. Robert Nicolls had gotten drunk and stayed that way until they poured him aboard his London-bound ship. In the course of his maunderings, he had regaled more than one crowded taproom with the story of our amours. My reputation was shredded beyond repair. All this was told to me with breathless wide-eyed pseudosympathy by my cousin Esther.

"So, miss," my Aunt Gertrude said to me that night at the supper table. "I hope you've found the truth of the Bible's warning of the wages of sin."

I said nothing.

"What is to become of you, I can't imagine. Any hope of finding a respectable husband has gone glimmering."

The next day I sought out Guert Cuyler in his father's law office. "Do you too believe the worst about me?" I asked.

He hung his head. "Robert Nicolls left little to the imagination."

"Do you believe in love—its power to invade the heart and annihilate sense?"

Guert nodded dumbly.

"I loved Robert Nicolls that way. I don't anymore. I assure you I'll never make such a fool of myself again. I'm here as a client—nothing less, nothing more."

He nodded again.

I told him about my uncle's treatment of my estate. Guert sighed. "It would be a very difficult case to prove in court. Especially in this province, as long as Nicolls remains governor. I would say for however long he stays, it's impossible."

"I don't understand it!" I cried. "As my father's only heir, don't I have a claim to half ownership of the New Netherlands Trading Company?"

He sadly shook his head. "Your grandfather gave the company to your uncle when he retired. His will only left you his immediate estate. He was afraid if he left you a half interest, and you married, the company might fall into division and quarreling. If you'd been a man, he might have acted differently."

"What a consolation."

Guert walked me to the street door. "Miss Van Vorst—Catalyntie—" he said. "I know the mere idea of what I'm going to say must provoke you. But at some future date—when your heart is healed of this wound—as I'm sure it will be—I wonder if you would consider the possibility of another suitor."

"You?"

"Yes."

"You're much too good—too kind—too honest—for a wretch like me," I said. "Find a woman with a heart that hasn't been corrupted."

Turning my back on what was almost certainly my one hope of redemption in New York, I trudged up the

Broadway in the spring sunshine. The street reminded me of Robert, of our expedition, mouth to mouth, on the king's birthday. I was about to turn off it into Wall Street when a large man came flying out of a tavern headfirst to sprawl in the muck at my feet. I gazed down at the soiled figure and muddy face of Malcolm Stapleton.

"What brings you from New Jersey?"

He reeled to his feet. I saw he was drunk. "Clara," he muttered.

"What about Clara? Have you lost interest in her? I've heard you were using her to save money on your whoring."

He shook his head drunkenly. "Loved . . . her," he muttered.

In my malevolent mood, the very word made me laugh. "What would a lout like you know about love? You're like your friend Nicolls. The morals of a whoremaster. Any woman who isn't for sale doesn't interest you."

Slumped against the tavern wall, the giant began to weep like a five-year-old. "Dying—Clara's dying," he said. "My fault."

"Dying?" I could not believe it. "Dying of what?"

He mumbled out the story. All my accumulated rage at Robert Nicolls exploded in his face. He, not Robert, became the paradigm of male cowardice and corruption. "I hope at least you have the decency never to show your face before honest folk again," I said. "I hope you'll go where some wandering Indian war party in search of amusement captures you and slowly peels the flesh from your bones and cooks it over an open fire. And you can easily imagine what part I hope they choose first!"

I rushed across town to the Van Vorst mansion. For some reason I was imbued with an absolute certainty that I could save Clara, no matter what had happened to her. Perhaps I was driven by the frantic realization that without her I was totally alone in this hostile New York world. I told Aunt Gertrude what I had heard and asked her for money to go to New Jersey. She refused. I damned her for a heartless bitch and rushed upstairs. There on my dresser was Robert Nicolls's gold locket. I seized it and ignoring my aunt's shrieks, raced to the nearest tavern.

I sold the locket for fifteen pounds, probably a tenth of what it was worth, and hurried to the Hudson River docks, where I found a ferryman in a stout rowboat who hauled me to Hoboken. There I hired a wagon and driver, who took the better part of the rest of the day to reach the Stapleton mansion near the falls of the Passaic.

By luck, Adam Duycinck was glancing out the window of Clara's room as I arrived. He greeted me at the door and led me upstairs without bothering about introductions to anyone. By the time I reached Clara's bed he had shamefacedly told me his role in what had happened. I saw at a glance that Clara's spirit was struggling to escape her body. She had given up her desire for existence.

I seized her in my arms. "I saw Malcolm Stapleton in New York," I said. "He told me you were dying. You can't. You mustn't. You won't. I need you. I need your love."

I have no idea how long I lay there with my arms around her. Eventually Georgianna Stapleton hovered in the background, shrilly explaining why the murder of the baby had been necessary. Duycinck and her husband hid behind her.

"Madam, you sicken me," I said. "Leave this room. No one shall enter this room except me until Clara is well again. If I have to write to His Majesty the King himself, I will have you prosecuted for this crime—if you stay in this room another ten seconds!"

For the next month, I was Clara's nurse. I demanded and obtained special, extremely expensive medicines

Duycinck recommended. I raged at George Stapleton as a worse murderer than his wife, utterly intimidating the man. I refused to speak to Georgianna Stapleton. I treated Duycinck like the whining moral vagrant that he was. Alone with Clara, I told her again and again she had a duty to live. She was my only friend in this treacherous world, where the Evil Brother ruled.

Slowly, Clara allowed herself to be dragged back from oblivion's precipice. By the time summer winds sighed through the opened windows of her bedroom, she was able to walk a few tottering steps—and began to think about the future. "Where is Malcolm?" she asked one day.

"Gone where I told him he should go," I said. "Where the scum of the colony drifts. To the frontier, where every man has something shameful to hide."

"You should have let me speak to him first!" Clara said.

"Why?"

"I loved him. He loved me."

"You were living in a dream. In the real world, love doesn't exist," I said. "People use the word but it's simply a disguise for animal desire—or some less obvious greed, like money or property."

"What's happened to you in New York?"

I told her, making myself as stupid, Robert Nicolls as venal as I could find words to describe us. "You didn't love him?" she asked.

"I thought I loved him. Until I awoke from my idiotic dream."

"I wasn't living in a dream," Clara said. "Love is as real, if not as powerful, in this world as money or desire. Don't we love each other?"

"We're exceptions."

"Didn't your grandfather love you—and me?"

"He was another exception," I said.

"Then Malcolm is another exception. He loved me

the way a great warrior makes war—with his whole soul.''

"Why didn't he protect you?''

"In his heart he wanted to protect me. But he was defeated by his God.''

"You're talking nonsense! What were you going to say, if you had a chance to speak to him?''

"That I forgive him.''

"No! You must never forgive. That's what makes women weak. They're preached at day and night to forgive their fathers, their husbands, their lovers, everyone who robs them of their happiness. Men don't forgive. Neither should we.''

For another hour, I poured out the details of the year of humiliations and insults I had endured in the Van Vorst household. I told her of my mulcted estate, of my cousins' perpetual envy and obloquy. I retailed my final conversation with Robert Nicolls.

"Revenge, revenge on them all—that's the only thing that keeps me alive,'' I said. "They hope my loneliness, my unhappiness, will kill me. But I'm a daughter of the Seneca. I'll never surrender to them. I'll cut out their lying vicious hearts before I die. I swear it.''

With no warning, my rage faltered. I was the Moon Woman again. "But I can't do it without you, Clara. I want you to hate them with me. You must, Clara! You must! You can't forgive this monster Malcolm Stapleton. The next thing you know you'll be forgiving his stepmother and Duycinck.''

"Oh my dearest friend,'' Clara said. "If you could see what I see—what evil is speaking in your soul— your heart would be filled with fear and doubt.''

I strode to the round mirror that hung on the wall beside the bed. "I see nothing but a woman who's going to become rich and powerful. A woman who's never going to allow a man's love to confuse her heart again.''

"I don't think we can control our hearts,'' Clara said.

"What enters them, what changes them, is part of our *ondinnonk,* our fate."

"No!" I said, furious again. "I've discarded that part of our Seneca inheritance. Indians are children of nature in all its blind stupidity. As Senecas, we starved each spring like animals in the forest. White men defy nature. They never starve. If their crops fail, they bring grain from across the ocean in their ships. Their money enables them to do anything. We're going to get some of that money, Clara. We're going to get a great mountain of it. Then we'll have the power to do whatever pleases our hearts—and what will please mine most will be *revenge.*"

It was wrong, Clara felt in her deepest self. They were blundering down a path that led to another precipice. But she was too weak, too uncertain, too drained by her illness and the sorrow of her failed love and lost child to oppose her willful Seneca sister. All she could do was silently vow that if she ever saw Malcolm Stapleton again, she would tell him she forgave him.

BOOK

THREE

ONE

BY THE FLICKERING LIGHT OF a lantern, I descended into the cellar of our house on Maiden Lane to gaze one more time at the trading goods. I fingered the swatches of deep blue and dark red strouds.[1] I locked the sea chests and turned to the barrels of imitation pearl necklaces and earrings and hand rings. The silver and gold gleamed in the lantern's glow, like my hopes. For a moment I could barely breathe. So much depended on these goods. I was looking at three hundred fifty pounds, half of all the money I had in this world.

Footsteps on the stairs. Clara stood a few feet away. The distance was a kind of statement. She declined to hover over these treasures like a mother over a promising child. The refusal implied a certain dislike, even a disapproval, of their meaning and purpose. Not for the first time, I struggled against irritation, even anger. Why didn't she feel the same way about this leap for independence?

"Come to bed. We have to get up before dawn tomorrow," Clara said.

"I just wanted to make sure everything was in order," I lied.

Clara laughed mirthlessly. "It's been in order for a week. Come upstairs. I've made some tea. It will help you sleep."

I sighed. It was pointless for me to lie to Clara. She

[1] *A coarse wool, named after the English city in which it was manufactured.*

could read my soul as plainly as if my thoughts, my desires, were printed on my face. That realization made me surly again. "Very well, Miss *Flowers*," I said.

"I'm sorry if I hurt you this morning," Clara said.

"You didn't—I understand, perfectly."

At 10:00 A.M. on this last day in New York, Clara and I had put on our soberest outfits, skirts of grey and bonnets of black, and hurried down to City Hall. We had stood before the same high walnut dais from which Judge Walter Van Staats had hurled imprecations on Clara and all the other members of her race. Old Staats was dead now. In his place sat the Englishman, lean, hawk-nosed Daniel Horsmanden.

I informed Judge Horsmanden that I wished to free Clara from slavery. The judge nodded perfunctorily. Last week, Guert Cuyler had visited him in his chambers and negotiated the matter in advance. This was a pro forma appearance, for legality's sake.

"Are you prepared to post a bond of five hundred pounds to guarantee that she won't become a charge on the public?" Horsmanden growled.

Guert had warned us that Horsmanden had grave doubts about freeing Africans, no matter what the law said. I knew nothing about his personal animosity toward Clara. I thought the size of the bond was his way of expressing his judicial disapproval. "Yes, Your Honor," I said.

The words drove pain through the center of my body. Clara frequently told me I loved money too much. Was this proof? If it was, I would prove to myself at least that I loved Clara more. I stoically signed the bond that the clerk of the court handed me. If I ever needed to borrow money, this obligation could be construed as a debt, inclining a lender to refuse me. There were too many merchants in New York who might look for such an excuse.

Judge Horsmanden asked me what last name Clara

was going to use. "Van Vorst," I said. Why not? We were sisters in everything but blood.

"Is that agreeable to you?" Horsmanden asked Clara.

"No," Clara said. "I would prefer another name."

I stared in astonishment—and anger. How could Clara refuse Cornelius Van Vorst's name?

"What name would you prefer?" the Judge asked sarcastically.

"I would prefer Flowers. Clara Flowers."

I struggled to understand. Clara was telling me we were still Seneca sisters. But she wanted to expunge from her soul the name that recalled her slavery.

"So be it," Judge Horsmanden had growled. "I'd rather see a Clara Flowers soliciting on the streets of New York than an African with a respectable name like Van Vorst."

Clara had borne the insult in silence. I had been ready to give Horsmanden a ferocious rebuke, which would probably have prompted him to raise the bond to a thousand pounds. Just in time, Clara's hand on my arm reminded me of my grandfather's advice about bowing down. On the way home, she told me about her encounter with the judge in New Jersey.

A year ago, I had brought a still-feeble Clara back to New York and rented a small house on Maiden Lane. Clara's abuse had been the perfect pretext for refusing to spend another day in the household of Johannes and Gertrude Van Vorst. With Guert Cuyler as my attorney, I had petitioned the court to allow me to live independently on the income from my estate, which I would legally inherit when I became twenty-one.

Behind the scenes, I had already done some vigorous politicking to guarantee a verdict in my favor. I told George Stapleton I wanted his backing as the price of my silence for his wife's treatment of Clara. There were laws against the murder or attempted murder of a slave—and abortion was an equally serious crime. Royal

Governor Nicolls was soon persuaded to say a word on my behalf. The court ordered Johannes Van Vorst to pay me five hundred pounds a year. Clara and I had lived so simply, we had been able to save two-thirds of this stipend, and I had invested half of it in a ship that carried four tons of winter wheat to England, doubling the money. I had used this profit to finance our trading expedition.

My uncle, who begrudged every farthing he had been forced to surrender, predicted—and hoped—his rebellious niece would fail disastrously. Most of New York concurred with this spiteful prophecy. A woman could not sell goods to Indians. Johannes Van Vorst declared the headstrong creature might as well take the money—which was really *his* money—and throw it into the Hudson.

I went grimly ahead with my purchases of trading goods. I bought jewelry that everyone said was much too expensive; I chose nothing but the best cloth, which drew more scoffs from supposedly knowing New Yorkers. Indians could not tell the difference between cheap and dear. More to the point, in regard to predictions of my failure, the frontier was in turmoil. At least eight traders had been murdered, their goods stolen by marauding bands of presumably French Indians in the last six months. A woman stood a very good chance of being raped as well as robbed and murdered.

Now, as we went upstairs to our narrow kitchen, I found myself brooding on our courtroom visit. I declined to be cheered by the pot of hot tea under the cosy or the plate of sugar cookies beside it. "I should have asked George Stapleton to intercede with the governor again. I should never have had to post a five-hundred-pound bond," I said. "Most people only have to post a hundred."

"Mr. Stapleton looks like a dying man," Clara said. We had seen Stapleton on the street on our way to court.

"He looks like a drunkard to me," I said. "Remember Leaping Bear? He turned yellow the same way, from whiskey."

Leaping Bear had been the great drunkard of our village. He lived to drink. He sold everything, his gun, his hatchet, he even gave his wife to traders for whiskey, until it killed him. George Stapleton's skin was a pale yellow, his hands shook, his shoulders sagged.

"Tell my son if you see him in Albany or the woods that I'll give him six more months to come home," Stapleton said when we met him. "If he chooses to remain a vagabond, I'll remove him from my will and leave all my property to his brother."

"Have you had any reports of his whereabouts?" I asked.

"He's been seen at Albany—and at Oswego," Stapleton said.

I was dismayed to see Clara brighten at this news. Oswego was the British fort on Lake Ontario where we planned to launch ourselves as fur traders. Could she possibly want to see Malcolm Stapleton again?

George Stapleton gazed mournfully at Clara. "As she lay dying, my first wife made me swear before God to be a good father to him. She's appeared to me in dreams every night since he left."

"We'll tell him he has a father with a troubled heart," Clara said.

"In exchange for that favor, would you loan us the services of Adam Duycinck?" I said. I was determined to wring every possible advantage from this man. "His ability to repair muskets could be very useful to us. It's a great problem in every Indian village—so many muskets are broken, useless. A trader who brings a gunsmith with her would be instantly popular."

George Stapleton was not enthusiastic. "My wife depends on him to run Hampden Hall—"

"He has great influence with your son. He might persuade him to return—"

"All right. I'll endure the thousand lashes I'll receive in New Jersey. Adam will be on the dock tomorrow morning when you sail."

What a strange man, I thought. He seems tormented in some deep way that goes beyond business or marriage. Why was he so afraid of his first wife's spirit? Why was she haunting him? Eventually I would learn that George Stapleton was more than strange.

As soon as we parted, Clara objected to Duycinck as a traveling companion. He summoned too many painful memories she would prefer to forget. She brought him up again as we drank our midnight tea. "You must learn to ignore your feelings—when they interfere with improving some moneys," I said.

"I don't think I'll ever do that," Clara said.

You will if you remain my partner or— I caught myself before I made the threat. Clara still meant too much to me. But the look on her face made it clear that she had sensed my unspoken words. Suddenly I found myself bewildered, almost afraid of my own nature. Could a mountain of money transform love into indifference, even hate? I did not know. But a vibration of future pain, grief, loss shook both our souls.

TWO

DUYCINCK WHINED—OH, DID HE whine!—all the way up the Hudson. It was March—still mostly winter in New York. The river was full of floating ice. The little Dutchman predicted a blizzard that would leave us frozen to death somewhere along the Mohawk. If the weather did not get us, the French and Indians would finish us off.

"You females are *ignorant*. You think you can disregard politics," Duycinck said. "I've heard my master talking to Governor Nicolls. There's dirty work afoot in the north. The French in Canada are determined to run the English out of the fur game, if they have to kill every trader in the province. I don't want my scalp drying on some Ottawa lodgepole. Or Seneca, for that matter. I don't trust your wonderful tribe. Didn't they slaughter your parents?"

Tears welled in Clara's eyes. I told Duycinck to shut up. At Albany we hired wharfmen to unload our trading goods and took rooms at the Crown Tavern on State Street. It was where Clara and I had spent the night with our parents on our journey to the Mohawk fifteen years ago. Clara trembled and wondered if there was some place else we could sleep.

I shook my head. "It's better to face it all. We're going to stop on the way up the Mohawk and walk through the ruins of the house, if they still exist."

"No!" Clara said. "That place is certain to be haunted. The way they died—"

The innkeeper, a squat pug-nosed Dutchman wearing a greasy grey wig, interrupted us: "Slaves sleep in the cellar. Ten pence a night."

"Miss Flowers is as free as you are—or I am," I said. "She'll sleep upstairs with me."

I brandished Clara's manumission certificate in the man's fat face. The innkeeper was still reluctant, but when I flung two Spanish dollars in front of him, he gave us the rooms. After a dinner in the smoky taproom that mixed pork with roasted potatoes in a puddle of grease on our plates, I asked the innkeeper where we could hire bateaumen for a trip up the Mohawk.

"No one's going up the Mohawk alone these days,"

he said. "No one who wants to keep his scalp on his head. Traders band together, twenty or thirty to a group."

"See what I told you?" Duycinck whined.

"We're going up the Mohawk," I said. "We've got five hundred pounds of trading goods sitting on the town wharf."

"I'll buy them from you for two hundred pounds," the innkeeper said.

"Go to hell," I said.

In the morning I strode down to the waterfront and sent Duycinck scampering through the alehouses and brothels that clustered there, spreading the word that someone was ready to pay double wages for a trip up the Mohawk to Oswego. Eventually a dozen boatmen came shambling into the chilly morning, blinking blearily at this strange apparition in skirts, talking confidently about how much money she planned to make in the fur trade.

The last bateauman to arrive was preceded by a capering Duycinck. "I've found him. I've found the lad. God knows he don't look like much but I've found him."

It was Malcolm Stapleton. He wore buckskin breeches and a shirt that had not seen a laundry in a year at least. It was smeared and splotched with grease and grime; not a little dirt was also on his face. He stood there, patently bewildered by the sight of me and Clara.

"I'll hire the worst scum in Albany before I hire you," I said.

"Catalyntie—" Clara said.

"I'm in charge of this expedition," I said.

"But you promised his father."

"I promised to give him a message. Which I will do, forthwith. For some unknown reason, your father wishes to see you before he dies."

"Is he ill?"

"He doesn't look well. But that may be simply the effects of living with your mother."

"She's my stepmother!" Malcolm roared.

"Whatever the reason, he wants to see you. If you need money for your journey downriver I'll lend it to you."

Malcolm barely listened to me. He was gazing mournfully at Clara. "You're . . . well?" he said.

"I'm well," she said.

"I was sure you were dead. I never tried to find out. I was afraid if I heard the worst, I'd sink to the bottom of a bottle and never come up."

"Do you want to borrow some money?" I asked.

"No," Malcolm said and shambled back down the wharf into the narrow alleys that led to State Street.

"Malcolm!" Clara raced after him, ignoring my call. She caught up to him as he was turning into an alehouse. An ugly red-faced woman sat at a table, slurping liquor from a mug. "Malkie!" she chortled.

For Clara, it was a vision of the way the Evil Brother was devouring the lost warrior. Malcolm's soul had been far more damaged than her woman's body by the debacle of their aborted child in Hampden Hall.

Clara dragged Malcolm back into the street. "What happened to us was terrible," she said. "But I want you to know I forgave you long ago. In my heart you're still the warrior, the soldier I dreamt of loving—and I still love."

Malcolm turned away, as if the mere sight of her was unbearable. "I should have brought you up the Mohawk and lived where there are no laws. I was a coward."

"That's impossible . . . you . . . a coward," Clara said. "There's no man who could make you a coward. You were overwhelmed by your god, speaking in your father's voice. I think he's a false god. But he was still . . . god. Perhaps a face of god. I begin to think he wears many faces, just as men do."

Malcolm listened mutely, understanding but not understanding. The words did not touch his heart. He was still irretrievably lost to the world of the spirit, to meaning, hope, love.

"Clara!" I stood at the head of the narrow lane, determined not to let Malcolm seduce her again. "I've hired the bateaumen. We leave in an hour."

"Where are you going?" Malcolm asked.

He shook his head angrily when Clara told him our plans. "You'd better select the right men. Otherwise you may never be heard from again."

"What do you mean?"

"There's a dirty game being played along the Mohawk," he said. "Some people in Albany are in it."

His words were almost an echo of what Duycinck had said to us coming up the Hudson. Perhaps that made me more inclined to ignore them. "Clara!" I called. "We mustn't waste a moment—"

I wanted to reach the Indian country as soon as possible to meet the hunters as they returned with their furs from their winter of trapping in the woods. Back at the Crown Tavern, as we packed our clothes and Duycinck railed at me for dismissing Malcolm Stapleton, Clara wondered if we should take his warning seriously.

"I have an answer to that," I said. From my trunk I drew three pistols. I gave one to Clara, one to Duycinck, and kept one for myself.

"You expect me to shoot someone?" Clara said, fingering the carved stock, the stubby ugly barrel.

"I expect you to try, if it comes to that," I said.

In an hour we were jolting overland to Schenectady in wagons with our trading goods and bateaumen. By afternoon we were heading up the Mohawk in a bateau manned by six oarsmen. As we struggled against the swift current, the bateaumen began talking in a language we did not understand.

"What are they saying?" Clara asked me in Seneca.

"I don't know. It's French," I said, suddenly regretting my failure to study the language more diligently during my time in Madame Ardsley's finishing school with my Van Vorst cousins.

I asked our boss boatman, a thickset Dutchman named de Groot, why they were speaking French. "We go up the lake to Quebec as often as we go up the Mohawk to Oswego," he said.

"The lake" was the Lake of the Sacrament,[1] the long narrow inland sea north of Albany that stretched almost to the Canadian border. "I thought trade with the French was forbidden by law," I said.

"North of Albany, nothing is forbidden," de Groot said. "Their money is as good as yours."

They went back to talking French, leaving me with a growing suspicion that they were saying things they did not want us to hear for the worst possible reasons.

When they hauled ashore to cook an early supper and answer nature's calls, Duycinck, who had been riding in the prow of the bateau, strolled over to me and Clara and said in a low voice: "My French isn't very good, but I heard enough to tell you this—they're going to cut my throat tonight and throw me into the river. They plan to enjoy you and Clara for a while—and do the same thing with you. Then they're off to Montreal with your trading goods. They'll come back to Albany with a story about an Indian raid. You couldn't have found a worse set of villains if you advertised for them."

"That's why I gave you a pistol," I said, struggling to control my pounding heart. "We'll fight them."

"Have you ever tried to shoot a man with a pistol? You can't do it at more than ten feet. A musket can kill you from fifty yards."

"Then they'll kill me," I said. "I'll die here if that's

[1] Now Lake Champlain.

my fate. But I won't give up those goods! My life is in those goods!''

"Don't be ridiculous,'' Duycinck growled. "You can always buy more goods. You're a bloody heiress. If you want to live, we've got to disappear into the woods.''

I shook my head. "I'll die here. Before I go back to New York and listen to them laugh at me for a fool.''

"Talk to her,'' Duycinck said to Clara. "I'm running at first dark. If you want my company, come along. I've got a compass. We can get back to Albany in a day or two.''

"Damn you for a cowardly son of a bitch!'' I said.

The little Dutchman was hurt. "Adam's not a coward,'' he said. "He'll fight as bravely as the next man if he thinks he's got a chance of winning. But one crookback and two women armed with pistols against seven brutes armed with muskets is not what he computes as a chance.''

He strolled off to snatch a piece of venison from the fire. "He's right,'' Clara said. "It makes no sense for us to die here.''

"It makes sense to me,'' I said.

"Then I'll die with you,'' Clara said. "I owe you my life. You can have it now—or any time in the future.''

I gazed at Clara through a blur of bitter tears. Duycinck was right. The pistols were useless. "We'll go back to Albany and find some honest men,'' I said. "I can't—I won't—let them rob me as if I were a child.''

"Do you want some dinner?'' de Groot called. Now there was no mistaking the malice in his leering smile.

"Pray to the Master of Life,'' Clara whispered. "Nothing else will save us.''

I was too angry to pray. While we ate, more French flew between de Groot and the other boatmen and rage condensed like a chunk of ice in my body. As our escorts chomped on their venison and bread, I conceived a plan.

I would not flee into the woods like a frightened rabbit. I would take a witness back to Albany with me.

Among the goods piled in the center of the bateau was a canoe, which we planned to use to travel down Lake Ontario to visit the village of Shining Creek, after we finished our trading at Oswego. I drew Duycinck aside and told him what I wanted to do with it. He called it madness at first but finally agreed to my plan. A canoe ride back to Albany was far more appealing than an overland trek.

As twilight deepened and the boatmen busied themselves setting up tents, I ordered the youngest of them, a short, button-nosed boy of sixteen or so named Brunck, to unlash the canoe. I said Clara and I disliked venison and wanted to fish for supper in the middle of the river. Brunck told us we could catch more fish in the shallows by the shore. The sneer on his face bespoke his contempt for female stupidity.

"Unlash it anyway," I said.

He muttered something in Dutch about the canoe soon changing owners. The moment he got the craft in the water, I drew my pistol and put it to his head. "Get in," I said. "Don't make a sound, if you don't want a bullet in your skull."

The terrified Brunck cowered in the bottom of the canoe. Duycinck and Clara sprang into the craft and I shoved it into the current. Within minutes we had vanished downstream in the gathering darkness, Brunck in front paddling literally for his life, with my gun at his back, and Clara wielding the other paddle in the rear.

We reached Schenectady by midnight, snatched a few hours' sleep and hired a wagon to take us to Albany in the dawn. At 9:00 A.M. I paraded the sullen Brunck up State Street to the courthouse at gunpoint while dozens of Albanyans gaped. I demanded to see a magistrate. In ten minutes we were standing before a thin-lipped older man named Oloff Van Sluyden.

Judge Van Sluyden's eyes were not friendly from the moment he saw us. When he heard my name, he grew visibly hostile. He listened with barely concealed contempt to my story of premeditated murder and theft and asked young Brunck in Dutch: "Is there a word of truth to this?"

"Not a word," said Brunck, readily picking up the signal. "It's all female moonshine. They ran off when one of them got it into their heads that we was in love with them. An uglier pair of whores I never seen. You couldn't have got me to stick one of'm for a hundred pound."

"Do you have a witness to this attempted battery?" Judge Van Sluyden asked me.

Duycinck told his story. The judge looked sourly at him. "You're in this woman's employ?"

"Yes, Your Honor."

"Is this a scheme to defraud these poor fellows of their wages?"

"No, Your Honor. I'm ready to swear—"

Judge Van Sluyden was too busy working himself into a rage to let Duycinck swear to anything. "Do you think you can go to Oswego with an order from me to repossess your goods and clap honest men in jail—on hearsay evidence like this? Get out of here before I arrest all three of you for vagrancy and false testimony and give you a hundred lashes each at the whipping post!"

Outside, I stared down State Street in the thin March sunshine, while Duycinck urged me to go back to New York. The whole thing was unspeakable, intolerable. But what could a woman—or two women—do about it? We needed a man's protection—or help. A man might persuade some other honest men to do something about de Groot and his thieves. But where could I find this paragon in a town where we did not have a single friend?

"It's exactly as Malcolm warned us—a dirty game with some in Albany in on it," Clara said.

Malcolm Stapleton. The vision of that morning when he defeated Bold Antelope leaped in my memory. Was he capable of helping us? He looked like a dirty dissolute sot. That could simply be evidence of his poverty. He was still a pine tree of a man. Could I ask help from someone whom I had told to his face I considered lower than the worst scum in Albany?

No—but Clara could ask him. Maybe there was something to be said for a forgiving heart, after all—although I still vowed never to tolerate one in my body.

I outlined the proposal to Clara. "Cry a little," I said. "Appeal to his manhood."

Clara curtly told me she would not have to descend to such hypocrisy. In a half hour, Malcolm Stapleton stood on the wharf. "Do you have any money?" he asked me.

"Not a great deal," I lied.

"You'll have to pay more than bateaumen's wages if you want men to risk a bullet in the belly for you," he said.

"Does that include you?" I said.

"I don't want a farthing of your miserable money. I'm doing this for Clara's sake. She's told me what you've done for her. There must be some good in you, even if it escapes me."

I swallowed this insult and agreed to pay triple wages to any man Malcolm persuaded to join us. In an hour he had three men on the wharf, each armed with a long gleaming musket and a cartridge case with thirty rounds of bullets and powder. I can still remember their names: Peter Finch, Andrew Berner, and Michael Malone. They were all younger than Malcolm. "I can vouch for these fellows," Malcolm said. "We've spent time in the woods together, learning to be rangers. When the war begins with the French, we'll be the first to fight."

"Why should we have a war?" I said.

"The French want one. They see no other way to stop

the English from spreading over this whole continent. But you'll never hear that from anyone in Albany. They're making too much money trading with the murdering bastards.''

I marveled at the confident way Malcolm spoke. Despite his sloppy clothes, he was much more than a dispirited vagabond. Clara's would-be soldier had become a man during his adventurous year in the north. But I stopped short of endorsing his readiness to fight the French.

''Let's regain our goods and worry about a war some other time,'' I said.

''These men don't give a damn for your goods—or your money, for that matter,'' Malcolm said. ''They want to deal with de Groot and his gang of traitors. Right, men?''

A growl of agreement came from Peter and Andrew and Michael. ''They're patriots, sick of the way the king's interests are being sold by the greedy politicians in this traitorous town.''

I had the good sense to say nothing to this speech. I saw its galvanizing effect on Malcolm's three followers. I also realized that Malcolm Stapleton had acquired some interesting information about the way things worked in Albany. I had never forgotten my grandfather's suspicion that my parents and the others had been murdered by men in Albany who profited from their deaths.

We hired horses who carried us to Schenectady in a few hours. By midafternoon, we headed up the Mohawk in a large canoe. We traveled at twice the pace of the heavily laden bateau we were pursuing. By dark we had reached the campsite from which Clara and I and Duycinck had fled. ''They can't be more than ten miles ahead of us,'' Malcolm said. ''Twenty at the most. Let's keep going.''

Far into the night the men bent to their paddles. Finally Malcolm ordered them ashore and sent Peter Finch up the riverbank on foot. He came back in an hour to report he had located de Groot's camp. "We'll attack at first light," Malcolm said.

"Are there enough of us?" I said. De Groot had six men.

"There's enough," Malcolm said.

We slept in relays until the first hint of the sun began greying the eastern sky. Malcolm assembled his men. He told Clara and me to stay with Duycinck, guarding the canoe.

"I'm coming with you," I said. "I've got a pistol. I want the privilege of killing that son of a bitch de Groot."

Malcolm shrugged and put me at the end of his little column. For an hour we followed the river until Peter Finch, in the lead, held up his hand. We filtered into the woods on two sides of de Groot and his bateaumen, asleep in three tents in a clearing by the river.

The sky was brightening but Malcolm ordered everyone to stay among the trees until he gave the signal to attack. "What are you waiting for?" I said.

"Enough light to aim a gun," Malcolm said. The light along the river was still grey and thin.

A half hour later, as the sky began to redden, Malcolm borrowed my pistol, aimed it in the air, and pulled the trigger. The bateaumen came tumbling out of the tents, led by de Groot with his musket in his hand. "Get down to the river," he called, crouching low. "Form around the boat."

"De Groot," Malcolm called. "I've got men all around you. Anyone who tries to launch that boat will be shot down without mercy. We're here to regain Miss Van Vorst's stolen goods. We don't want to kill anyone unless you make it a necessity."

"It's Stapleton, goddamn him," de Groot said to the

men around him. "Here's my answer, you English son of a bitch."

He fired his gun in the direction of Malcolm's voice. The bullet hissed through the trees a foot away from me. So that is what death in battle sounds like, I thought. It did not frighten me. I liked it. I liked being exposed to the sort of danger men claimed no woman could endure.

The bullet did not frighten Malcolm either. He took careful aim and pulled his musket's trigger. The crash deafened me and the gush of acrid smoke from the barrel almost blinded and choked me. Other muskets were booming from the woods. The men around de Groot fired back but soon three of them were sprawled on the green grass, dead or badly wounded.

Another bateauman raced up to the Dutchman clutching a bloody arm and shouted: "It's death down by the boat. They shoot anyone who goes near it."

"Load and follow me," de Groot shouted. He and three others still on their feet raced toward the woods on the north side of the clearing. Malcolm fired another round and dropped the last man as he entered the trees.

Peter Finch crept through the trees to join me and Malcolm. "Should we go after them?" he asked, his eyes shining with excitement.

Malcolm shook his head. "De Groot would have all the advantages on the run in the woods."

He sent Michael Malone back to bring Clara and Duycinck up to the clearing in the big canoe. Matter-of-factly, we buried de Groot's four dead men in unmarked graves. Malcolm turned to me and said: "You've recovered your property. Now what? Have you had enough of the north woods? Is it back to safe comfortable Manhattan Island?"

"I'm going to Oswego," I said. "Will you come with me? You and your men?"

"From what you told me about my father, I should go back to New York as soon as possible—"

"Then Clara and I and Adam will go on alone. I think you must know by now our fate is in these goods. We're as determined as any soldier to conquer or die."

"Let me talk to my men," Malcolm said.

While Malcolm conferred with his recruits on the other side of the clearing, Clara glowered at me. "He should go back to his father."

"Why should you give a damn for him or his father after what they did to you?" I said.

Before Clara could answer me, Malcolm sauntered across the clearing. "How much will you pay?" he asked.

"I'll double the wages you're getting, which are already treble."

The thought of risking so much money almost made me ill. But I needed this glowering giant's protection. In my mind he was still lower than the lowest scum in Albany for what he had done to Clara. But he was a fighter—and that was what I needed to survive in this vicious northern world, where nothing was forbidden.

As we took over the bateau and prepared to resume our journey up the Mohawk, I noticed Clara gazing at Malcolm. He was issuing crisp orders to Duycinck and Peter Finch, who would lead the way in the canoe. He wanted them to stay alert for any sign of de Groot and his two friends. They were more than capable of ambushing them.

"Don't you think he's redeemed himself?" Clara said.

"I thought only Jesus could redeem people," I said.

"You know what I mean," Clara said.

I knew exactly what Clara meant. She was still in love with this blond behemoth. She had told me as much a dozen times. Why did it dismay me to hear it now?

THREE

OSWEGO AT LAST!

It had been an exhausting journey up the Mohawk to the great portage, where we dragged the bateau and canoes on rollers to Wood Creek. On this narrow winding watercourse, a huge fallen tree blocked our passage. It had to be sawed up and hauled out of the water with backbreaking labor. Next we paddled across the lake of the Oneidas. They had a great palisaded castle on its shores. Their chiefs made no secret of their expectation of generous presents and we took pains to please them, not wanting to find ourselves on the wrong end of their hatchets. Finally we traversed the Oswego River to the British bastion on the shore of Lake Ontario.

The bulky stone fort loomed against the skyline of the immense empty lake. From its ramparts a huge red British flag whipped and crackled in the cold March wind, a symbol of royal power and pride. The geometry of the jutting parapets and casements proclaimed order and dignity and strength. For the first time, I glimpsed the meaning of the word *empire*.

Then I got a closer look at the world that surrounded the fort. Like pygmies at the feet of a giant, a clutter of wooden huts and tents and tepees created a veritable slum where fifty or sixty traders and several dozen Indians mingled in the mud. We had arrived an hour before sunset, a time, Malcolm Stapleton remarked, that was almost guaranteed to give the worst possible impression of the fur trade.

Their business finished for the day, white men and

Indians were getting drunk as fast as possible. While venison and fish broiled over open fires, card and dice games raged on all sides. As we watched one of the nearer dice games, an Indian lost his last beaver skin and bet his powder horn on the next roll of the dice—and lost that too.

Clara was repelled by the scene. I tried to revel in it. "The drunker they get, the more they gamble, the less business they'll do," I said. "We'll keep our heads clear and make a fortune."

I saw skepticism in Malcolm's eyes—an opinion he had exhibited once or twice as we labored up the Mohawk—and I had rejected in my headstrong way. In private, Malcolm had told Clara he had made many trips to Oswego over the past year. He thought we would have a very difficult time buying furs. He grew even more emphatic when he discovered we had no rum in our baggage. Rum was the heart of the business, he told her.

Leaving Adam Duycinck and the other men to guard the bateau and canoes, Clara and I and Malcolm hurried through the noisy chaos of the trading village to the gate of the fort. After Malcolm exchanged a few words with the sentry on duty, we were beckoned inside. In a few minutes we were meeting an unshaven slack-jawed man in a soiled red coat—Captain Henry Hartshorne—the commander of His Majesty's Independent Company at Fort Oswego.

Hartshorne listened to my complaint against de Groot and his henchmen with an air of weary resignation. He seemed almost annoyed at me for bothering him with such trifling crimes as theft and attempted murder. He was far more amazed to discover that I had come to Oswego to trade with the Indians.

"Don't you have parents, a guardian?" he asked. "Surely someone must have told you that any woman who spends a night here without a proper escort has lost her reputation forever.''

''My parents are dead. I have no guardian I trust nor reputation to forfeit,'' I said. ''Mr. Stapleton will tell you why, if you're truly interested.''

''I'm acting as her escort, Captain,'' Malcolm said. ''I advised her against coming here. But she's not inclined to take advice from anyone.''

Hartshorne pointed to Clara and said: ''This wench is much too pretty. You'll have a hell of a time protecting her from the traders.''

''She's not a wench. Her name is Clara Flowers,'' I said. ''She's my partner in this business.''

''Is all this true, Stapleton?'' Hartshorne asked, more and more astounded.

Malcolm nodded. He gave him a somewhat labored explanation of when and where he first met me and Clara, stressing our years as Senecas. ''Miss Van Vorst—and Miss Flowers—are worthy of whatever protection you can offer them, sir. They've withstood great misfortune with a resolution that speaks well of their characters.''

''How am I supposed to protect them?'' Hartshorne said. ''You know my difficulties. I have a grand total of thirty-six men in this garrison, half of them sick on the miserable rations they get. They haven't powder enough to fire more than one round a man. If I got in a quarrel with those trading brutes, they'd cut my throat quicker than any Indian.''

''At the very least I hope you'll arrest de Groot and his men if they come in here,'' I said.

Hartshorne shook his head. ''My jurisdiction extends only to the trading area around the fort. If he behaves himself here, I have no right in law to lay a hand on him.''

Back at the boats, Malcolm told us what he knew about Captain Hartshorne. His father had been a wealthy merchant in the West Indies sugar trade. A madness for gambling had beggared the son. He had fled to America to escape debtor's prison and took the command at Oswego as an alternative to starvation.

Malcolm was inclined to sympathize with Hartshorne. The captain had encouraged his ambition to be a soldier. "He's convinced unless we show some talent in the military art, the French will destroy us," Malcolm said. The penny-pinching New York legislature had reduced the funds for Oswego every year since Hartshorne arrived. Militarily speaking, the fort was a joke. The French could come down from Canada and take it anytime they chose.

I listened impatiently to this tale of woe. I was thinking of how I could persuade Malcolm to protect us from de Groot and like-minded denizens of the frontier. "I can't pay all your men the triple wages they're getting while we try to do business here," I said.

"They wouldn't take it if you could," Malcolm said. "They want to be on their way home. No one but a fur trader or a fugitive from the law spends any time in this place if he can help it."

"Would you stay—for an honest wage?"

"I'll stay for Clara's sake."

I realized it was time to suspend my animosity toward this man. "I want to apologize for the obnoxious things I said to you in Albany," I said. "Your good conduct on the Mohawk—and several rebukes from Clara—have made me realize I was unjust."

Around us drifted the raucous voices of the fur traders and the Indians as their celebration grew more and more boisterous. An Indian woman, completely naked, burst out of one hut and fled into the woods, pursued by two white men in dirty red coats.

"There goes some of the garrison to their sport," Malcolm said. "It's a wonder they have the strength to lift a gun."

Was he unwilling to accept my apology? I struggled to take my grandfather's advice and bow down a little lower. I needed this young giant. But I vowed I would never bow down to him—or any other man—in my heart.

"Will you stay?" I asked.

"I told you I would," Malcolm said.

"Look!" Clara cried.

From one of the trader's huts had staggered an Indian we instantly recognized: Bold Antelope.

Malcolm nodded. "I've seen him here once or twice. He's changed his name. He calls himself Grey Owl. When he gets drunk he talks the damnedest stuff you've ever heard."

Clara called to him and Grey Owl—or Bold Antelope—approached us, blinking with disbelief. "What are you doing in this place?" Clara asked him in Seneca. "Why aren't you back at our village, contented and happy, with a wife and young sons at your side?"

"They laughed at me in Shining Creek after I let this white man take you away from me," Grey Owl said, glaring at Malcolm. "Even the women said I was like a damp stick, all smoke and no flame. They were right, too. I have seen a different destiny for my soul. I have the dreams to prove it."

"What is it?" Clara asked.

"To preach the truth that all Indians are one people," he said. "To urge them to cease to live as separate tribes and unite as a single nation. Otherwise the white man will devour us one by one."

"And your *ondinnonk* sees the day when the tribes will unite?" Clara said.

"Yes. I have dreamt it many times. I see a great army of warriors as numerous as the leaves on the trees assembling to drive the white men back to the great ocean."

"Oh, my friend, I don't think it is possible," Clara

said. "Remember what our sachem, Black Eagle, told us? It is the white men who are numerous as the leaves on the trees. I have seen them in their great cities and on their farms."

"It will happen, nevertheless. The white men cannot fight the Indians in the forest. We will draw a line on the ground and tell them to come no farther. When that happens, they will lose heart and begin to quarrel with each other over the way they have divided this land. Then we will play them against each other as they have so long played us."

"It would be better if you went back to Shining Creek and made peace with your family and friends," Clara said. "Forget me and what happened at the great council. I'm only a woman. Other women will make you happy again someday."

"Never!" Grey Owl said. "I cannot forget Bold Antelope. He died on that day of shame and rose again as Grey Owl. He lives to revenge his warrior ancestor."

Clara almost wept. "I'll pray to the Manitou for you. I will ask him to give you peace."

"You may do what you please. You cannot change my fate now."

Grey Owl drifted back into the cluster of huts. "How does he live?" Clara asked Malcolm.

"Many Indians consider him a prophet," Malcolm said. "They give him clothing and food. He comes here to make converts of the warriors who drink too much rum and get cheated out of their furs."

Smiling drunkenly, the two soldiers who had run into the woods returned with the Indian woman. They gave her some coins and she went back into a nearby hut. Clara and I were appalled: Indian women becoming prostitutes!

We set up tents on the outskirts of Oswego's trading town and tried to get some sleep. The drunken shouts and laughter continued far into the night. The noise was not much worse than we had encountered in New York, where parties of drunken sailors or roistering apprentices regularly clashed with the Night Watch. But what it signified made sleep elusive.

Clara told me what Malcolm had said about the importance of rum. "Now that I've seen this place, I fear he may be right," she said.

"I'll go bankrupt before I sell rum," I said. "On that point I'm still a Seneca."

The next day, Malcolm's recruits headed back to Albany in one of the canoes, each with triple wages of eleven pounds clinking in their pockets. Before they departed, they lugged our trading goods from the bateau to the tents and opened the boxes and bales. Malcolm bought a bottle of rum from one of the traders and went down to the river with Adam Duycinck to see them off.

As Clara and I unpacked our goods, word of our presence swirled through the huts and tepees. A semicircle of traders and Indians soon surrounded us. The white men rubbed their unshaven faces and scratched their unwashed armpits and all but smacked their lips with anticipation as they contemplated us.

"How much?" asked one of them. He was a big-bellied tub of a man with a loud, authoritative voice.

"These goods are not for sale. I'm here to trade for furs," I said. I added in Seneca to the Indians: "You will get honest prices from me. I'm a daughter of the Turtle Clan. My friend Clara is of the Bear Clan."

"I mean how much for her?" the questioner said, pointing at Clara.

"She's not for sale. She's as free as I am," I snapped.

"You mean you're going to give it away?" the big-bellied questioner asked.

Roars of laughter. I stubbornly tried to ignore what they were talking about. "What's your game? Do you aim to be queen of Oswego?" another man asked.

"We're here to trade for furs—and nothing else!" I said.

Incredulity on every face. "If you aim at bargaining, here's the going rate," the fat man said. "A squaw charges a shilling or a bottle of rum. Assuming you're both free of the pox, we'll pay three, maybe four, shillings for your Negro friend—and five for you. No one's seen a white woman here in years."

"I'll go double that!" shouted another man, a wiry, hook-nosed fellow with a cleft lip. He threw his arm around my waist and leered into my face. "When you're this ugly you've got to pay extra!"

The next sound was the crack of my open hand against his cheek. As he stumbled back, astonished, I snatched my pistol out of one of the boxes of strouds. "I know how to use this. Anyone who thinks he can abuse me or my friend Clara had better wear chain armor on his balls—"

I was talking like a Seneca—but it only convinced the traders that we were prostitutes. The hook-nosed suitor clutched his burning cheek and burst out laughing. "Why, hell, she's got enough spit and fire to keep a seventy-four-gun man-of-war busy. I'll double my double offer. Who would think the devil would bring such a piece to Oswego! It's enough to make me believe in divine providence all over again!"

"Enough bullshit," said the big-bellied man. He had an odd way of talking. The words seemed to come out through some kind of horn in his nose. His accent was strange. We later learned he was from Connecticut. It was our first encounter with a Yankee. "Set your price and we'll guarantee you protection against the fort and anyone else. But we're not about to let you sell this stuff to the Indians. It makes our goods look too cheap— which they are. We'll take it off your hands for a fair price—"

A half dozen traders began pawing the strouds and

examining the jewelry. They all agreed the stuff was too expensive for profitable trading.

"Who the hell sent you here with these goods? Someone who wants to run us out of business?" one asked. He had buck teeth that gave his mouth a mean, sly expression.

"Get your hands off our goods!" I cried, shoving them away from the boxes and bales.

"Listen, bitch—" the big-bellied man said, rapidly losing patience.

"What the hell's going on here?"

Malcolm Stapleton had returned from his farewell party with his men. He loomed over the circle of traders like a frontier Hercules.

"It's none of your affair, Stapleton," the big-bellied man said.

"I'm afraid it is, Stannard. I've made myself responsible for the safety of these two women," Malcolm said. "They're paying me eighteen shillings a day. I would take it seriously amiss if they were disturbed in any way."

"You must be crazy," Stannard said. "What Indian will trade with a woman?"

"We'll soon find out," Malcolm said.

"That we will, my friend," Stannard said. "Let's go back to business, men."

The traders drifted back to their huts. Clara and I conferred with Malcolm on where to find customers. He recommended patrolling the shore of Lake Ontario. Many Senecas from villages along the lake arrived by canoe.

I took his advice and soon had my first prospect, a burly brave with a great pack of beaver skins on his back. "Greetings, Brother," I said. "I'm a daughter of the Seneca. I spent twelve years in the village known as Shining Creek on the shore of this lake. I want to pay you a fair price for your skins. I have cloth and jewelry that your wife and daughters will like very much.''

The man was so amazed to hear a white woman speaking his language, he willingly accompanied me to our tents, where Clara further amazed him by also speaking Seneca and offering him a selection of our strouds and jewelry. His name was Leaping Deer, he said, and his wife had in fact told him to come back with strouds like these.

I began counting his pelts. "We're paying a fair price, not like the rest of the thieves in this place," I said.

Leaping Deer told us he had been robbed here once before. Last year he had gone to the French fort at the other side of the lake, called Frontenac. But their cloth was no good and neither was their jewelry. His wife had made his life miserable for the rest of the year, complaining about them. So here he was, risking robbery again. He was glad he had found two honest women.

Out of the clutter of huts strode the Yankee trader with a bottle of rum in his hand. "Leaping Deer!" he called. "Remember me? Your friend Stannard? What a fine time we had on your last visit. Have a drink of this.''

Stannard spoke very bad Seneca, mingling words from other Indian languages in his well-rehearsed speech. "It's the best rum in the world. From an island in the ocean far to the south. My father is a ship captain. No one else in America gets rum this good.''

"Ho!" said Leaping Deer. "I remember you, Stannard. But I don't remember you as my friend. When I left here I had no skins and no money.''

"We played at dice. A fair game. One of your own people won your skins. Come on, have a drink. This year maybe your luck will change—if you want to play with the dice. If you don't, I'll pay you the best price in the fort for your pelts.''

He thrust a tankard into Leaping Deer's hand and

filled it with rum. Clara and I could only watch in dismay as our customer stared at the brown fluid.

"Don't!" Clara said. But Leaping Deer drank it down in one long swallow.

"Ho!" he said. "That is good rum."

"The best in the world," chortled Stannard.

"Listen, Brother!" I said. "We have a man here who will repair your gun if it needs it, and show you how to keep it working well."

"What do women know about guns?" Stannard said. "Do business with them and they'll soon treat you like a husband, complaining and whining at you. Worst of all, they have no rum. They don't think Indians should drink rum. Doesn't that sound like your wife?"

"Ho!" said Leaping Deer, holding out the tankard. "That is *very* good rum."

Stannard filled the tankard again. Leaping Deer drank it down, shouldered his pack of skins and followed him into the twisting streets of the trading town. Over the next two days, this scene was repeated a dozen times. Stannard or someone else armed with a bottle of rum stationed himself close enough to our tents to intercept every Indian Clara or I persuaded to look at our goods. It soon became painfully evident that rum was the missing ingredient in Catalyntie Van Vorst's wonderful plan to grow rich in the fur trade.

By the end of the second day, I was so humiliated I could not face Clara or Malcolm. Especially Malcolm, whom I was convinced still disliked me and was hoping I would fail. I wandered down to the shore of the lake in near despair. Maybe I should sell our goods to Stannard and his friends and let them have me for five shillings a night. Everyone in New York assumed I was a whore. Why not act like one—and make enough money to go back to the city in triumph?

No—Clara would never let me do such a thing.

"Now what are you going to do?" said a voice in the

twilight. It was Malcolm Stapleton. He loomed against the shadowy lake, a tower of mockery. Clara was with him. Had they been enjoying each other in the tall grass along the shore? The possibility redoubled my bitterness.

"Go ahead," I said. "Laugh at me. I've made a fool of myself."

"Maybe there's another way to sell our goods," Clara said. "If we went to the villages, where the women could see the stuff firsthand—"

"That would violate the treaty," I said. "The chiefs of the Iroquois want to keep the traders out of the villages—because of the rum."

"But we have no rum."

"How can two women call a council to change the treaty?"

"You don't need every tribe's permission," Clara said. "Why not start with the Seneca? If we give presents to one of the chief sachems—"

Clara was right. Presents, to an Indian, were not a bribe. They created an obligation to grant favors in return. They formed a kind of alliance between the giver and the receiver.

"Where can we find one of the sachems?" I said.

"Perhaps our friend Leaping Deer would know."

We plunged into the trading town around the fort. In a few minutes we located Leaping Deer. He was playing a favorite Iroquois game, casting three dice in a bowl. Around him was piled two packs of beaver skins, as big as his own. "Ho," he said, recognizing us, although he was very drunk. "You women have brought me much luck. I'm winning on every toss. Look at how much I've won."

He offered us rum, which we politely refused, and asked him if he was acquainted with any of the Seneca's ruling sachems. He said one of them lived in his village. His name was Peaceful Lake. He said the village was less than a day's paddle away toward the setting sun, on the lake shore. "Tell him you are a friend of Leaping Deer. Tell my wife I will soon be home with enough goods to shut her mouth for ten winters!"

The next day we left most of our goods in the padlocked fort armory, piled enough to trade in a single village into the large canoe, and headed down the lake. By the end of the day we reached the sachem's village, where we were greeted with vast excitement. Everyone marveled at Malcolm's stupendous size, the hump on Duycinck's back, and the white woman and the African woman who spoke their language so well. We were soon in the presence of the grand sachem, Peaceful Lake. He was a stern old man who bluntly asked if we were witches come to enchant the village.

I assured him we were not witches and offered to let the village shaman examine us to prove it. I presented the sachem with a belt of white wampum, a bright red and blue blanket, and a pearl necklace for his wife or daughter. "We seek your permission to trade here and in the other villages of the Seneca," I said. "We have tried to trade at the fort of your father and mine, King George, at Oswego, but it was impossible because we refused to give rum to any Indian. Apparently there is no law that prevents this—or if there is one, the king's people do not enforce it."

Peaceful Lake's expression remained grave. It was impossible to tell if he was offended by my suggestion that there was a defect in the treaty the Iroquois had negotiated with the British to create Oswego. There was no reason for him to be impressed with my words, which were spoken in the apologetic manner of a lowly member of the Turtle Clan.

The meeting still hung in the balance when Clara stepped forward to speak. She exuded the serene self-confidence she always displayed in public, thanks to her privileged childhood. Clara presented the sachem with a silver horn filled with gunpowder. "Help us to begin a new kind of trading, in which no rum will be permitted. Let us show it can be done, from the quality of our goods," she said.

With vivid detail, she denounced the drunkenness and cheating that prevailed at Oswego. "The League of the Iroquois has acted wisely, as always, to keep the evil drink out of our villages. But they must renew their efforts to purify Oswego."

Clara painted a heartbreaking picture of a warrior starving and freezing for months in a winter camp to gather his furs, then losing his hard-won catch in a night of dice and drinking. "In the end he comes home to his family and village empty-handed. Can such a man find it within himself to be a great warrior, after such a defeat? I do not believe I exaggerate when I say Oswego is in the grip of the Evil Brother. We serve the Master of Life."

As always, Clara's *orenda* had enormous impact on her audience. Even the village shaman, who usually disliked admitting anyone else had spiritual gifts, confessed she spoke with the power of the Manitou on her tongue.

Peaceful Lake had listened to Clara's speech in dignified silence, as befitted a grand sachem. Now he rose, raised his hand palm outward, the traditional gesture of peace and friendship, and spoke. "These are true daughters of the Seneca," he said. "You may trade in this village or any other village of our tribe, under my protection. If anyone challenges you, tell him to send a swift runner to me and I will confirm your privileges in my own voice."

My reaction to this good news should have been exultant. We had won an opportunity to trade in a way that was almost guaranteed to make us successful. But my euphoria was curtailed by the way Malcolm Stapleton was gazing at Clara with unqualified admiration. By returning to the Indian world, I had become awkward She-Is-Alert, the Moon Woman, and Clara was ever triumphant Nothing-But-Flowers once more. For the first time I questioned this arrangement, which had seemed for long years to be part of the natural order of things.

Four

WITH CRIES OF DELIGHT, THE women of Peaceful Lake's village swarmed to examine our goods. They draped the deep red and dark blue bolts of cloth around each other and hefted the blankets and exclaimed over their quality. The know-it-alls of New York, who had sneered that "savages" could not tell one piece of cloth from another, did not know what they were talking about. Clara and I had grown up listening to our Seneca mothers compare the quality of the goods their husbands had brought home from the French in Montreal and the English in Albany. The English cloth was superior in every way—better woven, a thicker, finer nap, warmer, more durable. We also knew what every Seneca woman liked—deep shades of color, a blue that was almost black, a red that was almost burgundy.

"My husband returns from winter camp tomorrow. He will stop here to see me for a few days before going to the Oswego fort," one woman said. "We will trade with you—I promise you."

"My husband will soon be here too," pleaded another woman. "Çan you wait for him?"

"My husband is here already," announced another woman in triumphant tones. "I will speak to him. We will trade—now!"

The third woman's husband soon appeared lugging a huge pack of beaver skins. I carefully explained the prices we would pay for each skin—and how much we would charge for each yard of cloth. The husband, a tall, fierce-looking warrior named Stalking Bear, protested that he could get better terms at Oswego.

"You are talking nonsense!" his wife said. "You have never brought a decent piece of cloth back from that place. You want to go there for the rum. For once you will consider your wife and children before your gullet!"

Stalking Bear's expression suggested he would gladly tomahawk me and Clara if he ever encountered us in the woods. Clara drew me aside and wondered if we were wrecking every marriage in the village. But I dismissed such troubling thoughts. I urged Stalking Bear's wife, who was named Light-On-Snow, to choose a bracelet from the jewelry cask, free. Light-On-Snow selected a bracelet and added one for her daughter, plus a necklace and a set of earrings, which they paid for in well-cured beaver skins.

"You have made me a happy wife!" she cried, as they headed for their longhouse with a roll of strouds, the jewelry, and several blankets.

"I hope you will make your husband happy in return," Clara said.

Light-On-Snow, who was at least forty years old and growing fat, contemplated Stalking Bear's glum expression and sighed. "I will try," she said.

Stalking Bear and succeeding warriors were somewhat mollified when I urged them to let Adam Duycinck repair their muskets, free of charge. In a half hour Adam was up to his knees in broken guns, cursing under his breath, demanding a charcoal fire hot enough to bend metal. He said it would take him a week, at least, to repair that many guns.

I soothed him by going to Peaceful Lake and asking if one of the village's unmarried young women could overcome her dislike of Adam's hump and come to him that night. I told the sachem that Adam was a sorcerer who would reward the girl with the power to repel evil spirits. There was nothing unusual about entertaining visitors in this fashion, and Peaceful Lake agreed. Adam's attitude was transformed from glum obedience to cheerful industry the instant he heard the news.

The following night the village had a feast. Malcolm Stapleton had gone into the woods that afternoon with several warriors and they returned with a great buck. The women roasted it over the fire and we ate it with fish from the lake and corn cakes from the village granary. The harvest had been good last fall. There had been no starving time this spring. After the food, the women, led by the matron of the Bear Clan, announced they wished to perform the Eagle Dance.

Four of the village's prettiest young women stripped off their clothes and coated their bodies with bear grease. They chose four young men and stripped away their leggings and breechclouts and greased their bodies too, while drums began to beat and the village shaman shrilled the music of the four winds on his pipe. The women sprang into the firelight and caressed each other, weaving and whirling in front of the shaman. They were the flowers, the grass, the green corn of spring and summer.

The women sprang over the blazing coals and whirled around the warriors, standing as silent as trees, watching them. Then the young men raised their arms, like green boughs greeting the warm sun, and began to move in circles around the weaving writhing women. I sat beside Malcolm Stapleton and Clara, watching this, remembering how I had felt in our girlhood village when this dance was performed. Clara was often chosen to lead it. I remembered how beautiful her brown body had been in the firelight, how violently every young man in the village had desired her. While the Moon Woman sat disconsolate, ignored, among the lesser members of the Turtle Clan.

Now, on Malcolm Stapleton's face I saw the same desire the dancers were saluting with their cries and gestures. It was stirring in my body too. I was part of the earth again, part of the vast slow movement from winter to spring to summer and back to winter. In my white life on the streets of New York, I had almost forgotten this fundamental reality. City people separated themselves from the earth, they almost ignored its irresistible powers.

I saw desire on Clara's face too as the naked dancers awoke memories of her triumphant youth. I saw Malcolm's arm encircle Clara's waist, his lips brush her neck. She did not shun him—as any sensible denizen of the white world, with its laws and maxims and supposed wisdom about the wages of sin and lessons learned the hard way, would do. Here in the wilderness we were restored to a world without clocks or calculation, to the simplicities of impulse and wish, to happiness seized as a moment without reference to tomorrow.

Now the dancing warriors were circling the women, waving their arms in great loops, like the wings of eagles, sweeping the winds of spring around them, asking them if they were ready to accept the seeds of life, the gifts of the Manitou, in their bodies. Yes, no, yes, the women said, covering their eyes, their mouths, their cunts, with the same reluctance that the winter earth yielded to spring.

Malcolm's lips were on Clara's throat, he was whispering in her ear. Yes, she nodded, yes—and no. Tears streamed down her face. She was haunted by winter memories that no spring wind, however warm, however scented, could dispel. Watching, the Moon Woman of the Turtle Clan rejoiced—and a moment later wept, horrified by the wishes of her treacherous heart. For the rest of the night I lay a few feet from the fire, pretending to sleep, while my mind exploded with images of warriors and women, husbands and wives in the longhouses, satisfying the desires aroused by the Eagle Dance.

By the end of the next day we had traded all the goods we had brought from Oswego. I decided to leave Adam and Clara in the village and return to the fort with Malcolm Stapleton and the purchased skins. Clara would obtain from Peaceful Lake and other warriors the information to sketch a map of the Seneca villages to the west. We would come back with more goods and paddle down the lake to trade with them.

The wind blew from the northeast and paddling the heavily laden canoe was backbreaking labor. Malcolm had urged me to hire two Indians but I said I did not want to spend the money—or be responsible for bringing them to Oswego and its temptations. Actually, I had other reasons, which only became apparent to me as the afternoon waned and I said my arms were breaking and we would have to camp for the night.

We went ashore and I briskly built a fire on the beach. By now I knew why I had arranged to leave Clara behind. The drums of the Eagle Dance still thudded in my blood, the images of the naked warriors and women whirled in my brain. Were they doing the same thing in Malcolm's brain? I hoped so.

"I'm so hot from all that paddling," I said. "I think I'll take a swim before supper."

Slowly, deliberately, I pulled off my clothes and plunged into the freezing lake. How wonderful the water felt on my skin! But it did nothing to extinguish the conflagration in my soul. Malcolm Stapleton sat on the shore, watching me, bafflement and desire mingling on his face. He did not realize he was no longer in the company of Catalyntie Van Vorst, the virago who had hurled vituperation in his face in Albany. My Seneca self had consumed that city creature.

"Why don't you join me?" I called from the water. "You must be as hot as I am. Can you swim?"

"I can swim," Malcolm said.

"Then what are you waiting for?"

Malcolm stood up and stripped. When I saw him naked, I knew the Evil Brother had possessed my soul but I did not care. The massive chest covered with light blond hair, the rippling muscles of his arms and neck were more beautiful than any sculptor or painter could ever create. I wanted wanted wanted him and whether he loved or hated me did not matter. I was the earth and he was the west wind, born to caress me. It was totally different from the sentimental literary love I had felt for Robert Nicolls.

Malcolm dove in and disappeared for a full minute. Terror clutched at my heart. Had he drowned? He burst to the surface only a few yards from me, a strange half smile on his face. I could not tell what he was thinking.

"Did you like the Eagle Dance?" I said.

"Yes," he said. "Did you?"

"I've seen it many times," I said.

"It didn't arouse you?"

"Did it arouse you?"

"What do you think? What do you think you're doing now? Are you trying to drive me crazy?"

He swam toward me as he said this. It occurred to me that he might be going to drown me. I did not care. Before he killed me, I wanted him to take me. I wanted him so badly, my life had ceased to matter.

"I know you love Clara. But you can't have her anymore. Why not take me?" I said.

"Do you mean that?" Malcolm said.

"I seldom say anything I don't mean."

Now I knew the Evil Brother was in control of my heart. He was forcing me to deny my love for this man—the love I had felt from the moment I saw him on that morning in the meadow of the peace council.

But what else could the Moon Woman do when she was competing with Nothing-But-Flowers?

Malcolm's lips, cold from the frigid waters of the lake, were on my mouth. His hands roved my body, clutched my breasts, my rump. Then his long legs found the lake's bottom, he opened my thighs and filled me with the pine tree of his manhood, filled and filled and filled me but without leaving the bone-chilling waters that surrounded us. Clutching fistfuls of my streaming hair, he thrust his tongue down my choking throat and filled me again and again with an icy angry passion that was the total opposite of what I had imagined and desired. But I told myself it was enough, it was better than nothing, it was all the Moon Woman could expect.

Then Malcolm's seed leaped in me and I thought my heart would explode. It was beyond anything I had ever felt or imagined with Robert Nicolls in our fevered trysts. For the first time I saw a hope, however faint, that I might have a contented life. But the hope vanished in the very moment of its birth.

"Is that what you wanted?" Malcolm said, holding me at arm's length, empty yet full, satisfied but not happy.

"Wasn't it what you wanted?" I said.

"Yes," he said.

He shoved me away—as if he wished I would float into the lake's vastness like a piece of driftwood, or sink like a stone to the muddy bottom. I did neither, of course. I swam ashore and lay on the sand, letting the wind dry me, thinking: without a single caress. Maybe the wind can console me. Maybe the wind will become a caress. But the wind remained the wind.

Eventually Malcolm swam ashore. He dried himself with a blanket and pulled on his clothes. "I know you love Clara. But I don't want you to hate me. Can we manage that?" I asked.

"We can manage that," Malcolm said.

He did not know he was talking to the Moon Woman. He thought he was talking to Catalyntie Van Vorst, acting like a slut. For a moment I was so ashamed I wanted to die. But I gripped my writhing heart with an eagle's claws and vowed: *No*. Let the Evil Brother do what he pleases with me. I will have my heart's desire.

"Get dressed," Malcolm said.

I ignored his command—hoping he might take me again. Instead, he whirled and strode down the beach. The Evil Brother's voice mocked me: *Not a single caress*. The wind remained the wind.

At about a hundred yards, Malcolm turned and glared at me. "Get dressed!" he roared.

This time I obeyed him.

The next day at Oswego we stored our beaver skins in the fort's armory under the sullen eyes of the fur traders. As we lugged the rest of our trading goods back to the canoe, we encountered a short, pompous Dutchman in a beaver hat and greasy leather coat, accompanied by Captain Hartshorne in his soiled red one.

"Be you Catalyntie Van Vorst?" the Dutchman said.

I nodded.

"I am Willem Van Schenck, appointed by the Albany County Commissioners of Indian Affairs as the Right Honorable Commissary of this, His Majesty's fort and fur-trading emporium of Oswego. You are under arrest."

"For what?" I said.

"For violating the treaty which His Majesty's commissioners have negotiated with the Six Nations of the Iroquois, limiting all fur trading to an area within five hundred yards of Fort Oswego."

I curtly informed Willem Van Schenck that I had negotiated permission to trade in the Seneca villages with one of their grand sachems. Malcolm summoned a few phrases from his year with lawbooks and declared that the most the commissary could do was serve me with a writ that would have to be adjudicated in an Albany courtroom.

Malcolm asked Hartshorne if he agreed. The captain said he was no lawyer, but it sounded sensible to him. "I told the commissary that in my seven years in this post, I had yet to arrest anyone," he said. He was obviously on our side. The commissary had no authority to make him do anything.

"You'll be far better off if you accept arrest and discharge here and go straight home, young woman," Willem Van Schenck spluttered. "You won't relish a term in an Albany jail."

"I'll take that chance," I said. "Serve your writ and be damned."

"You're likely to join her in the jailhouse," Van Schenck said to Malcolm. "With none of the access to her private parts you've no doubt enjoyed up here in the woods."

Malcolm picked up Willem Van Schenck by his greasy leather coat and slammed him against the wall of the fort. "You've just insulted this lady—and me," he said. "Apologize if you want to keep your head on your shoulders."

"Captain!" Van Schenck squawked. "Call out the guard!"

"I think you've misjudged Mr. Stapleton, Commissary," Captain Hartshorne said. "He's a gentleman— and no gentleman accepts an insult meekly."

"I . . . apologize," gasped the terrified Van Schenck.

Malcolm let the commissary slide to the floor and we resumed loading our canoe. Soon it was up to its gunwales in the water. Malcolm advised me to buy another canoe and hire some homeward-bound Senecas to paddle it. I found my old friend Leaping Deer snoring off a drunk in one of the cabins. He had lost all his furs at dice, as well as his musket and powder horn and even his moccasins. He agreed to paddle our second canoe in return for a roll of strouds and some jewelry, which might prevent his wife from murdering him. A friend from the same village, Sitting Otter, was in a similar plight and accepted the same terms.

At Peaceful Lake's village, we picked up Clara and Duycinck, who had repaired the local muskets at a record pace, giving him time to talk several other young women into sharing his bed at midnight in return for a portion of his supposedly supernatural powers. Clara had completed an excellent map of the villages along the lakeshore, all the way to our girlhood home, Shining Creek.

That evening, we camped by the lake and Malcolm went into the woods with Sitting Otter, hoping they might spot a deer before darkness fell. We had left Leaping Deer trying to mollify his outraged wife and daughters, under the stern eyes of Peaceful Lake. Clara and I chopped down a small birch tree to make a fire.

"Do you still love Malcolm?" I asked, as we hacked the tree in pieces with hatchets.

"Yes."

"Why didn't you give yourself to him, after the Eagle Dance? I could see he wanted you."

"I can't—I'm not sure I can ever be with a man again," Clara said. "What happened was so terrible."

"On the way back to Oswego, I let him take me. He wanted a woman so badly. Do you hate me for that?"

Clara split a piece of wood in a single blow. "You know I can never hate you."

"Why not? I almost hate myself for letting it happen. I . . . I wanted him—as much as he wanted me."

Clara split another piece of wood with the shining hatchet. She could bury it in my skull with the same swift motion, I thought. I studied the sinewy brown flesh of Clara's arm. Why doesn't she kill me, I wondered? She knows I'm lying. She knows I seduced him.

If I died now, my soul would be seized by the Evil

Brother. But I did not care. All I wanted was my heart's desire. The Seneca years stormed in my soul. The years of the Moon Woman. Then Robert Nicolls's betrayal. Didn't I have the right to some happiness?

My conscience tormented me. How could I compare my petty suffering to Clara's? My only hope of escaping the Evil Brother was her forgiveness. But I could see Clara was not ready to forgive me. Perhaps she would never be ready. That would mean I could never escape the Evil One.

"Since you can't please him that way, would you care if I did now and then—presuming he's willing?" I asked.

Clara split another chunk of wood. Did she see it as the Moon Woman's lying heart? Her *orenda* gave her almost infallible judgment in such matters. But the grip of the Evil Brother was so strong, I did not care if Clara loathed me. Nothing mattered but my heart's desire.

"Why would he be willing?" Clara said. It was clear by now that she was very angry. But I still did not care. The wind was the wind. Anger was anger. I only wanted my heart's desire.

"Because he's a *man*," I said.

"Oh," Clara said. She split another chunk of wood. "Why wasn't he willing with the women in Peaceful Lake's village? A half dozen offered themselves to him after the Eagle Dance."

Clara knew everything. Her *orenda* was implacable, irresistible. "He was willing with me. *Very* willing," I said.

"If he's that way again, of course I have no objections. How could I?"

Clara threw down her hatchet and walked off along the shore, leaving me sitting there, filled with shame and self-hatred. The Evil Brother grunted and heaved in my soul like a sow giving birth. He was laughing at the Moon Woman's dream of escaping him.

Tears blinded me. When Malcolm and Duycinck and Sitting Otter emerged from the woods with a young deer on a sapling, they found me crouched beside the still-unlit fire, sobbing uncontrollably, smashing my hatchet into the sandy earth again and again.

"What the devil are you chopping up? Ants?" Malcolm said.

"Go to hell!" I said and fled down the shore in the opposite direction from the one Clara had taken, leaving the three men to puzzle over what was wrong with their female employers.

FIVE

THE REST OF THIS TRADING trip was a peculiar blend of misery and triumph. Clara barely spoke to me and Malcolm Stapleton frequently glared at me as if he was only waiting for an opportunity to strangle me. At some point Clara had told Malcolm what she had learned about our trip back to Oswego. Meanwhile, at village after village, our strouds and blankets and jewelry were received with wild approval by Seneca women, who eagerly traded beaver and marten and even bearskins for them, ignoring the occasional feeble protests of their husbands.

By this time, summer was replacing spring on the lake and in the forest. We paddled through days of dazzling sunshine and slept beneath the stars with only a single blanket. Lying a few feet away from Malcolm on the lakeshore or in a village, my soul was crowded with images of surrender, tenderness. I saw us alone in the forest, the sun gleaming on that magnificent male body, while I whispered how much I adored him. But Clara's presence mocked these febrile hopes.

Once, in near despair, I got up at dawn and wandered into the woods and clutched a pine tree and rubbed my face against the bark until my cheek was almost raw. Above me in the branches, a blackbird went *caw caw caw*. The Evil Brother was mocking me. I would never escape his grip.

We sold the last of our goods before we even got close to our childhood village of Shining Creek. Nevertheless, I wanted to press on to it, because I was determined to begin the search for our parents' killers. To my surprise, Clara objected strenuously. "We know who they are," she said. "The very same people we learned to love and respect. I don't want to face them with such a question on my lips."

"I mean the white men who lied the Senecas into the raid," I said.

Clara shook her head. "The whole idea makes me see the wisdom of Jesus's Sermon on the Mount. It's better to pray for your enemies. Far better than blundering back into the past in search of revenge. Hatred wounds and disfigures both sides in a quarrel."

"What do you think, Malcolm?" I said.

His mighty brow furrowed, his soldier's brain tried to comprehend loving an enemy. "I'm inclined to agree with Catalyntie," he said. "A crime—especially murder—demands punishment."

It was a glimpse of how far we two ostensible Christians were from Clara's vision of life. But the more we debated the decision, the less enthusiastic I became. For one thing, we had no presents left to give our mothers and grandmothers and the village leaders. There was also something to be said for getting our furs to market as quickly as possible.

Finally, in two overloaded canoes, we turned our backs on Shining Creek and began our return to Oswego. At Malcolm's urging, I hired four muscular Seneca warriors to help us paddle our weighty cargo of skins. Toward the middle of the first day, one of the warriors, a sharp-featured man named Little Wolf, pointed to the horizon of the lake. "French!" he said.

Malcolm followed his pointing finger and shouted to Duycinck: "Load your gun!" He quickly loaded his gun and told me to urge the Senecas to load their guns as well.

I peered into the noonday glare and saw a ship at least as big as a Hudson River schooner heading toward us. Its white sails were taut in the strong breeze. "What is it?" I asked.

"A French gunboat. They have two on the lake," Malcolm said. "They may try to seize your furs."

"Why in the world?"

"Because they consider this the territory of their king. They've told Hartshorne they plan to knock down Oswego the minute a war starts. They don't want anyone coming this far west to mess with their Indians."

"The Senecas aren't their Indians."

"Sometimes they aren't, sometimes they are. You better make damn sure these warriors are on our side."

I turned to the warriors, unnerved and uncertain. Malcolm was right about their divided allegiance. Who could testify to it more bitterly than Clara and I? The Senecas had murdered our parents in the service of the French and their treacherous Dutch collaborators in Albany.

"Brothers!" I said. "A ship of the French king approaches. I hope you will stand by me and my sister, Nothing-But-Flowers, if they try to seize our furs. Otherwise I will not be able to pay the money I promised you when we reach Oswego."

"The French give us many presents," Little Wolf said. "They have obliged us to consider them friends."

The other warriors nodded, obviously confused by the

possible confrontation. "All these guns are from the French," one of them said, holding up his musket. "It would be treachery to kill a Frenchman with one of them without an act of war on their side."

"We can't let them shoot first," Malcolm said. With some help from Clara and me, he had learned quite a lot of Seneca, although he could not speak it very well. "Tell them to load their guns."

"Clara—?" I said, confessing the Moon Woman's inadequacy again.

"Brothers!" Clara said. "We think it would be best to load your guns because the French have treacherous hearts. They may make war on us without warning. They secretly hate the Senecas for our allegiance to the King of England. For the sake of your wives and children, and the honor of the Senecas, load your guns and prepare to defend yourselves."

"The woman speaks well!" Little Wolf said. All four warriors loaded their guns. We continued paddling toward Oswego, staying about a half mile from the shore of the lake. In an hour the gunboat was close enough to hail us.

"Who are you?" called a blue-coated officer in French, using a tin speaking horn. Beside him, two sailors waited beside a cannon, whose ugly black snout jutted from a gunport. In the stern, a helmsman steered the ship. A half dozen other men lounged on the rails.

"Talk to him, Duycinck," Malcolm said.

"English subjects, trading for furs with the permission of the Grand Sachem of the Senecas," Duycinck replied in halting French.

"You are violating the territory of the King of France," said the Frenchman, whose voice resounded through the horn like the buzz of a giant hornet.

Duycinck translated and Malcolm said: "Tell him if he wants to start a war, we're ready for it."

"Are you crazy? That cannon's pointed straight at us," Duycinck said.

"My gun will be pointed at those sailors in exactly one second if they try anything," Malcolm said.

"The territory belongs to neither the King of France nor the King of England. It is the territory of the Iroquois," Duycinck shouted.

"You will surrender your furs and come with me to Fort Frontenac," the Frenchman said. "There French justice will decide the matter."

Duycinck translated this ultimatum. "Tell Little Wolf and his men to shoot at the sailors. I'll take the officer," Malcolm said. "Duycinck, go for the helmsman. Wait until I shoot."

I passed along the order to Little Wolf. The warriors cocked their muskets. Was Malcolm right, I wondered? How could we survive a fight with this ship, armed with cannon, in our frail canoes? We would all end up at the bottom of the lake.

A second later, Malcolm's gun boomed in my ear. The speaking horn fell from the officer's hand and he crumpled to the deck. In the same instant, Little Wolf and his fellow warriors fired at the sailors manning the cannon and Duycinck shot at the helmsman. The cannoneers and the helmsman toppled, killed or wounded. Shouts of anger erupted from the ship. Men ran down the deck toward the fallen officer. Without a helmsman, the ship slewed off course and lost the wind. Her sails flapped helplessly, like the wings of some great crippled bird.

"Head for the beach!" Malcolm said.

We leaped to our paddles and in ten minutes our bows grated on the sand. "Unload everything. Get it into the trees," Malcolm said.

In another ten minutes of frantic work, we had the bales of skins well into the trees. We dragged the canoes after them. By this time, the French gunboat had regained headway and sailed toward us. They stood off-shore and their cannon boomed angrily. Ball after ball whistled into the trees. Malcolm told everyone to lie down. "You'd have to be very unlucky to be killed by this kind of shooting," he said.

The French lowered a small boat and a half dozen sailors armed with muskets got into it and rowed for shore. When they were about two hundred yards off the beach, Malcolm ran out of the woods and knelt on the sand to take aim at them. The ship's cannon boomed and a ball flung up sand only a few yards from him. *If he dies, I'll kill myself,* I told the Evil Brother. *Preserve him and I'll be your servant forever.*

Malcolm's musket crashed and one of the oarsman tumbled into the thwarts. The rowboat slewed to the right and sailors fell into confusion. The Senecas were amazed. It was considered impossible to hit a man at such a distance. Few muskets could hit anything beyond fifty yards.

"That fellow has great magic on his side!" Little Wolf exclaimed.

"Is it from the crookback, or from the women?" one of the other warriors asked.

"I don't know," Little Wolf said. "But I would not want to face him in battle."

The rest of the Frenchmen in the rowboat had an agitated conference, while the cannon from the ship flung more balls at Malcolm. The rowboat returned to the ship, where they lifted aboard the wounded man and sailed up and down, silently proclaiming their determination to sink us if we dared show ourselves on the water.

"Now what do we do?" I said.

"Wait until dark," Malcolm said, "then load up and pull away, staying close to the shore. If they come after us again tomorrow, we'll just run ashore and repeat the performance. But I don't think they'll bother chasing us. They're beaten and they know it."

"How did you hit that man at such a distance?" I asked.

"Adam deserves the credit," Malcolm said. "He made this gun for me. It's got a rifled barrel."

He explained that a rifle's barrel was full of grooves that gave the shooter far better control over a bullet. "It's got twice or three times the accuracy of a smooth-bore musket," he said.

So it was human ingenuity, not the Evil Brother, who saved him, I thought. In my soul, the Evil One mocked this attempt to evade him. *You promised me,* he whispered. *Anyway, without me you know you will never have him again. How else can the Moon Woman hope to overcome Clara's orenda?*

As darkness fell, the French ship sailed off to the north, probably to Fort Frontenac. Their wounded men needed a doctor's skills. Malcolm announced we would paddle all night to try to reach Oswego before the French returned with reinforcements.

We arrived at the fort at dawn. In the grey half light, its frowning bulk seemed enormous. But Malcolm said it was not much of a fort. If the French brought heavy cannon down the lake in ships, they could pound the masonry walls to rubble in a few days. Captain Hartshorne was not exaggerating the weakness of the place.

"No wonder the French can't wait for war to start," Duycinck said.

"Why should there be a war?" I asked, as we hauled the canoes ashore.

"There's always been a war between us and the French here in America," Malcolm said. "They know it, we don't. We keep hoping it will go away. While they build more and more forts and gunboats and shower the Indians with presents."

"They can't compete with English goods—so they'll try to drive us out of the fur business with guns?"

"Exactly," Malcolm said.

"I don't see why they can't negotiate peace," Clara said. "There are enough furs for both sides."

"But if one side or the other wins, they can set the prices as they please," I said.

"Your grandfather said monopolies were bad," Clara said.

"Not if you have the monopoly," I said.

"Monopoly has nothing to do with it," Malcolm said. "It's a war between liberty and enslavement, between Protestant freedom and Popish tyranny."

We did not realize we were renewing the international argument that Clara and I had first heard from our tutor, Harman Bogardus. We still could not believe it would embroil our lives. For the time being, there were other concerns that soon distracted us at Oswego. With the gloating approval of the other fur traders, Commissary Willem Van Schenck served me and Clara with a writ charging us with violating the treaty between the government of New York and the Iroquois. We were to answer it in the Court of Common Pleas in Albany. If found guilty, we faced heavy fines and other punishments.

"Those damned witches deserve a lot worse than a fine," shouted a familiar voice in the crowd. I soon located the ugly face of our would-be murderer, de Groot. Two of his men were with him. They shouted incendiary nonsense about me and Clara being the slayers of their friends. Malcolm roared an angry rebuttal to this slander. For a few minutes, it looked as if there would be a riot, which might have ended in bloodshed—probably ours. For all his size, Malcolm was outnumbered twenty to one.

Captain Hartshorne rushed to our rescue with a half dozen men behind him. "There'll be no drumhead justice while I command this fort," he said. "These people have broken no law nor killed anyone except in self-defense. Get back to your business."

Growling, the mob returned to their huts, leaving de Groot and his confederates nonplussed and deserted. "You'll hear from me one of these days. My voice will speak from the muzzle of a Brown Bess,"[1] de Groot snarled.

Malcolm thrust the muzzle of his rifled gun in de Groot's chest. "Here's a look at how you'll be answered," he said.

How could we have survived without this man? I wondered. By now, Clara and I would have been robbed, raped, and murdered. My brain raced ahead to future years. Was there some way I could retain Malcolm's services? I could not imagine finding any other man who would risk his life for eighteen shillings a day to help me grow rich. Scarcely had this thought winged through my head before it was answered by the Moon Woman's sardonic voice: *He'll do it for Clara—and no one else.*

The next day, we prepared for our trip back to Albany. We had twelve packs of furs, weighing a hundred pounds each. I could not find a single bateauman who would work for me. They all sided with de Groot and the traders. I was about to despair when Little Wolf staggered out of one of the huts. He and his friends had spent their pay on rum. Two of them had lost their muskets and powder horns at dice. They glumly accepted my offer of four shillings a day to paddle us to Albany.

Before we departed, Malcolm insisted on making a full report to Captain Hartshorne of their encounter with the French gunboat. The captain was not pleased. "Do you realize you may have started a war?" he said.

"You know as well as I do if we went to Frontenac, we would never have seen our pelts again," Malcolm said.

"You took that risk when you elected to trade in the villages," Hartshorne said. "You better get on your way

---

[1] *British army nickname for a musket.*

to New York as soon as possible. I'm sure the French will be here trying to arrest you for murder before the next sunset."

"I'm sorry to leave you the headache, sir," Malcolm said. "I'm obliged to you for the great kindness you've shown me since I came here."

"Would there were a few more patriots like you in America," Hartshorne said. "We'd be far more ready to deal with these arrogant frog-eaters."

I was fascinated by this conversation. It was an educational glimpse of how much the English feared and hated the French. At least as interesting was the way Malcolm seemed to look upon the captain as a kind of father, and Hartshorne regarded him as a sort of son. It was not unlike the way the Senecas adopted a captive or a wanderer into a family to replace sons or daughters who had died. In the white world, where men defied their fathers and roamed off to the frontier on their own, it was equally logical for a young man to look for a second father.

And a wife? No, men did not go to the frontier in search of a wife. In search of a woman—or many women, perhaps—but not a wife. For a moment I was seized by the heaving, strangling desire for Malcolm that the Evil Brother could now invoke in my soul whenever he chose. Was the Evil One trying to tell me I might find my heart's desire in the word *wife*? Somehow I doubted it. But I did not forget it.

Malcolm made no secret of his admiration of Captain Hartshorne as we began our journey to Albany. He told Clara and me how much he had learned from him, not only about soldiering but about England. Malcolm's father had a placeman's view of the crown. He thought only of how much money he could get from the government. But in England there was a party of high-souled honest men who called themselves patriots. They struggled, mostly in vain, to resist the rule of the king's first or prime minister, Robert Walpole. He was the ultimate placeman, corrupting everything. Malcolm set himself firmly in the Patriot Party. He wanted to be a patriot in America.

I pretended to be impressed by this oration. Clara certainly was. But I doubted the virtue of these patriots. Already I had concluded almost everyone in this world looked first to his own advantage. It was true among the Senecas and among the whites. Warriors fought for fame and booty and the admiration of women. Sachems loved power. Women yearned for the greatest warriors. In the white world, power begot money and money begot power and everyone hungered after both. I was determined to get my share, and I did not much care whether that made me less than a patriot. But for the time being I held my tongue and pretended to admire Malcolm's noble ambition.

Across Lake Oneida and down Wood Creek to the portage and along the Mohawk we paddled, eight hours a day, camping at night in the woods with huge fires to keep the wolves at bay. We could hear them howling and snarling in the trees, only a few yards away. Occasionally Malcolm fired his gun at them. Little Wolf and his friends thought this was a waste of powder. They knew wolves never attacked a human unless he or she was alone. For all his talk of fighting in the woods, Malcolm knew little about the ways of the wilderness.

By now it was August—summer in its glorious prime. Above us the sky was a dome of cloudless blue. The trees and grass along the river brimmed with green glowing life. The river itself was a shining ribbon of light in the beating rays of the sun. By noon, it also became a tunnel filled with thick moist waves of heat. Paddling, Malcolm stripped to his waist, like the Indians. Soon his massive torso gleamed with sweat. I yearned to touch him, to run my hands, my lips, down his gleaming flesh.

Clara and I, paddling as hard as any of the men, were even more sweaty in our long dresses and underskirts. It was white stupidity—this insistence that women had to cover their whole bodies with cloth at all times. On the morning of the third day, I said: "I'm going to dress like a hunting woman."

In the spring when the hunting women returned from the winter camp with the trappers, they paddled beside them in the canoes, wearing nothing but breechclouts. I cut one of my skirts into strips of cloth and fashioned a breechclout.

Clara watched, frowning. "He still won't be willing," she said.

She snatched the shears out of my hand, stripped off her dress and petticoat, and made herself a breechclout. My heart clotted with dismay.

We emerged from our tent, both wearing breechclouts and nothing else. Malcolm Stapleton and Adam Duycinck almost choked on the tea they were drinking beside the campfire. "Ho!" said Little Wolf in Seneca to his friends. "Here is a good sight for our eyes in the dawn. Wouldn't you like to get one of them alone in the woods?"

"I'll take both of them," said one of his fellow warriors.

"What's so strange?" I said. "You've seen hunting women before."

"Will you behave like hunting women for us?" Little Wolf asked.

"No," I said.

For another eight hours we paddled down the river through the thick warm air, while dread gathered in my soul. When we camped that night, Malcolm ignored me. His eyes sought only Clara. After a hurried supper of dried beef, corn bread, and tea, Clara walked away from the fire. In a moment she was only a blur against the dark shine of the river. Malcolm followed her. After a while, I could not bear it and went down to the water's edge. There was no trace of them.

Then I heard the sounds from the trees: the small cries, the violent breathing of desire. Clara had overcome her dread of another child. I turned and stumbled back to the campfire. I touched Little Wolf on the shoulder and said: "Maybe I will behave like a hunting woman after all."

In the trees on the other side of the camp, Little Wolf soon grunted above me. *Are you satisfied?* I asked the Evil Brother, as the warrior thrusted and thrusted, occasionally growling like a cougar. *Is this what you want me to become?*

No, said the Evil One. *I have much more ambitious plans for you. You will not become a whore. Whores don't grow rich. This is a mistake. You must bide your time and win him by becoming* respectable. *Of course, you will always be a whore in your heart. That is the fate of any woman who pledges herself to my service.*

We are agreed once more, my dark master, I whispered, as Little Wolf filled me with his seed. What would I do if he gave me a child? An Indian bastard would prove everything New York already thought about me. But the Evil Brother would not permit it.

I thanked Little Wolf in Seneca, as I had thanked the other warriors who had taken me into the woods around Shining Creek. The Moon Woman was always grateful for the smallest male attention. Back in our tent, I stared into the darkness until Clara returned.

"Was he *willing*?" I asked.

"Yes," Clara said.

She was silent for a long time. "But it wasn't the same," she said. "It will never be the same again."

She began to weep—great choking sobs, as if she were mourning her own death. Why wasn't this good news? the Moon Woman asked herself. Wasn't this exactly what she had been hoping for? *Of course it was*, mocked the Evil One.

With a cry, I flung myself across the narrow tent and embraced Clara. We clung together, rocking back and forth, both weeping, for a long time. "Pray for us," I whispered. "Pray to the Master of Life. Somehow you can save us both. Ask him to help you forgive me. Ask him to help me forgive myself."

SIX

THE NEXT DAY WE PREPARED to resume our journey in an exceptionally morose mood. Malcolm Stapleton responded with curt monosyllables to Duycinck's attempts at conversation. Clara and I were at least as downcast. The only cheerful traveler was Little Wolf. He considered his enjoyment of the white hunting woman last night a tribute to his manhood. The rest of the warriors gazed hungrily at the Moon Woman, wondering if they too would get a turn.

They soon learned the Moon Woman had become Catalyntie Van Vorst again. I hauled out my purse and paid them all off. We were only a dozen miles from the falls of the Mohawk at Schenectady and the river's swift current would carry us there without lifting a paddle. I thereby saved a day's pay. For good measure, I subjected them to a lecture from Clara, exhorting them not to go home via Oswego and lose their wits and their money at rum and gambling. They stalked into the forest, subdued warriors all.

"If we ever have a war up here, I'm going to stick close to you two," Duycinck said. "You'll browbeat the entire Iroquois Confederacy into burying their hatchets before they can get close to my scalp.''

Clara and I put on our dresses and petticoats again and resumed our civilized identities. At Schenectady, I hired three wagons at the usual outrageous prices to lug our skins the final sixteen miles to Albany. There we found more malice awaiting us. Willem Van Schenck, the commissary at Oswego, had sent two men in a swift canoe to carry his writ to the sheriff of Albany County and that dignitary was waiting for us on the docks.

He was another Dutchman—a huge fat fellow named Roelof Janse Van Maesterland, with the gold chain of his office clanking around his neck. ''You will haf to surendar dem furs and yourself for seizure, damn you,'' he thundered. ''Vat's a fine-lookin' young wommens like you mixin' met dem scum at Oswego for, riskin' yer immordal soul for miserable pelts?''

I decided to bow as low as possible before this fearsome figure, who I perceived was not very intelligent. Reassured by the Evil Brother, I had regained my devious self.

''I'm a poor orphan, trying to make her way in a cruel world,'' I said in Dutch. ''Oh, Your Honor, don't send me to prison. Let me carry these furs to New York and sell them so I can pay a lawyer to defend me. I broke no law of God or man, I swear it.''

I wept pathetically and told Sheriff Van Maesterland how all the traders at Oswego had persecuted me because I was Dutch. ''Everyone of them is a damned Englishman,'' I said. ''You should have heard the things they called me—Dutch whore was among the mildest insults. I appealed to Willem Van Schenck to stand by me but I fear he's been corrupted by their pounds sterling—and a habit of toadying to that English officer who rules the fort.''

The dismay on Clara's face made it clear that she knew I was telling prodigious lies, even though she did not know enough Dutch to understand them. "Is dis true?" Roelof Janse Van Maesterland asked Clara. "Yer midstress vas insulded by dese traders?"

Clara managed to swallow the assumption that she was still my slave. "Oh yes," she said. Insults had unquestionably been exchanged.

"Sooch demmned insulds I vill not condone to a vo-man of Dutch blood, no madder vat her bad judgment is," growled the sheriff. "I vill get dis writ nolle pros-sed[1] dis day or my name is not Roelof Janse Van Maes-terland!"

He lumbered off to the courthouse. Duycinck, who had followed the whole conversation in Dutch, gazed at me in awe. "She's the only woman I've seen who's a match for your stepmother," he said to Malcolm. "She could lie the devil out of his pitchfork."

I was tempted to shove the little Dutchman into the Hudson. The last person I wanted to be compared to was a woman Malcolm loathed. But I had more pressing problems. In an hour Roelof Janse Van Maesterland was back with another man, far younger and much more intelligent. He was unquestionably Dutch, with clever blue eyes and hair as blond as mine.

"Dis be my nedphew, Nicholas Van Brugge," the sheriff said. "He's a counselor at de bar. He vill defent you for nodding."

"I will pay full fees the moment I lay hands on ready money," I said. I still had fifty pounds in my purse but I thought it better to play the helpless female.

"Dat bastard Oloff Van Sluyden vill not dismissed de charge," the sheriff said. "Maybe now I remember your name I suspect why. Dat man and his whole family ist a bunch of demmned scoundrels!"

"What do you mean?" I asked in Dutch.

"I mean I remember an evil thing that happened to

your father and mother on the Mohawk,'' the sheriff replied in Dutch. ''There are people in this town who thought the Van Sluydens were parties to that crime. But proof was totally lacking. They will have to answer to God for it.''

''I'm too young to remember what my uncle is talking about,'' Van Brugge said in English. ''But it's become a sort of secret scandal here in Albany. These people have controlled the fur trade with the French in Canada for a long time and they've never wanted any competition from the west. They fought the proposition to build a fort at Oswego. They continue to harass it in every way they can.''

It made murderously perfect sense. I whirled and spoke to Clara in Seneca. ''They know the men who killed our parents. Now we know them too. We must find a way to kill them.''

Clara shook her head. ''It happened too long ago.''

''It happened *yesterday*,'' I hissed.

Malcolm Stapleton understood enough Seneca to grasp this part of the conversation. He said nothing but I could see he was more inclined to side with me than with Clara.

I thrust aside this hopeful observation and concentrated on my current dilemma. Plaintively, I brushed tears from my eyes and asked Nicholas Van Brugge what we should do. Did the Van Sluydens control the courts of Albany? I gave him a heartbreaking rendition of our nasty dismissal when we sought Oloff Van Sluyden's help against de Groot and his confederates.

''They have considerable power. But it's not absolute, thank God,'' Nicholas Van Brugge replied. ''We'll ask for a three-judge panel to hear your case.''

We spent the night in the Crown Tavern, Malcolm and Duycinck sharing a room, while Clara and I slept next door. We spent much of the night arguing about whether we should seek revenge on the Van Sluydens.

"How do we know any of those who are still alive had anything to do with it? It happened almost twenty years ago," Clara said.

"That doesn't matter," I said. "A Seneca would wait for the right moment and drench their houses in the blood of their children, their wives, their daughters! A Seneca never forgets, never forgives an injury."

"We're not Senecas anymore."

"In our hearts, we'll always be Senecas."

"I hope that isn't true. If it is—we'll die hating each other."

"Why?"

"You know why."

She was talking about Malcolm. "Maybe we can find a way to talk peace," I said. I was willing to share him, to accept any terms Clara offered, however humiliating.

Clara's eyes said *never*. She turned in the bed and blew out the candle. I lay there in the darkness, waiting for tears. But my eyes remained dry and cold. If Clara wanted war over Malcolm, she would get it.

The next morning the courtroom on State Street was surprisingly crowded. Roeloff Janse Van Maesterland and Nicholas Van Brugge had spread the news of the trial among their friends. On a front bench sat a group of men who Van Brugge said were members of the Van Sluyden clan. I saw venality and worse on their tense faces.

"They look like they would do anything for money," I said.

"I fear you're right," Van Brugge said.

Clara and Malcolm and Duycinck sat in the rear of the courtroom. I wanted to bring Clara forward as my partner but Van Brugge ruled against it. "Let us not distract the judges from the main point," he said.

The sheriff presented Commissary Van Schenck's writ to the court and explained why he had chosen not to execute it. The three judges included Oloff Van Sluyden, a red-cheeked Dutchman named Bleecker, and a sallow Englishman named Parton. Van Brugge argued that I had not violated the treaty with the Iroquois. I had received permission to trade with them from one of their grand sachems, who had the power to grant exceptions. The young lawyer stressed the importance of my refusal to trade in rum, wryly suggesting it would be good for both races if liquor was banned from the trade at Oswego as well.

Then he added: "This is a peculiar case, Your Honors. It stirs memories of a crime which took place on the Mohawk many years ago, involving this young woman's parents—"

By the time he finished, Judge Van Sluyden had tried three times to gavel him into silence but the other judges overruled him. The young Dutchman closed with a plea against permitting the "persecution" of a blameless young woman to go unchallenged.

The three judges retired to their chambers for a consultation. While they waited, a half dozen older men bowed before me and whispered in Dutch: "I knew your grandfather. He was a true man."

It was amazing to discover so much goodness in the world. Had I sold my soul to the Evil Brother prematurely? Was there some way for honor and love to overcome the iniquity that seemed to lurk in so many hearts? The judges returned to the courtroom with clumping old men's gaits and ascended the bench. The central judge, the red-cheeked Dutchman named Bleecker, announced the verdict: "The court rules the writ of Commissary Van Schenck is without merit."

I was bewildered. What began as outrageous lying to Sheriff Van Maesterland had ended in a modest triumph of truth and justice. Before I could begin to sort out this conundrum, I had to decide where and how to sell our skins.

"Do you plan to stay in the trade?" Nicholas Van Brugge asked me.

"Most assuredly."

"Then I advise you to sell here in Albany and make your peace with the Van Sluydens in the bargain. Our biggest buyer and shipper of furs is Philip Van Sluyden, Oloff's son."

"Make peace with my parents' murderers?" I cried.

"There's no proof that they murdered your parents," Van Brugge replied. "It's never been more than a nasty rumor, propagated by people who resent the Van Sluydens' wealth and power."

"Is that true?" I asked his uncle the sheriff.

Roeloff Janse Van Maesterland struggled between a desire to give me good advice and a need to take a legal view of the matter. It was true, the story was never more than a rumor. But he thought I would be better off if I sold my furs in New York and stayed there.

"I will not be driven out of business by threats!" I said. "Do you agree, Mr. Stapleton? Will you let them do that to me?"

"Not while I'm in your employ," Malcolm said.

The implication was all too clear. He hoped to be out of my employ as soon as possible. Disconsolate, I allowed Nicholas Van Brugge to lead me to the dockside office of Philip Van Sluyden. Expecting a younger version of his dour father, I was taken by surprise. The man was as handsome and as suave as Robert Foster Nicolls.

"Ah," he said to Nicholas Van Brugge. "I'm glad you persuaded Miss Van Vorst to see me." He offered me a grave bow. "I told him at the very least I wanted to apologize for my father's atrocious conduct on the bench. I fear he's getting old. He resents terribly the vicious rumor that he was in some way responsible for your parents' death. Nothing could be farther from the truth."

He uttered this pronouncement in the manner of a man

who expected everyone to agree with whatever he said. Although he wore ordinary business clothes, Philip Van Sluyden virtually emanated wealth and power. He was the crown prince—or the young king—of Albany.

"I hope I may come to believe that, sir," I said. "It would put my heart and mind to rest."

"You must believe it because it's true," he said, as if he were talking to a child. I suspected this man had a rather low opinion of women's intelligence. "To prove my point, I want to give you the best price in my power for your furs."

Philip Van Sluyden went briskly to work, examining our pelts. He said they were "good quality" and offered me seven shillings a pound for them. I was dismayed. Our four months of work and peril in the wilderness was going to net us only four hundred twenty pounds. I had paid three hundred fifty pounds for our goods and another fifty pounds to transport them to Oswego. That gave us a profit of twenty pounds—less than one percent. When I added in the cost of paying Malcolm Stapleton and his friends for their protection, we would show a loss of more than eighty pounds.

"If this is the best price possible, how does any trader make a profit in this business?" I asked.

"I've heard you carried no rum."

"True."

"You can buy a three-gallon keg of rum for twelve shillings. If you know what you're doing, you can trade that for eight pounds of beaver worth fifty-six shillings. If you add water to the rum—the Indians never notice—you can double that exchange rate. No trader can make a profit unless he deals in rum."

"I'll . . . never do it!" I said, although the words almost killed me. Clara was watching me, wondering if that was another lie. I could see her growing disgust with the whole system.

"I can get better prices in London," I said. "I'll take

my pelts there myself.'' I had no idea if this was true. I felt a need to defy this arrogant man.

''You'll lose more money if you do,'' Van Sluyden said with a complacent smile. ''The voyage alone will cost you a hundred pounds. Then there are warehouse fees, duties. A single trader can't make a profit shipping his own skins. I own a ship that carries the catch of a dozen traders to London.''

His logic was crushing. On Malcolm Stapleton's face was a barely concealed satisfaction. Was he secretly pleased to see this headstrong female encountering hard truths about the man's world she talked about conquering? Aside from our various collisions, I suspected he disapproved of the very idea of women in business.

I struggled for self-control. I was a small fish in the fur trade for the time being. I saw that the real money was made by men like Van Sluyden, who had a store attached to his office where traders bought strouds and jewelry and rum on credit and paid for them in beaver skins at the end of the season. His markup on the goods was over a hundred percent.

Some sort of native Dutch stubbornness prevented me from submitting to this cold-eyed scion, who had made himself the ruler of the fur trade. I remembered that my father had hoped to become a manor lord on the Mohawk. If the Evil Brother—or this man's father—had not destroyed that hope, I might be presiding over a store this size on the river, which traders would prefer to this Albany emporium because it was far closer to Oswego.

''I thank you for your good advice, Mr. Van Sluyden,'' I said. ''But I will sell my furs elsewhere.''

The crown prince found it hard to conceal his displeasure. ''Where the devil do you think you can do that at better prices?'' he said. ''No one outbids Philip Van Sluyden in New York. If they do, they soon find they can't sell their furs in London for more than a penny on a pound. My friends there see to it.''

Like my Uncle Johannes, Philip Van Sluyden had made his peace with the English system by carving himself a juicy slice of it. "I'll take my chances, nonetheless," I said. I strode into the street, leaving the great man muttering about female stupidity.

We retreated to the modest home of Sheriff Van Maesterland. Both he and Nicholas Van Brugge were dismayed by my intransigence. "You're pursuing a pointless vendetta," Van Brugge said. "He could have smoothed your way with the traders at Oswego. No one dares cross him up there. They owe him too much money."

"What good would that do me, if I can't make a profit?" I said.

The lawyer shrugged. "You can make one if you deal in rum."

"Yah," said the sheriff. "Der savages moost have der drink."

"Never! Can't you see the whole thing is a rotten English scheme to keep prices down? They don't care what the rum is doing to the Indians. I do."

Van Brugge laughed. "You remind me of my mother. She was always telling my father not to truckle to the English."

"All der vimmens in der family vas the same way," Sheriff Van Maesterland said, gazing fondly at me. He seemed ready to adopt me as his daughter.

Van Brugge, having discharged his duty to me as my lawyer, now spoke more as a friend or relative. "Maybe there's a way to sell your furs for more money. But it's risky."

"What is it?"

"Send them to Amsterdam."

"Out of the question!" Malcolm Stapleton said. "Parliament's passed a law requiring all the goods shipped from New York and any other colony must pay duties in London before going anywhere else."

"Parliament passes many laws," Van Brugge said. "Not all of them are obeyed. There are men in Albany who still trade direct with Amsterdam. In time of peace, the British seldom interfere with a vessel on the high seas. Their frigates keep to home waters."

"As sheriff I'm supposed to arrest such fellows," Roelof Janse Van Maesterland said in Dutch. "But a man can't enforce the law day and night. Their ships sail after dark." He added a huge wink to make sure I got his point.

"Where can I meet one of these brave Dutchmen?" I asked.

In another hour I was sitting with Killian Van Oorst in his house off State Street. He was a compact man with a secretive air about him. Yes, he had a ship. Yes, he was planning a voyage to Holland. Yes, he had heard about my extraordinary trip to Oswego and my vindication in court. Yes, he knew what beaver pelts were selling for in Amsterdam. He had a letter from his brother only yesterday, stating that the price, translated from Dutch guilders, was the equivalent of sixteen shillings an English pound. Two and one half times what Philip Van Sluyden had offered.

"Would you consider shipping my pelts on consignment, for ten percent of the sale price?"

"My usual commission is twelve percent."

"Eleven?"

"Agreed."

If Killian Van Oorst made a successful voyage, my furs would sell for eight hundred fifty-four pounds—which meant I would clear roughly three hundred pounds, a profit of about eighty percent. I signed a contract with him on the spot. It said nothing about shipping furs, of course. There was only a vague reference to "goods." But Sheriff Van Maesterland and Nicholas Van Brugge assured me Captain Van Oorst was an honest man and would never cheat a fellow Dutchman—or

woman. Encouraged by this testament to Dutch solidarity, I empowered Van Oorst to find an Amsterdam merchant who would ship me goods on credit to open a store
in New York.

I insisted on Clara signing the contract too. I wanted
to make it clear that we were partners in this final step
of our joint venture. Malcolm Stapleton infuriated me
by advising Clara not to do any such thing. "You're
breaking the law. You could end up in prison if this
attempt to defraud the king fails," he said.

We were having dinner at Sheriff Van Maesterland's
table when this quarrel erupted. "Oh, young fella, you
ist too padriotic for me," chuckled the sheriff, as he
sliced a well-pickled ham and his wife filled flagons of
beer so large Duycinck was almost invisible behind his.

"That's a title I'll never apologize for," Malcolm
said. "Without the king and his fleets and armies, what
would we be today? The victims of Spanish and French
butchers, who'd raid our ports, capture our commerce,
and reduce us all to beggary."

"Does the king and his great fleet and victorious army
mean his rule is right?" I said. "A robber who has the
power to take your property and your life is still a robber."

Malcolm grew almost incoherent with indignation.
"You're talking treason, Miss Van Vorst. It's a good
thing you're a woman. You can say such things without
fear of punishment."

"Let them punish me as much as they dare!" I said.
I was putting on a show for Sheriff Van Maesterland,
who beamed at me and said with more women like me
and a few good men, the Dutch would never have lost
New York.

Clara, mainly to please Malcolm, declined to sign the
contract. The next day I paid Malcolm the thirty-eight
pounds I owed him for his protection and asked him if

he was returning to New York with me and Clara and Duycinck.

"I've told him he *must* come back," Clara said. "The other night I dreamt of his father. He seemed crushed by unhappiness. I fear he's in great distress."

Malcolm paced the Van Maesterland parlor and finally decided he should go with us. We embarked on a Hudson River schooner that afternoon and in four days were in New York. The city sweltered in the August heat. On the wharfs, sweating whites and blacks unloaded ships and cursed at cartmen, who cursed them in turn. Clara offered Malcolm a room in our house on Maiden Lane but I feared it would cause too much gossip for a young man to stay with two unmarried women. This might have made some sense if the two unmarried women had reputations to lose. My real fear was what might happen if Malcolm spent any time with Clara in domestic circumstances that might arouse their wounded love.

Malcolm curtly told me that he would stay at his father's town house on Broad Street. Parting company, Clara and I hurried through the noisy smelly city streets to our house. After four months in the wilderness, where silence reigned most of the time, except for the wind and the occasional voices of birds and animals, the city's clamor was almost unbearable. So was the stench of rotting food and offal in the humid streets, with wandering pigs the only hope of cleaning it up.

Clara found the atmosphere distressing. "Maybe we should have stayed at one of those Seneca villages," she said, half seriously.

"And starved each spring?" I said. "No. It's better to grow rich down here, even if the noise and smells are unpleasant."

In our relatively cool parlor, I began telling Clara my plans for the immediate future. In December I would be twenty-one and I hoped to get control of the inheritance my grandfather had left me. We would use some of the money to expand the store I hoped to open with the goods Captain Van Oorst was bringing from Amsterdam. I would invest more of the money in shares of various ships and their cargoes and the rest in opening a trading post on the Mohawk that would rival Philip Van Sluyden in the fur trade.

"We'll run that bully out of the business," I said. "Without selling an ounce of rum. Then we'll go to work on proving his father was a murderer."

Someone rapped the brass knocker on our front door. Clara opened it to find a dazed Malcolm Stapleton and an alarmed Duycinck. "My father's dead," Malcolm said. "There are strangers in his house."

He slumped in a chair and Duycinck continued the story. "That's but the half of it. We met our old friend Cuyler in the street. He tells us Malcolm's disinherited. His father's left everything to his brother, with his stepmother in charge until the quarterwit gets to be twenty-one. If there's a penny left in the till when that year arrives, I'll be the most surprised man in America."

"But he said he wanted to see Malcolm," Clara said. "There was something he wanted to tell him."

"And what did the lad do? He went off chasing beaver skins on the shores of Lake Ontario for the next three months. You ladies warned him of disaster—and then persuaded him to ignore it."

"*I* didn't," Clara said.

"Whether you did it jointly or singly doesn't matter much," Duycinck said. "The lad's ruined."

I too might be ruined. The death of George Stapleton, my advocate, however reluctant, with His Honor, the royal governor, would give my Uncle Johannes a wonderful opportunity to try to defraud me of my inheritance. But I was amazingly indifferent to this probability. I was too busy thanking the Evil Brother for the chance to acquire Malcolm Stapleton.

"It was my fault. But Malcolm will never be ruined as long as I've got a pound in my pocketbook," I said. "I'm ready to declare him a partner with an equal share of our profits from the furs Captain Van Oorst will sell in Amsterdam. I'm sure Clara will agree. Won't you, Clara dear?"

"Of course," Clara said.

"I'm ready to form a joint company for future trading, with him as full partner," I said. "Don't you also agree to that, Clara dear?"

Clara glared at me. She knew exactly what I was doing. I was purchasing Malcolm Stapleton. Transforming his dislike into grudging gratitude, corrupting his patriotic conscience, making a mercenary of the idealistic soldier Clara had loved and lost. But she could not oppose me without seeming to be an ungenerous, unreasonable purist.

"Did you hear that, lad?" Duycinck said. "All's not lost. You've got true friends here. Now if we can find a way to pry me and my indenture out of the hands of your Cleopatra of a stepmother—"

"We'll do that too," I said. "Damn the expense."

"By God, I take back every dirty thought I've had about you," Duycinck said. "Come on, lad. Let's go find our friend Cuyler and drink to your father's memory."

Malcolm allowed Duycinck to lead him out the door. I realized he had yet to say a word to indicate he accepted—much less was grateful for—my generosity. Was the Evil Brother mocking me again?

The moment the door closed, Clara whirled on me. "Even if he marries you, he'll never be willing," she said.

It was more than a prophecy. It was a curse. How could I persuade Clara to revoke it? Should I weep and beg her forgiveness, plead the madness of desire? Confess my surrender to the Evil Brother and implore her help?

No, the Moon Woman whispered. *You will do none of those things.* "I haven't the slightest intention of marrying him," I lied.

SEVEN

THE NEXT MORNING, I was up at dawn, gulping down iced tea in the stifling heat and writing a letter to Guert Cuyler, begging him to take charge of winning my inheritance from my uncle. On the way to Guert's law office with the letter, I encountered none other than my esteemed guardian, stalking down Wall Street, as hatchet-faced and morose as ever.

"Good morning, Uncle," I said.

He passed me as if I were invisible. "Uncle!" I called. "Don't you remember me?"

He turned and contemplated me with gloomy disdain. "I no longer consider you part of our family," he said.

"What do you mean?"

"I read in the newspaper about your atrocious conduct at Oswego. It's been verified by friends in Albany. You've confirmed our worst fears about your character. You're an utterly debased creature."

"My conduct at Oswego was beyond reproach!" I said. "I did nothing but defend myself against a bunch of drunken swine. What friends in Albany confirmed these lies?"

"Judge Oloff Van Sluyden, for one," Johannes Van Vorst said.

Passersby loitered to pick up the gist of this angry

exchange. Artisans and customers crowded the doors of their shops. From the expressions on their faces, it was clear that they already believed the worst about Catalyntie Van Vorst.

"Oloff Van Sluyden is a lying son of a bitch. He's also very probably the murderer of my father, your brother," I shouted. "Where is this newspaper story?"

"Go read it for yourself in the *Gazette*."

The *New York Gazette* was published in a shop next to the post office. I stormed into the back room, where the owner, a short balding Englishman named Birch, was setting type for the next edition with the help of two young apprentices wearing soiled black aprons and little else. It was well over a hundred degrees in the room. I demanded to see the story about me. Birch grumbled and groused but he finally produced a copy of the month-old paper.

The story was entitled: "News from Oswego," and described the difficulties traders were encountering from marauding Indians on the Mohawk and a glut of pelts which was driving prices down. Toward the end came a paragraph that made me cry out with rage.

A certain Miss Van V. of New York arrived a few days ago with a black doxy in tow and set up a bawdy house in a tent within hail of the fort. Business was brisk until it was rumored that the black doxy had the pox and then trade fell off steeply in that venue. But Miss Van V. more than made up for the loss by doubling her hours. She accepts pay in beaver skins, wampum, or rum. Some say she will clear 500 pounds if her health holds.

"How dare you publish these lies?" I said. "I'll sue you for damages and own your paper before I'm through."

"Sue and be damned. It was your own uncle who

carried the story to me," Birch said. "He confirmed every word of it. He said he had it direct from a trader who saw you playing the strumpet with his own eyes."

"My uncle!"

This passionate conversation had a curious effect on me. By the time I finished it, I saw uses to which this libel against me could be put. In a half hour I was in Hughson's Tavern on Pearl Street, where Malcolm Stapleton and Adam Duycinck were living.

I found them having breakfast. Malcolm was demolishing an entire pound of ham and a half dozen eggs, washing it down with a flagon of hard cider. He gave me such a wary look, I decided a few histrionics were in order. "I need your help but I'm almost ashamed to ask it," I said. "My reputation—and Clara's—are totally ruined. You may not want to be seen in public with us." Whereupon I burst into tears. The two men wanted to know what was wrong. Sobbing, I told them about the libel and its source.

"Would you testify to our good conduct at Oswego?" I asked Malcolm.

"You're damned right I will!" he said.

"How can we get the editor to publish it?"

"Let's pay him a visit."

Down to the *Gazette* we strode in Malcolm's wake. We found editor Birch in his front office, selling advertisements to a half dozen merchants. "Here is a gentleman of unimpeachable character, sir," I told him. "He was with me at Oswego and is ready to deny every word of that vile story you published about me and my friend, Clara Flowers."

"It will cost you a shilling a column inch to publish a denial. The same price I charge for advertisements," Birch said.

Malcolm seized the little Englishman by the shirt, dragged him over his counter and hoisted him to eye level. "Did I hear you correctly?" he said. "You've libeled two *ladies* and you expect them to *pay* for their justification?''

''You . . . misunderstood me,'' Birch gasped. ''I meant I'll print it gratis—although it will cost me several advertisements.''

''That's too damn bad,'' Malcolm said, returning him to terra firma with a thud.

Watching, I could only think how much I adored this huge male creature. I wanted to fling my arms around him and kiss him. I wanted to lead him directly to the nearest bed. But I remained outwardly calm and composed—except for expressions of extravagant gratitude.

Malcolm demanded to see the offending column and with Duycinck's help dictated a refutation which the quaking Birch promised to have in next week's paper. We strolled back to the tavern, where Malcolm decided he could stand another breakfast. I thanked him again for his help.

''It's the least I could do, after your kindness yesterday,'' he said. ''But I can't accept your generous offer.''

''Why not?'' I said, my heart plummeting.

''I want to earn my own way in this world.''

''But you would be earning it. Just as you earned it this year, providing us with protection—''

''Clara told me she's never going to trade for furs again. She wants nothing more to do with the rotten business. I don't think you should either.''

I was numb. The Moon Woman could not challenge Clara's moral judgment. ''How do you propose to earn your way?''

''I may go to the West Indies. Governor Nicolls says he'll recommend me to the governor of Jamaica. I can probably get a commission in a regiment stationed there. The mortality is heavy. There's often places open which you can buy for very little money, which Nicolls says he'll lend me.''

"But you might die of some malignant fever," I said, my flesh shriveling at the thought.

Malcolm shrugged. "We must all take our chances."

Men! They loved challenging death for its own sake. I glanced at Duycinck and saw he had no very high opinion of going to the West Indies. Here was an ally, if I could get him alone.

"We must discuss buying your indenture, Adam," I said. "Do you know the terms?"

"All too well."

"Why don't you write them out and bring them to me this afternoon."

That afternoon, I claimed to be busy preparing papers for the coming legal struggle with my uncle and easily persuaded Clara to go buy the food and drink we would need for the next week. When Duycinck arrived, I wasted no time getting to the point. "I can't abide the thought of Malcolm Stapleton dwindling into insignificance as an ensign or lieutenant in some damned British regiment in Jamaica."

"Nor I," Adam said. "You know what I think of those lime suckers."

"Why is Nicolls so eager to see Malcolm out of the country?" I mused. "Didn't you or Clara tell me His Honor the governor was known to enjoy Mrs. Stapleton's bed?"

"All too often," Adam said. "But the lad bears him no resentment for consorting with the bitch. He's too busy despising her."

"I smell something. Why don't you go off to New Jersey for a few days, pretending to rejoin the family—and see what you can find out about how George Stapleton's will was drawn and when it was signed."

I had no idea whether there was any basis for my suspicion. But what better way to keep Malcolm Stapleton in New York than to embroil him in a lawsuit? Presuming my Uncle Johannes intended to cheat me, we would share a grievance, always a good way to link feelings. I would sympathize with him, he would sympathize with me.

Duycinck, of course, would give me plenty of credit for first suspecting Georgianna Stapleton of malfeasance. After the little hunchback left with money to take him to New Jersey, I walked from room to room, thanking the Evil Brother for keeping his promise. My heart's desire was still within reach.

When Clara came home followed by two dusky Africans carrying a veritable cargo of meats and grains and vegetables, I was so cheerful, so agreeable about helping her put the food away in cupboards and bins and in the ice cellar in the backyard, I was almost ashamed of myself. She listened somberly while I told her how Malcolm had terrorized Birch, the editor of the *New York Gazette*, and then announced he was departing to the West Indies.

"We can't let him go to those godforsaken islands, Clara. We need him here in New York. Can't you stop him, somehow?"

As I surmised, Clara knew nothing about Malcolm's future plans. She was more than a little shaken to discover he had shared his thoughts with a woman she assumed he disliked and never mentioned them to her. She was soon on her way to Hughson's Tavern to talk to him.

She found Malcolm in his room at the tavern, reading a book on the West Indies. "Are you really going to the islands?" she said.

"Who told you?"

"Catalyntie. You seem to share a great deal with her these days. You don't have a qualm about leaving me alone here in New York?"

"Alone? I thought you and Catalyntie—"

"I don't think I can live another month with that creature. All she cares about is money. She'll use me, you, anyone and everyone, to get it.''

Malcolm was bewildered by the emotional maelstrom he was inadvertently creating. ''You could come to the West Indies with me,'' he said.

There was a hollow sound in Malcolm's voice as he said those words. His gaze broke away from hers. His love had become a compound of guilt and remembered happiness, which they both knew could never be regained.

''When you die of fever, what then? Will I be sold into slavery again? Or become some other officer's whore?''

''Clara!'' Malcolm said. ''Don't ever use that word to describe yourself. Between you and me there will always be the purest, the truest love that ever existed in this miserable world. It will live in my heart until the day of my death.''

Clara clung to him, weeping. ''I want you but I don't want you. Can you understand that? I don't want any man that way again.''

''I understand it. I understand it all too well.''

''But that could change. I think it will change.''

Again, Clara sensed an almost invisible withdrawal, a virtually imperceptible loss of fervor in Malcolm's manner. ''I hope so,'' he said. ''I hope so for your sake.''

But not for his sake. He was telling her that he was prepared to live without her love. He was now a man who must make his way in the white world and he had resolved to live without her whether she liked it or not. His dead father's words ravaged their love again. *Are you planning to marry this woman? If so, you will have to live in the forest with the Indians.* Was he going to the West Indies to escape her? Was that the bitter truth behind this decision?

''A day doesn't pass without my thinking how much

I want you. I don't think a day will ever pass without that yearning,'' he said.

Perhaps that was enough. Perhaps she should let him go to Jamaica or Barbados and she would try to live on that sad pledge. She kissed him and returned to Maiden Lane, where she told me that she had had made no objection to Malcolm going to the islands.

"How can you be such a fool?" I cried. "He'll die down there. Then both of us are at a total loss."

"I'd almost rather see him die—than fall into your clutches."

"Clara—I care about him—love him—as much as you do. Can't we agree on what's best for him? Instead of letting him destroy himself?"

I wanted, needed, Clara's love—and Malcolm's. Somehow, I vowed to keep one and win the other. The next morning, I crossed the Hudson to New Jersey and hired a horse in the little Dutch settlement of Hoboken. In four hours I was at Hampden Hall—where I found a chaos of confusion and despair. Packing boxes and barrels stood everywhere. Morose Africans wrapped sailcloth around furniture and chandeliers and statuary. A departure was unquestionably under way. In the middle of it all stood Adam Duycinck, poring over a list.

He led me out in the yard. "Cleopatra is about to return to her native Egypt," he said. "She's planning to run the place with an overseer to keep her in silks and madeira. Everyone in the house tells me she drove George Stapleton to his grave with her screaming, raging demand for a new will—and his refusal until he saw Malcolm. Suddenly he dies and presto—there's the document with his signature at the bottom, witnessed by no less than Governor Nicolls and his secretary."

"We must get you back to New York as soon as possible."

Adam led me to the library, where Georgianna Stapleton was conferring with a ship captain. I knew I was unlikely to receive a warm reception after my brawl with this woman over Clara. I spoke the curt cold language of business. "It's come to my attention, madam, that you're planning a return to England. I'd like to buy Adam Duycinck's indenture from you for the remainder of his term. He's proved extremely useful to me in the fur trade."

"What did he do? Hold the candle in your tent?" Georgianna Stapleton said. "From what I read in the papers, your trading placed no greater burden on Adam's skills."

"That story is an atrocious libel, I assure you," I said, barely managing to keep my temper. "Adam will testify to that."

"I already have," Adam said.

"To tell the truth, I'll have no great use for the scoundrel in London, where I intend to live. He was indented for fourteen years to pay his court costs and passage, which rounded off to two hundred pounds. He has seven years to go. You can have him for a hundred pounds."

I haggled the price down to seventy-five pounds and rode back to Hoboken with Adam jouncing behind me in the saddle. In New York, I was delighted to find Guert Cuyler waiting for me at Maiden Lane. With him was a cousin, a suave young Dutchman named Peter Van Ness, whose father had a law office on Broad Street. Clara was serving them tea.

I immediately set Adam to testifying about George Stapleton's suspicious will. Poor Guert was confused. "I thought we were to assail your uncle," he said. "I've spent a dozen hours tracking down what happened to your father's property on the Mohawk."

"That can wait," I said. "This Stapleton matter concerns me far more. Clara and I feel we owe a debt of gratitude to Malcolm for the courage he displayed on the Mohawk. Isn't that right, Clara dear?"

Clara murmured something that might have been an

assent—or an attempt to breathe without asphyxiating herself with rage. I did not care. The Evil Brother assured me that I could eventually deal with Clara's wrath. The two young attorneys conferred and agreed that there would be little hope of preventing Georgianna Stapleton from leaving the country. No slave could testify in a New York court. Duycinck, as an indentured servant, could do so but he would be relying on hearsay from the slaves. If the will was to be challenged, it would have to be in England. That would require a great deal of money.

"Money is not a consideration," I said.

We sent Adam to bring Malcolm into our conference. He listened to a rehearsal of the details with astonishment, disbelief—and rage, in that sequence. I could barely conceal my joy.

"This is not a matter that can be pursued on an officer's pay in Jamaica," I said. "I think you had better cancel your plans to embark on that career."

Guert Cuyler agreed. He told Malcolm that he would want him in New York to recruit witnesses who might testify that George Stapleton did not intend to disinherit his older son.

"You'll do all this for me on the chance that if we succeed, I can pay your fees?" Malcolm said.

Cuyler and Van Ness looked uncomfortable. "Miss Van Vorst has guaranteed our fees," Van Ness said.

"I presume you'll reconsider my offer to become my partner in the fur trade—so if all else fails I can take the money out of your share of our profits," I said.

I sounded so earnest, so honest, I could scarcely believe myself. The Evil Brother was coaching me to conceal my heart's desire. Clara, watching helplessly, could only glower—making the worst possible impression on Malcolm, I hoped.

"You're almost too generous," Malcolm said.

"How true," Clara said. But she could not bring herself to interfere in an offer that was so clearly to Malcolm's benefit.

I watched Malcolm bite his lower lip, thinking how much I wanted my mouth to be there instead. "How can I say no?" Malcolm said, succumbing, as men like to think they do, to the inevitability of fate. He never really wanted to go to the West Indies in the first place, of course. He felt guilty about leaving Clara. His boyhood dreams of military glory were in the northern woods—and now he could still cherish them. His conscience, like most men's, was pliable, realistic. The fur trade might have its faults—but so did other businesses. It was the way of the world and who was he to set about changing it? He was a soldier, not a reformer.

It would be a difficult case, Van Ness warned. With the governor known to be Mrs. Stapleton's protector, few people would be willing to testify against her. But the governor's tenure was rumored to be expiring. Without the power of his office, she might be far more vulnerable. We parted with handshakes all around and optimistic words about future triumphs.

I waited a day—which I spent conferring privately with Cuyler and Van Ness about my case against my uncle. Guert Cuyler had discovered that my father's Mohawk lands had been sold to Oloff Van Sluyden for half their value—and the Van Sluydens had become major customers of the New Netherlands Company, exporting almost all their Canadian-bought furs on Johannes Van Vorst's ships. Clearly, Uncle Johannes was a man who would do anything for money.

I hurried to Malcolm Stapleton's room in Hughson's Tavern and found him alone, reading a copy of his father's will. I thought of the despair in which I would have plunged if he had sailed to the West Indies and tears poured down my cheeks.

"What's wrong now?" Malcolm said.

"I don't know what to do," I sobbed. "My attorneys

tell me I'm liable to be driven from the courtroom by that story in the *Gazette*. Even with the retraction you've obtained, they say my reputation is ruined and this will weigh heavily in a judge's decision. The court may regard me as a person without moral standing—a vagrant—and deprive me of everything I rightfully own, just as your stepmother has deprived you.''

''I never heard of such a thing,'' Malcolm said.

''It's not a *certainty*,'' I said, pretending to be telling as much of the truth as possible. ''But they say my chances would be vastly improved if I married a respectable man. Where can I find a husband after a story like that?''

Malcolm was mute. ''It's not the only reason I should marry, Mr. Van Brugge says. He claims it would be a great advantage in doing business with Oswego traders and shippers like that bully Philip Van Sluyden. Men always think they can take advantage of a single woman. They almost have a compulsion to cheat her. A woman with a husband is much more formidable.''

Malcolm remained mute. Was he beginning to glimpse where the conversation was going? If so, his face betrayed nothing. I retreated several steps, as if I was far too unworthy even to hope that he would consider for a moment what I was about to say. I was bowing as low as possible, perhaps lower than any woman should bow. I was in the grip of the Evil Brother—and my heart's desire—which began to look more and more like the same thing.

The city bawled and racketed outside Malcolm's open window. I lowered my eyes until they rested on that enormous chest, the huge arms, the massive thighs of this creature I valued more than riches, more than honor, pride, or the truth.

''Would you—could you—consider marrying me?'' I said in the hushed voice of a penitent in a church. ''I know I'm not a very lovable woman. But I would be a good wife to you. I can bind myself to that promise. I know you'll always love Clara—I understand that. I'd even understand it if you felt compelled to go to her at times."

Mute. The man remained mute, expressionless. His eyes were opaque. The city clamored outside the window. Was this the Evil Brother's ultimate mockery? If he said no, I vowed to go directly from this room and fling myself into the East River. I refused to endure another moment of existence, knowing Malcolm would tell Clara, Duycinck, a dozen drinking friends what this outrageous slut Catalyntie Van Vorst had proposed to him.

"If I married someone else," I resumed in an even more abject voice, "he might dispute my promise to pay your legal fees. That would pain me greatly, to think we would not have a chance to see justice done on your behalf—when the injustice was committed partly through my fault. I think I would rather lose my own suit against my uncle than see that happen to you."

I raised my eyes. Malcolm Stapleton was standing up. He pushed himself away from his chair in an odd lumbering gesture as if he was too paralyzed with astonishment to walk properly.

"Miss Van Vorst," he said. "Catalyntie."

It was the mere pronouncement of my first name. He had never spoken it before. It had been either "Miss Van Vorst" or "You." I flung myself against that massive chest. "I also love you," I whispered. "I *love* you. *Love* you. In spite of Clara."

"Of course I'll marry you," he said, taking my hands.

My mind went blank, my body emptied of flesh, blood, bone. I was a dry husk of bewilderment. The Evil Brother had fulfilled his promise. Where were the gusts of joy, the thunder peals of happiness? Was it because I knew that the Evil One would now exact his payment? Or was it Clara's voice, hissing: *never*?

BACK IN OUR HOUSE ON Maiden Lane, I made tea and set about convincing Clara that she should be glad Malcolm Stapleton was going to marry me. "Isn't it best to face the truth? You could never marry him, Clara. If you oppose us, he might change his mind. You'd be condemning him to a miserable existence. There's nothing more pathetic in this world than an aging bachelor. And a bankrupt in the bargain. He has no head for business. Unless he regains his estate, he's ruined."

"Malcolm is free to do what he pleases, with whom he pleases," Clara said.

I winced at the contempt in her voice. But I could not stop myself. "He isn't free. He still loves you, Clara."

I could see how delicious those words were in Clara's ears. She could see it almost destroyed me to say them. "He chooses a strange way to express it—marrying you," Clara said.

"Oh, Clara." My throat filled with genuine tears. "Surely you know I love you too. I'd give my life—almost—to prevent what's happened. But—"

But it has happened, I could all but hear Clara thinking. Malcolm has chosen the Moon Woman's white skin over my brown skin. Catalyntie Van Vorst's money over Clara Flowers's wounded love. The white world, where money ruled everything, would praise his shrewdness—if they ever bothered to examine the exchange. To them it was mere common sense. A man had to consider his self-interest above everything else.

I gulped my tea and struggled to mitigate the brutality

of this conclusion. ''There's advantage in it for you, too. You've got not one but two loyal friends who'll never abandon you, if they have a shilling to share. I swear that, Clara. If I took another husband, he might not let me help you. The law gives a husband great control of his wife's property.''

''You're going to give Malcolm control of your money?''

''To some extent. There'll be a marriage settlement, of course. You remember what my grandfather said about keeping control of money that's rightfully mine.''

Liar liar liar. I could hear the word raging in Clara's throat like a war cry. For a moment she wished us both five hundred miles away, out of this painted parlor with a portrait of Cornelius Van Vorst on the wall, back in the forest where Seneca justice ruled. Instead of a gold-rimmed Sèvres teacup, there was a bone-handled knife in her hand. She had her Seneca sister by the hair, threatening to cut her open from her lying gullet to her libidinous crotch.

No, no, no. Clara struggled to affirm her faith in the Master of Life. He was the father of the savior, Jesus, the Jew whose sayings had stirred her so profoundly. *I say unto you, forgive your enemies, do good to them who hate you.* What a marvelous dream of human life he proposed. But would it ever be more than a dream? She had yet to see anyone in the white or red or black world who practiced his superhuman precepts.

''Promise me this,'' Clara said. ''You'll never ask Malcolm to commit a crime in your name.''

''Why would I do such a thing?''

''Because you hate people. You wish them dead.''

I accepted the rebuke. ''I promise.''

''One more thing. You won't make him a mere mercenary. Use your money to help him became a true soldier, a patriot.''

I hesitated. Clara knew I thought patriots were fools.

But I did not really care what Malcolm did, once he left my bedroom. "I promise," I said.

"Not a promise. Swear on the blood of our parents. Swear on their dead faces. Swear on your grandfather's grave!"

"I . . . I swear," I said, intimidated, almost frightened by her fervor.

"All right. You have my blessing on your marriage."

"Truly a blessing, Clara?" I said.

"Not truly. But as close as I can come to it now."

"Not a curse—I couldn't bear a curse, Clara. I want you to take back that *never* you flung at me in Albany."

"I have no power over that word," Clara said.

It was arranged. Guert Cuyler drew up the marriage settlement. He was my attorney, and he naturally saw things from my point of view. The agreement stated that I would retain control of the as yet undetermined value of my inheritance, to the amount of one hundred thousand pounds. This was more money than the richest merchant in the colony of New York was worth but Malcolm signed the document without a hint of demur.

We were married on a Saturday afternoon in September at the altar of the New Dutch Reformed Church on Nassau Street. I wore white like a virgin bride and invited a half dozen friends of my grandfather to attend. I made no secret of viewing the ceremony as a chance to restore or at least repair my reputation. Clara sat in the church wondering what the Senecas would think of such elaborate nonsense to certify a woman's virginity. They would find it especially amusing in this case, when the entire community knew it was nonexistent.

Malcolm invited many of his own and his father's friends, but pointedly omitted the governor. By this time Guert Cuyler and Peter Van Ness had challenged George Stapleton's will. Van Ness was preparing to go to England to study at the Temple Bar, and would hire a London lawyer to pursue the suit there. There was no hope of winning the case here in New York. The governor had the power to create a special chancery court with himself as its chief judge. It had jurisdiction over any case he cared to choose from the dockets of other courts.

The city buzzed with the news of the Stapletons' assault on the governor's mistress. Several of our invited guests made excuses rather than risk His Excellency's wrath. At the wedding supper at the King's Arms Tavern, Clara sat opposite us, her expression mournful, as if she were at a funeral instead of a marriage. Malcolm betrayed his guilt by talking exclusively to her and barely saying a word to me. When toasts were offered to true love and perfect happiness, he gazed into her eyes as he raised his glass.

At last, the wedding couple went home to their rented house on Depeyster Street. I had left Clara in the house on Maiden Lane, with Adam Duycinck for a boarder. He was to be in charge of keeping the books for the store I hoped to open on Pearl Street as soon as possible. No doubt Clara lay in her lonely bed, trying to imagine—and then forbidding herself to imagine—what was happening in the redbrick house on Depeyster Street.

She would have been pleased, on the whole, by the scene that unfolded. Infuriated by Malcolm's attention to Clara, I berated him the moment we stepped in the door. "I can endure the knowledge that you still love her," I said. "But must you make a public statement of it?"

"I was only trying to make Clara feel at ease," he said.

We went to bed in less than a loving humor. I tried to rescue the night by telling Malcolm I forgave him. He curtly insisted he had done nothing that needed forgiveness.

By this time, if there had ever been anything of that ingredient called romance in the air, it had dissipated. We were closer to a quarrelsome married couple in a satire by Plautus. Malcolm could only remember the perfect bliss of his year of love with Clara. He abandoned our bed and sat in the kitchen, gloomy as a bear in winter. I pursued him, horrified to find myself the Moon Woman again. I tearfully promised I would learn to hold my tongue, I would please him in everything. He almost certainly thought I was lying but he returned to the bedroom.

"Will you tell me something?" he said, looming over me. "Why don't you realize how beautiful you are?"

Those were the most bewildering words I had ever heard. They sent my heart leaping toward the stars—and simultaneously plunged it into the icy depths of the Arctic Sea. He was paying me a marvelous compliment and simultaneously withdrawing it. Wasn't he saying that he would always consider me a slut? A beautiful woman did not scheme and sidle to ensnare a man. A beautiful woman allowed a man to love her—she did not solicit his ardor like a whore on the Broadway.

"Perhaps . . . if you told me that in a kinder way . . . I might begin to realize it."

"I'm not a complete fool—though I know you're inclined to think I'm one—I wouldn't marry a woman who . . ."

He let the words trail off. What was he going to say? A woman who disgusted him? Another compliment to treasure. At least I had escaped—no doubt by inches—that fate. I stopped his blundering mouth with a kiss. "I told you I *loved* you," I said. "Doesn't that mean anything?"

I could see it did not mean a great deal. "I need you in my arms. I need you and need you and need you," I whispered. "Without you I have no hope of happiness. Doesn't that mean something to you?"

Having seen what made me happy—money and more money—he could not swallow this extravagance. But he felt compelled to pay me some sort of compliment. "I wanted you—that day on the lake. When you took off your clothes, I almost felt you were obeying my secret wish.''

His kiss was serious. Mutual lust would be our bond. In my heart I knew it would be a temporary one—but the Moon Woman was used to taking the best offer she could find. The Evil Brother had only promised to deliver Malcolm to my bed—he had said nothing about love. In a desperate act of faith, I told myself I would outwit the Evil One. Somehow, somewhere in the indefinite future I would persuade Malcolm to love me. Meanwhile there was this magnificent male body to enjoy—and the knowledge that he desired me, he found me beautiful.

But She-Is-Alert could not stop her perpetually vigilant mind from noticing the same lack of tenderness that had pained her in the lake. There was more enthusiasm, perhaps. After all, he had made a pretty good bargain from his point of view and as an honest man he was more than willing to fulfill it. But there was an element of force, of rough willfulness in his lovemaking that gave our union a hint of a contest. I sensed that with every thrust he saw himself somehow subduing me—an idea I subtly resisted even while I struggled to banish the thought, to let him fill me with pleasure and more pleasure.

In the end there were sighs and groans of animal relish—a sense that we were joined in a way that satisfied some parts of our souls. But I had imagined an eagle's swoop of triumph and delight. I was left earthbound—not a complete surprise for someone who was born to be a creature of the city. Yet memories of my forest girlhood had left a kind of window of random freedom, of wildness, in my soul in which I wanted my husband to join me.

The Evil Brother had fulfilled his promise. I struggled to convince myself that I was satisfied. Wrapping my arms possessively around him, I began telling Malcolm what I saw as our joint future. "The first thing we'll do is run Uncle Johannes out of politics," I said. "You'll stand against him for the legislature and beat him silly in the vote."

"How will I do that?" Malcolm said. "He's held that seat for fifteen years. It was your grandfather's seat before his."

"We'll convince the voters he's not a patriot. He's selling out the king and the colony by trading with the French in Canada. We'll condemn him for voting against funds for the fort at Oswego."

"We need someone to say those things," Malcolm said.

"Why not you?"

"I'm no politician. I can't make a speech."

"You can learn. You can learn to make a soldier's speech."

I was remembering my Seneca days again—listening to the warriors boast of their prowess, their eagerness for battle. A warrior could not match a sachem in debate. But he could thrill and arouse listeners with his ferocity, his readiness for war.

"Meanwhile we'll track down the guilty parties in my parents' death. The next time we go to Albany, we'll lure one of the Van Sluydens into the woods and torture him until he confesses the whole affair."

Malcolm recoiled in horror. "You can't torture people! Clara warned me you'd have ideas like this."

"We wouldn't really have to torture him. Just threaten him enough to make him confess."

"It's still a crime. Clara—"

"Damn Clara! What did you do—ask her for permission to marry me?"

"We talked about it," Malcolm said.

Outside in the street, some drunken sailors began quarreling with the Watch. They flung obscenities at

each other. Dogs began barking and nearby house owners leaned from their windows to shout for quiet. Mr.
and Mrs. Stapleton lay side by side in their bed, stiff
with antagonism. I was discovering that possession was
nine-tenths of the law in business and war but not in
marriage.

The next day Guert Cuyler filed papers with the court,
contending that Johannes Van Vorst had sold his
brother's Mohawk lands for a fraction of their value in
order to curry favor with the Van Sluydens in the fur
trade. He demanded the restitution of the full five thousand acres or their current value. He also sued for payment in cash of the sale price of Cornelius Van Vorst's
New York house and the real value of the Long Island
property—rather than in New Netherlands Company
stock, which Johannes could manipulate as he pleased.
For good measure he had a political friend file a bill in
the assembly, calling for the creation of a special chancery court to oversee the administration of minors' estates—with the governor specifically excluded from its
bench.

Nothing makes a person more exultant than a lawsuit
in the early stages. Later the plaintiff discovers the endless delays, the unexpected interpretations, the dismaying equivocations of the lawyers and judges. But for the
first few days, victory seems to beckon like a flag in the
breach of a besieged fortress. I rushed home from court
to share my excitement with Malcolm Stapleton, my
husband. He was not there. I ate a cold supper in the
twilit kitchen, wondering where he was.

About ten o'clock I heard stumbling steps in the hall.
Adam Duycinck said: "All right, old pal. You're safe
in port now."

Another deeper voice spoke with an up-country New
York twang. "Easy now. Aim him at that chair."

In the entrance hall I found Malcolm Stapleton
slumped in a chair, obviously drunk. Staggering around

him were Adam Duycinck and John Hughson, the owner of Hughson's Tavern. "What the devil is this all about?" I cried.

Hughson smirked at me. He was a big stupid oaf, bald except for a fringe of hair around his ears. "It's nothin' to be alarmed about, Madame Stapleton. He'll be fine in the mornin'."

"Get out of my house," I said. Hughson vanished into the night, leaving Adam to deal with the wrath of the new owner of his indenture.

" 'Twas just a little postwedding celebration," Adam said. "A salute to the lad's lost bachelorhood."

"Get on your feet, Malcolm Stapleton!" I said. "Get on your feet and get out of my house. I won't have a husband who's a public sot. I'll annul the marriage tomorrow."

"Now now," Malcolm said. "Didn't you get your money's worth last night?" He grinned at Adam, who laughed nervously.

"Is this what you're telling the town? Talking about me as if I was a new kind of whore? One who has to pay men for her pleasure?"

"He never said a word that even hinted of such a thing," Adam said.

I did not believe him. "I won't be humiliated this way," I cried. "Get him out of my sight. Take him to Clara's house. Give her a look at the hero in his cups."

"I don't think that would be a good idea," Adam said, his head clearing rapidly. He was speaking as my confederate now.

"No, I suppose not," I said.

Together we half-dragged, half-pushed Malcolm into a spare bedroom and stretched him out on the bed. "Was Clara with you?" I asked.

"No," Duycinck said.

"If you're lying I'll sell your indenture to the first ship owner I find bound for the West Indies."

"She wasn't. It was just his friend Cuyler."

"My lawyer? I hope he didn't go home as befuddled as Malcolm."

"He says George Stapleton's will is cast iron. There's no breaking it. Georgianna's got the estate and that's all there is to it," Duycinck said.

"I begin to think you've led me on a goose chase— into your bedroom," Malcolm said.

"Didn't I tell you I loved you?"

"The lady's got a point, lad," Duycinck said.

"Stop calling him lad. He's a married man. He's going to run for the assembly and you're going to manage him. Before we're through we'll turn this province upside down. We'll put an end to this truckling to Englishmen."

In the morning, Malcolm was contrite. "I'll swear off rum. I promise you," he said.

"Don't be foolish," I snapped. "You can't win an election without drinking rum in every tavern in the ward. You must learn to drink it like a man—not a greedy slurping boy."

The words stung him like a lash in the face. I saw the dilemma of every woman who tries to guide a man. The male of the species regards every piece of blunt advice, every sharp word of correction, as an insult to his manhood. Malcolm seized me by the arm and roared: "I thought you promised to put a rein on that tongue."

"I'm sorry," I said.

That night he stayed home and I tried to cook for him. It was a disaster. The roast was overdone, the potatoes baked to cinders, the bread was the texture of clay. On Maiden Lane, Clara had done the cooking, I had done the shopping. There had been no pain in confessing my inability in the kitchen. Now I was mortified. "I'm afraid I'm not a *goede vrouw*,"[1] I said, as I cleared away the dishes.

---

[1] *Dutch for good housewife.*

"You remind me more of my stepmother every day," Malcolm said. "She never went near the kitchen if she could help it."

Another compliment? Was he finding some sort of strength in thinking he was fated to replicate his father's career: first a great love, then a lusty bitch? Once more I told myself to make the best of it for the time being. I would learn to curb my tongue and maybe he would learn to improve his compliments. Together we would learn to love each other.

The bad dinner did not diminish his ardor in the bedroom. My God, how he filled me! Great surges of pleasure that stirred a hope of an eagle's flight, in spite of the growling violence of his assault. There was still not an iota of tenderness but I began to wonder if that mattered in my hardened heart. Perhaps this rampaging desire was all either of us wanted, this mounting expectation of bliss that melted away with a grateful shudder of dissolution as his seed throbbed in my belly. The Evil Brother seemed disposed to let us annihilate Clara's *never*.

The next day I hired Shirley, my grandfather's old cook, for two shillings a day and board and a room for herself and her husband Peter, who was considerably older and too feeble to do any serious work. This rescued us from my cooking and allowed me to devote all my time to plans for the store. Captain Van Oorst would be arriving in October and there were advertisements to write, display shelves to build. I tried to involve Clara in the plans but she remained tepid about the prospect of becoming a saleswoman. She told me she would not be good at it.

Meanwhile, Malcolm had announced his candidacy for the colony's assembly in the fall elections. Running in a ward in which forty percent of the voters were Dutch, no one gave him much of a chance. But I wrote a circular letter in Dutch describing him as the candidate who would rescue New York from the wiles of Governor Nicolls and his corrupt administration. A typical Englishman, he only sought to suck money out of the province—without regard to its safety. I accused the governor of encouraging trade with Canada and profiting from it. But the real profiteer, the man who made even more than the governor from this illegal trade, was Johannes Van Vorst.

Meanwhile Malcolm made the rounds of taverns and coffeehouses, describing the way the French were trying to destroy New York's share of the fur trade. He enthralled audiences with the story of our encounter with the French gunboat on Lake Ontario. He liked the contest for votes, liked being a public man, orating on the importance of patriotism. He liked warning his fellow citizens of the potential treachery of France and Spain. He came home at night, boasting to me about how many voters he was convincing. In the bedroom, his ardor seemed to increase in tandem with his multiplying hopes of local fame. For a while something approximating happiness seemed about to occur in our lives.

In late October, a furtive knock on our door awakened us at midnight. Malcolm answered it and discovered Captain Killian Van Oorst. He sidled into the house and I soon joined them in the kitchen. The captain said he had a cargo of goods for the store. "Where?" I said, ready to rush out and examine them by lantern light.

The captain said the ship and its cargo were at Sag Harbor on Long Island. I poured him a tankard of rum and asked him why he had not landed in New York. He looked at me in his sly way and said: "Do you want to sell dear or cheap?"

I understood immediately that he was smuggling the stuff ashore to avoid the customs duties.[2] I smiled at my

---

[2]*At this time, the customs officers in New York did not own a single boat. They charged duties only on goods that came directly to the docks.*

fellow Dutchman and said I wanted to sell cheap and could hardly wait to see the goods. The captain assured me that wagons could be hired at Sag Harbor without difficulty. I could have the goods in New York in a day or two. He added that he had found a merchant in Amsterdam who said he would be very interested in sending me trading goods for the Indians. Finally, he handed me a bill of exchange from the same man, drawn on John Van Cortlandt, one of New York's most prominent merchants, paying me nine hundred sixty-two pounds for our furs. There was, of course, no mention of furs. The money was paid for ''goods.''

''That's more than I bargained for,'' I said, fingering the piece of paper, which would guarantee our solvency for another year at least.

''The price of beaver went up another shilling,'' Van Oorst said. ''And my brother said they were very good skins.''

Malcolm Stapleton sat at the kitchen table, frowning throughout this discussion, saying little. Captain Van Oorst went off to the King's Arms Tavern for the night. ''Didn't I promise you we'd be rich?'' I said, dancing around the kitchen, kissing the bill of exchange.

''You're breaking the law,'' Malcolm said. ''I won't be a party to it. You transacted for the furs before we married. But now your name is Stapleton. You must pay full duties on those goods, exactly as the law prescribes. That's an order.''

''Why should we pay money to that fat thief on his throne in London and go bankrupt trying to sell goods for twice what they're worth? They've jacked up the duties on everything from Holland to make their London merchants rich.''

''You can't run an empire without laws,'' Malcolm said. ''Here I am, promising voters to go to the assembly to pass a law forbidding trade with Canada. Aye, and prohibiting rum with the Indians. But what's the good of passing laws if my own wife will only obey those that please her?''

''I may have changed my name but I haven't changed my blood,'' I said. ''I'm Dutch—and Seneca—and American—and none of these inclines me to obey any pettifogging laws passed by greedy Englishmen three thousand miles away.''

''You will not bring those goods to town in wagons!'' Malcolm roared. ''You will hire a ship—or tell that Dutch trickster Van Oorst to sail them to a wharf here in New York and pay the duties.''

''I will do no such thing!''

We went to bed, too furious to sleep. In the morning, I dressed without speaking to my husband, collected Captain Van Oorst at the King's Arms and went over to Brooklyn on the ferry. There we hired a carriage and rode out to Sag Harbor to look at the goods. They were of the first quality—and in marvelous variety. There were barrels of choice ham and pork, dipped candles, silk, cotton and Kenting handkerchiefs, Muslin cravats and Scotch gauze, claret in bottles and hogsheads, damasks of sundry colors for vests, all sorts of cloth, from poplins to flowered dimity to plaid to broadcloth, ready-to-wear cloaks and cardinals, hair buttons, steel buckles, knives and forks, and a parcel of choice barley.

''It's beautiful,'' I said. ''Such variety. You've given me a name for my business. The Universal Store!''

The owner of the wharf at which Van Oorst was tied up said he had several farming relatives who would be glad to rent their horses and wagons. I stayed overnight aboard the ship and the next day said good-bye to Captain Van Oorst with fervent promises to do further business and headed for New York at the head of a six-wagon procession. By the end of the day, the goods were in the store on Pearl Street, ready to be spread on counters and sold as soon as we could get an announcement in the newspapers.

At home, I found a glowering husband awaiting me. "You're resolved to sell those things without paying duties?" Malcolm said.

"I am extremely resolved," I said. "How do you expect to pay the bills for those drinks you buy in taverns for would-be voters? We must be in business year-round, not merely three months of the year hunting furs."

"You promised before the altar of God to love, honor, and obey me," Malcolm said.

"I skipped the word *obey*. You didn't notice," I said. "If I said it, I skipped it in my mind."

"If you can absolve yourself that way, so can I—in regard to the other words."

The Evil Brother smiled in a corner of my soul. I could read the mockery in his cruel eyes. *I never promised you happiness. Only your heart's desire.*

"I talked to Clara. She agrees with me completely," Malcolm said. "She says this is a test of how we'll deal with each other for the rest of our lives."

"If Clara wants to work in my store—and share the profits—she'll change that opinion."

"'My store'? I believe it's our store. As your husband I have the right to decide a great deal about our affairs."

"You have no control over a cent of my funds—up to a hundred thousand pounds—and we're a long way from that."

I snatched the marriage contract out of a bureau drawer and thrust it at him. "There's your signature, agreeing to that arrangement."

Malcolm flung the paper on the table and stalked out of the house. No doubt to another conference with Clara, the keeper of his patriotic conscience. That night, after a silent, surly supper, I went to bed, expecting him to join me. Instead, he stayed by an oil lamp in the parlor, reading newspapers. Finally I went in to him and asked: "Shall I put out the light in the bedroom?"

"You can do what you please."

"I'm sorry about the goods. I wish there was some way we could agree."

"There is. But you won't do it."

Back in bed, I saw the future grinning at me like a skull. He would return to my arms when it pleased him. But it would not please him very often. He would find other women who pleased him more. Perhaps Clara, when and if she overcame her dread of another child. But Catalyntie Van Vorst still would not let him have his way. Her Dutch blood, her grandfather's words about independence—and her self-interest—stood in the path of such a surrender.

Did it mean that money meant more to her than her heart's desire? Or was money and the power it bought her real heart's desire? Was the other thing a trick of the west wind, the waft of eagles' wings in her Indian soul, dwindling now as the city and its clamor swallowed the memory of the forest and its dream of wild desire?

Perhaps, I thought. Perhaps. But I still hoped for love somewhere, somehow. I was a woman, after all.

BOOK

FOUR

ONE

"I'M SICK TO DEATH OF cringing before greedy stupid women," Clara said.

Adam Duycinck fluttered around the premises of the Universal Store like a broken-winged sparrow. "But Clara—they adore you," he said.

"I despise them all," Clara said.

"You're talking nonsense and you know it," I said.

This quarrel had been building for a long time. I knew how unhappy Clara was, truckling, as shopwomen must, to our customers, who were mostly the rich and powerful of New York. Something in her nature made it impossible for Clara to be insincere. She loathed herself for it. The advice Cornelius Van Vorst had given us—to bow before the powerful, but never to bow in your heart—did not work for her.

Another more visible reason for the quarrel was the bulge beneath my dress. I was eight months pregnant. I strongly suspected Clara's disgust with a shopwoman's life was mostly a desire to escape from the sight of me carrying Malcolm Stapleton's child.

There was another reason for the quarrel which neither of us was willing to confront: the color of Clara's skin. It made her hypersensitive to orders or remarks from our wealthy white customers that smacked of condescension or worse. A shopkeeper was in many ways a servant—and Clara was determined not to be treated like one. For Clara, freedom was a kind of hair shirt. To be treated like a servant was synonymous with being treated like a slave.

Still another reason for the quarrel was the success of the Universal Store. We were underselling most of the other stores in New York with our smuggled Holland goods. Ladies flocked to buy cambrics and woolens at bargain prices. I was by no means the only merchant of Dutch blood who dealt with Amsterdam via smugglers like Captain Van Oorst. But Clara found my evasion of the law particularly odious because it embarrassed Malcolm.

He had won his contest for the assembly, taking Johannes Van Vorst's seat away from him. That same year, Governor Nicolls had been recalled to England and George Clarke, the lieutenant governor, a longtime resident of the province, had encouraged Malcolm to introduce a bill, calling for a ban on trading with Canada. The Van Sluydens in Albany and Johannes Van Vorst's friends in New York had violently opposed it. They had challenged Malcolm to assure everyone that he was not profiting from another kind of forbidden trade. Malcolm had no answer and his bill languished while his enemies hooted.

"I've always said you were free to dissolve our partnership any time you chose," I said. "But I think you ought to give some thought to how you'll support yourself."

"Don't talk to me as if I were a child—or an ignorant servant," Clara said. "Of course I've given some thought to it."

"What are you going to do?" I said, abandoning my superior manner. I wanted Clara to stay in the store. Not only was she popular with the customers, it enabled me to feel I retained a semblance of our old friendship. Now I see I was trying to control her. I was mortally afraid she could take Malcolm away from me whenever she chose.

"How much is my share of the business worth?" Clara asked

"Adam, bring out the books," I said. I pulled out a chair and sat down, my hands clutching my aching back. It had not been an easy pregnancy.

The little hunchback hauled his ledgers out of the drawer. After two years in business, we had capital in cash and goods worth 4,278 pounds. Clara's share of that amount would be 1,426 pounds.

"I can't pay you that much in a lump sum," I said. "But I'll be happy to give you part in cash and the rest in credit to be paid off over the next five years."

"Five years! I could starve in five years. Is that how you treat a friend?"

"We're not talking friendship now. We're talking business," I said. "I would also want a sworn statement from you that you will not go to work for another store and try to take customers away from me."

"Didn't I tell you I hate this work? Every time I sell something to a woman like Eugenia Fowler, she makes me feel I've sold part of my soul."

Eugenia Fowler was the wife of George Fowler, the richest merchant in New York, the owner of the city's biggest distillery. She had her own coach, an Irish driver, and two black slaves as footmen. She lived to shop—and she loved nothing as much as a bargain. She had told all her friends about the Universal Store's low prices and our sales had boomed. This had added to Mrs. Fowler's already imperious style when she visited the store.

I had no trouble bowing low before Mrs. Fowler. I consoled myself with visions of the mahogany chests and walnut highboys I would soon buy for our house, making me Mrs. Fowler's social equal. I confidently expected to have as much money as Mrs. Fowler when I reached her ancient age of forty-something. Clara found no consolation in such a vision. Without a husband or a prospect of one, she saw no point in filling a house with fine furniture—or her wardrobe with expensive gowns.

In her loneliness, Clara prayed to the Master of Life to send her a purpose in this world. Prayer came naturally to Clara. Her Seneca grandmother had taught her all men and women were linked by their common descent from the Manitou. Her admiration for the teachings of Jesus had intensified this natural sympathy. She felt impelled to reach out, to help, whenever she saw people in pain or misery—sights by no means uncommon in 1730s New York.

One winter day a year ago, a red-haired young Irishwoman named Cicely, obviously a whore, had come into the shop. She had no money and her only dress had been torn in a fight with another whore over a customer. She wanted to know if she could buy a new dress on credit. Clara had given her the cloth and the name of a seamstress, telling her she would pay for the whole thing.

I grew livid when Clara told me about Cicely. "We'll become the whore's emporium!" I said. "No respectable woman will go near us. Keep your charity to yourself on Maiden Lane, if you insist on it."

Word of Clara's generosity had spread swiftly along Pearl Street and soon several other prostitutes were asking her help to refurbish their outfits. She told them to collect their cloth at her house on Maiden Lane. Often she gave them coffee and a meal—and heard their pathetic life stories. In almost every case they had been seduced and abandoned by a man they had trusted.

Others sought help in the form of wool blankets or cloth for a wool shawl to protect them against New York's cruel winters. Many of them were free women of her own color. Clara found it impossible to say no to them, too. She always scrupulously reported her generosity to Adam, who noted it in his ledger as a deduction against her share of the profits. I never made any objection to these charitable gifts but I never offered to share them either.

Now, my quick temper soured by my pregnancy, I

proceeded to use these debts as another argument against Clara quitting the store. "Don't you think we should deduct from your share the benefactions you've seen fit to bestow on beggars and whores?" I said.

"How much does it come to?" Clara asked.

Duycinck did some hurried addition. "Sixteen pounds six shillings," he said. "That's cash from the drawer. Then another one hundred one pounds eight shillings at going prices for dresses, blankets, and the like. Should I charge her wholesale or retail for that?"

"Retail," I said.

"Malcolm said he'd contribute his one-third share of our partnership to these gifts," Clara said.

"When did he say that?" I asked.

"Several months ago, when I told him about them."

"He never mentioned it to me."

"I'm not surprised."

"I will contribute nothing to a practice that still threatens us with ruin," I said, now determined to be completely obnoxious. "Only a few days ago, I saw a whore on Broadway dressed in the same cambric we sold to Mrs. Fowler for an evening dress!"

"I hope she saw it too," Clara said, unable to restrain her detestation of Mrs. Fowler. More than once she had watched her scream insults at her Irish driver or African footmen because they were not standing at attention, ready to receive her, when she left the store.

"Did you hear that, Adam? Can you blame me for being glad to be rid of her?" I cried.

Adam said nothing. The little hunchback shared Clara's sympathy for the unfortunates of this world— being one of them from birth.

"Damn you both," I said, struggling to my feet. "You enjoy making me out to be a hard-hearted bitch when all I'm trying to do is protect this business. How do you plan to make a living, Miss Flowers?"

"I think I may become a partner in Hughson's Tavern."

"With that lunkhead John Hughson? You'll lose your money in a year. If ever I've seen a man who's destined to go bankrupt, it's that dimwit."

"His wife runs the place," Clara said. "She has brains enough for both of them. She's a good woman—who needs help."

"Oh?" I said. "Has she already received some of your benefactions?"

I glowered at Adam, who paled visibly and admitted that for almost a year we had been carrying money Sarah Hughson owed us for sheets and pillowcases, curtains and tablecloths, purchased when they moved their tavern to a larger building on the Broadway, on the growing west side of the city. Six months was all the credit we normally allowed. But I had been so ill with my pregnancy, I had not given the books more than a cursory glance for a long time.

I looked at the ledger and exploded: "One hundred and fifty pounds! We'll deduct that from your share, you can be sure of it, Miss Flowers—or the Hughsons will see me in court."

"They've been struggling—but they'll pay it," Clara said.

She made no attempt to explain her friendship with Sarah Hughson, a dark-haired talkative woman whose life story reminded Clara of her own. From Yonkers, a town just north of New York, she had fallen in love with a big muscular farmboy and persuaded him to move to the city—where they soon found themselves with four growing daughters and little money. They had opened a tavern to supplement his earnings as a shoemaker. Adam drank at Hughson's and he had brought Sarah Hughson to the Universal Store, where her anxious flow of words about herself and her family had stirred Clara's sympathy.

From Adam and from several prostitutes, Clara learned that Mrs. Hughson let the whores use the tavern's rooms free of charge when they could not pay. When Adam dunned her for the unpaid one hundred fifty pounds she had told Clara about their shortage of cash and her desperate search for a partner. They owed money to their distiller and a half dozen other merchants. Adam had gone over their books and assured Clara it was a good investment. With better management and a more respectable clientele, the tavern could clear five hundred pounds a year—a juicier profit than the Universal Store, whose goods, even at smuggled prices, cost more than rum.

The Hughsons needed cash now to pay their creditors and they would not be thrilled to discover they would have to wait five years for Clara to pay in full her thousand pounds for a half ownership. Clara waited until I departed and asked Adam if I had the money in cash and was deliberately holding it back.

Adam shook his head. "She never lets money sit idle. Almost every cent is out at interest or invested in a ship or a cargo."

"Does that mean I'm doomed to spend the rest of my days here?" Clara said.

Adam winked. "She could write you a bill of exchange on any merchant in town for the full amount."

Bills of exchange passed from hand to hand and were used to pay debts. Very often they were never converted into cash. They were a substitute for ready money.

"I'll talk to Malcolm," Clara said.

Malcolm was at the King's Arms Tavern on Broad Street, reading the latest newspapers from London. Since his election to the assembly, he had become intensely interested in politics both in America and in England. As usual, he was surrounded by a group of young men his own age who were equally fascinated by this complicated subject, which did not interest Clara at all. She asked Malcolm if they could talk in private and they retreated to a corner of the shadowy taproom. She told him about her impasse with me and asked his help.

"You know how hard it is to change her mind about anything," he said. "It's no easier for me."

"Then forget the matter," Clara said.

"If I had funds of my own, you'd have the money in five seconds. But the latest news about my lawsuit is far from promising."

"We'll forget it," Clara said. "I can tolerate the shop-woman's lot. It's not so terrible."

"No!" Malcolm said, seizing her hand. "For your sake I'll dare the dragoness in her den."

"I'm sorry to add to your unhappiness."

"I can bear it well enough," he said.

In the momentary silence, they both knew a great deal was being left unsaid. He was half confessing that he enjoyed his wife in bed, in spite of her disposition. He was also admitting that he liked the life of a public man that I had helped him create.

"Do you think my investment in Hughson's is a good idea?" Clara asked.

"Good and getting better by the day." He waved a folded newspaper. "The word from Europe is war with Spain or France or both. That will bring the king's ships and maybe his troops to New York. Every tavern in town will become a gold mine. Even the whores will get rich."

He was still a warrior. Clara could see he loved the prospect of a war. "That's a good argument to use on Catalyntie," she said. "Nothing is more likely to convince her than the word *profit*." She told him about Adam's proposal of a bill of exchange.

"Consider it done," Malcolm said.

That night, over dinner, Malcolm went to work on me with a nice combination of pleas and threats. He confirmed his promise to share a third of Clara's charities on his own account and said if I declined to give her a bill of exchange for the full amount we owed her, he would write one himself. I furiously pointed out that under the law it would be my debt as well as his. "I know that," he said, complacently chewing his venison.

Almost casually, Clara had demonstrated who had more influence with my supposedly devoted husband. Trapped between my anger and old affection, I struggled not to hate my Seneca sister. The baby kicked in my stomach. Maybe he was telling me to bide my time.

The next day, Eugenia Fowler was the store's first customer. "Clara, my dear girl," she said. "That cambric you selected for my evening gown was the sensation of the King's Birthday Ball! Governor Clarke himself told me he's never seen anything quite as ravishing. I want to buy up every yard you have left, so no one else can get their hands on it."

"Of course, Mrs. Fowler. But other shops—"

"Other shops won't have your quality. Holland goods—at least the luxury sort—are so superior to English or French. The Dutch have a way with expensive fabrics. Rather like the Irish with their linen."

"I'll have Adam deliver our entire stock to your house this afternoon," Clara said.

As the great lady departed to her coach, I countermanded Clara's promise. "I'll be damned if I'll sell her all our cambric," I said. "Send her twenty yards and keep another forty for other customers."

"I gave her my word," Clara protested.

"I didn't see your hand on a Bible," I said. I clutched my back again and sank into a chair. "I'm sure this monster child is a boy," I said. "He does nothing but kick. His father adores it, of course. He puts his hand there and chuckles like an eight-year-old."

In fact, the baby had not stirred. I was telling Clara I had better hopes of keeping Malcolm than she did.

I gazed sourly at my Seneca sister. "So I'm to give you a bill of exchange for the full amount, is that it?"

"I hope so," Clara said.

"Oh, it must be so. That captain of finance, Malcolm Stapleton, explained it all to me at dinner last night. I'm to tie up a fifth or sixth of my credit to keep you happy. Because if darling Clara is unhappy, he's unhappy too."

"I think it's fair," Clara said.

"Oh, very fair. While I'm shaped like the sail on a Hudson River sloop in a stiff breeze, you go to him and sigh and sob. You know as well as I do what was stiff by the time you finished with him."

I was talking like a Seneca again. Clara did not mind that as much as the implication that she had seduced Malcolm into the arrangement. "He thinks it's a good investment," she said.

"Let's hope he's right," Catalyntie said. "If I die giving birth to this monster in my belly, I hope you marry him, no matter what anyone says. He'll need you in more ways than one."

"You won't die," Clara said. "You'll go on and on, insisting* on your own way in everything, becoming colder and more unloving. I often pity Malcolm."

"But never a tear for me?" I said. "Have you ever thought I'm doing the best I can? Have you thought of where you might be without me? I mean, since I rescued you from your adventure in New Jersey?"

"I know all that!" Clara cried, almost weeping. "But I still want to get away from you—before you destroy me."

"Nothing can really separate us," I said. "Here's your bill of exchange."

I handed her the paper and stumbled out of the store, managing to conceal my tears until I was a block away. The bill was for the full amount of Clara's share, 1,426 pounds. I had not deducted any of the gifts to the whores or her African supplicants—or the Hughsons' debt.

Would she see it as a forlorn gesture of love? Probably not.

That night, Adam drew up a letter of agreement and he and Clara hurried through a chilling October drizzle to the Hughsons' tavern. Adam gazed up at the brick-fronted, timber-roofed building and pronounced it a noble acquisition. Inside was the usual mixture of sailors, whores, and average New Yorkers, drinking, eating, arguing, playing cards or dice.

Malcolm Stapleton was there, orating on what was likely to happen if war broke out. "Between the Spanish and the French West Indies fleets, they could ravage this coast before help arrives from England. The Walpole ministry has let the army and the navy decline to a pathetic state of weakness. We must convince London to take steps immediately to create regiments here in America—"

They extracted Malcolm from his admirers and told him the good news of my capitulation. He nodded. "She told me at dinner," he said. "Maybe it proves she loves you, Clara, in spite of her hard heart."

For a moment Clara almost wept. "I'm afraid you're right," she said.

In their disorderly office on the tavern's second floor, Sarah and John Hughson joyously signed the agreement, making Clara a half owner for a thousand pounds. Clara handed over the bill of exchange and Sarah Hughson offered her a bill drawn on her mother's house in Yonkers for the difference of four hundred twenty-six pounds. Adam wanted to go to Yonkers to inspect the place first but Clara said she trusted the Hughsons. Sarah vowed that the bill would receive priority among the tavern's debts, as soon as the outstanding obligations were paid.

John Hughson insisted on opening a bottle of their best port to celebrate the deal. "You're the answer to a year of prayers to the Virgin,'' Sarah said, beaming at Clara.

"The Virgin?" Clara said.

"I was raised a Catholic. We pray to the Virgin Mary. She never fails to answer a prayer,'' Sarah said.

Clara knew little about Catholicism beyond what Bogardus had taught us. "Where does she get her power?" she asked.

"From being the Mother of Jesus, the Son of God."

In the office doorway swayed Mary Worth, one of the city's older, fatter whores. "Oh, Sarah,'' she said in a singsong voice. "There's a captain downstairs who's lost his purse at cards—but he has pounds a-plenty on his ship—"

"Take him to room number ten,'' Sarah Hughson said. "But mind you get the money out of him tomorrow, hear?"

"Oh, I will, depend on it.''

Mary vanished and Mrs. Hughson finished her port. "I think the Virgin finds little fault with the sins of the flesh,'' she said.

Clara was amazed, knowing the harsh puritanism of the Dutch Reformed and other Protestant churches. She looked forward to learning more about this strange faith.

Downstairs Malcolm Stapleton helped John Hughson hoist Clara onto the bar and introduce her as the new half owner of the tavern. Hughson tried to make a speech of it, but the port had addled his not very abundant wits just enough to get the facts all wrong. He told everyone Clara had borrowed a thousand pounds from the Stapletons to rescue him from bankruptcy. Clara saw dismay on Malcolm's face—he knew the story would convince everyone in New York that Clara was his mistress. Was he unhappy because the story made him an unfaithful husband—or because it was not true? Clara wondered.

While Hughson talked, the faces of the crowd swirled

before Clara's eyes in the light from two huge iron chandeliers, each with a dozen blazing candles. Some white, some black, mostly young, they were a motley group—but she felt closer to them than she would ever feel to the customers of the Universal Store. Even if the good cheer they displayed was mostly the product of rum, it was better than the brittle jealousy and petty envy she saw so often among the rich.

One face caught her attention: her old friend Caesar. "Hey, beautiful, remember me?" he said, pushing his way to the bar as Malcolm lowered Clara to the floor.

"Of course I remember you," Clara said.

"She'd rather forget you," Malcolm said, shoving him away. Everyone who drank at the city's taverns knew Caesar. He made the rounds almost every night, often peddling stolen goods in return for drinks.

"What's this?" Caesar said. "The great assemblyman doesn't give a damn for a poor nigger who can't vote for him? Your little piece of chocolate cake had a better time with Caesar than she's ever had with you."

Malcolm punched Caesar in the face, sending him flying backward across a table of cardplayers to land in a heap with cards and bottles and rum in a mess around him. "What the hell was all that about?" one of the cardplayers asked.

"He just insulted this lady," Malcolm said.

Blood streamed from Caesar's nose. "You son of a bitch," he shouted. "There'll come a day when Caesar will make you sorry for that."

"Oh?" Malcolm said. "How will Caesar arrange that?"

"He won't arrange it alone. There'll be an army behind him. An army that will make all you English bastards beg for mercy."

"Oh?" Malcolm said. "Who'll be the general of this army, Caesar? You?"

"Maybe. I'll be one of the generals. I wasn't named Caesar by accident."

"Step aside," Malcolm said to the cardplayers. He approached Caesar, his fists raised in the style of a prizefighter. "Come on, General. We'll make this our first battleground."

He was a head taller and at least thirty pounds heavier than Caesar. Something propelled Clara from the bar into the dwindling space between the two men. "You've hurt him enough," she said to Malcolm.

She turned to Caesar. "Go to Dr. Hopper. He'll give you something for your pain. Tell him to send the bill to me."

"Thanks, beautiful," he said.

Caesar retreated into the night. Clara turned to confront a frowning Malcolm Stapleton. He and everyone else in the place were wondering if Caesar was telling the truth about being her black lover. They had just finished presuming Malcolm Stapleton was her white lover. It was not a very good way to start trying to make Hughson's a more respectable tavern.

"Why did you do that?" Malcolm asked.

"It wasn't a fair fight," Clara said.

"Fair or foul, I'll break his neck the next time I see him," Malcolm snarled.

"Not if you want my . . . my good opinion!" Clara said.

Malcolm stalked out of the tavern, leaving Clara surrounded by staring eyes. The story of the assemblyman's embarrassment would be all over New York tomorrow morning. Did she care?

The answer was yes. She still wished Malcolm Stapleton well. But in another part of her soul, a second answer whispered: *no*. She gazed slowly around her, absorbing the reality of the white and black faces mingled here. Twisted mouths, low sullen brows, hard obtuse eyes—fate had consigned them to the bottom of life's heap. They would never be part of the world of power and wealth that Catalyntie and Malcolm were struggling to enter. But they were part of her world now.

Free, Clara thought. For the first time she was truly free. She had chosen to turn her back on Catalyntie and Malcolm, to separate from them in this fundamental way. Her impulse to protect Caesar from Malcolm's superior strength was part of this freedom. Perhaps she could use it to heal some of the bitterness in Caesar's soul—and help other Africans find a place in this misshapen American world.

"As long as I own a share of this place," Clara said. "Quarrels, brawls, hateful talk of any kind, will be forbidden here. Let's celebrate my partnership by treating everyone to their favorite drink."

A rumble of approval rose from the crowd. They swarmed to the bar. Cicely, the red-haired Irish whore, threw her arms around Clara. "I told them you had a heart as big as County Mayo!" she cried. "Sure now you've proved it."

Clara kissed her red mouth. "We're all brothers and sisters," she said.

"Oh, I don't know about that!" Cicely said. "My brothers never did the sort of things half the loafers in this place have done to me."

As laughter and good cheer became general, John Hughson lowered his big bald head and whispered to his new partner: "I'm glad you saved Caesar from a drubbing. I'm obliged to him for a good bit of income each year."

"How is that?"

Hughson winked. "You know how Caesar operates. He needs a place to stash his stolen goods. He's in business like you or me. We get a nice cut of the profits."

Around them, the whores and their friends were exchanging more jokes and insults. Why, surrounded by this cheer, did Clara sense evil in Hughson's offhand words? Was the big man's carelessness about the line between honesty and dishonesty as unacceptable in its way as Catalyntie's passion for profits?

Sympathy for the ill-fated warred with Clara's instinctive honesty. The memory of Malcolm Stapleton looming over Caesar, his white fist raised to smash his battered black face, suddenly became more important than the strictures of the law. She said nothing.

TWO

SWEAT MATTED MY HAIR, SOAKED the pillow, drenched my nightgown. The labor pains were coming every few seconds, each one like a spike driven through my back. But I had yet to utter a sound. The doctor, a young Englishman named Tracy, was amazed. For the third or fourth time, he told Clara most women screamed and moaned and sobbed.

Clara bathed my face with a cold cloth. "She's a Seneca," she said. "We learned to bear pain from our mothers' example."

I had sent for Clara when the labor began. It was not because I needed her to maintain a Seneca standard of stoicism—at least, that is what I told myself. I wanted Clara to see the impact of a son on Malcolm Stapleton. The Moon Woman was still trying to exorcise her fear that Clara could take Malcolm away from her.

"I can see the head," the doctor said. "Push! Hard! Harder!"

The pain came in blinding flashes now, darkening the room. I clutched the bedposts with both hands and pushed. Once and for all, I was freeing myself of this monster. He seemed to be sucking my insides with him. How could anyone call this natural? It was enough to make me believe the priests and ministers were right— some original sin had inflicted this ordeal on women.

"I've got him!" the doctor cried.

Triumphantly, he held up a red creature with the pinched face of a corpse. He whacked him on the bottom and the baby unleashed a howl that shook the roof.

"A boy?" I asked. There was so much sweat in my eyes, I saw everything through a salty haze.·

"A boy."

The Evil Brother was keeping his part of the promise. Now Malcolm would never leave me. After the doctor cut the umbilical cord, Clara wrapped the child in a blanket and held him in her arms, exuding the tenderness that came so naturally to her. "He's beautiful," she said. "You must be so happy."

Good riddance, was all I could think. Until I watched Clara give the baby to Malcolm. He cradled the infant in his huge arms, gazing at him with total rapture. "Now we have a reason to get rich," he said.

Rubbing the salty sweat from my eyes, I studied Clara's face. I saw regret and disapproval flicker there at hearing Malcolm subscribe to his wife's view of life. But Clara managed to maintain her smile. "I'm sure he'll be a warrior like his father," Clara said.

The hell he will, I thought. No son of mine was going to die in battle. I would raise him to be the most successful merchant in America—and Europe. He would learn to speak Dutch and French and German and trade with all of them. He would inherit my money and quintuple it. But for now the main source of contentment was his power to bind Malcolm to me forever. Let the Evil Brother demand his reckoning eventually. I had my heart's desire, beyond all blandishments.

"What shall we name him?" Malcolm said.

"Cornelius," I said. "After my grandfather."

"I was thinking of Hugh, after my grandfather," Malcolm said. "The one who fought in the Civil War."[1]

"That can be his middle name."

"Cornelius Hugh Stapleton," Clara said. "He sounds powerful. Important."

"He will be," I said.

"God willing," Malcolm said.

Whether God wills it or not, I thought.

The next day, I was out of bed, working in the store, while the doctor tut-tutted and half our customers warned me I was risking my life. I ignored them. I had seen Seneca mothers give birth in the morning and hoe corn in the afternoon. I carried the baby with me in a sack on my back, well wrapped in a warm blanket, and nursed him in the rear of the store when business was slow.

Business was soon worse than slow, it was terrible. We had sold the best cloth and a hefty percentage of the rest of the stock that Captain Van Oorst had brought from Holland on his most recent voyage. I had been forced to replenish my shelves from Nicholas Cruger and other large importers from England, driving my prices up and my profits down. As I fretted over the prospect of a sinking income, Captain Van Oorst arrived in town with a cargo of beaver skins and suggested I join him on his voyage to Amsterdam. I could meet my Dutch suppliers and perhaps persuade them to give me enough credit to launch the Mohawk store I planned to compete with Philip Van Sluyden's monopoly of the fur trade. My pregnancy—and the slow pace of my lawsuit against my uncle—had forced me to postpone this grand ambition.

Over Malcolm's objections—he feared for the baby's health while I was gone—I decided to make the voyage. Once more I was calling on my Indian heritage; Seneca

[1]*He is referring to the English Civil War of 1642–49.*

men took care of the children while the women worked in the fields. I hired a wet nurse—an Irishwoman named Bridget McCarthy who had recently given birth and whose breasts still had plenty of milk—and was ready to depart.

"Adam can run the store," I said. "Malcolm, you must press the new governor to settle the suit against my uncle. You're in a perfect position to do it. He needs you in the assembly. Get him to issue a writ of error and set up a special chancery court with him as judge and jury."

"But that's so dishonest. People will say we're misusing the law—exactly the way Nicolls did."

"Who gives a damn what people say? We've got Uncle Johannes on the run. He's lost his assembly seat, his protector Nicolls. Now is the time to finish him off. I thought you were a soldier—a warrior."

Fury mottled Malcolm's face. "I can see motherhood isn't going to change you."

Slamming doors behind him, he stamped out of the house. For the rest of the week, the argument raged, with Malcolm resisting my idea. I mocked him. Did he or didn't he want to get rich? Did he care about our son? I was risking my life on a winter passage to Amsterdam to expand our business. Still he said no.

I suddenly realized why. "You've talked to Clara about this, haven't you?"

He said nothing. "Damn her! Why and how has she appointed herself the keeper of your conscience?"

"She said I should remind you of a promise you made her—about me. What was it?"

"Never mind," I said. The memory unnerved me for a moment. Quickly, the Evil Brother whispered: *But you promised nothing about your own actions.*

On the day before I sailed, Cornelius Hugh Stapleton was christened at the First Dutch Reformed Church. Governor Clarke and his wife were among the guests at a reception we gave for our friends after the ceremony. A portly, avuncular man, the governor had already displayed more than ordinary friendship for Malcolm. Like him, he was a member of the Patriot Party's American branch. His Excellency was convinced it was time to assert English power in Europe and America instead of trimming and truckling to the French in Prime Minister Robert Walpole's style. He was in thorough agreement with Malcolm's ideas about the importance of winning the fur trade war with the French in Canada.

Finding Malcolm and the governor chatting in a corner of the front parlor, I joined them. "Your Excellency," I said. "I'm sailing to Holland tomorrow to attempt to borrow enough money to save my business. If I don't survive the voyage, I wonder if you would consider doing a kindness for my little son—"

While Malcolm watched in mute dismay, I told the governor the story of my lawsuit against Johannes Van Vorst. I produced enough tears to dampen my cheeks and melt his politician's heart to putty, describing my parents' murders, adding spontaneously invented horrors of my Indian captivity, and embellishing my return to find my estate looted.

"My dear Mrs. Stapleton," the governor said. "When you return from Holland, you'll find your estate restored to you—or my name is not George Clarke. This is something we shall undertake together, eh, Stapleton?"

"I would be . . . honored," Malcolm choked.

That night—which we both knew might be our last night together—Mr. and Mrs. Stapleton lay beside each other in the darkness after Malcolm snuffed out the candle. An autumn wind howled off the Hudson, suggesting the dangers of an Atlantic passage at this time of year. But Malcolm could find no words of tender farewell.

"You're determined to turn me into a scoundrel, aren't you?" he said. "Have you thought about what might happen if you succeed?"

"I'm trying to turn you into a man who sees the world as a place of strife—as demanding of nerve and courage as your imaginary battlefields. There's no room in it for your patriotic moonshine."

"You're wrong. Every man needs a cause—king and country, Protestant freedom against Catholic tyranny."

"Bosh. Men fight for glory, power, fame."

We left it that way—my Dutch alienation from English patriotism and his worship of it lay like a wall of brass between us. Bitter experience would teach me that Malcolm was right, especially in his case. Without his ideal vision Malcolm would become a hollow man in front of my mortified eyes.

Only as I said good-bye to the baby did I waver about leaving him. What if this little creature died? The Evil Brother was capable of every imaginable treachery. Malcolm would blame me and I would lose him forever. I clutched the child to my breasts, then handed him back to the wet nurse.

"If there's the slightest concern for his health, consult Clara Flowers at Hughson's Tavern. She'll know what to do."

"Aye, ma'am."

I had more confidence in the prayers and spells we had learned as Senecas than I had in Dr. Tracy's pills and potions. I had seen the village shaman retrieve more than one member of my longhouse from the brink of death.

Sending my trunk to the ship, I rushed to Hughson's. Clara was behind the bar, serving drinks. The taproom was quiet at midday, but none of the customers were the sort of people I would let into the Universal Store. Once more I was confounded by Clara's preference for the poor and downtrodden of this world. I felt no such pity. It was simply foreign to my soul.

"I'm sailing with the tide, as you probably know," I said. "If the Atlantic swallows me like the first Catalyntie, I will you the child—and Malcolm. Find a way to love him in spite of your infirmity. Consult Adam. He may know something about such things—having committed the original hurt.''

We embraced, almost sisters again for a moment. ''I wish you wouldn't go,'' Clara said. ''I had a bad dream about you last night.''

I almost abandoned the voyage on the spot. ''What was it?''

''Never mind.''

''Did I looked drowned?''

''No. Very much alive.''

''Then dream on. I'll dare the Evil Brother to do his worst as long as I have life in me.''

Clara looked grave. Did she sense I was serious? Whatever she thought, she said nothing. We kissed good-bye and Clara said: ''I'll pray for you every day.''

For the next six weeks, I clung to these words as Captain Van Oorst's ship battled the howling winds and mountainous seas of the North Atlantic. I was the only passenger. More than once I wondered if the leaky old freighter, quaintly named *The Orange Prince*,[2] could possibly hold together as immense waves laid her on her beam ends. Several times, the mainsail sheets parted and the sailors had to struggle aloft to seize the flailing lines before the great square of canvas flapped itself to pieces.

But Killian Van Oorst was a canny sailor. He conned his ship through the murderous waves and winds and by December 1, we had passed the French and English coasts and were in the whitecapped Zuider Zee. Soon, under bright sunshine, we were gliding up the ice-choked estuary of the Amstel, the river that had given Amsterdam—originally *Amstelleddamme*—the dam in

[2] *After William of Orange, the Dutch Protestant ruler who became King of England in 1689, in the revolution that expelled the pro-Catholic James II.*

the Amstel—its name. Snowflakes swirled down as Van
Oorst expertly docked at one of the wharfs. I gazed in
astonishment at the thousands of ships and the immense
city they sustained.

I staggered like a sailor as I tried to negotiate a paved
sidewalk that did not pitch and toss like the *Orange
Prince*'s deck. Captain Van Oorst laughed and caught
my arm. Two of his sailors commandeered a wheelbar-
row for my trunk and followed us inland to a street of
magnificent houses overlooking a canal. Their fronts
were lined with marble and dozens of servants were out
scrubbing every inch of them, standing on ladders and
platforms.

Although hundreds of people hurried along the sidewalks, wrapped in cloaks or fur-lined greatcoats against
the intense cold, there was none of New York's clamor.
All was quiet and orderly. Even the horses pulling big
sleighs across the numerous canal bridges were sedate
and virtually noiseless. There was also not a trace of
New York's stenches and garbage in the streets. The
sidewalks and gutters were as clean as the floor of my
New York parlor. The size of the houses, the glimpses
of countless other streets radiating from some central
point to the horizon, were overwhelming. How could a
stranger make an impression in such a place?

"This is the Heerengracht," Van Oorst said. The
Lord's Canal, I quickly translated.

He led me to the door of one of the largest houses on
the street and rapped the brass knocker. A plump young
pink-cheeked maid answered it. She greeted the captain
with a curtsy and a broad smile.

"Tell Mrs. Hooft her uncle is here with the Indian
princess," the captain said.

He gave me one of his sly smiles. On the long voyage,
we had dined together in his cabin every day. We had
talked mostly about New York politics. I had learned
little about him—beyond his remark that he was the

youngest of ten brothers and that was why he had gone to America to make a living.

The interior of the house was awesome. The huge rooms had marble walls and floors, each of a different color. Behind a half dozen breakfronts gleamed a fortune in fine china. Oriental rugs like Cornelius Van Vorst had owned—but three times the size—were everywhere. On the walls were dozens of paintings of individuals and groups of men and women, as well as summer scenes on rivers and canals, brightened by fields of tulips.

Into the parlor strode a tall, remarkably attractive young woman in a dark green satin gown decorated with exquisite arabesques of white lace. Her chestnut hair was lightly powdered beneath a lace cap and she wore far more lipstick and rouge on her face than any respectable woman in New York would dare to use. Captain Van Oorst introduced his niece, Tesselschade Hooft.

"How wonderful to meet someone with a new story to tell!" she cried and embraced me.

"I took the liberty of telling my family and friends about your captivity among the Senecas," Captain Van Oorst said. "They were fascinated and urged me to bring you to them in person."

"You must stay with us as our guest," Mrs. Hooft said. "As soon as you recover from your voyage, we'll give a dinner party in your honor. All our friends are in a passion to meet you. We know so little of the savages of America."

"I'll be honored—but I must warn you I'm no scholar on the subject of the Indians. I only know what I experienced," I said.

"That's precisely what will create a sensation in Amsterdam," Mrs. Hooft said. "Let me show you to your rooms."

On the second floor, I was ushered into two large rooms, each the size of the second floor of my New York house. A coal fire crackled in a grate. A huge canopied bed had been turned down and a tray with a bottle of wine and sweetmeats stood on a small table beside it. My trunk soon arrived and two cheerful maids helped me hang my clothes in a great mahogany wardrobe.

That night I dined with Mrs. Hooft and her husband in a dining room with walls and ceiling of alabaster. The husband, Philip, was a short, plump man of thirty-five or forty, with an ugly, froglike face. But he had the manners and *savoir-faire* of a prince. I soon learned that my hostess was the daughter of the captain's oldest brother, who had made a fortune in the East Indies trade. Philip Hooft was the son of another wealthy man, one of Amsterdam's burgomasters. He had died ten years ago and Philip had inherited this splendid house and the bank his father had founded.

"When Uncle Killian told me the barbarities the English had tried to perpetrate on you in Albany, I immediately urged Philip to endorse the credit you needed to outfit your store in New York," Mrs. Hooft said. "Has it prospered?"

I told her I was making a profit of thirty percent and had brought with me payment in full for the latest shipment of goods. Both Hoofts were delighted. "One or two people at the bank had doubts about loaning money to someone so young," Philip Hooft said.

After dinner, Mrs. Hooft introduced me to her son, Willem, a thin, nervous eight-year-old who proudly informed her that he spoke English and French and could read Latin. His mother gazed at him with almost overwhelming affection, smoothing his blond hair, patting his rumpled jacket. "He has great promise. I pray that God will protect him. I lost another boy to the smallpox three years ago," she said.

The remark filled me with nameless terror for my infant son in New York. I pleaded with the Evil Brother to befriend him. He could have my soul for two eternities.

The next day, Philip Hooft invited me to join him in a trip to the bank, which was in a building on the Dam, Amsterdam's great square. "You may be interested in how we make money over here," he said.

What an understatement. I sat beside him at a massive gold-trimmed teak desk, studying the documents that were brought from other floors for his approval. Should they risk two hundred thousand guilders to insure an East India ship, which was now two weeks overdue? The owners were willing to pay forty thousand guilders for the coverage, in a desperate attempt to cover their losses.

"I have a feeling you're bringing us luck," Philip Hooft said, as he approved the insurance. "If the ship returns, half the payment will be yours. It will be your St. Nicholas Day present."

December 6, the feast of St. Nicholas, was less than a week away. I had almost forgotten this gift-giving tradition, which had been abandoned by the Dutch in English New York. My head swam. This man was rich enough to casually give me twenty thousand guilders, five thousand pounds—more than my total capital!

This was only the first of many transactions I witnessed that day that made my breath catch. A certain Madame d'Urfe of Paris wished to sell ten thousand shares in the Swedish East India Company for two million guilders. Philip Hooft bought them for half that price, convincing the lady's Venetian agent that the weakness of the Swedish thaler made an immediate sale advisable. After the agent departed, he coolly informed me that the Swedish thaler was expected to rebound and he would probably clear one hundred thousand guilders on the deal.

"How much capital does the House of Hooft have at its command?" I said.

"Oh, about a hundred million guilders," Philip Hooft said. "We're not very big compared to the House of de Neufville and the other giants."

Once more, my head whirled. A hundred million guilders was twenty million pounds. In New York, a merchant was considered rich when he was worth a hundred thousand pounds. For the rest of the morning, Philip Hooft swapped currencies with half the nations of Europe, bought and sold stock in the Dutch and English East Indies companies and the Bank of England, and purchased a ten percent share in next year's Baltic grain fleet, which was a major source of Amsterdam's wealth. Finally he decided we had done enough business for the day and escorted me across the expanse of the Dam to visit the Stock Exchange, on the river side of the great square.

Two hundred feet long and 124 feet wide, with a majestic carillon and clock tower at one end, the Exchange had an inner courtyard where the brokers in their black hats and black breeches clustered in good weather. In the numerous arcades were merchants who dealt with the Levant, with Russia, with the West Indies and other parts of the world, as well as specialists in timber, stone, grain, and other commodities. Whenever a deal was struck, the payer and payee adjusted their trading balances in the Bank of Amsterdam, across the Dam on the first floor of the City Hall.

"The Exchange is very democratic," Philip Hooft remarked. "Anyone who keeps a balance of a hundred thousand guilders can trade in his own name."

My guide inhaled a pinch of snuff. "Eventually, you must keep an account here, yourself," he told me. "A bill of exchange drawn on the Bank of Amsterdam is as good as gold or silver anywhere in the world. We can trade for you on the Exchange while you're in America."

"If our East India ship comes in, I'll open an account with my share immediately," I said.

"In that case we'll try to build it up before you leave," Philip Hooft said.

That evening, Mrs. Hooft gave a dinner party for twenty-four people in her splendid dining room. The table was a blaze of fine silver and china. Tulips and other flowers grown in nearby hothouses filled the room with color. I wore my best New York gown—a sea green damask that was tasteful, yet basically simple in design and decoration. I did not attempt to use lipstick or rouge in the Amsterdam style—I decided to be nothing more or less than an American, not an imitation European.

At the table, the guests asked me a hundred questions about my Indian life. They seemed particularly anxious to discover if Indians were cannibals, like the tribesmen Dutch sailors encountered in Africa. I assured them that the Senecas ate only captured warriors—after subjecting them to torture to enable them to demonstrate their courage. I talked at much greater length about the virtues of the Senecas, their sense of honor, their hospitality to visitors, their loyalty to their clans and nation, and the league of the Iroquois.

"Did they eat your parents?" asked one plump woman who wore a glittering necklace of diamonds across her ample bosom. She was both horrified and titillated by the possibility.

"An enemy is eaten only to acquire his courage. My parents were not warriors."

Another urgent question was whether Indian women were chaste. "Once a woman marries, she's as chaste as any white woman," I said. "But before marriage she may have several lovers."

"Just like the Dutch," said a man named Vondel. He had a sly arrogant expression that reminded me of Robert Foster Nicolls. The grandson of a famous playwright, he seemed to be a particular friend of Philip Hooft.

Vondel's remark stirred a vehement argument about the chastity of Dutch women, which ended with the general agreement that they were taught to be chaste and generally were, but they were not entirely sure they would be unhappy if they were not.

"Can you advise the ladies on this point, Mrs. Stapleton?" asked Vondel.

I liked this cynical man-about-town less and less. "Do you want me to speak as a Seneca or a white woman?" I said.

"Either," Vondel said.

"I think in either case it's a cause of regret in a woman's soul—if she gives her love and discovers it's unrequited. But it's especially sad if she's white. Because our moralists are so unforgiving."

Tesselschade Hooft raised her wineglass and said: "To our American cousin and her profound morality!"

As the guests departed, Philip Hooft announced an intention to stroll home with his friend Vondel for a taste of his superfine gin. Alone, Tesselschade embraced me and told me I had been "magnificent." She especially liked my answer to Vondel. "He was my faithless lover," she said. "Fortunately, I had wealth and an understanding father. Do you love your husband?"

"Yes," I said.

"How fortunate. I don't. My father arranged the marriage. That's the way it's done here. It's almost always a matter of money marrying money."

For a moment I was assailed by an overwhelming desire for Malcolm Stapleton. Was it the Master of Life, not the Evil Brother, who had arranged that eruption of desire on the shore of Lake Ontario? I suddenly wanted to spend the rest of the night talking to this gentle sensitive woman about the meaning of the word *love*. Was it impossible to love a man with a frog's face? Or was it the lack of free choice? Or some kind of wound inflicted by the faithless Vondel? Had Robert Foster Nicolls inflicted a similar wound on me?

"Is your husband faithful to you?" I asked.

"Of course not. I told him I didn't want more children. I didn't enjoy the whole process. Did you?"

"Not the labor pains but the rest—"

"How lucky you are," Tesselschade Hooft said.

The next day, Mrs. Hooft awoke me with a cheerful cry: "You've become famous! I told you all Amsterdam would be enthralled."

She handed me a newspaper. I was horrified by the story, which was not even close to the truth. It quoted me as saying I had watched the Senecas eat my parents and claimed I admitted to dining on human flesh in my later years as a captive. It portrayed the Senecas' sexual habits as a series of orgies—with the clear implication that I had been involved in more than one.

When I expressed my dismay to Tesselschade Hooft, she dismissed it with a wave. "It was written by Vondel. He owns the paper. No one believes anything in it but the shipping and stock reports."

In my head, something or someone whispered *beware*. At breakfast, Philip Hooft was all smiles and compliments about my "performance" last night. Vondel said he had never met anyone so exotic in his life. A beautiful Dutch woman with the mind of an Indian! I saw there was no point in complaining to him about the newspaper story.

Once more I was invited to the House of Hooft on the Dam. There delightful news awaited us. The East Indiaman had arrived safely in the dawn. The owners had already paid their forty thousand guilders of insurance money with thanks. Philip Hooft promptly wrote a bill of exchange on the Bank of Amsterdam for twenty thousand guilders and strolled across the Dam to help me open my account in the bank's gilded offices.

Back in the Hooft bank, Philip announced it was time to improve my account. The bank would buy in my name four hundred newly minted gold ducats for four million guilders. The price of gold on the Exchange was low. A trusted friend would carry them to Frankfurt, Germany, where gold was selling three points higher. They would exchange the ducats for bills on the Bank of Amsterdam—and make an instant profit of forty thousand guilders.

"Where can I find someone to carry four million guilders of gold to Frankfurt?" I said.

Philip Hooft shrugged. "After that story in Vondel's paper, I'm sure you can command almost anyone. Vondel himself. Or me."

"I can't imagine how I could persuade him—or you— to undertake such a large task," I said.

In fact, I saw exactly what I was expected to do. "We could discuss it at Vondel's rooms over a good dinner," Philip Hooft said. "Tesselschade is taking our son to visit his grandfather. She won't return until tomorrow."

Forty thousand guilders. Eight thousand pounds. In return, I would let Messrs. Vondel and Hooft do what they pleased with me for a day and a night. *Was it so terrible?* the Evil Brother asked. I would have Philip Hooft hungrily awaiting my next visit to Amsterdam. Meanwhile he would be making strenuous efforts to improve my account on the Exchange.

Suddenly Clara was whispering in my head: *This will prove you love nothing but money.* Somehow I found that unacceptable. I wanted to believe I loved Malcolm— and our son. I wanted them to love me. But how would accepting Hooft's offer affect this love, which only existed in distant New York? They would never learn about my infidelity in Amsterdam. When I was in New York, I would continue to love them extravagantly. Money would enable me to prove it with gifts, power, influence.

It will prove it to the only person who matters: yourself. Did the resistance hardening around Clara's words mean Catalyntie Van Vorst had a soul? A spiritual self that she valued more than money, perhaps even more than her heart's desire? It was not a Dutch or an English soul—any more than it was an American soul—though it partook of that last word. It was a woman's soul and in the name of that invisible, evanescent inner self, was I going to say no to Philip Hooft's tempting offer?

Not quite. I would show him that Americans, particularly those raised by the Seneca, had more than their share of guile. How often had I heard stories in the longhouse of warriors who were trapped by their enemies and outwitted them with clever words or stratagems?

I smiled boldly into Philip Hooft's protruding frog's eyes. "Dear Philip. I wouldn't dream of putting you or Mr. Vondel to such a journey. I'll take the ducats to Frankfurt myself. If I can survive in America's forests, surely I can manage in civilized Christian Europe."

"I wouldn't dream of letting you do it. Unscrupulous men are always—"

"Perhaps your uncle, Captain Van Oorst, can accompany me."

Stymied, he had to let me go in search of Captain Van Oorst. One of the servants at the Hooft house said he was staying at the inn, Ster Van Oosten. By now it was noon. The innkeeper told me the captain was still in his room. I mounted to the second floor and pounded on the door. The captain opened it in his woolen underwear. Behind him a slouching dissolute-looking young man peered impudently at me.

"Let me in, goddamn you," I said. I shoved my way into the room and began telling the captain how low I thought he was. "You transported me to Amsterdam like a piece of goods to be auctioned off to your nephew-in-law and his friends for a few thousand guilders. When I get back to New York, I'll tell my husband and he'll fillet you like a flounder and feed you to the sharks."

"I don't know what you're talking about!" Van Oorst protested.

"The hell you don't," I said. "Get on your clothes. You and I are going on a little trip to Frankfurt."

"Who *is* this creature?" asked the young man. He talked and acted more like a woman, flouncing around the room, picking up his clothes.

"A passenger," Captain Van Oorst said. Something in the way he said this made me wonder if I should return to America aboard his ship. I might join the first Catalyntie in the depths.

The muttering captain got himself dressed and accompanied me to the Hooft Bank on the Dam. There we found an agitated Philip Hooft on his way out the door. "I'm so sorry," he said. "I'm afraid the deal with the ducats is off. The price of gold has just gone down in Frankfurt. A messenger arrived with the news only a half hour ago. Are you sure you won't join me for dinner at Vondel's? There are many other opportunities we could explore."

"I'm *so* sorry," I said with the same exquisite courtesy. "But I must begin buying the goods I'll need for next season. I have a long list."

"She's a woman of business, isn't she, Captain?" Philip Hooft said. "The Senecas couldn't change that Dutch trait."

"Aye," said Captain Van Oorst sourly. Once more I thought I saw murder in his eyes. Was a fat commission vanishing?

Suddenly my heart, which had been clutched like a fist in my breast, soared into the blue December sky. I almost wept with gratitude for Clara's presence in my soul. Perhaps with her help I was destined to outwit the Evil Brother after all.

THREE

FOR THE NEXT TWO MONTHS, Philip Hooft watched hungrily as I came and went from his splendid house on the Heerengracht. Each day his eyes seemed to protrude a little further, his pendulous lower lip seemed to thicken and droop another fraction of an inch. Soon I could think of him only as the Frog. Behind this derision I was scrupulously polite and occasionally flirtatious. I complimented him on his colorful Parisian clothes. Everyone in Amsterdam aped the Paris fashions. I let him take me iceboating on the frozen Amstel, and rode with him and Tesselschade in a *schuit*—a canal boat, towed by horses—for a visit to the Hague, the ornate capital of the Netherlands, where I was presented at the court of the current Prince of Orange, the country's theoretical ruler.

I attended concerts, plays, readings of poems as Philip Hooft's ghostly third, the woman of his wilderness desires. Occasionally we encountered Vondel, who one night asked me candidly how long I was planning to torture his friend. Was my skill in this black art something I had learned among the Senecas?

I pretended I did not know what he was talking about. "In America, we women are *innocent* about such matters. Why don't you put that in your paper?" I said.

At the Hague, we met a fat cheerful older woman, the Countess Van Osteen, who greeted Philip with great affection. She had read about me in Vondel's paper but assured me she did not believe a word of it. The countess talked in brilliant spurts of sarcasm and wit about the probability of war in Europe between the Catholic and Protestant powers. The Spanish were prodding the French into it, hoping they would demolish the Netherlands. The Dutch were depending on the English to protect them, in the name of Protestant solidarity. "We certainly can't protect ourselves," she said. "Our so-called government is a joke."

Tesselschade Hooft agreed. She explained to me that the Prince of Orange was more figurehead than ruler. Fearing tyranny, when the Dutch won their independence from Spain they had left most of the power in the hands of the cities, who frequently chose to ignore the Hague's feeble attempts at guiding the country. "Politics bores us. We prefer to make money—or love," Tesselschade said.

"At my age, money is more interesting," the Countess Van Osteen said. She began quizzing Philip Hooft about the best buys on the Amsterdam Stock Exchange.

On the way back to Amsterdam, Tesselschade told Catalyntie that the countess had been a great beauty in her youth. "Philip's father was one of her lovers."

Philip Hooft gazed longingly at me, his frog's eyes pleading. *See?* they groaned, *I am asking you for nothing truly forbidden.* Over the past three months, I had almost grown sorry for him, watching him endure the icy irreversible loathing with which his wife regarded him. However, in the best Dutch tradition, I did not permit pity to interfere with business. I used Philip's name to obtain a line of credit from the Bank of Amsterdam to finance the Mohawk River store, as well as to buy two thousand pounds of luxury merchandise for the Universal Store in New York City.

As I bought my goods at shops and warehouses in the port section of the city, I saw women from the *speelhuisen* or "musicos" where men went for the satisfaction they could not obtain from their wives. Like most prostitutes, they were sad tattered-looking creatures by day. Was Philip reduced to these women? I wondered. But I remained firmly anchored to the resolution I had made that morning in the Hooft Bank on the Dam.

Finally, the last of my goods was safely stored in the hold of *The Orange Prince*. It was time to depart. I had decided to sail with Captain Van Oorst after all. I had said nothing to the Hoofts about his fondness for young men—and this had restored our relationship to something approximating an armed truce. The longer I stayed in Amsterdam, the less fault I found with his advertising me as an acquiescent Indian princess. Everything in this vast commercial city had a price.

Rarely did the Hoofts invite people to dinner without the prospect of improving some moneys. Vondel's paper was wholly owned and financed by Philip Hooft. He used it not merely to further his erotic ambitions but to spread news that made his speculation in currencies and commodities and investments in cargoes more likely to succeed. A Vondel-pushed rumor of war between Spain and England sent the price of grain soaring, doubling the value of the bank's investment in this year's Baltic fleet.

Politics both in Holland and England were viewed entirely in commercial terms. The Protestant succession, the English Patriot Party, were amusing—or annoying—excrescences to the main point: profits on land and sea. England's corrupt prime minister, Robert Walpole, against whom Malcolm Stapleton and his friends railed in the name of patriotism, was a hero in Amsterdam. Philip Hooft praised the way Walpole had ignored for years now the demands of the Patriots for war against Spain for seizing British ships and abusing British seamen in the Caribbean. With the largest merchant marine in the world and no army or navy worth mentioning, the Dutch wanted war with nobody. As they saw it, only fools and fanatics fought wars, which multiplied death, debt, and taxes—and interfered with business. On this point Philip and I were in hearty agreement.

On the day I sailed, Tesselschade Hooft revealed how much she knew about the inner drama of her American guest's visit. "I can't decide whether I should thank you or chastise you for failing to requite my husband's passion," she said in her aloof way.

"Do you really wish I had?" I asked.

"I suppose I would admire you less," she said. "But I would have understood. He would have showered you with guilders. He calls out your name in the night. I've never seen him so obsessed."

"I would have admired myself less."

"Are you sure your husband has been faithful to you all these months?"

"We can't be sure of anything in such matters," I said. "But I hope so."

"I hope so too, for your sake," Tesselschade said.

Those last words coiled around my throat and burned there like the switches of a thornbush for the entire voyage back to New York. Sailing on a springtime ocean, we scarcely saw a single angry wave—but that only made me more anxious. By the time we sighted the looming highlands of New Jersey, I could barely think about anything but Malcolm Stapleton crushing me against his huge chest with a welcoming kiss.

I left Captain Van Oorst unloading the ship in Sag Harbor—yes, I was still a smuggler—and hired a horse and chaise that took me to the Brooklyn-Manhattan ferry. Rushing up the muddy garbage-strewn streets to our brick house on Depeyster Street, I found only Shirley, our African cook, and my son, Cornelius Hugh Stapleton, with his nurse, Bridget. The two servants were both cooing over the baby, who was sitting up, gazing with alert but puzzled eyes at this strange lady looming over him. When I picked him up, he burst into tears and reached for his nurse.

"Aw now, Hughie darlin', it's all right," Bridget said.

"Hughie?" I said. "That's not his name."

"It's what his father calls him. I don't think we could break the habit now," Bridget said.

"Where is his father?" I said.

"Like as not he's at Hughson's."

"Go down there and tell him I'm home," I said.

In ten minutes Malcolm was in the hall calling: "Catalyntie?"

I handed the baby to Shirley and ran to meet him. My kiss was violent enough to meet any standard of romance—but the ferocity all came from me. He barely responded with any force of his own.

I clung to him, burying my face in his shirt. "I thought of you every night," I said. "Did you think of me?"

"Of course," he said.

The words were flat, perfunctory. There was no vibration of desire in them. My heart struggled to accept the inevitable. He was a man, after all. He had gone to the whores to relieve his need. What else did I expect? Still, Tesselschade Hooft's thorny words tightened cruelly around my throat.

Malcolm decreed a dinner party to welcome me home. Adam Duycinck, Clara, her partners, the Hughsons, Guert Cuyler and his wife, and two Patriot assemblymen friends and their wives joined us for a merry feast. We had something to celebrate besides my homecoming. Governor Clarke had settled my lawsuit against my uncle resoundingly in my favor. Johannes Van Vorst had been ordered to pay the full value of Cornelius's property in cash—and the Mohawk lands had been wrested from the Van Sluydens and restored to me.

"You're a bloody princess!" Adam Duycinck howled.

"The question is—shall we live to spend the money," Malcolm said.

"Why shouldn't we?" I said.

"Haven't you heard? We're at war with Spain."

I listened, bemused, as Malcolm discoursed passionately on the way the Patriot Party had finally embarrassed Prime Minister Walpole into declaring war. A sailor named Robert Jenkins, who had been seized by the Spanish eight years ago during a Caribbean melee in which they had severed his ear, had appeared before Parliament calling for revenge, with the ear pickled in a jar. The uproar in the newspapers had been so severe, Walpole had been forced to declare war on the unrepentant Spanish.

Now the question was how hard the "Great Corrupter," as Malcolm and other Patriots persisted in calling Walpole, would fight the war. Would he abandon the exposed American colonies to the depredations of the Spanish fleet—or would he take the offensive and seize the Spanish islands of the Caribbean? Malcolm hoped New York would play a leading part in such an assault. He was calling for a militia bill to raise an American army that would be ready to sail as soon as the British fleet arrived to transport them to the Caribbean. He had sent messengers to New Jersey and Pennsylvania, urging them to join New York in this warlike measure.

Listening to my husband and his excited friends, I could only imagine how they would be viewed at a dinner table in Amsterdam. I could hear Vondel or Philip Hooft dismissing them as naive idealists, colonials hopelessly out of touch with Europe's reality—and menaces to business in the bargain.

Clara had little to say during the dinner. She and her partners, the Hughsons, did not seem enthusiastic about the war. "I've never seen a war do much but drive up the price of bread for the poor," Hughson said. Clara seemed more interested in persuading New York City's Common Council to give more help to the poor—which the cost of fighting a war would prevent. She talked of several people who had frozen to death in unheated rooms during the bitter cold of January and February.

Finally, the guests departed and Malcolm and I were alone. I kissed him boldly on the mouth and whispered: "That party could have waited until tomorrow night."

"I thought you'd want to celebrate the good news about your lawsuit," he said.

"There's only one thing I want to celebrate," I said.

In bed, I readied myself for the usual swift, almost violent assault. He was still my heart's desire—that was the only thing that mattered. I would not insist on niceties. But a different man took me in his arms. The bedroom gladiator had vanished. He kissed me softly, tenderly, and said: "We must become more like lovers. Don't you want that?"

"Yes, of course," I said, barely disguising my amazement.

Instead of a swift fierce conquest, there was a slow dreamlike mixture of kisses and caresses, a minuet instead of the throbbing drums of an Eagle Dance. When he entered me, he was gentle, almost meditative. Slow careful thrusts were followed by more kisses, more caresses. I began to puzzle over the mystery of this transformation. What explained it? I had expected the old mixture of anger and lust. Now I began to wonder if I preferred it. This gentle dance was lasting too long; my blood was barely stirring.

No, there was a rising tide of desire, it lapped at the edges of my mind. But it never engulfed that restless entity as he came with a small groan of satisfaction. In that instant I found the answer to the mystery of my new lover-husband. He had gone back to Clara. He was loving his wandering wife with some if not all of the tenderness, the gentleness he had learned in Clara's arms.

As he drifted off to sleep, I lay there, stunned, bewildered—and finally enraged. I did not want Malcolm Stapleton's tenderness on Clara's terms. It was a bor-

rowed commodity, something I could never regard with
an iota of pride or satisfaction. Should I accuse him
now? Shove him out of my bed forever? That was what
I was tempted to do. I was ready to revoke my agreement with the Evil Brother. Surely this was a violation
of our contract!

In his mocking way, my dark companion offered me
his rueful wisdom. I would lose far more than I could
ever hope to gain if I furiously denounced Malcolm. I
should play this game as a sophisticated Amsterdamer,
rather than a naive American.

In the morning, I returned to Sag Harbor and hired a
dozen wagons to transport my smuggled goods to Manhattan. I paid Van Oorst and told him about the declaration of war. Would it interfere with future voyages to
Amsterdam? He shook his head. The Spanish navy was
a lackluster affair. But if the French came into the war
on Spain's side, that might upset things at sea.

Back in Manhattan, with the goods safely in Cruger's
warehouse, I headed for the shop. Adam Duycinck was
there, waiting on a customer. The woman left without
making a purchase. A discouraged Duycinck told me
business had been poor since Clara left. The place
needed a woman's touch.

I barely listened. "When did Malcolm go back to
Clara?" I said.

"Has he?" Duycinck said. "It's news to me."

"Liar," I said.

I strode over to the Broadway and found not a sign
of Clara in Hughson's Tavern. At the house on Maiden
Lane, a slattern of a girl answered the door. She was no
more than sixteen but she had slut all over her shifty-
eyed face.

"Where is Miss Flowers?" I said.

"Upstairs."

I brushed past her and mounted the familiar narrow
stairs. In the front bedroom, where I had slept, I found

Clara giving a drink to a shrunken, red-haired woman who lay gasping and groaning in the bed. It was Cicely, the Irish whore who had been the first object of Clara's charity.

"What the devil is going on here?" I said.

Clara shut the bedroom door and stepped into the hall. "She's dying," she said. "The pox has eaten her insides away."

"And the creature who answered the door is another whore?"

"That's Mary Burton. She's trying to reform. She's indentured to the Hughsons. I let her live here to keep her out of temptation."

"Clara! This is a respectable street. Do your neighbors know what you're doing?"

"Oh yes. They don't like it. They've got a complaint against me before the Common Council."

"You're in no position to make enemies."

"Because of my color?"

"Yes."

"I'll take that risk."

I flung aside my cloak. "I'm not here to argue about that. Though I think it worsens what I am here to say."

"I've gone back to Malcolm. Who told you?"

"No one. I figured it out for myself," I said. "There are no secrets in the bedroom."

Clara pointed downstairs, suggesting Mary Burton might be listening. We retreated to Clara's bedroom, where she displayed a disconcerting mixture of guilt and defiance.

"You're partly responsible—what you said to me about marrying him if you were lost at sea. You've been gone six months. Malcolm was so miserable—I went to Duycinck about my infirmity. He told me I'd probably never have another child. No one his mother aborted ever conceived again. To make sure he gave me some secrets from an old book of his mother's—by some ancient Greek doctor.''

''Why don't you lie? Tell me you heard I was dead?'' I raged. I did not know how to deal with this mixture of adultery and pity.

''Would you rather have had him go to whores?''

''Yes!''

''They're all diseased. The pox, the clap—do you want him to bring those things into your bed?''

''I'd rather risk them than put up with your insufferable condescension!'' I cried.

''What are you talking about?'' Clara said, honestly bewildered. ''I don't consider you my inferior.''

''You do! You always have! You always will! For you I'll always be the Moon Woman.''

I began to sob. I had just made the most terrible confession of my life. I had admitted to myself and to Clara that those years of derision in Shining Creek had half convinced me I was an incomplete woman, a freak of nature. Ironically, Clara more than anyone could trigger this demoralizing sensation—and the rage it stirred in me.

Clara threw her arms around me. ''Catalyntie! Don't you remember how I tried to protect you from that cruelty?''

Tears trickled down Clara's cheeks. I saw her pain, different but no less real than my own. ''Listen to me,'' she said. ''Malcolm loves you for his son's sake—and for your own sake. He and I love each other in a different way—but it isn't going to last. He wishes he was still the man I loved at Hampden Hall—and I was the simple adoring Indian girl. Eventually he'll realize we've both changed. In a few years I won't mean anything to him. He'll be completely yours.''

''No he won't. He'll always love that vision of you and him in the wilderness—even though it almost killed you.''

"Perhaps," Clara said. "Neither of us can do anything about that. Try to share that much of him with me."

"I could have come home rich. There was a man in Amsterdam who would have given a hundred thousand guilders to sleep with me. I let you talk me out of it."

"You won't regret that," Clara said.

"I was so proud of myself. Now I think I was a fool."

"You won't—in time."

As we talked, I began to realize something more remarkable than resuming her love affair with Malcolm had happened to Clara. There was a new authority in her voice, a new confidence in her manner. I was meeting the Clara who had created her own freedom, a reality infinitely more profound than the legal fiction I had purchased for her.

"Hey, beautiful," said a dark voice downstairs. "Got a minute for a good story?"

I followed Clara out on the landing. Downstairs in the hall stood a tall muscular African with the sharpest features I had ever seen. His nose, his mouth, his chin, seemed carved out of blackest basalt. He had slitted, harshly intelligent eyes. Mary Burton had let him in. Her slattern's mouth wore a welcoming smile.

His sudden appearance had a notable effect on Clara. Not a little of her coolness vanished. She seemed unnerved by his mere presence. "I'm visiting with my friend Mrs. Stapleton," she said. "Catalyntie—this is Caesar. John Vraack's Caesar."

"Oh yes," I said, recalling his performance in the courtroom four years ago.

Caesar went on his way. "I hope to buy his freedom," Clara said, still agitated. "He has . . . abilities."

"If I remember correctly, they were closer to agilities," I said. "He seemed mostly expert at climbing in second story windows."

"He lives dangerously—because he has no hope,"

Clara said. "Would you—enslaved to a wretch like Old Vraack?"

Everyone in New York knew and disliked John Vraack for his bad temper and second-rate bread. "Probably not," I said. I was not prepared to give more than a tiny fraction of attention, much less sympathy, to Caesar. I saw nothing remarkable about him visiting Clara's house.

I hurried down Maiden Lane toward our house on Depeyster Street. As I rounded the corner I almost collided with a hatchet-faced figure in black: my uncle, Johannes Van Vorst. "What's this?" he said, noticing traces of tears on my face. "I thought you'd be prancing around the town, whooping like an Indian, waving my bloody scalp."

"It's none of your business, I assure you," I said, wiping my eyes.

"You've proven yourself quite a nuisance," Johannes said. "But my turn will come. An old friend in Amsterdam sent me a copy of Vondel's paper, which leaves no doubt about your morals. I mailed your husband a copy today."

"He doesn't read Dutch."

"I had it translated for him."

"I can explain it to him in five minutes."

"I had a letter the other day from Oloff Van Sluyden. He hopes you'll venture up the Mohawk again. He guarantees it will be your last trip."

Johannes's hatred was like a pail of cold water in the face. My rage at Clara abruptly dwindled. I walked home to Depeyster Street in a meditative mood. Maybe it was best to look upon Malcolm's return to Clara as a temporary thing. Clara was probably right, it was better than him going to whores and getting an infection which might sicken us both. Maybe I should be consoled by my profits in the fur trade, my success in Amsterdam, my triumph over my uncle.

In the house, I found Bridget McCarthy playing with the baby. I sat him on my lap and Bridget asked what they should call him, now that his mother was home. "Shall it be Cornulus, ma'am?" she said, mangling the name in a typically Irish way.

"Hugh will be fine," I said. I would yield in little ways to Malcolm. What did it matter what the child was called? My grandfather would understand, if he was aware of my continued existence in this bizarre world. I was bowing down in my struggle for my heart's desire. Soon, I was sure, larger stratagems would occur to me. *You're not as lovable but you're far more clever*, whispered the Evil Brother. Fool that I was, I accepted the compliment without demur.

※

FOUR

THAT NIGHT AT SUPPER, I sighed theatrically over my tea. "The most awful thing happened to me today," I said.

"What?" said Malcolm, halfway through his third piece of apple pie.

"I was told my victorious lawsuit means nothing. We'll never be able to go near our Mohawk Valley lands."

"What? Why not?" Malcolm said, putting down his fork.

"I met my Uncle Johannes on the street. He told me Oloff Van Sluyden has sworn to kill me if I so much as set foot in the Mohawk Valley again."

"The son of a bitch!" Malcolm growled. "What do you plan to do with that land? Five thousand acres is almost eight square miles. I'm no farmer—as you well know. I'm principled against hiring slaves—''

"I am too," I said, giving Clara her due. "I have a better idea. In Amsterdam I obtained enough credit to open a trading post up there. We could sell off most of the land to small farmers in two-hundred-acre tracts. Eventually, we'd have a countryside of prosperous customers and meanwhile we could do a fine business with the fur traders going up the Mohawk to Oswego. We could put that bastard Philip Van Sluyden out of business."

"Sounds good," Malcolm said, scraping his plate.

"But it's all dwindling away to a mere dream," I said. "How can we do anything in the face of the Van Sluydens' promise to massacre us?"

"By putting ourselves in readiness to massacre them first," Malcolm said.

"You'd do that—for me?" I said.

"You're my wife, damn it!" Malcolm said. "It's land our son will inherit someday. Of course I'll do it. I'll do it for us—and for the colony of New York. We must have law and order on our frontiers, just as we have it here on Manhattan Island!"

By now you must be wondering: Is this the same Catalyntie Van Vorst? The headstrong virago who seldom knows how or when to hold her tongue? Yes, it was the same woman but she was learning to apply some of the philosophy she had recently acquired—in the service of her heart's desire. She wanted to open a trading post on the Mohawk. But she wanted something else even more, something that made this idea irresistibly attractive. It was a perfect way to separate Malcolm Stapleton from Clara Flowers.

As I purchased a fortune in strouds and jewelry and blankets and other goods on my Amsterdam line of credit, I met Clara on Pearl Street and told her we would soon be leaving for the Mohawk. I looked for a hint of distress, some sign that she would miss Malcolm. I saw nothing.

"I hope it goes well," she said. "There's so much evil involved in that disgusting trade."

I slept poorly that night, wrestling with Clara's ominous words. I struggled to convince myself all over again that the fur trade was a business like any other business, no worse, no better. Where did Clara find the gall to call it evil? Uninspiring, difficult, dangerous, perhaps—but evil?

No sooner had I resolved that large question than I found myself wrestling with whether to sell rum to the fur traders, who would inevitably resell it to the Indians. Should I be the middleperson in this destructive process? I asked Malcolm what he thought. He began with an oration about how little he liked the fur trade in general and finally said rum was absolutely necessary if I hoped to attract customers. If the traders had to go to Philip Van Sluyden for their rum, they would buy his goods too.

Still I could not bring myself to purchase the stuff. The next night at dinner, my husband was unusually silent. Finally he confessed he had discussed the rum with Clara. "She thinks we should quit the business rather than sell it," he said.

"How can she object, when she sells the same vile stuff each day at Hughson's?" I said. "There are drinkers in New York who don't handle rum much better than the Indians."

"That's true," Malcolm said. "But—"

It was demoralizing. Could I have changed his mind about rum as swiftly as Clara? I doubted it. But I agreed with her and ruefully abandoned the vile potion—and a decent profit from our venture. "We'll cut the prices on our goods," I said. "They'll buy from us rather than Van Sluyden—and maybe resell them to the Indians without using rum. They won't need it to make a good profit."

After another long silence, Malcolm warily added: "Clara thinks we should hire free blacks for our work force."

"What if it comes to fighting?"

"I can train them to fight as well as any white man," Malcolm said. "If all goes well, we could settle them on farms up there. Clara thinks it might be a step toward freeing other blacks and letting them create their own towns and villages. Perhaps their own colony."

"Why not?" I said.

I was getting Malcolm out of New York—that was the main thing—perhaps the only thing—that mattered to me. In a month, we headed up the Hudson to Albany. It was a far different expedition from the parlous little band I led the last time. Malcolm had recruited two dozen sturdy young African dock wallopers who liked adventure and a chance to own their own farms. Guert Cuyler, who was in love with soldiering almost as much as Malcolm, abandoned his lawbooks to serve as second in command. His family owned lands along the Mohawk and he planned to survey them and begin selling them off. For a share of our profits, he would lend his survey skills to us as well. Adam Duycinck was our bookkeeper, organizer, and paymaster. On his advice, we had bought two three-pound cannons to help defend our outpost.

All in all, I had invested ten thousand pounds in this venture—far more than the value of the Mohawk lands—in fact, almost all the money I possessed. I was violating my grandfather's primary rule, never to risk more than half my money on a single enterprise. But I recklessly thrust his warning voice out of my mind. I was getting my heart's desire. Nothing else mattered.

In Albany we made no secret of our plans. On the contrary, Malcolm invited every fur trader he met to examine our goods—which were superior in variety and quality to Philip Van Sluyden's wares—and undersold him on every item. We distributed maps of the Mohawk, specifying our location on the very site of my parents' ruined house. We retained Nicholas Van Brugge to draw up a charter for The Stapleton Trading Company and commissioned him to be our land agent.

Finally we hired wagons and bateaux and sent a messenger up the river to Peaceful Lake's village, asking the sachem if he would permit us to hire a half dozen warriors as scouts. Malcolm was determined not to be surprised. We mentioned this alliance to no one, not even Van Brugge, who told us the Van Sluydens and their allies were talking bloodily in the taverns about our invasion.

I gloried in the way Malcolm took charge of this enterprise. I never stopped descanting to Guert Cuyler and Adam about his good judgment, the masterful way he handled the traders, even when some of them, Van Sluyden loyalists, flung insults in his face. Our old enemy de Groot was much in evidence along the docks, warning everyone that if they traded with us, they would never do business with Philip Van Sluyden again. More and more, it became apparent that there was not going to be any quarter offered in this war.

For a while, Malcolm was the midnight lover I had known in New York, when he first went into politics. He reveled in my double need for him, as a protector and a husband. But our rapture abruptly dwindled the night we reached the site of my parents' house. I remembered so much, I crept into his arms more like a frightened child than an ardent woman. I wanted his strength to exorcise memory's nightmare. He responded with wonderful compassion. For any other man and woman, it would have been the most memorable night of their marriage. Instead his tenderness reminded me of Clara and my ardor faltered. I struggled to escape my fearful inferiority, to achieve the spiritual sharing Clara urged. But it was beyond me.

When our Seneca scouts arrived, a different kind of trouble began. They were led by our old Oswego friend, Leaping Deer. Inevitably, as soon as he discovered we gave a daily ration of rum to our soldiers, he wanted some. The other braves echoed his demands. Malcolm was inclined to give them a ration. I absolutely refused.

This made them less than enthusiastic scouts. They skulked in the woods a half mile from our camp, instead of ranging in a ten- or twelve-mile arc. Malcolm accused me of usurping his authority and was almost as sulky. "I wish we'd brought Clara along," he growled. "You don't know how to talk to Indians."

That inflicted another wound on the Moon Woman. I found myself tormented by terrible nightmares. Again and again, I saw the Senecas rampaging through our house, my father toppling through the years, his blood staining my pathetic love. No wonder I was such an easy prey for the Evil Brother. In one of the dreams I recognized Clara's Seneca father, Hanging Belt, the greatest warrior of our village. How could such a noble figure commit such a crime? I remembered the gentle way he had played with me and Clara when we were children. How he had brought us presents from his trading voyages to Oswego, dolls and bits of jewelry.

Soon, no matter how passionately Malcolm loved me, I found no pleasure in it—or anything else. Day and night, my head ached, my stomach churned with nameless fear, my heart was like a piece of icy mud in my breast. I began to feel doomed, defeated. The energy, the enthusiasm I normally summoned for business seemed to have evaporated. Gradually I began to realize I was spiritually sick. Clara was right. This was a haunted place. I should have never come near it.

One of the people I saw repeatedly in my dreams was Joshua, Clara's father. He prowled the wrecked house, clutching his scalped head, a spirit in torment. At times he knelt beside my father's corpse and wept. For some reason his ghost seemed trapped in this world. Had he failed to prepare himself for death? As Senecas we were taught that everyone must gather his spirit for the passage from the land of the living to the land of the dead. Those who fail to do so roam the night forever.

Meanwhile, our Africans labored to build a small stone fort from the ruins of the house. It was hard, slow work. Along with the masonry and timbering, Malcolm insisted they spend three hours a day rehearsing various military maneuvers and sharpening their marksmanship on targets in the meadow. After a full month, we had only three walls and half a roof.

On the river a steady procession of traders passed us on the way to Oswego. Only a handful stopped to examine our wares—and all deprecated our lack of rum. Overthrowing Philip Van Sluyden was going to be equally hard, slow work. The realization that I might soon be facing financial disaster did nothing for my troubled spirits.

Leaping Deer and his Senecas decided to go home. I had to pay them a month's wages for doing nothing. As they headed for Oswego with enough money to stay drunk for a week, I seized the arm of the youngest brave, a slim swift warrior named Little Beaver. I asked him if he would take a message to the village of Shining Lake. "Tell Hanging Belt if he will come to the place where he first found She-Is-Alert and Nothing-But-Flowers and bring the shaman, Flying Crow, he can wipe away the bad blood he spilled here."

Little Beaver agreed to carry the message for an extra five days' wages. Next I dispatched one of our hired soldiers down the river to New York and asked Clara to join us as soon as possible. I wondered if I were going crazy. I was abandoning one of the primary purposes of this journey. I was inviting Clara to join us in the wilderness, where she and Malcolm would be tempted to resume the unreal love that still haunted them.

Two weeks later, Hanging Belt and two younger warriors appeared before our still-unfinished fort. With them was the successor of Flying Crow, the shaman I had known in Shining Creek. His name was Black Wing. Hanging Belt was at least sixty. But he still carried himself like a warrior. I told him how I had seen him in my dreams—how the whole place was haunted by the ghosts of those he had killed here.

"Why did you attack these people?" Malcolm asked in his bad Seneca.

"We were told they were here to steal away our fur trade," Hanging Belt said. "It would come down the river of the Mohawks and avoid our lands."

"Who told you?"

"A trader from Albany. I don't remember his name. But he had red wampum[1] and a promise from the governor that we would have a special place in the trade if we killed them. He said they would build a fort near Shining Creek and we would be paid for each pelt that crossed our lands. Instead they built Oswego and the promise was forgotten."

Hanging Belt gazed mournfully at the ruined house. "It is not a deed of which I have ever boasted," he said.

It was exactly as my grandfather suspected. The Van Sluydens had committed murder to protect their illegal trade with Canada. But our first task was to pacify the souls of the slain. "When Nothing-But-Flowers arrives, we'll begin the ceremony of mourning," I said.

Clara arrived the next day. She embraced Malcolm and kissed me with special fervor. "I've been having the same dreams about my father," she said. "It was almost as if I were here with you. Your letter was like a message of deliverance."

---

[1] A summons to war.

She greeted Hanging Belt and the shaman, Black Wing, and the other two braves with her usual warmth. They were delighted to see her, especially when she told them about her dreams. "Now we know there is work to be done," Black Wing said. "Our long journey has not been in vain."

The implication was not flattering to the Moon Woman. Her dreams might be caused by eating rotten fish or too many walnuts. But the power of Nothing-But-Flowers's *orenda* was uncontestable. Once more I found myself struggling with my old feelings of inferiority.

That night, Black Wing instructed us to build a great blaze in the ruins of the old manor house. He donned one of his false faces, seized his rattles and his shield on which were painted signs so ancient no one knew their meaning. They belonged to the warriors who first came to the forests and lakes of New York, a thousand years ago.

"Listen to me," quavered Black Wing, in the chanting voice of the priest. "I speak as one who knows the way to the land of the dead. It is written on this shield. Read the signs of deliverance and speak them when the Evil Brother or one of his devils bars your path."

In the grass outside, Clara and I and Hanging Belt and the other Senecas shook rattles and chanted ancient prayers. "No one can trap your soul!" we cried. "See how the Evil Brother flees before the False Face. Draw hope from our voices. Begin your journey now to the land of the dead, where those you love await you."

Around and around the blaze Black Wing raced, flaunting his sacred shield, shaking his rattles. His false face, red and black and twisted to one side, so that one eye was higher than the other, gleamed in the firelight. Slowly, I began to feel the grip of the evil spirits loosening. My heart began to beat freely.

I turned to Clara. Her eyes were shining in the firelight. "I feel it too," she said. Tears poured down our cheeks.

"Grieve no more, Father, your daughter is here," Clara cried. "Accept your fate, however cruel it was. None of us can choose our deaths."

The fire blazed into the night. In its dancing glow I glimpsed Malcolm and Guert Cuyler watching us, astonishment on their faces. We were revealing the depth, the reality, of our Indian selves.

Somewhere in the forest, a cry of pain interrupted us. "Help. Catalyntie! Malcolm! Help!" A minute later, Malcolm half led, half carried Nicholas Van Brugge into the firelight beside Black Wing. Blood drooled from his mouth. He had been shot in the chest. "They're coming!" he said. "I heard about it—by accident. They're only a few miles away, downriver."

We abandoned the ceremony of mourning and rushed the wounded man to a tent beside our half-finished fort. "I followed them up the river," Van Brugge said. "They shot me yesterday. But I managed to escape into the forest. They didn't find me."

"Who is it?" Malcolm said.

"Philip Van Sluyden and that bastard de Groot," Van Brugge said. "They've got a hundred men. Fifty Ottawas led by a French officer—the rest traders."

A hundred men. We had twenty-four, plus Malcolm and Guert. I turned to Hanging Belt. "These are the same men who brought you here to kill innocent people a hundred moons ago," I said in Seneca. "Now they are bringing fifty Ottawas from Fort Niagara and another fifty white men from Albany. They're coming to kill me and Nothing-But-Flowers. Will you stand with us?"

"Of course," said Hanging Belt. "But we cannot sit here and wait for them to devour us. We must ambush them before they see our weakness."

I called Malcolm away from the dying Van Brugge.

"Hanging Belt says our only hope is an ambush," I told him.

"Where?" Malcolm said. "I'm more inclined to retreat upriver to Oswego as fast as possible."

"It's too far. They'll overtake us. And we'll have to abandon all our goods," I said. "We'll be bankrupt."

"Better bankrupt than dead."

"Listen to Hanging Belt," I pleaded. "He's fought a hundred battles like this."

"Catalyntie's right," Clara said.

Still reluctant to admit an Indian was his military superior, Malcolm listened. "First," Hanging Belt said. "Let us think no more of sleep tonight. Let's explore the river and see where these enemies might land. They won't come ashore here. They know you have cannon in your fort. They will come ashore nearby and approach through the forest and attack without warning. We must be waiting for them as they land and surprise them."

As I translated this for Malcolm, Hanging Belt ordered the two young Senecas to go downriver in a canoe and try to locate the enemy. Meanwhile, Malcolm and he and I (as a translator) went downriver in another canoe, looking for a likely landing place. The moon was almost full. The river and the shore glistened in its yellow light. We traveled less than a mile when Hanging Belt said: "There is the place."

A bend in the river had created shallows that were thick with tall fernlike reeds with finely divided fronds. This bracken blended into a grassy bank up which boats could be hauled with little effort. "They will come ashore here," Hanging Belt said.

"What if they don't?" Malcolm said to me in English. "We're nowhere. They can burn our fort and goods at leisure."

"And us in the bargain if we sit there waiting for them," I said. "Trust this man."

"All *right*," Malcolm said.

"We will do as you say," I told Hanging Belt.

Back at our fort, we discovered Guert Cuyler was dealing with a mutiny. At least half our hired soldiers were inclined to take to the woods. They had no stomach for fighting four to one odds. As Malcolm argued with them, the two Senecas returned to report that they had located the enemy. They were about three miles downriver.

That was a moment when Malcolm proved himself a leader of men. "We can beat these bastards if you stand with me," he shouted. "Do you want Africans to be remembered as soldiers or cowards? We hired you to give you a better life up here on the Mohawk. Are you going to let these murderers steal it from you? Hanging Belt, one of the greatest Seneca chiefs, is going to fight with us—"

He outlined the tactics for the ambush. Hanging Belt had suggested them to him coming back upriver. A dozen men would hide in the shallow water among the bracken. Another dozen would take cover in the woods on one side of the clearing. Hanging Belt and his Senecas would raise a war whoop at the back of the clearing. Then the men in the bracken would fire, followed by the flankers in the woods.

"I want everybody to whoop and yell like a tribe of devils," Malcolm said. "Make us sound like a hundred and fifty, two hundred men."

Hanging Belt beamed when I translated this. The white chief was getting in the spirit of the ambush. His confidence may have helped steady the Africans as much as Malcolm's speech. The rest of the night was consumed by preparations. Each man was issued thirty rounds of ball and powder. At Guert Cuyler's suggestion, one of the cannon was lugged downriver in a canoe and positioned in the woods where the second detachment would fight. It was loaded with grapeshot—small deadly pellets that turned it into a giant shotgun. Hanging Belt and his warriors carefully applied the violent colors of their war paint—and urged it on Malcolm, Guert, and the Africans as well.

At 4:00 A.M. the ambushers were ready to depart. Malcolm turned to me and Clara, his streaked face weird in the fading firelight. "If we fail, head upriver as fast as you can paddle. Keep going until you reach Oswego."

"I want to go with you—to fight!" I said.

"Out of the question. Duycinck will bring you the news, one way or another. He'll be back in the trees with Hanging Belt."

He kissed me briefly and said: "You've been a good wife. Raise our son to be a good man."

He turned to Clara. "Wherever I go, whatever I become, I'll remember you."

"You'll come back," she said. "You'll come back to both of us."

I was devastated. My expedition to the wilderness to make Malcolm mine forever had produced this testament of undying love to Clara. As we watched the canoes vanish down the darkened river—the moon had long since descended—Clara said: "I didn't ask for that."

"I know."

."You brought me here."

"I know. I needed you more than I feared you. I still do."

"How many times do I have to tell you it won't last? He's yours in the long run."

I struggled against my combative, avaricious nature, the soul that fate had bequeathed me. "I'll try to believe that," I said.

Clara began loading a canoe with food and muskets and ammunition. "If they lose, you must stay alive for Hugh's sake," she said.

"I suppose so," I said, still disconsolate. Motherhood barely mattered. I only wanted my heart's desire.

The light along the river began changing from inky black to grey. It was less than an hour to dawn. "I can't stand waiting here," I said. "Let's join Hanging Belt in the woods. We can yell as loud as a warrior."

"I feel the same way. Shall we put on war paint?" Clara said.

"Why not?"

We found the paints that Hanging Belt and his Senecas had used to streak themselves in red and blue and yellow. Quickly, we coated our faces and arms and pulled on leggings and moccasins I had brought with me to wear in the wilderness. In less than an hour, we crept through the trees to the place where Hanging Belt and his warriors were lying in wait with Adam Duycinck.

"The blood of our fathers brought us here," Clara said in Seneca. "We want to help you wipe away the stain on your honor."

"Do you think we shall win?" Hanging Belt said. "We are few and many of the black men are terrified."

"They're new to this kind of war," Clara said. "But they are led by a true warrior."

"The one you call Mal-colm?" Hanging Belt said. "Yes. He has a warrior's heart. Let us hope he acquires a war chief's head."

The rising sun was beginning to tint the eastern sky. On the river, with its great guardian trees on both banks, the light remained grey. Morning fog added to the dimness.

Panting into our midst came one of Hanging Belt's Senecas. "They come!" he said. He had been scouting downriver.

Hanging Belt rose to his knees and hooted like an owl three times. From the bracken in the shallows came three answering hoots. Malcolm was ready.

Around the bend in the river came a squadron of canoes. In the lead was de Groot, studying the forest with his murderer's eyes. Behind him in another canoe was

Philip Van Sluyden. In each craft, a half dozen Indians drove them toward the bank with swift strokes of their paddles.

They cut through the bracken on the downriver side of the little bay. Malcolm and his men were crouched less than two dozen feet away. They had cut some of the fronds and planted them in their caps, so they blended perfectly with the swaying greenery.

One after another, the canoes landed and their occupants sprang out and congregated in the meadow. Soon the last canoe was making for the bank. Crowded by the others already ashore, the rear paddler steered for the bracken where Malcolm and his men were hiding. As the prow entered the weeds, Malcolm's gigantic form rose from the shallows and dragged the lead paddler out of the boat, cutting his throat in the same deadly motion. Behind him his men repeated the murderous performance on the others in the boat.

In the same instant, Duycinck, Hanging Belt, and his warriors opened fire from the rear of the clearing and the dozen men in the woods on the left flank poured in another volley. Within sixty seconds, Malcolm and his men had unlimbered their muskets and blasted the stunned foe with a volley from the river. It had not gone exactly according to plan but ambushes seldom do.

Hanging Belt and the Senecas bellowed war cries as they swiftly reloaded their muskets. Clara and I shrilled them as vigorously as the warriors. They were a terrifying combination of the howl of the wolf and scream of the panther. Anyone who had spent some time in the north woods recognized a Seneca war cry. It struck consternation into our frantic opponents.

Similar if less recognizable howls poured from the flankers in the woods, as they too reloaded and blasted another volley into the milling mass in the clearing. "No quarter!" roared Malcolm from the bracken. "No quarter for traitors.'' His muskets boomed again and another half dozen Van Sluydenites went down.

Such punishment would have been too much for even professional soldiers to endure. These were not professionals. The traders were mostly bullies who were heroes only when they were dealing with drunken Indians. Their coup de grâce was the cannon, which Guert Cuyler had shrewdly kept silent. Just as de Groot managed to form some of his men into a shaky battle line, the gun boomed, flinging hundreds of deadly chunks of metal into their ranks.

Wailing with terror, the survivors took to the woods. Several who could swim leaped into the river, where Malcolm and his men finished them off. The surviving Ottawas also fled. Indians do not believe in fighting to the death. If the enemy has outgeneraled you, far better to run away and fight another day.

In five minutes the battle was over. At least fifty of our would-be attackers lay dead or dying in the meadow. The rest were in frantic flight, a demoralized rabble. I leaped into the clearing, only one idea blazing in my mind: *revenge*. Among the tangle of bodies, I soon found Philip Van Sluyden. He was barely alive, with two gaping wounds in his chest.

''Hanging Belt!'' I cried, as I straddled my quarry. ''Give me your scalping knife!''

''Let him die in peace,'' Clara said.

''Give me your scalping knife!'' I said.

''Don't give it to her,'' Clara said.

Hanging Belt gazed steadily at us. He saw two daughters of the Seneca. He had seen many Seneca women scalp the dead. There was nothing unusual about it. He could not understand why Clara was objecting to it.

Hanging Belt handed me his knife. Grunting, snarling, I hacked off Philip Van Sluyden's scalp, exactly as I had seen my father's slashed off twenty years ago. With a final groan Van Sluyden died in the midst of the amputation. I held up the bloody object and realized Malcolm and Guert Cuyler and almost everyone else except the Senecas and Clara were watching me with mute horror. In Clara's eyes I saw understanding and sympathy—and sorrow. Did she already know what this savage act would cost us?

Five

THE DRINKERS AT HUGHSON'S TAVERN gathered around Clara in a pastiche of wide-eyed white and black faces as she read the story of the Battle of the Bracken in the *New York Gazette*. I had commissioned Adam Duycinck to write an account of the clash. Duycinck was honest enough to admit the plan for the battle came from Hanging Belt but his version gave Malcolm most of the credit for leading the fray. He also praised "the brave Africans" who had defeated four times their number in the forest.

"That's the part I want you to remember," Caesar said. "What black men can do with guns in their hands."

Caesar had no interest in the rest of Duycinck's story, which dealt with political warfare. Because one of the dead was the officer in the French army who had led the band of Ottawas from Fort Niagara, Duycinck argued the affair was proof of French treachery—and the readiness of some New Yorkers, such as the Van Sluydens, to do business with the Catholic enemy. Duycinck worked into the story a graphic description of Malcolm's rout of the French sloop on Lake Ontario—making him sound like a one-man army on the northern frontier.

Malcolm had come to New York with an advance copy of the story for acting governor George Clarke, urging him to send it to the British secretary of state for America. If that gentleman showed it to Prime Minister Robert Walpole and George II, it might trigger a declaration of war on France. That would clear the muddle of an undeclared war from the atmosphere—and might very well make Malcolm Stapleton the leader of an American army that would invade Canada and settle the question of who would rule North America once and for all.

War was raging all around the perimeter of England's North American colonies. Only last week, the *New York Gazette* had reported that on almost the same date as the Battle of the Bracken, a Spanish army numbering over a thousand men had landed on St. Simon's Island off the coast of Georgia. Timely warning of their arrival had been brought to Savannah by a privateer.[1] The royal governor called out the colony's militia and ambushed the Spanish on the march. The enemy soon fled to their ships, leaving behind more than a hundred dead.

"Read us the other story," Caesar said. "The Stono River Story."

Clara drew an older copy of the *Gazette* from beneath the bar and read the story of a slave uprising in South Carolina. The paper was almost six months old now. Caesar had asked her to read it a dozen times to various Africans he brought to Hughson's to drink with him.

"A traveler lately arrived from Charleston reports an alarming upheaval on the Stono River, about twenty miles from the capital of that colony. Some twenty slaves from plantations along the river, where rice is grown in great abundance, met secretly at night over several months. Inflamed by reports of Spain's declara-

---

[1] *A merchant ship, armed and commissioned to attack and seize enemy ships in time of war.*

tion of war and the hope of freedom, they formed an army, joined by a blood oath, and on an appointed Sunday, while most of the white people were at church, broke into a local store, stole guns and powder and left the heads of the two white owners on the store's steps to demonstrate their desperate intentions. They marched south for the Spanish colony of Florida, shouting 'Liberty.' Along the way they were joined by numerous other Africans. Any whites they encountered on the road were slaughtered without mercy, except for two, whose slaves pleaded for them as kind masters. Fortunately, several whites escaped their vigilance and sounded the alarm. The militia was called out and soon blocked their route. In a pitched battle, the Africans were totally defeated. Most of those who surrendered were executed on the spot, saving a half dozen who pleaded they had been forced to join the revolt at gunpoint. The greatest perturbation now reigns in the whole colony with extra patrols mounted on all roads at night and Africans kept closely confined, even in the city of Charleston.''

''Fools,'' Caesar said. ''They should have waited for the Spanish to attack, then risen. The whites would have been fighting the Spanish and been caught between two fires.''

Fat moon-faced Cuffee, Caesar's closest friend, asked Clara to get out her book of maps and show them where it had happened. Clara opened the big atlas of the world she had bought from Harman Bogardus, our old teacher. She showed Cuffee the location of South Carolina on the American coast and ran her finger along the King of Spain's dominions, which included the entire continent of South America and Mexico and islands in the Caribbean and the long peninsula of Florida.

''How far is it from here to there?'' Caesar asked, running his finger from New York to the island of Cuba, which everyone knew was the headquarters of the Spanish fleet. Caesar had been fascinated by the book of

.maps since the first time he saw it. He had learned the names of the islands and countries from Clara.

"Over a thousand miles," Clara said.

"How long would it take a ship to sail that far?"

"I don't know."

"Three weeks," said one of the sailors in the crowd.

"That ain't long," Caesar said. "We could have a Spanish fleet and army here anytime."

"Or French, if the Battle of the Bracken gets read in Paris," Cuffee said. "My master claims it's all stuff. The Stapletons murdered that Van Sluyden fellow and his French Indians on their way to Oswego to talk peace."

"That's a lie," Clara said. "I was there. They came to kill the Stapletons—and they would have killed me too. Van Sluyden got exactly what he deserved. He was a murderer—and a traitor in the bargain."

The words made little impact on the drinkers. English patriotism was not popular at Hughson's. Luke Barrington, an elongated hooknosed Irish schoolteacher who frequently drank at the tavern, raised a tankard of rum. "Here's to King Philip of Spain and King Louis of France. Either one's my king more than that fat Protestant bastard on his throne in London. If a Catholic king comes here with an army, I'll carry a musket for him and knock the bloody English on the head."

"Amen to that!" Caesar said, clinking his glass of ale against Barrington's tankard. "There's a thousand black men ready to join you. All we need is some guns."

"That's crazy talk. It can get you all hanged!" Clara said.

The war with Spain had turned Caesar's dream of a slave revolt into an obsession. The Stono River uprising and the Battle of the Bracken had redoubled the intensity of his ambitions. At first Clara had merely scoffed at them. But as more and more Africans began listening seriously to him, the memory of her vision of disaster on her first night with Caesar had returned to haunt her.

"Listen to her," Caesar said. "Since she peddled her ass to the great Malcolm Stapleton, she's been hoping it'll turn white."

Clara poured a tankard of ale—and flung it in Caesar's face. "Get out of here," she said. "And stay out until you learn to hold your tongue."

Everyone roared with laughter—including Caesar. "Ever seen a bitch like her?" he said.

Mary Burton, waiting on tables, offered Caesar a dirty napkin to wipe his face. It was not the first time Clara had expelled Caesar from the tavern. He would come back. He knew she wanted him to come back. They were linked in a strange dangerous way that neither completely understood.

Hughson's was one of the few taverns that allowed Africans to buy rum at its bar. It was against the law to sell a drink to a slave. It was also against the law for more than three slaves to meet anyplace, even on the street. New York still remembered the African uprising of 1712. But the laws were seldom enforced by the overworked handful of constables who composed the city's Night Watch.

If Caesar returned before dawn, he would come not to drink but to sell another bundle of stolen silver plate or candlesticks or a dozen yards of cloth. Sarah Hughson would buy them for ten percent of what they were worth and sell them to shopkeepers like Adam Duycinck for three times that much—and Adam would sell them to rich New Yorkers for ten times as much.

It was wrong—it was dangerous. The legal punishment for theft was death—but the law was seldom enforced in New York. In England, it was a different story. The British soldiers from Fort George had told Clara of seeing a hundred people a month hanged in London alone—some as young as twelve years old—for stealing a loaf of bread when they were starving.

Clara heard little about England that inclined her to respect its government or its laws. But she said nothing about the Hughsons' business in stolen goods with Caesar for a deeper reason. Some sort of rough justice was accomplished by it. The longer she worked at Hughson's, the more Clara felt she had emigrated to another world where different laws prevailed.

The poor drank at Hughson's. The rum was the cheapest—and worst—in the city, so raw Caesar swore it was burning his guts out. From the mouths of the Africans and the poor whites—the sailors, the dockworkers, the whores, and schoolteachers like Luke Barrington who were not paid much better than the dockers—Clara heard about a different New York, where there was a daily struggle for enough food and shelter to survive. Those who failed—who became vagrants on the streets—were thrown into the almshouse, a prisonlike building on the northern edge of the city, where they froze and semistarved on miserable food or sweated in the summer months and frequently died from the numerous diseases that raged through the place.

"Clara!"

Shoving his way to the bar was the towering figure of Malcolm Stapleton. He pointed to the *New York Gazette*. "Has everyone read the bad news from Georgia?" he said. "It's what happens when your fleet and army lie supine and the enemy can seize the initiative. We should have twenty ships of the line and a hundred transports in the harbor at this moment, ready to attack Cuba. You wouldn't find any Spaniard within a hundred miles of Georgia. Instead we idle here, our cities open to attack, while the Great Corrupter soothes the king with empty promises of action next year. It's enough to make a man repent of patriotism or consider himself a damned fool."

Malcolm's diatribes against Prime Minister Robert Walpole had long since passed into the realm of hyperbole. But no one disagreed with him. Luke Barrington, the schoolteacher who had just pledged his allegiance to the Spanish king, was silent as a statue. No one was ready to argue with a man of Malcolm's size and political importance. Although he was under savage attack for his role in the Battle of the Bracken, he remained a leader, even a heroic figure, to many New Yorkers.

His victory in the northern woods had added several inches to his military stature. The governor had made Malcolm brigadier general in command of the state's militia. He was at Hughson's to talk up this year's militia bill. In spite of the declaration of war on Spain, the New York assembly had refused to vote money for a local army. They told the fuming governor they would only do it on explicit orders from the king. They implied that the king and his friends had started this war and they were the ones who should pay for it. It was hardly patriotic and Malcolm and his militant friends were left in the dismayed minority.

Clara served drinks while Malcolm argued with those who saw no point in spending money on soldiers until a genuine French or Spanish threat appeared on the horizon. Malcolm vehemently maintained that an untrained army would be worse than none at all. Finally, the drinkers drifted into the night and John Hughson came downstairs and said it was time to close. Mary Burton got out her mop and pail and began swabbing the taproom floor.

Hughson peered at Malcolm in his stupid way and said: "You're all wrong about raising men to fight for King George. He ain't a proper King of England."

"Who is?"

"He's living in France at this moment. Charles Edward Stuart is his name."

Malcolm seized him by the shirt. "What the hell are you talking about, man? That's treason. Treason to the

Glorious Revolution of 1688, to the heroes who threw the pope off the throne of our country!''

''Call it what you want. It's the truth,'' Hughson said.

Malcolm whirled on Clara. ''Where the hell is he getting these ideas?''

''I have no idea,'' Clara said, dismayed at Malcolm's passion. She suddenly remembered Harman Bogardus warning her and Catalyntie that no one could be neutral in this quarrel, with its explosive mixture of religion and politics.

Hughson broke Malcolm's grip on his shirt. He was a match for him in size and strength. ''I thought you was our friend, thanks to Clara,'' he said.

''I won't be a friend to anyone who has such dirty ideas in his noodle,'' Malcolm said. ''My advice to you is wipe them out, fast. Or you'll be talking to a magistrate.''

Hughson waited in sullen silence while Clara got her cloak and said good night. As Malcolm walked her home to Maiden Lane, he again demanded to know where Hughson had gotten his traitorous ideas. ''From his wife,'' Clara said. ''She was born a Catholic. Her relations were principal officers of this colony before your so-called Glorious Revolution of 1688.''

Malcolm stopped in the street as a sailor lurched by them with his arm around a whore. ''Clara—it's your Glorious Revolution too.''

''That's so much stuff, Malcolm. It was all about plunder, power. Who would get rich or stay rich. Look who rules England now. Doesn't Walpole the Great Corrupter prove the whole thing was about money?''

Malcolm struggled to find an answer—and failed. ''Where . . . where did you get these ideas?''

''From thinking. From books.''

''Whose books?''

''Never mind. I don't like your readiness to arrest everyone who disagrees with you.''

"Do you think the Spanish or the French will let you have your own ideas if they conquer New York? We'll all become papists or die at the stake with the most hideous tortures you can imagine. I'll die fighting so it matters little to me. But I loathe the idea of you and Catalyntie and my son at their mercy."

There it was, Malcolm's little trinity of devotion, Clara thought mordantly. Did she still want to belong to it? She had begun to doubt it. Perhaps because of what she heard and saw each day in Hughson's tavern. Perhaps because she could not forget the pain on Catalyntie's face when Malcolm said good-bye before the Battle of the Bracken. Perhaps because there was someone else who needed her love.

"Clara," Malcolm said. "I know you told me—"

"And I meant it. I should never have gone back to you. Now you have a wife at home—"

"Is that the only reason?" Malcolm said.

"No," Clara said.

"Is it Caesar? I've heard reports of him visiting you at very unusual hours."

"No more unusual than your visiting hours," she said. "I'm teaching him to read."

"Isn't that against the law?"

"Damn the law."

"Clara—I've never felt so low. The governor is at his wits' end with this militia bill. They're making him look like a fool—and me in the bargain. Our store on the Mohawk is a total loss. Not a trader will come near us. They all curse us for killing their friends. Johannes Van Vorst and the Van Sluydens are on their way to convincing half New York we're murderers and worse. They play up Catalyntie's scalping Philip Van Sluyden as if that was the only reason for the battle."

Clara sighed. She mourned the decline of her warrior lover into this harassed ambitious man, plunged into a world he did not really comprehend, buffeted by its con-

fusions. "All the more reason why Catalyntie needs you.
Every·time you touch me, I begin to feel it diminishes
her."

"This will be the last time, I promise you."

"No, Malcolm. Once and for all—no."

Malcolm trudged into the darkness. In the back bedroom of her house, Clara could hear Adam Duycinck
laughing with one of his whores. He was the most popular lover in the city, since he began advertising himself
as an expert in preventing conception. He had attracted
swarms of customers to the Universal Store, where he
gave consultations between sales. Catalyntie and other
theoretically respectable women had begun using his
techniques.

The rest of the house was empty. Malcolm had persuaded Clara to abandon her nursery for sick and dying
prostitutes. He had probably saved her from being accused of keeping a bawdy house and thrown into the
street by her irate neighbors on Maiden Lane. Now she
boarded two or three of these unfortunate women at
Hughson's or some other tavern.

Upstairs, a voice whispered. "Hello, beautiful." It
was Caesar.

"I'm too tired to give you a reading lesson now," she
said.

"I didn't come for a reading lesson. I came to find
out what you want from me."

"What do I want from you?" The question was un-
cannily apt. Did he somehow know she had just refused
Malcolm Stapleton's love, finally and forever? "I
think—or hope—that someday we might become lovers.
Maybe even husband and wife. We might have our own
tavern. We might adopt one of the African orphans in
the poorhouse and become a family."

"How do you expect that to happen when I'm old
Vraack's slave?"

"In a year I'll have enough money to buy your freedom."

"So that's it."

"What do you mean?"

"You think you can buy Caesar. You think you can make him into your nice quiet obedient husband."

"I can't imagine you ever being either quiet or obedient."

Throughout this conversation, Caesar sat on the edge of her bed, a black blur in the room's darkness. Clara was standing in the doorway. He suddenly stood up and drew her into the room. She realized he was naked. Slowly, methodically, he undressed her. She did not try to stop him. She did not protest. An enormous *fate* kept echoing in her soul. Caesar was her black fate, as Malcolm had been her white fate.

Naked, she received him into her body like a wife, she mounted him and played the whore, she let his rough hands gouge her breasts, her rump. She was not surprised by his violence. Caesar was a walking cauldron of anger. She could only hope that her love, the most extravagant love she could summon from her soul's depths, might transform that black anger into acceptance, hope, peace.

When it ended at last with a shiver of mutual bliss, she waited for a sign that they had begun a journey together. Instead, Caesar's voice came out of the darkness again, as harsh and angry as ever.

"Let's understand something. Caesar don't want you to buy his freedom. Caesar ain't goin' to be any woman's bought man. Caesar's goin' to win his own freedom in his own way in his own good time. Then we can begin to talk about bein' lovers."

"You can't do it. You can't conquer a city without guns. Even if you seize it, then what? Caesar—it's madness."

"No it ain't. We're goin' to get some guns. We'll

take New York like Hangin' Belt won the Battle of the Bracken. By ambush, surprise.''

"I won't help you.''

"I'm not askin' for your help. But I want an absolute end to your mouthin' against it—and me.''

Clara said nothing. But her silence was consent.

In the morning she walked to Hughson's through a spring rain, feeling bewildered. She had been ready to arrange her life in a new way. But Caesar was impervious to the language of love and forgiveness.

At the tavern, buxom Sarah Hughson greeted her with a conspiratorial smile. Clara wondered if Caesar had robbed the governor's silver. Were they all about to become rich?

"I feel like a new woman,'' Sarah said.

"Why?'' Clara said.

"I've been to confession for the first time in twenty years.''

"To whom?''

"His name is John Ury. He's a priest.''

"A Catholic priest?''

Sarah nodded. "We must keep it the deepest secret,'' she said. "They'd hang him if they knew.''

"What do you do in confession?''

"You tell the priest your sins and he forgives you. It's what Catholics call a sacrament. Jesus gave his apostles the power to forgive sins and the power has passed down to Catholic priests through St. Peter, the first pope.''

What nonsense, Clara thought.

"The Protestant priests lost the power when they killed the English bishops,'' Mrs. Hughson said.

"Will he stay here long?'' Clara asked.

"I hope so. He plans to make a living as a tutor. He's in search of a place to board. Would you rent him one of your rooms?''

"I'd have to meet him first. Does he have a wife?''

Mrs. Hughson shook her head. "Catholic priests don't marry."

"Never?"

"Never," Mrs. Hughson said. "They take a vow of chastity forever."

A man who never touched a woman? Clara found this priest harder and harder to believe. She followed Sarah Hughson upstairs. In one of the tavern's third-floor rooms, they found a short dark-haired man reading a thick book, the pages of which were edged in gold. He had a slight stoop to his narrow shoulders, as if he carried a perpetual burden. A deep vertical line above the bridge of his nose suggested grief—or care—or intense thought. His mouth was kind, except for a single crooked tooth, which gave him an ambiguous expression. His eyes were dark and hooded, with bushy brows that seemed combative. He was wearing ordinary brown cloth breeches, with a patch above the knee, and a worn brown coat and tan waistcoat.

"Father Ury," Sarah Hughson said. "This is Clara Flowers. The woman I told you about. Who saved us from ruin."

"Please don't call me Father," Ury said with fierce urgency. "We must break that habit immediately."

"I'm sorry," Sarah Hughson said.

Sarah Hughson seemed to vanish from Ury's field of vision. His dark eyes focused totally on Clara. "My dear. They didn't tell me you were so young."

"Oh—I'm not that young," Clara said.

"You did something worthy of a woman far older, rescuing these good people from debtor's prison. I've spent some time in prison myself."

"So have I," Clara said. "That was one of the reasons—"

"I'm not surprised," Ury said. "So often we must suffer first before we learn to help others. Suffering is God's chain of grace in this cruel world."

This was a new idea to Clara. She shook her head. "I'm afraid I don't understand that kind of god."

"None of us do," Ury said. "We can only struggle to obey His teaching, through the example of his son, Jesus."

"I've read about Jesus. He was a good man," Clara said. "Why do you think he's a god?"

"Because his life teaches us God's central message—to accept the way of the cross—the way of suffering—without losing our faith in the mystery of God's goodness—in the hope of salvation after death."

The man spoke with such calm assurance, Clara was momentarily speechless. "Do you think you could rent Father—I mean Mr.—Ury a room?" Sarah Hughson said.

Clara contemplated this strange man. Why not? It would be interesting to hear Adam Duycinck argue with him. Adam did not believe there was anything after death but darkness. It would be even more interesting to see if he really lived without touching women. That would truly amaze her.

"Yes," she said. "I have a room."

"How much?" Ury said with a wisp of a smile. "I have very little money and don't expect to make much more."

"You can pay me whatever you think it's worth," Clara said.

"You're very kind," Ury said.

"No—just curious," Clara said.

Outside, the sky had darkened; a heavy rain began to fall. As Clara glanced back, the light seemed to drain from the room and John Ury was suddenly a blurred figure, shrouded in gloom. He might have been a spirit from the other world. Was he evil or good? Clara felt powerful emanations of both forces in the room as she closed the door.

As Malcolm intimated in his conversation with Clara, by becoming a Seneca again for that passionate moment at the close of the Battle of the Bracken, I had damaged my business reputation and his political career. Our enemies, the Van Sluydens and my Uncle Johannes and his wife and daughters, both of whom had married wealthy husbands, eagerly spread the slander that we had murdered Philip Van Sluyden and his trader friends. Customers deserted the Universal Store. In the next election, one of my uncle's sons-in-law beat Malcolm for his seat in the legislature.

On the Mohawk, customers for our fur trading store remained scarce. Our enemies among the traders called us "The Negar Store" and accused us of trying to create an African colony that would seize control of the river and waylay whites. Unable to continue paying our black soldiers, we gave them each two hundred acres of land along the river and closed the store. We retreated to New York where I sold the goods for half their value.

Soon we were desperate for cash. With the rising tide of war between the Spanish and the English and the likelihood that France might enter the conflict at any moment, the British navy roamed the high seas, making it almost impossible to smuggle goods from Holland. I was forced to buy English goods from New York importers, and the profits from the Universal Store plummeted.

There seemed to be only one somewhat forlorn hope— Malcolm's lawsuit to recover his New Jersey lands. This

prime topsoil, five square miles in extent, already in cul-
tivation, could be borrowed against almost indefinitely.
We decided to go to London and prosecute the case
personally. After years of legal paralysis, it seemed
hopeless to try to accomplish anything at a distance.

I also needed a London merchant to back me in New
York and ship me goods at prices that would let me meet
the competition. Much as it pained me, I saw it was time
to take my grandfather's advice and submit to English
power.

When I told Malcolm this side of my plan, he laughed
sardonically and said: "Don't tell me you're going to
start obeying the law." Our economic debacle on the
Mohawk had shaken his confidence in me. He still
yearned for Clara. We were far from a happy couple.

Malcolm went off to search the wharfs for a ship to
England. I wrote an ad for the *Gazette*, advertising the
Mohawk lands for sale or rent—and went over to the
Universal Store to discuss with Duycinck the possibility
of hiring Mrs. Hughson to manage the place while we
were in London. She had two daughters who were old
enough to work as clerks. She seemed to be making a
success of the tavern she owned with her husband and
Clara.

Duycinck declined to say yes or no to the proposal.
"Why so doubtful?" I asked.

The little hunchback squirmed and twisted his face.
"There are certain points to her character I'd rather not
discuss," he said.

"That's not good enough. Tell me the truth or—"

I had reduced terrorizing Duycinck to an art. He capitulated instantly. "She's a fence, madam. She and her
husband deal in stolen goods. I bought some stuff from
them. But I stopped. It made me too nervous. I could
feel the hemp around my neck."

I was stunned. I knew there was random thievery in

New York but I never realized it was a business. "Does Clara know?"

"I think so. I've never discussed it with her. I've never discussed it with anyone."

"I'm glad you stopped," I said. "But why did you start? Did you have so little confidence in me as a businesswoman?"

"Your success or failure had nothing to do with it, madam. I sold the stuff off the books and kept the money for myself."

I was deeply, painfully hurt. I had come to regard Adam as a trusted friend as well as an employee. "What have I done to deserve such treachery?" I said.

Adam tried to play the man at first. "You don't pay me enough to satisfy my appetite for good rum and pretty girls," he said.

He crumbled under my accusing stare. I paid him very well and he knew it. "Maybe this hump on my back makes me a kind of outlaw," he said.

The fact that the little fellow confessed his own guilt to protect me from Sarah Hughson was to his credit. "I wish I could pay you more," I said. "But we're closer to ruin than to prosperity at present. You know that. Still, in return for your somewhat peculiar honesty, the rest of your indenture is canceled forthwith."

"I'll spread the news when I celebrate tonight. Catalyntie Stapleton has a woman's heart—even if she wields a wicked scalping knife."

"That was a terrible mistake. I think it's changed Malcolm's feeling toward me."

"I've told Malcolm he should have scalped that swine Van Sluyden for you."

It was bewildering to discover that this little man, a total cynic about most people, admired me. I thanked him for his support and turned to go.

Adam seized my arm. "Promise me you won't tell

anyone—even Clara—what I said about Sarah Hughson. Her behemoth of a husband might wring my neck.''

''I don't know what to say to Clara.''

''Nor do I,'' Adam said.

Back at the house I found Malcolm waving a newspaper. He had located more than a ship. A fine brigantine, *Raleigh*, was just in from London. She would be sailing as soon as they loaded a cargo of grain. The captain had brought the latest London papers and they were full of momentous news. Malcolm read the story aloud to me from his favorite paper, *The Craftsman*.

''The time of the Patriots has come. The Great Corrupter has finally been called to account by our gracious King. Prime Minister Walpole has been forced to resign his place and the nation and the empire confidently expect that with him will go the army of vipers, bloodsuckers, thieves, and arsekissers who have so long disgraced the halls of our government. Not a few citizens hope the Great Thief himself will be placed on trial for his innumerable peculations and treacheries— but that is probably too much to expect from our benumbed benighted age. Perhaps, once the Patriots sweep out the accumulated filth of Walpole's reign, there will come a time for retribution. But for the present, let us simply rejoice in the nation's salvation.''

Malcolm was ecstatic. He saw a divine intervention in our favor. Justice was returning to the British Empire and he would be one of the beneficiaries. Remembering how much my Dutch friends admired Walpole, I was not so sure the change was for the better. But I had learned to hold my tongue in matters political.

I decided to take five-year-old Hugh Stapleton to London with us. I persuaded our cook Shirley's daughter,

Amelia, to come along as his nurse. To manage the Universal Store, I enlisted the wife of my old friend Guert Cuyler. She was a buxom intelligent Dutchwoman named Sophia, who was eager to try it. Her mother had managed a store for her late father, Harman Kierstede, a successful merchant of my grandfather's era.

As we began packing for our trip, we were interrupted by a visitor—our old friend Captain Hartshorne. The doleful countenance, dirty coat, and tattered wig that had characterized him at Oswego had vanished. He was dressed in the latest style, a bright blue waistcoat, a mauve swallowtail coat, and buff breeches. The silver buckles on his shoes must have cost him a year's pay. A new optimism pervaded his fleshy face.

"I'm on my way back to old England," he said. "I thought I'd give my friends the Stapletons a call."

Malcolm was delighted—and soon learned the reason for his military father's transformation. The death of Hartshorne's bachelor uncle—his father's brother—had left him a fortune almost as large as the one he had gambled away ten years ago. He was to receive it only if he swore a solemn oath in front of a clergyman never to touch cards or dice again. Malcolm easily persuaded the captain to join us aboard the *Raleigh* and insisted on putting him up in one of our spare rooms until we sailed.

This hospitality proved useful. A day or two later, another knock on the door introduced us to one of the most attractive young men I had ever seen in New York. William Johnson was about six feet tall, with a muscular physique that emanated vitality and a convivial Irish manner that more than matched his handsome face. He had seen my ad about the Mohawk store and was interested in managing it. He had plans to settle on the river to supervise the settlement of some lands belonging to his uncle, Sir Peter Warren. With Captain Hartshorne on hand to explain the politics of the fur trade and glorify Malcolm with a recitation of the Battle of the Bracken, the young Irishman was quickly convinced that he had found friends and business partners. Naturally pugnacious, like most of his race, he had no fear of the Albany conspirators, if they had the stomach for another foray against the store. He had a half dozen relatives with him, all of whom knew how to use a gun.

With our businesses in good hands, Malcolm and I sailed for England aboard *Raleigh*. The captain was a garrulous old salt named Jones, who predicted England would be at war with France within the year. Malcolm spent much of our six weeks at sea discussing with Hartshorne the fall of the Great Corrupter, Walpole, and the transformation they were both sure it would make in English politics.

I remained skeptical. I had no faith in moral transformations—especially English ones. I spent the voyage teaching little Hugh arithmetic. By the time we landed, the boy could add, subtract, and multiply simple sums and Hartshorne declared he was a prodigy.

Hartshorne's predictions of a political resurrection had Malcolm in a state of wild excitement as we glided up the winding Thames with the incoming tide, admiring the neat green fields and handsome houses that dotted the countryside along the river. Compared to forested mountainous America, England was one vast garden. It all looked so peaceful, so well ordered, I was almost ready to believe Hartshorne's optimism.

Soon London appeared on the horizon. The dome of a great church, identified by Hartshorne as St. Paul's, rose above the numerous spires of lesser churches. Malcolm stayed at the rail with Hartshorne while I retreated to the cabin to pack our trunk. Through an open porthole I overheard my husband say: "You can't begin to realize how much it will mean to me to have a decent competence of my own to put me on an equal footing with my wife."

"No doubt, no doubt," Hartshorne said. "She does seem a bit *strong-willed.*"

The words stung. So this was all I had to show for my years of trying to persuade him to love me—paying his tavern bills and the cost of keeping him in good clothes to play the politician in New York. He still resented my insistence on managing our finances. A bitterness crept into my heart that I found impossible to wish away.

With Hartshorne as our guide, we landed at a wharf not far from the remains of the old royal palace of Westminster.[1] Pointing downstream to where boatmen were ferrying people back and forth between two landings, Hartshorne remarked that it was the route King James II used to escape to France when he was deposed in the Glorious Revolution of 1688. "They say he dropped the Great Seal in the river midway across," Hartshorne said.

Not far away were the twin towers of St. Stephen's Chapel, where Parliament met. The residence of the Speaker of the House of Commons was a huge stone pile, more imposing than the chapel. We hired a coach from a nearby inn and drove down a wide street full of majestic old grey stone buildings around which numerous taverns clustered. "This is New Palace Yard," Hartshorne said. "The law courts. You'll no doubt be spending a lot of time here."

Next came narrower streets lined with cross-timbered houses which Hartshorne described as "ancient." The streets had picturesque names, such as "Thieving Lane" and "The Little Sanctuary," so-called because it was once a place where fugitive criminals could escape arrest. It was still populated by "the worst sort," Hartshorne said, adding it was "not a place to frequent after dark." A glance at the ugly faces and ragged clothes of

[1] *Now the site of the Houses of Parliament.*

the passersby readily convinced us that the captain knew whereof he spoke.

We progressed up King Street to Whitehall, site of a palace which had burned down forty years ago, prompting the royal family to move to St. James. The nobility rushed to buy the land and now it was populated largely by "great folks," Hartshorne said. He pointed to spacious three-story mansions in red brick or ochre, some overlooking the Thames, and reeled off the names of their owners—all dukes and marquises.

Soon we were in the heart of the city, and the streets and names became a blur. London was immense. Hartshorne said it had upward of six hundred thousand people. Three Amsterdams, I thought. Around us traffic thickened, a confusion of coaches and wagons and open carriages and a sprinkling of sedan chairs. These enclosed little houses made of leather, carried on the shoulders of two sturdy men, shocked Malcolm. "I didn't think you could get free Englishmen to do such degrading work," he said.

"Hunger is a great persuader," Hartshorne said in his offhand way.

I was fascinated by the incredible number of shops, each with a colorful sign swinging from it. When we passed through Leicester Square, Hartshorne pointed to the huge mansion at one end as the residence of the Prince of Wales. In front of it were four crude wooden shops. Elsewhere, whole streets of shops were devoted to a single industry, such as snuff or candle making or cabinet making.

On Holborn Street, our carriage was brought to a halt by an enormous crowd following a man and woman standing in a cart. There were women with young children in the procession, as well as couples smiling and chatting as if they were going to a play. "Someone on their way to be hanged at Tyburn," Hartshorne explained. "It's only about a half mile off, on the Oxford-Bayswater Road."

He leaned out of the carriage and asked a man selling sweetmeats what crimes the offenders had committed. "Thievery" was the response. "They was in service. Caught them with a half dozen spoons in their pockets."

"How many have they hanged this month?" Hartshorne asked.

"It's been brisk. Twenty-five!" the man said. "I've sold out me tray almost every day."

"Twenty-five in a month?" Malcolm said. "We don't hang five in a year in New York."

"Maybe you should multiply that number a bit," Hartshorne said. "The town would be a lot more quiet."

Finally we reached our destination—the White Horse Inn on Piccadilly, which was run by a Hartshorne relative, John Williams. He was a short rotund man with a red nose and vivid red dewlaps under his chin that made him resemble a rooster. He regarded Hartshorne with amazement, as if he had come back from the dead.

"I thought your head would be decorating some redskin's lodgepole long since," he roared.

Hartshorne introduced Malcolm and me as his "American" friends. Williams stepped back to get a better look at Malcolm's bulk. "Are they all this size?" he said.

Hartshorne shook his head. "They come in all shapes, like us," he said. "His mother was Scottish. I think that's where the size originates."

Hartshorne said we were all eager to hear the latest news about the political situation. Had the Patriots formed a government? Was Walpole's army of placemen about to join him in headlong retreat?

Williams shook his head and beckoned us into his empty taproom, where he opened a bottle of sherry to celebrate our arrival. "There's naught but trouble in the wind," he said. "The Patriots is fighting among themselves and Walpole's army shows no inclination to retreat.''

He began discussing Parliamentary politics, with a profusion of names and nicknames that left even Hartshorne confused. Malcolm looked completely bewildered. Though I paid little or no attention to politics, I was able to grasp the essence of the story. Walpole had left behind him two major generals in his political army, the brothers Pelham. The elder was the Duke of Newcastle, who had immense estates and influence in the north, around the city of that name. With twenty-five thousand voters among his tenants, he controlled a formidable bloc of seats in Parliament. As secretary of state, he had vast numbers of government jobs in his control. His brother Henry, as paymaster of the forces, had access to millions of pounds for bribes.

''But the country gentlemen,'' Hartshorne said. ''What's happened to them?''

''Tories, most of'm. The king won't let one of'm in the cabinet. He claims they're all Jacobites at heart. He may be right.''

''I thought the Patriots would end that old quarrel between the parties,'' Hartshorne said. ''To me the names Whig and Tory are meaningless.''[2]

''You've spent too much time in America,'' Williams said. ''They'll be Whigs and Tories as long as James Edward Stuart is sittin' across the channel, backed by French money and politics.''[3]

''You mean the Tories are loyal to the Pretender?''

[2]*The terms Whig and Tory went back to the previous century. The Whigs backed the revolution of 1689; the Tories remained loyal to the deposed James II and his family.*
[3]*James Edward Stuart was the son of the deposed James II, who died in 1701. Whigs called James Edward ''The Pretender.'' Tories called him James III.*

Malcolm said. "There are still people of that persuasion in England?"

"Hah!" Williams said. "I've had my windows broke once a week since Walpole went down. There's plenty in London who are ready to throw rocks at my sign. But it'll swing as long as I'm proprietor and my son after me."

"The White Horse is the emblem of the House of Hanover," Hartshorne explained to an amazed Malcolm Stapleton. Thanks to my thorough grounding in recent English history from Harman Bogardus, I knew this was the family of the current king, George II. The British had imported them from Germany when William of Orange failed to produce an heir.

The next morning we rose early and with directions from our innkeeper set out for St. Martin's Lane, where our lawyer, Peter Van Ness, had rooms. As we strolled down this narrow winding street, past numerous shops of cabinetmakers and other craftsmen, we suddenly found ourselves in the middle of a riot. A mob of several hundred people had gathered before a brick house with barred windows in the basement. On the sidewalk lay about a dozen women, most of them apparently dead. Friends and relatives wept over them.

"Murder the bastards!" screamed one woman. A rock sailed through the air and demolished a window on an upper floor.

Malcolm asked a ruddy-cheeked older man on the fringe of the crowd what had happened. "The constables was drunk last night and they gathered up all the streetwalkers they could find and stuffed them into the loft of the Round House here with all the doors and windows shut," the man said. "There wasn't enough air in the place to keep a canary alive. They was piled on top of each other like logs. The poor women died like pigs in the slaughterhouse. Is this arbitrary power at work or ain't it? What a hell of a country!"[4]

His words worked him into such a rage, the old man pried a paving stone out of the road and demolished another window of the Round House. "Burn it around their ears," he howled.

The mob stormed into the house and began throwing furniture out the windows. Soon flames and smoke swirled from the top story. Bells clanged and tradesmen rushed from their shops. Down the street came a bright red fire engine, pulled by a half dozen men. New York had bought two of these machines, which were a great improvement on buckets.

At first the crowd refused to let the firemen into the house. A magistrate appeared and threatened to read the riot act. That would enable the authorities to call for the army. The mob fell back and sullenly allowed the firemen to run their hoses into the building. Malcolm volunteered to help work the pumper that sent the water gushing up the hoses to douse the flames.

The old man Malcolm questioned now began to harangue the crowd. "This wouldn't happen in a country with an English king. We've got a king who speaks better French and German than English. Three cheers for the true king over the water!"[5]

The crowd sent up three treasonous cheers with the greatest enthusiasm. Malcolm could not believe his ears. We continued down St. Martin's Lane to Slaughter's Tavern, where we asked for Peter Van Ness.

"The American poet?" said the smiling proprietor. "He's no doubt hard at work upstairs."

---

[4]The London Weekly Journal *reported this incident more or less as Catalyntie Stapleton tells it. The Round House on St. Martin's Lane was district police headquarters where prisoners were held overnight.*
[5]*This was a popular way of referring to James Edward Stuart.*

We mounted to a room in the rear of the third floor and discovered our once hard-eyed young New York attorney had in fact become a poet. He wore a loose-fitting kimono and skullcap, making him look more like a Jew than a Dutchman. His desk was littered with books; a skull peered at us atop one pile. He was pleasantly surprised to see us, but treated us more like creatures from another life.

"New York seems so far away and long ago," he said.

Malcolm's case against Georgianna Stapleton? Oh yes, he would give us the name of the barrister he had hired. He had heard nothing from him for months—perhaps a year. Van Ness was far more interested in telling us that he was publishing a book of poems and through one of the many literary men who drank at Slaughter's, he hoped to win the approval—and generosity—of the great Tory politician Lord Bolingbroke. There was a very good chance that Bolingbroke might soon become prime minister—which would mean fame and limitless fortune for his protégés.

I strongly suspected literature had stolen our lawyer's wits. He read us several poems, which extolled the "rustic peace" of the American forest, the unspoiled beauty of the Hudson or the Mohawk River. I did not associate peace or beauty with either place. For me the forest would always be haunted by terror and death—and the Hudson and the Mohawk were no more than tedious highways. Van Ness called his poems *Iroquois Odes*—a title which had already won him a publisher, but which struck me as absurd.

Restraining my sharp tongue, I let Malcolm congratulate Van Ness and wish him every success. He gave us Georgianna Stapleton's address and the name and address of our English lawyer. Malcolm decided to visit his brother first. We trekked back down St. Martin's Street and along a dozen more streets to Golden Square, a splendid set of four-story houses around a fenced green park. Strollers readily guided us to the house next to the Portuguese Embassy.

A maid led us to a well-furnished parlor, with a marble mantel and overdoors enriched by scrollwork and flowers. Georgianna Stapleton swept into the room in a dress which was the equal of anything I had seen in Amsterdam. It was a rich damask, embroidered with golden lace, cut low in the front to display her splendid breasts.

"Stepson!" she said, boldly kissing Malcolm on the mouth. "And his commercial wife. What brings you to London?"

"My wife is here to do business on behalf of her store in New York, madam," Malcolm said. "I'm here to see my brother and discuss the matter of my father's estate with him—and perhaps with you."

"Jamey left London for the Scottish border six months ago. We've bought him a commission in the army."

"He's only fifteen," Malcolm said.

"Most ensigns are fourteen,"[6] Georgianna said. "Governor Nicolls thinks it will be the making of him. Jamey wanted to go."

"Is it part of your plot, madam, to hope for his early death, so you can completely loot our estate?"

Infuriated, Georgianna returned this insult to Malcolm with interest. "Once and for all, let's make a few things clear. Hampden Hall was not built with your mother's money. When she died that was all gone, thanks to your father's feckless ways. I procured him credit to build the house and play the rich man. Whatever money I spend from his estate, which is still up to the chimneys in debt, I've earned it. You might even say I'm still earning it,

[6]*Ensign was the equivalent of a second lieutenant.*

since without Mr. Nicolls's intervention, it would have been sold for its debts long ago.''

''I don't believe a word you say, madam,'' Malcolm said. ''I never have and never will.''

Georgianna's smile became a sneer. ''Still a booby, aren't you,'' she said. ''Do you think you can win a war with us? Mr. Nicolls sits in Parliament for the Duke of Newcastle. He and his brother, Henry Pelham, will soon be running the country. This Patriot stuff is so much moonshine.''

While Malcolm fumed, my ever-active brain was concluding that Georgianna Stapleton's comments about the estate had a ring of authenticity. This was a woman who had rescued herself from the pit of poverty by her wits and beauty and she was clearly proud of it. There was a mystery here—a mystery I had long sensed about the late George Stapleton—and I did not know the answer.

We left Georgianna's house after she and Malcolm exchanged more warm words about her treatment of Jamey—and she triumphantly informed me Robert Nicolls was about to marry a Miss White, who had a dowry of one hundred thousand pounds. A furious Malcolm rushed to Old Palace Yard with me gasping in his wake. He was much too angry for me to discuss my intuition about Georgianna. In the Yard, we quickly located our lawyer, Thomas McDuffie. He was a small morose man, whose office was cluttered with dust-covered lawbooks.

''Stapleton? Stapleton?'' he said, his snub-nosed face a blank. It took a paragraph of explanation for Malcolm to refresh his memory. ''Oh, the American will! A very difficult case, young man. I've applied for a writ of mandamus, which would have returned the matter to a court in your colony, but the will has been filed and executed here as well as in New York, which complicates the matter—''

McDuffie paused and his eyes drifted from Malcolm

to me. "Let's be blunt. How much money are you willing to spend to settle this?"

"What do you mean?" Malcolm said.

"I mean a bribe or two. Or maybe three."

"I will pay no man a bribe. With Walpole down, won't there be a restoration of honesty and integrity here?" Malcolm said.

McDuffie regarded him with the sort of kindly smile people give harmless lunatics. "When that day comes, you may also look for Jesus Christ and a brace of Archangels to sail up the Thames. It will be the advent of the Second Coming, I assure you," McDuffie said.

"How much money are you talking about?" I asked.

"At least two thousand pounds. Possibly three."

"We don't have it."

McDuffie sighed. Hurling more legal terms at us, he made it clear that he thought we had no case. "But it was my mother's money that was taken from me," Malcolm said. "I heard her say a hundred times that the land was bought with her money and it would come to me—"

"Do you have a copy of a marriage settlement?" McDuffie asked.

Malcolm shook his head. "Where did your mother come from?" McDuffie asked.

"The Scottish lowlands. The town was called Thornhill."

McDuffie became almost cheerful. "In Dumfries. My home county. What was her maiden name?"

"McCullough."

"Was she related to *the* McCulloughs?"

He rapidly explained that the McCulloughs were the most powerful family in that part of Scotland. They had led a revolt in 1715, which had attempted to place James Edward Stuart on his father's throne.

"I never heard her mention such a thing," Malcolm said.

"She wouldn't, by any means. Half her family was wiped out in it. I lost a few of mine. The McDuffies were retainers of the laird, David McCullough. He was a thorough Jacobite."

"She taught me nothing but loyalty to the king!" Malcolm said.

"But did she say which king?" McDuffie said, with a lively sneer. "There's a good many of us who toast the king and then pass our tankards over the nearest water glass to signify which king we mean."

I was enjoying this more and more. But I said nothing. I could see Malcolm was all but undone by the idea that his mother may have been a Jacobite. McDuffie decided Malcolm should go to Thornhill and consult his mother's family. If they could testify to a marriage settlement which restricted the disposition of his mother's money, it might affect the validity of his father's will.

Back in the White Horse Inn, I urged Malcolm to head for Scotland as soon as possible. It was costing us a pound a day to live in London. The less time we spent here, the better. He agreed without enthusiasm. Neither of us imagined McDuffie was sending him north to make the most demoralizing discovery of his life.

SEVEN

IN NEW YORK, CLARA'S LIFE was moving down another path, crowded with the faces and voices she encountered each night at Hughson's. Primary among them was Caesar, who seemed to take savage pleasure in mocking her silent reproaches by recruiting in front of her eyes for his plot to seize New York. Lately he had been buying

drinks for six Africans who had been captured aboard a
Spanish merchant ship taken by a privateer off Cuba and
sold as slaves in New York. They maintained they were
free men and should be held as prisoners of war for
exchange, just as white sailors were. But no one paid
any attention to them. They had been bought by George
Fowler to work in his distillery.

Clara's pity for them knew no bounds. Especially for
Antonio, the youngest and boldest of them. He was a
handsome fellow, straight-backed, with broad shoulders
and fierce warrior eyes. He told her in his halting English that he had been engaged to marry a woman whose
freedom he had bought with his earnings as a sailor.
Now she was weeping for him in Cuba, while he faced
a lifetime of slavery here in New York.

"Clara's been praying for you every day since she
heard your fate," Caesar said.

Antonio glared contemptuously at Clara. "I say no
prayers to her God or any other god," Antonio said.
"Why should I pray to a power that's condemned me
to slavery a thousand miles from my home?"

"If you took up arms and won your freedom," Caesar
said, "you wouldn't have to pray to any god."

"You mean kill old Fowler?" Antonio asked. He was
not taking Caesar seriously. "Don't they hang people in
New York for that sort of thing?"

"They wouldn't hang you. If all goes well, they'd all
be dead—or our prisoners. Others would act with you.
Are you interested?"

"Of course I'm interested," Antonio said. "I'd gladly
kill old Fowler and his whole miserable family and
many more."

Caesar smiled mockingly at Clara. *See?* his smile said.
See how I'm going to win my freedom?

Three hours later, Caesar was back in the taproom.
The shutters were closed, all the lights out except a lone
candle. On the bar were a dozen silver forks and a silver

plate and a lush black bearskin coat—Caesar's swag for the night. With him was his button-nosed moon-faced helper, Cuffee. He was wearing his usual expensive clothes—castoffs from his master's wardrobe. His owner was one of the city's wealthiest men, Adolphus Philipse.

"What do you think of this?" Caesar said.

"I don't think anything of it. I don't even see it," Clara said.

"You got to admit he's the best burglar in New York, Clara," Cuffee said.

Clara said nothing.

"He's going to be king of New York. Going to make you his queen," Cuffee said. "You is all he talks about when he's drunk."

"Shut your mouth for once, Cuff," Caesar said.

Clara said nothing. She was keeping her promise of silence. But she had stopped teaching Caesar to read. She had refused to let him touch her again. She was letting Caesar go his own destructive way—hoping—occasionally praying—that he would change, that his desire for her would persuade him to abandon his mad scheme to conquer New York.

Sarah Hughson's heavy steps echoed on the stairs. Sarah's hair was down, she was wearing a green nightrobe and little else. Her cheeks were flushed. There was not much doubt that she had just finished a tumble with her husband. How she loved that big stupid lout. It was a puzzle, how an intelligent woman could become all but enslaved by desire. Was Catalyntie the same way with Malcolm in private—forever gazing hungrily at him? The thought made Clara flinch. She almost wished she had not been born a woman.

Sarah Hughson gazed admiringly at the loot. "Good stuff," she said. "Where did you get it?" It was always important to know where stolen property came from. It made disposing of it far less risky.

"Fowler's. Her upstairs maid left a back window unlocked. I'll take care of her."

"Good. I'll give you three pounds for the lot."

"Four. The coat alone is worth five pounds."

"All right. Tell Mary to put it away in the usual place, Clara. I'll give Caesar the money from the drawer."

Sarah Hughson counted out four pounds in Spanish gold dollars, the common medium of exchange in New York. Tomorrow, John Hughson would sell the silver plate and candlesticks to a ship captain sailing for the West Indies or England. The bearskin coat would sell in Boston, with a coastal shipper. Everyone profited. Only the very rich owners, George and Eugenia Fowler, were the losers.

Was that wrong? Clara wondered again, after Mary Burton had put the goods away in the secret room beneath the stairs. Eugenia Fowler was a despicable woman. Her husband made a fortune selling cheap rum to New York. He gave little to the poor. He was a friend of Johannes Van Vorst. Why not steal from him?

As Clara walked home to Maiden Lane in the warm spring night, the question ached in her mind. She found John Ury reading a book by the light of a single flickering candle. He seldom slept more than four hours a night. He had nightmares from his years as a priest on the run in England. Impulsively, she asked him what he thought of Caesar's thievery.

"There are some philosophers who argue that people living under tyranny can resist it by any means in their power," he told her. Since slavery was the greatest of all tyrannies, Caesar's petty crimes could easily be justified in the eyes of God.

Not for the first time, Clara was struck by how much more loving and forgiving Ury's Catholic God was than the stern deity the Protestants worshipped. The Protestant God forgave no one and demanded ferocious punishments for sin. The Catholic God forgave sins again and again in the ritual of confession. Surely this was closer to the spirit of Jesus, which both churches claimed to represent.

But was any of it true? To guide her, Clara depended on her *orenda*, the inner voice that separated spiritual truth from falsehood. Over the past four months, she had felt great power flowing from this priest. She had become convinced that he was a holy man. Not once had he suggested she give herself to him. He remained immune to the invitations of the whores who crowded Hughson's taproom.

Mary Burton, still one of Clara's boarders, set out to seduce him. Ury ignored her thinly veiled invitations to sleep with her. Finally, Mary wept and said she loved him and wanted to marry him. It revealed a startling degree of ambition in Mary's misshapen soul. Few slatterns like her ever dreamed of marrying a man as well educated and well born as John Ury.

Ury patiently explained to Mary that he had chosen not to marry, so he could preach the gospel more fully. "There are two kinds of love in this world, my dear Mary," Ury said. "One the ancient Greek philosophers called eros. This is the love most men and women know—the love of passion and possession. The other nobler love is called agape. That is the love Jesus preached. It is purely spiritual. It seeks nothing for itself."

"Sounds loony to me," Mary said.

To Clara the concept of the two loves was like a burst of brilliant light in her mind and heart. For the first time she understood herself and her place in the spiritual order of things. She understood her youthful fascination with Jesus. She understood why she and Ury shared a special sympathy for the slaves and whores of the city.

"I'm beginning to think I'd like to know more about

your Catholic God,'' Clara said. ''Is there any point in praying to Him? Why did He create so many different races? Why does He permit wars and slavery?''

Ury impressed her by admitting he did not know the answer to those deep questions. He could only tell her that prayer had enlarged his soul and filled him with love for his fellow men and women. Ultimately, he only knew that God had called him to follow in Jesus's footsteps. That was the heart of his priesthood.

From his trunk Ury drew a book about women from Spain and other Catholic countries, who had been given special gifts from the being he called the Holy Spirit. He suspected Clara possessed similar gifts. But first she would have to accept baptism and make a confession of faith. Clara resisted until Ury assured her that she could continue to believe in the Manitou, the Master of Life, the Evil Brother, and the other gods of her Indian faith. These were simply different ways of recognizing the Catholic God's presence in the world.

In a ritual witnessed by Sarah Hughson and her husband, Clara permitted the priest to baptize her. He trickled water through her hair and anointed her forehead with sacred oils. She felt no different after the ceremony. That night, at Ury's urging, she knelt at the window of her room and opened her mind and heart to God. The priest had told her to seek nothing, to ask no favors, simply to imagine herself as a lover waiting for her beloved.

The stars blazed in the inky depths of the heavens. She had read another book Father Ury had given her, by an Italian follower of a man named Galileo, describing the wonders of the universe. The earth was not the center of creation as it seemed but merely a speck in an immense abyss, with the sun and other planets and the moon for companions and the stars at a distance beyond imagining. This God was infinitely greater than the Manitou of her childhood. She thought of Jesus, his mysterious life, his brutal death.

Suddenly a woman's voice whispered in her soul: *forgive*. A strange sweetness flooded her flesh; a mixture of music and forest sounds murmured around her. The raucous clamor of the city vanished. She was alone on a vast river, winding through a forest of brilliant green trees. Deer and bear and wolves gamboled on the banks, unafraid. In the distance she heard a woman singing a sweet sad song in a language she did not understand.

All the pain of the past, her parents' violent deaths, the lost child, Malcolm's sad transformation, Catalyntie's corruption, the sufferings of the whores and the slaves vanished like smoke from a spent fire. She was filled with an incredible sense of glory. She stood on a cliff, looking across a tremendous continent, peopled with farms and villages and teeming millions of white and black and red and yellow-skinned people. Within her the voice whispered: *Heed me, O daughter of the morning.*

Clara stayed on her knees until dawn. When she told Ury about the voice, he embraced her. "I knew it, I knew it, from the start. Let me give you my most precious possession."

From his trunk he took a small statue of a woman in a blue robe, her hands outstretched. He told Clara it was the Blessed Virgin, the mother of Jesus. "I used to hear her voice when I prayed before this. Before the world and time corrupted me."

"Corrupted you? What are you talking about?"

"Never mind. I asked God for a sign and he gave you to me. No matter what happens now, I'll die consoled and content."

"What do you mean, what happens now?" Clara said. "Why are you thinking about dying?"

"We're in the midst of a war," the priest said. "That makes all our affairs uncertain."

For the first time, Clara felt he was being less than honest with her. She would soon discover that in John Ury's wounded soul, honesty was rather low on the ladder of virtues.

EIGHT

"WHY AAN'T YOU HOME MINDING your kiddies?" grunted the latest in my dwindling list of London merchants.

"I have my kiddy with me here in London. He's being very well minded, thank you."

As Malcolm rode north in jouncing stagecoaches to find out if his mother had negotiated a marriage settlement with his father, I had begun calling on London merchants to locate someone who would ship me goods on credit. I had acquired a pretty good list from several sources in New York. So far I had met with nothing but curt refusals and, occasionally, lectures on the incompatibility of females and business, like this one.

Soon I was down to the last name on my list, a cloth merchant named Chesley White. He was a short rotund man with red cheeks and kindly eyes. "I was expecting a creature with horns. At least a Jezebel with the airs of a Covent Garden strumpet," he said.

"Why?"

"You don't know about the letter that's been circulated about you? I'm a believer in fair play, even though I can't imagine what a woman's doing in business, when she supposedly has a husband to support her."

He fished around on his desk and produced a letter

from Johannes Van Vorst to another London merchant, named Beckley.

> *I have news that my niece, Catalyntie Stapleton, my late brother's child, is about to descend on London in search of credit to rescue her from her debts here. She is the most willful creature in the world—and, I regret to say, possibly the most depraved of her sex in this city. Captivated by the Indians in her infancy, she learned nothing but their godless ways until the age of seventeen. It has left her without a trace of virtue or trustworthiness. She launched her business on Dutch goods, smuggled brazenly into this town under cover of favoritism purchased, you may imagine how, from the governor and his friends. Lately, she married a fellow named Stapleton, a lout with nothing to recommend him but a taste for rum. What he doesn't drink away of her profits, he gambles. Since the good name of New York is dear to me, I hope you will circulate this letter among your friends to make sure she receives no credit or consideration from any worthy man of business in London.*

I burst into tears. They were tears of rage but Chesley White thought they were born of regret or remorse or both and pitied me. He took me to a nearby tavern and bought me a plate of oysters, while he partook of one twice the size. "I've found there's nothing like oysters to settle the temperament," he said. "They soothe the blood marvelously. Is there any truth to that letter?"

"None," I said.

"I fancy myself a judge of character. You don't look the part of a depraved woman," he said. "I have a daughter about your age. She's about to marry a fine young fellow named Nicolls, who's spent time in America. Before I ship you any goods, I'm afraid I must meet your husband.''

Bow down, bow down. I could hear my grandfather advising me. Fate seemed to be requiring ever-lower declensions. Not only was Malcolm to be examined like a potential felon—I had to do business with the man who was about to make Robert Nicolls rich. What next? Would I have to kowtow like the Chinese, knocking my head on the floor? ''My husband's in Scotland on business,'' I said. ''I'll be happy to introduce you when he returns.''

The business in which Malcolm Stapleton was involved when I exchanged those polite words with Chesley White was not the sort that would have induced White, a loyal follower of George II and a warm friend of Robert Walpole, to ship me anything but condemnations. Malcolm was in the manor house of the McCulloughs, a few miles from the town of Thornhill. More and more he felt like a man who had somehow wandered off his home planet.

He had ridden north with his friend Hartshorne, who had bought himself the colonelcy of the 20th Regiment, which was stationed in Carlisle.[1] By happy coincidence, Jamey Stapleton was serving as an ensign in another regiment, the 24th, stationed in the same border town. Malcolm had stopped for a few days to see his brother. It was not a reassuring visit. Jamey had not grown into a man of any size. He resembled his father, short, with a snub nose and lank brown hair. He told Malcolm he had chosen the army as better company than his stepmother, whom he called ''The Great Whore.''

Jamey's enlisted soldiers were the worst scum Malcolm had ever seen. Every one of them looked like a broken-down drunkard or fugitive criminal. Hartshorne

---

[1] *Commissions were bought and sold, usually for substantial sums, in the British army of this era.*

offhandedly admitted private soldiers were "the sweepings of the streets." No one else joined the British army but people so desperate they regarded the sixpence a week they received for pay as decent wages. Jamey proudly assured Malcolm that his men had learned to fear him. He called one private, Tracy, and told him to go to his quarters in the rundown inn where they were billeted and bring him a guinea[2] from the cashbox in his desk.

"Yes, Mr. Stapleton," the man said. He was a hulking brute twice Jamey's size. He returned with the guinea and Jamey told Malcolm if there was any money missing from the box, Tracy would get one hundred lashes in the morning. It was all so different from Malcolm's romantic vision of the British army, staffed by bold yeomen ready to die for their king, he could only shake his head in dismay.

Malcolm rode on to Thornhill through a countryside that seemed barren and almost uninhabited, compared to the teeming towns and villages of the English midlands, surrounded by their lush green fields. The humpish mountains of the borderlands were practically devoid of trees. Everywhere there were signs of war—ruined houses and abandoned farms. But the few people he met on the road were friendly. Their faces lit at the sight of him with a readiness that almost seemed a personal recognition.

Finally, a laborer with a shovel on his shoulder led him to the McCullough manor house, asking offhandedly in a Scottish burr: "Is it from London you're cooming, me laird?"

"Laird?" Malcolm said. "I'm no lord."

"Excuse me," the man said and hurried off, after ringing the bell at the gate of the sprawling walled house.

A bent old woman opened the gate. "Jesus, Mary,

---

[2] *A gold coin worth one pound and one shilling.*

and Joseph!'' she cried when she saw Malcolm. She crossed herself several times, trembling as if she were on the verge of a seizure.

Malcolm introduced himself and said he had been told his mother, Mary McCullough, came from these parts. He was searching for someone who knew her. ''From these parts! She came from this house!'' the hag cried. ''I nursed her at my breasts, bare dugs they are now but once full of milk for the most beautiful babe that ever was born in the kingdom of Scotland!''

''I remember her as very beautiful. I was eleven years old when she—''

''Mistress!'' screeched the old woman. ''Mistress. Come see a ghost in the flesh! Help me God, before I faint away. Come see him one and all.''

People poured out of the house, young, old, and middle-aged, all women except for one grey-haired man. They clustered at the gate, staring in a strange combination of horror and bewilderment.

''Is one of you the master of this place?'' Malcolm asked, with some exasperation. He had begun to wonder if it was a madhouse.

''I'm best qualified to speak for him,'' said a tall, grey-haired woman in a flowing blue gown. ''My name is Mildred MacDonough. It was once McCullough. I'm your mother's sister.''

''Why is everyone staring at me this way?'' Malcolm said, as they led him into the grounds. Several of the servants shrank back as if they feared his touch.

''You remind them of someone long dead,'' Mildred MacDonough said. ''They believe in ghosts. I was ready to believe in them myself when I saw you.''

In the house, servants set out glasses and jugs full of malt liquor and the women and the servants and the old man gathered at a long table in a big bare room and toasted his arrival. Everyone was still in a state of high excitement.

"It's a sign, I think—I hope—I pray," Mildred MacDonough said.

"A sign of what?" Malcolm said.

"That history won't repeat itself," the old man said.

"To the king!" a younger woman said. "May he not be much longer over the water."

"May he be on Scotland's soil at this very moment," said the old man, whose name was David MacGregor.

Malcolm thought it best to drink and say nothing. He soon learned the old man was his mother's cousin. The house and lands were owned by Mildred MacDonough's husband. He and his three sons were in France, soldiers in an army James Edward Stuart was creating to invade England with French help. But she still regarded the estate as McCullough property.

"They were conveyed to my husband in my father's— your grandfather's—will to prevent them from being seized by the English after the failure of the rising of 1715," she said. "They issued bills of attainder on every prominent man who served the true king in that cruel war. My father fled to France with King James Edward and died there."

These references to King James Edward made Malcolm so nervous he drank even more of the malt liquor than he was inclined to by nature, and everyone happily joined him, until there was a roaring party in full swing. They brought in a fiddler and several of the young women taught Malcolm some Scottish dances, which he performed with agility, being a natural athlete. Not until well after dark did anyone think of food. Someone in the kitchen had kept enough of her wits to slaughter a lamb, and they ate roasted lamb and haggis and other native dishes with gusto until close to midnight.

Finally Malcolm found a chance to tell Mildred MacDonough of his mother's fate and the disposition of the lands in his father's will. "That bastard George Stapleton, may his miserable thief's soul burn in hell for all eternity!'' Mildred said.

Malcolm felt compelled to defend his father. ''I'm afraid I gave him great provocation to disinherit me,'' he said. ''I resisted his wish to make me a lawyer. A soldier is all I've ever wanted to be.''

''And why not?'' Mildred said.

She caught herself. All conversation in the room had abruptly ceased. ''You and I must talk in private,'' she said.

She led him upstairs to an alcove beside her bedroom and sat him down on a footstool. The light from a full moon filled the room with a ghostly glow. ''This was once your mother's room,'' she said. ''It overlooks the garden. In the spring of 1715, all Scotland was in a ferment with the hope of putting our true king on the throne in London. For once, the lowlands and the highlands were both aflame with that single wish. To us here in Dumfries came Duncan MacGregor, younger brother of the greatest of the Scottish chieftains, Robert MacGregor, whom we called Rob Roy. Duncan was your image. As huge and as handsome. Your mother melted at the sight of him and he at her. Through that garden and up a ladder supplied by me he came to see her for a month. In this room you first leaped in her womb.''

No longer drunk, Malcolm gazed into the moonlit garden, trying to assimilate what he was hearing. ''Who was George Stapleton—the man I thought was my father?''

''He was the younger son of a barrister from Carlisle who was in charge of confiscating estates in the wake of the defeat of 1715. He kept wretched books and was a thief in the bargain. The authorities soon were on his track. He saw a chance to save his neck, we saw a chance to rescue some of the family's wealth from London's slavering greed. We proposed to hand over to him all our silver plate and almost every shilling of money, our jewels and our best bedclothes and raiment if he would marry your mother and flee with her to America. He agreed and sailed from Perth with a number of other refugees. Your mother was at that time four months pregnant.''

"What happened to my . . . my father?" Malcolm said. He was almost unable to pronounce the word.

"By that time, Duncan MacGregor was in his grave, slain in the Battle of Preston, fighting single-handedly at the last against a hundred English, according to legend. He refused to surrender like the others and tried to cut his way out.''

The Battle of Preston meant little to Malcolm. He had heard nothing from George Stapleton but denunciations of Jacobites. To think that his mother had sat in silence through these harangues, concealing her ruined hopes and broken heart. He saw why, of course. To tell him the truth would have required a confession too difficult for a boy to understand.

Mildred MacDonough left Malcolm to sit by the window until the moonlight vanished from the garden and the room. He threw himself on the bed but it was impossible to sleep. He was not Malcolm Stapleton, except by an accident of law. He was Malcolm MacGregor. What did that mean? Shaken beyond all measure, he drifted into a shallow sleep—to be awakened by wild shouts in the yard.

"He's landed, he's landed!" cried a man's voice.

"Where?" cried a woman's voice.

"At Moidart, the country of the MacDonalds. With only seven men. But the clans are rising. We'll see his standard fly from London tower in a month's time. Mark me!''

Malcolm rushed downstairs and soon learned they were talking about Prince Charles Edward Stuart, the twenty-five-year-old son of James Edward Stuart. He

had landed in the north of Scotland and called on the
nation to support him. At breakfast, Mildred calmly informed Malcolm that the prince's arrival had been plot-
ted for a year. Her husband, Robert MacDonough, had
gone north with her three sons to join the prince's ranks.
When he came down to Dumfries, they planned to rally
the country around him.

David MacGregor announced they would all celebrate
mass in the courtyard. He was, Malcolm soon realized,
a Catholic priest. From somewhere in the cellar the servants retrieved sacred garments, a green chasuble and a
white surplice, and set up an altar. His mother had been
a Catholic! So much for his devotion to the Protestant
cause. He felt compelled to kneel with the others in pretended reverence but he declined to receive the host,
explaining he had been raised a Protestant.

Malcolm did not know what to do. England and Scotland seemed about to erupt in civil war. The days and
nights were filled with messengers galloping down from
the north, reporting one clan after another had declared
for "the Bonnie Prince," as everyone in the house called
Charles Edward Stuart. Soon came news of victories—
British armies routed and the capitulation of Scotland's
chief cities, Edinburgh and Glasgow. Malcolm feared for
me and our son, marooned in London. But Mildred
MacDonough told him he would be mad to try to travel
there now. He looked too much like a highland Scot.
All roads south were under guard to prevent the revolt
from spreading to England.

"They'll hang you without even a show of justice,"
she said.

In London, I watched with amazement as the English
government wavered and wobbled and seemed on the
verge of collapse. When the Bonnie Prince landed,
George II was in Germany, inadvertently emphasizing
he was a foreign king. Most of the British army was in

Holland fighting the French and there seemed to be no rush to bring them home. Then came news of the prince's victories in Scotland. Next, the prince and his army of mostly highland Scotsmen invaded England.

In a week the Jacobites were at Derby, more than halfway to London, calling on the countryside to support them. Prominent English noblemen and their followers joined the prince's army. Peter Van Ness told me that he expected his patron, Lord Bolingbroke, to arrive from France at any moment to form a Tory government. Panic gripped the capital. The headquarters of the Bank of England was mobbed by thousands of depositors, trying to withdraw their money for possible flight. The tellers paid them in shillings, a desperate measure designed to slow the outrush of funds and stave off bankruptcy.

Intensifying the crisis, Walpole's heirs, the Duke of Newcastle and his brother, Henry Pelham, clashed head-on with King George II and led a mass resignation from the government to force the king to accept their policies and placemen. The Patriot newspapers screamed outrage and mobs swirled through London, shouting for a new king and a new Parliament. Jacobites broke every window in the White Horse Inn and beat up proprietor John Williams when he tried to stop them. I moved across the street to the Black Horse Inn and rushed to Chesley White for advice.

White told me to stay calm. ''The Pelhams are old gamesters like their master, Walpole,'' he said. ''They're betting everything on this toss—but I'm inclined to wager with them. The army's come back from Holland. You'll soon see the Bonnie Prince on the run.''

In Scotland, Malcolm shortly witnessed the truth of this prophecy. He had watched the prince's army stream south through Dumfries. He declined to join them—a decision that caused not a little coolness toward him among the McCullough servants. But Mildred Mac-

Donough defended his right to choose neither side. "This is not his country. It's birth, not blood, that gives a man a country," she said. Malcolm was grateful to this large-hearted woman. She obviously regarded him as a kind of son.

Soon the prince's army trudged north again and the wild optimism that had permeated the McCullough house trailed away like fog before a harsh wind. The English Jacobites had failed to rise and the British army from Holland was on the march. All the cattle—the chief wealth of the property—vanished into the highlanders' hungry jaws as they passed. Mildred MacDonough vowed she did not regret the loss of a single beast— though the house was reduced to eating bread and salt fish.

Hunger was only the beginning of their troubles. One cold grey morning, Malcolm was awakened by shouts and cries that were stitched with terror. Peering from his window, he saw about three hundred red-coated British soldiers outside the gates, escorting wagons on which two gallows had been mounted. "Open up, rebels!" roared a beefy officer on horseback.

Downstairs, Malcolm found Mildred MacDonough confronting a half dozen soldiers, led by the officer, who continued to speak in a voice that was never less than a roar. He was Brigadier Henry Hawley, commissioned by the Duke of Cumberland, commander of the Royal Army, to root out disaffection in the countryside. They had information that Mildred's husband and sons were in the rebel army.

"I am authorized by His Grace to hang every male person found in this house and burn it to the ground," Hawley thundered. "You have five minutes to collect what clothes you may need for warmth and get your-selves into the road. These men will hang."

He pointed to Malcolm and David MacGregor, who had joined them in the hall.

"Why would you murder a man of his age? And a young man from America—my sister's son," Mildred MacDonough said.

"I would murder a man of his age because according to our informers he's a papist priest. As for this fellow," Hawley said, glaring at Malcolm, "I've spent enough time in your miserable country to recognize a highland scoundrel, with or without his kilt."

"He was born in America. Let him speak. He hasn't a trace of Scot in his tongue!"

"I don't care how or what he speaks," Hawley roared. "Get busy gathering your things, woman, or I'll burn the house with you and your damned treasonous bitches in it."

"Do as he says, Mildred, dear," David MacGregor said. "I've long been resigned to such a death."

Mildred MacDonough dropped to her knees. "Bless us one last time, Father," she said.

All the other women in the house joined her on their knees. The priest drew a sign of the cross in the air and murmured something in Latin.

"We'll soon shut off that mumbo jumbo," Hawley said. "Drag him out and get the hemp around his neck. Take this highland scum with him."

Malcolm simply could not believe he was going to be hanged. In the garden he spoke to the young officer and two privates who were leading him to his doom. "My name is Malcolm Stapleton. I was born in the colony of New York. This is a mistake. I'm ready to swear I'm no rebel."

"He's telling the truth," David MacGregor said.

"Malcolm Stapleton," the young officer said. He was straw thin, with pipestem wrists and a face almost devoid of a chin. But his eyes glittered with intelligence. "Did you fight a battle in the forest? The Battle of the Bracken?"

"Yes."

"I'll be damned. Your brother's outside with our regiment. I'm Major Wolfe. He gave me your account of that scrape. He overheard me declaring in my portentous way that the British army must begin learning how to fight in the forests of North America."

"Am I still to hang for visiting here at the wrong time?" Malcolm said.

"I hope not," Wolfe said. "I'll speak to the brigadier."[3]

The sobbing women streamed out of the house. Soldiers wrestled David MacGregor up on one of the wagons and placed a noose around his neck. Another soldier ran out with the priest's chasuble. "Let's dress the papist devil up right!" he shouted.

"Good work," said Brigadier Hawley, standing at the gate. He gave the man a shilling. The soldier draped the chasuble over the old man's shoulders. MacGregor's hands were clasped, his head was bowed in prayer. In the background, smoke swirled from the house, flames gushed from the lower-floor windows.

Major Wolfe spoke to Brigadier Hawley, who glared at Malcolm and shook his head. "That's so much stuff. I say hang him!" he roared.

Disgust evident on his face, Wolfe turned to the regiment in formation across the road. "Ensign Stapleton. Step forward, please," he called.

Jamey Stapleton, in red coat and white breeches, a sword on his hip, emerged from the red mass. Wolfe led him over to Hawley. "This young officer will identify him, General," he said.

Jamey vigorously affirmed Malcolm as his brother. "I don't believe a word of it. I'm inclined to hang both of

---

[3] *Biographies of James Wolfe, later the conqueror of French Canada, sometimes called the grandfather of the American Revolution, confirm that he served with Brigadier Henry "Hangman" Hawley in the ugly business of pacifying the Scottish countryside.*

them,'' Hawley bellowed. ''We'll carry him with us to headquarters and see what the duke thinks of such folderol.'' It dawned on Malcolm that Hawley was drunk.

At a gesture from Hawley, the soldiers hoisted David MacGregor on the gallows, where he quietly choked to death. They left the women of the McCulloughs and the MacDonoughs weeping before their burning house and headed north to rejoin the main army. Father MacGregor's body swung on the gallows behind them as a grisly trophy. Along the way they burned two more houses and hanged another aged man, though he was not a priest.

''The brigadier tends to be a literalist about his orders,'' Major Wolfe said. He had invited Malcolm to double up on his horse with him.

Personally, Wolfe said, he thought such random murdering was beneath his dignity as a soldier, but he had to obey orders. In between hangings and burnings, he quizzed Malcolm about the tactics of the American Indians and compared them to the partisans that had harassed the Greek general, Xenophon, on his famous march.

At the end of the day, Hawley led Malcolm before His Grace, the Duke of Cumberland, second son of George II. ''Major Wolfe says this piece of highland dross is American as he claims. I'm for hanging him to satisfy my doubts,'' the brigadier roared.

The duke was sitting in an open field, drinking champagne with his staff. His tents were spread along the bottom of a hill a few feet away. Cumberland was a stocky young man of twenty-five with a weary bemused manner. His entourage wore the same attitude as they examined Malcolm.

''How many did you hang today, Hawley?'' the duke asked.

''Only two. But one was a priest.''

"Better luck tomorrow. If Major Wolfe vouches for this fellow, that's good enough for me," the duke said.

"I propose we enlist him as a volunteer aide, Your Grace," Wolfe said. "He's already won a battle in America, in which he defeated a swarm of Indians and irregulars with a mere twenty men."

"He must have Scotch or Irish blood, to tell such lies," the duke drawled. "Maybe we should hang him after all." This drew a laugh from his entourage.

Malcolm felt shame suffuse his flesh. He could almost hear his stepmother sneering "Booby." These English considered themselves a superior race. Where had he gotten the idea that he was one of them? More to forestall hanging than anything else, he stumbled out words about being ready and eager to serve.

The duke told Wolfe to find him a uniform. "It may take two coats to make one for him," Wolfe said. "But we'll be training up a Samson for our defense overseas."

"Let's see if we rule here first before we worry about that," the duke said.

Three nightmare weeks later, Malcolm Stapleton sat on a horse beside Major James Wolfe on the flank of the British army as it deployed onto a barren Scottish moor known as Culloden, from the name of a nearby castle. They were far to the north of Dumfries now, near Inverness. On a low rise about a quarter of a mile away was the army of Prince Charles Edward Stuart. Bagpipes skirled across the distance. Highlanders in kilted plaids waved long broadswords called claymores.

Malcolm had ridden out with Wolfe and Hawley every day of these three weeks, watching them spread death and flaming terror through Scotland. Hawley's rolling gallows seldom returned without trophies swinging from both ropes. At night Malcolm tried to blot out the memory by getting drunk. Almost every officer in the army did the same thing, except Wolfe, who stayed in his tent reading Xenophon and other military classics by candlelight.

Again and again Malcolm wanted to cry out against the slaughter. These were his mother's people, yes, his father's people too, now that he knew his origin. He was finding out that kings ruled by spilling blood, oceans of it. Now he was about to watch a far more terrific slaughter.

The armies were roughly equal in size. But the English had two cannon positioned between each regiment, while the Scots had only a few paltry guns on their flanks. With a mighty howl, the Scots charged, claymores whirling. The English cannon, firing grapeshot, tore horrendous gaps in their ranks but they kept coming, a plaid wave, kilts flashing in the sunlight. Malcolm had his eyes on the left of the British line, where his brother's regiment stood, muskets leveled. Beside him, Major Wolfe was explaining how important it was to wait until the enemy reached point-blank range before firing a volley.

"You're about to see the advantage of trained troops, Stapleton," Wolfe said.

At one hundred paces, the order to fire rang out. A tremendous blast leaped from the British muskets, a hellish mixture of smoke and flame. The whole front rank of the Scottish line toppled to the grassy earth but behind them came the next wave, their fearsome claymores raised. The British infantry had been training for weeks to meet this weapon. Every private had orders to bayonet the man to his right, so his thrust would go under the upraised arm of the attacker.

Most regiments obeyed this order with fierce élan and highlanders fell by the hundreds. But in Jamey's 24th Regiment, panic shook half the line. They dropped their guns and fled to the rear. Malcolm caught a glimpse of his brother, screaming curses at the running men. Without asking permission, Malcolm leaped from his horse and flung himself into the melee. The Scots, decimated elsewhere, tried to break through the 24th's splintered ranks. Malcolm waded into the confused struggle, his eyes on Jamey, who stood his ground and labored to reform his company. Malcolm reached him just as a highlander raised his sword to split Jamey's head like a melon. Seizing an abandoned musket, Malcolm bayoneted the Scot in the heart. Then, armed with his claymore, he stood in the breach like a maddened Hercules, felling his Celtic kinsmen left and right.

Jamey Stapleton pointed to Malcolm and shouted: "See what we have for reinforcements! Stand by him, men. Stand by the hero of the Bracken." The boy had told his company about his brother's American exploits when Malcolm visited their camp on the march north. Other officers took up the cry and the regiment rallied. It was an amazing example of what courage can accomplish on a battlefield.

A few minutes later, the Duke of Cumberland ordered his cavalry, led by Hawley and Wolfe, to strike the Scots from both flanks. The shattered clansmen fled, leaving over fifteen hundred dead and dying men on the field.

An aide rode up to Malcolm and ordered him to report to His Royal Highness immediately. Was he to be hanged for disrupting the regularity of the battle line? Malcolm wondered.

He found the duke on horseback, surrounded by aides and generals, including Hawley. "Mr. Stapleton," Cumberland said. "I want to apologize for any aspersions Brigadier Hawley and I may have cast on your loyalty and courage. You're a soldier after my own heart. Take this as a small gesture of my appreciation." He handed Malcolm a leather purse containing one hundred guineas.

The duke invited Malcolm and Wolfe to ride across the battlefield with him in the place of honor, on either side. It was a scene of carnage, dead and dying men everywhere. When the rebels saw the royal standard flying from the flagstaff of the dragoon at the head of the troop, several hurled Gaelic curses at them. One man, slumped against a rock, his chest soaked in blood, simply stared, defiant to his last breath.

"Wolfe," the duke said. "Shoot me that highland scoundrel who dares to look on us with such contempt and insolence."

"My commission is at Your Royal Highness's disposal," Wolfe replied. "But I can never consent to become the executioner of a brave enemy."

"What a peculiar fellow you are, Wolfe," His Royal Highness said. "Don't imitate his example, Stapleton. You'll never get promoted."

The duke, having disposed of the Bonnie Prince's army, now planned to extirpate rebellion from the Scottish soul by multiplying Hangman Hawley a thousand-fold. Not a glen in the highlands would be safe for disloyalty. Malcolm begged to be excused from this duty and turned his face south to London. He was worried about his wife and his son but his chief motive was escape from his Scottish nightmare. His brain seemed split into atoms by it, his heart was a torment of confusion. He stayed drunk from the beginning to the end of his journey.

You can imagine his amazement when he arrived in the metropolis to find he was London's hero. Perhaps worse, from his point of view, it was his wife who had worked the miracle.

NINE

COLONEL HARTSHORNE HAD WRITTEN ME a letter, describing Malcolm's heroism at Culloden. Hartshorne's regiment had been in line beside Jamey Stapleton's and the older man was an eyewitness to the whole performance, which he naturally thought was motivated by patriotism and the military prowess he had encouraged in Malcolm at Oswego. I showed it to John Williams, the owner of the White Horse Inn. He took the letter to the *Daily Courant,* a paper financed by the Walpole-Pelham regime. They published it immediately, with embellishments that had "the American volunteer" sustaining the entire right wing of the Duke of Cumberland's army.

John Williams offered me free room and board if I would move back to his establishment. Even before Malcolm arrived in London, crowds showed up at the White Horse to ogle the American hero. When the giant appeared in the flesh, all he had to do was dine twice a day in the inn's taproom to pack the place. The government was equally delighted to hail a champion from distant America. Malcolm's readiness to risk his life for their cause seemed to prove their popularity, although half of England and three fourths of Scotland despised them. Chesley White assured me that my credit would be good with him until my debts mounted to the moon— if I would bring Malcolm to dine at his house on Leicester Square.

Before I could accept that invitation, we were invited to a dinner at the Old Lodge in Richmond Park, one of

the many houses of the Great Corrupter himself, Robert
Walpole. We were escorted there by Colonel Hartshorne,
who had returned to London to enjoy his money and
bask in a share of Malcolm's fame, leaving his regiment
to fend for itself in Scotland. He told us the Patriots were
no longer a political force. They had been routed by
Walpole's Parliamentary army as thoroughly as the
highlanders had been broken at Culloden. Half had made
their peace with the Duke of Newcastle and his brother,
Henry Pelham, who was now prime minister, in return
for a nice raffle of offices. The rest had taken to drink
or gone to France to commune longingly with James
Edward Stuart. Hartshorne had bought a seat in Parliament[1] and was hoping to obtain the rangership of a royal
park in Surrey in return for his vote.

Richmond Park was part of the king's demesne, not
far from London. Walpole had made his son Ranger of
the Park and appointed himself his deputy. The son had
given his father the Old Lodge, on which Walpole had
spent a reported fourteen thousand pounds. The house
was magnificent. Damask draperies on every window,
French and Italian and Dutch paintings on every wall,
statuary inside and outside, French furniture that rivaled
Versailles.

The dinner was a private celebration of the victory at
Culloden. The Duke of Cumberland was there with his
generals, including Hangman Hawley. The Duke of
Newcastle and his brother Henry Pelham and a half
dozen other notables from Parliament were also in the
crowd surrounding Robert Walpole. The Great Corrupter
was one of the fattest men I had ever seen: a huge hearty
slab of a fellow, with the hard knowing eyes of a successful highwayman. He exuded power; it seemed to

[1]*Seats in Parliament could be purchased in so-called "rotten bor-
oughs," usually controlled by a great landowner.*

emanate from his bulk as well as from the total assurance of his manner.

Walpole pounded Malcolm on the back and joked about his size. "If the latest crop of Americans are as big as you, the damn colonies may be worth the money we spend on them after all."

Mrs. Walpole was nowhere to be seen, but the great man's mistress, a tall thin dark-haired woman, was in cheerful attendance. Most of the women in the party were mistresses, not wives, Hartshorne offhandedly told me, confirming everything I had heard from Robert Nicolls about marital fidelity among the British upper classes.

The conversation was mostly about who among the captured Jacobites would be hanged, who would be beheaded, who would be shot. A half dozen noblemen were consigned to the ax at the Tyburn Gallows, the rest to the noose at the same site. Deserters from the army, mostly lowland Scots, were to be shot against the wall at Hyde Park. "Let's appear generous," Walpole said. "There's no need to kill more than a few hundred." His successor, Henry Pelham, cheerfully agreed. They were, of course, not counting the thousands of garden variety Scots who were being slaughtered at that very moment in Scotland.

The principal business of the evening settled, they sat down to a stupendous feast. There must have been a hundred dishes on the table—beef, venison, geese, turkey, lamb, fish of a dozen varieties. Everyone imitated the former prime minister and the present chief, Pelham, who was almost as fat as Walpole, and dug in with a gusto that I soon found beyond my capacity. Pelham seemed determined to outeat Walpole. He frequently had venison on his fork and a turkey leg in his other hand, chomping back and forth, while gravy drooled over his double chins. Never had I seen such gorging, except in my Seneca village after a starving time.

Even more abundant were the drinks, jeroboams of Château Lafite, Latour, and other French clarets, as well as strong beers, punch heavily reinforced by gin and brandy, and champagne. All this was poured down in staggering quantities as toast after toast was shouted along the table—from the king to the Duke of Cumberland to the army to the navy down to Walpole's favorite racehorse. Soon everyone was as drunk as the Iroquois at Oswego. The Duke of Newcastle, who lacked the flesh of his brother and Walpole, toppled from his chair, unable to stand the pace. He was left flat on the floor and was soon joined by a half dozen others.

Finally, Malcolm was asked to provide them with entertainment. Someone produced a huge gleaming broadsword. A chair was brought in from the kitchen and Robert Walpole shouted: "Show us now, Stapleton, how you cleaved those highland scum. I'll wager a hundred pounds he can break this thing apart with a single stroke."

Brigadier Hawley maintained that was impossible. The chair was a stout piece of work. Malcolm might split the back but he would never get through the seat, which was solid oak. The bets flew around the table while Malcolm hefted the sword. He was as drunk as anyone in the room. Beside me, I heard Colonel Hartshorne, the man who had solemnly vowed never to make another bet, wagering two hundred pounds that Malcolm could do the job.

Planting his feet wide, Malcolm raised the broadsword until its tip vanished into the shadows of the ceiling. Down it came with a fearsome hiss and *whack*—the chair, back and seat, was in fragments on the floor. Malcolm stared at the ruins as if they were somehow repugnant to him. Robert Walpole staggered from place to place, collecting his winnings, and deposited a small mountain of guineas before Malcolm's plate.

" 'Tis yours, my friend," he shouted. "Fairly won."

There had to be two thousand pounds in the pile. I could scarcely resist counting it. Clutching the broadsword, Malcolm staggered back to the table. He gazed down at the money and began to weep. No one in the room, including his wife, knew what was going on in his head. He had told me nothing about his discoveries in Scotland.

With a snarl, Malcolm flung the back of his hand against the money, sending the coins flying across the table at the astonished Walpole and Prime Minister Pelham, who was sitting beside him. "A patriot," Malcolm said, laboring out each word as if it were a ten-pound weight. "A patriot doesn't fight for gold. He fights for his country."

A hush fell over the room. To fling the word *patriot* in Walpole's face was the greatest political insult imaginable. For twenty years the opposition had used it as a club to belabor his corruption.

"I think we can lay claim to that word, patriot, as well as anyone in England," Pelham said.

"Can you, sir? Can you?" Malcolm said. "I wish to God I could believe that!"

For a horrendous moment, I wondered if Malcolm was going to slaughter everyone in the room with that broadsword. I saw myself hanging from a gibbet at Tyburn as a conspirator in the most sensational murders in English history.

Robert Walpole seemed oblivious to this possibility. He barely looked at Malcolm. Instead, he glared up and down the table. "If a word of this reaches the newspapers, we'll spend ten thousand pounds of secret service money to track down the whisperer."

"Twenty thousand," said Prime Minister Pelham, whose face had acquired a grim cast.

Walpole ordered a servant to gather up the scattered coins and put them in a purse. He handed it to me. "Take this with my compliments, madam. You seem to be an intelligent woman. Tomorrow or the next day, when your husband regains his wits, talk some sense into his head.''

Colonel Hartshorne helped me half drag, half carry Malcolm to a carriage. ''I fear this is my fault,'' the colonel said. ''I gave the lad these patriot notions when he was at an impressionable age. I never realized he would take them so seriously. In Oswego, in the middle of nowhere, patriotism was an easy note to strike. In London it's another matter.''

''Don't blame yourself. He's always been inclined to see himself as a knight errant,'' I said.

Malcolm said nothing. Slumped in the carriage, he stared out at London's passing parade. The whores, the beggars, the gorgeously dressed gentlemen and their ladies were on full display everywhere on this warm spring night.

''What would Clara think?'' Malcolm said.

''I beg your pardon?'' Hartshorne said.

''What would Clara think of that dinner tonight? The plunderers of our country, gorging and swilling over the bodies of poor starving Scotsmen who had the courage to believe in a cause.''

''Now, now,'' Hartshorne said. ''You can't let wild men like that run the country—any more than you could let the bloody Iroquois run New York. Right, Mrs. Stapleton?''

''Of course not,'' I said. I still had no more idea than Hartshorne of the war that was raging in Malcolm's brain.

On Piccadilly, as we approached the White Horse Inn, Malcolm saw a boy and girl selling flowers to the patrons who lurched from the taproom door. They were about ten years old and very emaciated. Business was far from brisk. ''Fresh roses and daffodils,'' they piped in pathetic voices.

''Where's that purse Walpole gave you?'' Malcolm said.

I handed it to him as we descended from the carriage and Hartshorne paid the driver. Malcolm staggered over to the flower sellers. "How much for the lot?" he said.

"For all of them?" the boy said. Each had four bouquets in wicker baskets suspended from their necks. "Three shillings, sir."

"Here's three pounds instead," Malcolm said.

He poured a dozen coins from the purse into the basket. "Sir," said the astonished boy. "That's more than three pounds."

"Keep it," Malcolm said and stumbled upstairs and fell facedown in the bed, unconscious. I lay awake beside him, listening to his snores, trying to decide what to do. He was out of control and I did not know why. He had thrown away a chance to win preferment from the men who ruled England. One side of my mind thought it was madness. The other side thought there was a certain nobility to it.

Good God. I was thinking like Clara. The Evil Brother leered in the far corner of my soul, whispering: *Worse is to come*. Clara somehow helped me defy him. I began to see myself loving this reckless madman who flung defiance in prime ministers' faces. We would somehow survive his outrages. I would make enough money for both of us.

As dawn greyed the windowpane, I pressed myself against Malcolm. "Husband," I whispered. "You've barely looked at me since you returned from Scotland. You know how much I need your kisses."

It began well enough. He caressed me sleepily. I took his hand and placed it on my mound. "There's where I want you," I said. "Where I belong to you, no matter what befalls us."

I felt his lips stiffen. His hand lay there, inert. No fingers caressed my thighs, explored my creamy interior. For a moment or two he fumbled with my breasts, then turned away, leaving me with nothing but a view of his mountainous back and shoulder. "Some other time," he said.

I was overwhelmed by rage and shame. All the memories of my Moon Woman days assailed me. "What is it?" I said. "Have you given your all to some Scottish slut?"

"No," he said.

"Am I so repulsive?"

"No," he said.

"What is it, then?"

No answer.

Two nights later we went to dinner at Chesley White's house. He had explained in his invitation that he was giving a party for his daughter Elizabeth and her fiancé and her friends. They were eager to display Malcolm as a catch that would make them the envy of London. Meanwhile, I entertained acid thoughts about my approaching encounter with Robert Foster Nicolls. As I expected, the fox was more than a little discomfited to discover his future father-in-law beaming at his former love.

"Mr. Nicolls and I are old acquaintances," I told White. "We knew each other well in New York."

"I hear he played a soldier's part in more than one broil with your Iroquois," White said.

"Really?" I said. "That must have been in my captivity days."

The Whites and everyone else at the party immediately wanted to hear the story of Malcolm's exploits at Culloden from his own lips. He declined to utter more than a few monosyllables, which only made them admire him all the more for his modesty. I sat beside Robert Nicolls at the table, and as the other guests reiterated Malcolm's heroism, we gazed into each other's eyes without illusions.

"I trust Miss White's dowry is satisfactory," I said

in a low voice, smiling as if we were chatting about the latest play in Covent Garden.

"Eminently," Robert said.

"And of course you're in love."

"Eminently," he said.

Beneath the table, he took my hand. "But there's a part of my heart that remembers and regrets. Is that true for you as well?"

I trembled inwardly. It was amazing. I was still vulnerable to Robert's charms. "I remember a great many things—and regret all of them," I said.

Elizabeth White was a sweet, totally innocent young woman, with plaintive eyes and a face like a teardrop. She had been raised in a highly protected atmosphere which rendered her singularly susceptible to Robert's poetic apostrophes. The thought of her hundred thousand pound dowry made me taste again the humiliation of the day Robert rejected me and my paltry fifteen hundred pounds. Out of old anger and shame, I suddenly conjured an exquisite idea for revenge.

Walking back to the White Horse Inn along the Strand, London's most fashionable street, the masses of prostitutes that prowled this part of London by night assailed us, making lewd suggestions about three in a bed. Were they the reason Malcolm was shunning me?

"I've thought of a way to regain your estate," I said. "If I threaten to tell Chesley White about the way Robert Nicolls seduced and abandoned me for want of a dowry, I think Robert might persuade his father to settle the lawsuit in your favor."

"Do what you please," Malcolm said. "Though it sounds like ill-gotten gains to me."

He began comparing me to Walpole and the Pelhams in my lust for money and raved about his detestation of my mockery of patriotism and the sordid life I had forced him to live. Still unaware of the chaos in his soul, I let the bitterness he had already ignited in my heart burst into a wicked flame, all but consuming my love for him. I could hear the Evil Brother laughing in that dark corner of my soul. *I only promised you your heart's desire.*

In the morning, I summoned Barrister McDuffie to discuss the Nicolls situation. The shrewd little fellow thought that my threat might very well settle the lawsuit and readily agreed to play the negotiator. Within the hour Robert showed up at the White Horse Inn for a parley. In the shadowy taproom, he looked sadly diminished, in spite of his stylish clothes.

"This is unworthy of you—of our love," he said.

For a moment my resolution almost faltered. Was he right? I reminded myself of the mercenary way he had abandoned me and cold anger armored my heart. "The issue here is not love but money. All you have to do is persuade your father to help us regain Malcolm's property. Get him to deny he and his secretary witnessed George Stapleton's will. If the signatures are forged—the case is over."

Robert fiddled with the watch fob dangling from the pocket of his mauve breeches. "I'll see what my father thinks. May I say this only convinces me that my intuition of your money-grubbing soul was correct?"

"When it comes to money grubbing, you're hardly in a position to cast stones."

When Lawyer McDuffie visited later in the day, I told him our prospects looked favorable. "It's a simple matter of computation," the little Scotsman chortled. "Old Chesley White is probably worth a half million pounds, every cent of which will go to his daughter. That's ten times what the Stapleton lands are worth."

Malcolm joined us and McDuffie told him the good news. He sloshed down a tankard of rum and snarled: "How can the two of you sell that innocent girl into the arms of a whoremaster like Nicolls?"

"Damn you and your morality!" I said. "How can

you be so high-minded when you've seen the true state of this country. Is there a scrap of morality visible anywhere?''

''There's nothing I can do about that,'' Malcolm said. ''But I won't be a party to selling an innocent girl to a rascal!''

''He's no more of a rascal than any other fortune hunter she's likely to encounter,'' I said. I managed to convince myself this was more or less true. Robert could be charming when his financial needs were satisfied.

McDuffie, a total cynic about the English like most Scots, agreed with me wholeheartedly. But Malcolm declined to be persuaded. ''Ill-gotten gains,'' he said, sloshing down more rum. ''I don't know whether I can live with them.''

I had no idea how ominous those words would soon prove to be. ''Show me some gains that aren't ill-gotten, one way or another, in this great and glorious empire,'' I said.

The following day, a note from Robert Nicolls was delivered by a panting messenger. The bargain was sealed—and it only remained to work out the conditions. These turned out to be rather sticky, since mistrust and resentment were rampant on both sides. Would the lawsuit be settled before Robert married Miss White? Or would the wedding take precedence? I insisted on being first in line and the governor, after some grumbling, gave way.

Georgianna Stapleton was another sticking point. She was enraged by the whole negotiation. Not until Governor Nicolls's lawyer pointed out that forgery was a hanging offense did she finally consent to signing an agreement which turned over the estate to Malcolm and his brother, to share equally. Jamey had already indicated his readiness to accept the settlement.

To soothe Georgianna's temper—and no doubt to retain access to her person—Governor Nicolls persuaded the Duke of Newcastle to find her a sinecure in the royal household. She became a lady of the stole, with duties so nebulous she only had to appear once a year at the Queen's Birthday Ball. This single attendance was worth four hundred pounds from the treasury annually. That was as much—possibly more—than Georgianna was getting from Hampden Hall.

A week later, Robert Foster Nicolls married Elizabeth White at St. Clement Dane's church on the Strand. As a client of Chesley White, I had to go. Malcolm refused to join me. "Make an excuse for me with your forked tongue," he said.

"Is this all the thanks I get for regaining your property?"

Again, there was no answer.

When I returned from the wedding, I found Malcolm in the taproom of the White Horse Inn with his friend Hartshorne. They were both somewhat drunk. "I've been trying to cheer up this fellow," Hartshorne said, beaming at Malcolm in his asinine way. "I took him to one of London's best entertainments, the Royal Cockpit. The cocks were in fine fettle and the lad was soon a match for'm. I've seldom seen a fellow as fond of bold wagers. 'Pon my word I had trouble matching him."

"Did you win?" I said.

"I'm afraid not. Between us we must have lost five hundred pounds, eh, Stapleton?"

Malcolm glowered defiantly at his wife. "At least," he said.

"Five hundred pounds!" I cried.

"From his Walpole wallet," Hartshorne said, foreseeing my tantrum.

"We needed every penny of that to begin paying off his father's debts!" I said. "What about your oath not to make another wager?"

"Oh, I've kept that promise long enough. Upward of

six months now,'' Hartshorne said. "A man isn't a *man*, Mrs. Stapleton, unless he bets now and then.''

"Tonight we're going to Almack's," Malcolm said. This was one of the most notorious gambling clubs in London. "I'll win it back, never fear. You'll see I'm not the only one who can make a fortune in this family, Wife.''

For the next week Malcolm went off with Hartshorne to Almack's or some other gambling club or the Royal Cockpit every night and came home drunk, sometimes with hundreds of pounds of winnings which he flaunted at me, sometimes with empty pockets and copies of promissory notes for as much as a thousand pounds. I saw that behind his mad flamboyance, he wanted to lose all our money. Somehow that would purify him of the taint of corruption he associated with it. As for Hartshorne, he was as addicted to gambling as some men were to liquor. He was on his way to losing his second fortune.

In our room, I pleaded with Malcolm. But he remained beyond my reach, inside his perpetual drunkenness. He became even more unreachable when the government began executing the Jacobites at Tyburn. He went to the beheadings of three noblemen (several others were pardoned) and returned declaring they had died like brave men and he wished he had taken their side.

I persuaded our innkeeper, John Williams, to pay one of his waiters to trail Malcolm to the gambling dens but his only value was the accurate reports he gave me of the latest losses. One night I carried little Hugh to the taproom, where Malcolm and Hartshorne, after a lucky run at Almack's, were treating the whole establishment. "If not for my sake, will you stop this madness for his sake?" I pleaded.

Malcolm sat the boy on his lap and contemplated him mournfully. The child was half asleep. "I wish I could, I wish I could," he said.

Chesley White summoned me to his office to show me a squib in the *Public Advertiser.*

A certain American hero is fast using up the credit he won at Culloden. Rumor has it that he's now 50,000 pounds in debt at the gaming tables and no one in the administration is inclined to lift a finger for him. Worse rumor has it that his simple noggin has been infected by Patriotism.

White said he would find it hard to extend me credit if the story were true. "It's nowhere near fifty thousand pounds, I can assure you," I said, wondering if someone in the government who had not forgiven Malcolm for his outburst against them at the Old Lodge had supplied this information to the paper. It was hardly surprising to discover we were under secret service surveillance.

"Do you have money to pay these debts?" White asked.

"I have ample funds in Amsterdam, where I've traded for years," I lied. "Philip Hooft of the Hooft Bank will vouch for me."

Chesley White was impressed by the Hooft name. He let me go with renewed promises of friendship and credit which I was using to make extensive purchases of cloth and other goods for the Universal Store. Robert Nicolls and his bride were in Bath, London's favorite resort, penning White letters full of gossip and good cheer. All I had to show for my scheming was George Stapleton's debt-laden estate in New Jersey and his quondam son here in London, drunkenly gambling away its value.

Back in the White Horse Inn, I found two burly fellows talking to the proprietor, John Williams. "Here's his wife," Williams said.

The two visitors were bailiffs. They had a warrant to take Malcolm Stapleton to Old Bailey, the debtor's prison, if he could not produce the ten thousand pounds he had lost last night at Almack's, playing faro. I was tempted to let him go to jail and sail back to America without him. But how could I explain such a disgrace to our friends—much less our enemies—in New York? I could practically hear my Van Vorst relatives cackling with glee.

I told the bailiffs Malcolm had sailed for America that morning. Innkeeper John Williams loyally confirmed the lie. Upstairs, I routed him out of his drunken sleep and sent Williams rushing to the Thames's wharves to find a ship that was sailing for New York on the next tide.

"Are you happy now?" I said, showing him the bailiff's order. "You've brought us to the brink of ruin. I can't pay this without ruining my credit here in London."

"Let them have me," Malcolm said. "Go back to New York and forget me. Tell the boy I died of smallpox over here or some other lie that will make him at least mourn me."

"What's *wrong* with you? Why do you want to destroy all we've tried to build?"

Finally, he told me what he had learned in Scotland about his real father. "Don't you see what I've done?" he said. "Betrayed my own people, spilled their blood in the name of a gang of plunderers like Walpole and Pelham." Marrying me was of a piece with this theme of moral capitulation. He reiterated his comparison of my ethics and the Great Corrupter and his crew. "Between you, you've made me a traitor to everything I believe," he raved.

"I think God—or whoever runs this miserable disordered world—is far more responsible," I said.

Even if he were not accusing me, I could not have sympathized with him. Perhaps it was my Seneca contempt for pain, perhaps it was the bitterness my uncle Johannes and Robert Nicolls had steeped in my soul, but

I was incapable of tolerating weakness. It seemed especially offensive to discover it in the spirit of this gigantic man whom I had chosen as my protector, my prize in the lottery of love.

I could not help him. I could not even bear the sight of him. I summoned Hartshorne to persuade him to flee. The colonel continued to assume Malcolm's funk was caused by the way the Patriot Party had collapsed. With that marvelous ability to turn his opinions inside out, Hartshorne assured Malcolm patriotism was moonshine and eventually grown men faced up to that hard truth. He added a graphic portrait of the sordid life of debtor's prison. He himself was rejoining his regiment in Scotland to escape the bailiffs on his trail.

"For your son's sake, you must go back to New York on the first ship," Hartshorne said. "You can teach him the ideals of the patriot for use in a better age."

Over my dead body, I thought. But I vigorously seconded Hartshorne's sentiments. "You must go for the boy's sake," I told Malcolm. "I'll join you there in a month or two. You'll see a reformation in me, I swear it."

I was lying, of course. I wanted to rid myself of him for a while—maybe forever. I saw—I even hoped—he might turn to Clara in New York for the consolation he so badly needed. I did not care. I was sick of him, sick of my heart's desire.

"Where are you going?" Malcolm asked.

"To Amsterdam to try to repair our fortunes," I said. "There's a banker there who'll lend me money."

And what will you lend him in return? whispered the Evil Brother.

There was no need to answer that question.

BOOK

FIVE

ONE

IN HUGHSON'S TAPROOM CLARA WAS glancing at the latest edition of the *New York Gazette* when a familiar name caught her eye amid the shipping news. *Arrived on the* Mayflower: *Malcolm Stapleton, Esq. his son Hugh and a servant.* She wondered where Catalyntie was. Clara decided there were numerous reasons why her Seneca sister might have decided to stay in London or go to the Netherlands and thought no more about it.

Two nights later, Mary Burton approached the bar with a crafty look on her plump face. Was she about to tell Clara she was going upstairs with another customer? Mary regularly deserted her post to make a little extra cash that way. "Do you have an order?" Clara asked. She repeatedly had to struggle against her dislike of this girl. Along with her other flaws, she was always prying into everyone's business and spreading gossip about them around the town.

"Two flagons of strong beer," Mary said. "There's a fellow in the corner who says he'd like you to drink with him."

"I'm not interested."

"I think you would be, if you took a look at him."

Clara asked the drinkers at the bar to step aside and saw Malcolm Stapleton sitting in the corner. She instantly knew something serious was wrong. The politician, the victor of the Battle of the Bracken, the man who thrust his way to the bar and talked down everyone in sight, had vanished. He was still as huge as ever, but defeat, loss, were stamped on his face.

Other drinkers followed her gaze and a general hub-bub rose. The entire room swarmed around Malcolm to toast the hero of Culloden. The New York newspapers had all reprinted the London stories of his exploits. He acknowledged their cheers with a pale smile. He deprecated his heroism, claiming there were a thousand other soldiers on the field who did as much. This only swelled his popularity with the crowd.

Eventually, the congratulators drifted back to the bar. Clara left John Hughson in charge there and sat down with Malcolm. "There's talk of giving you a dinner. A hero's welcome home," she said.

"I can't face it. I'm going out to Hampden Hall. I've gotten it back from my stepmother, thanks to Catalyntie. Will you come with me? We can live out there, without reference to marriage vows. Catalyntie can stay here in New York and plow up her profits."

"I have a business to run here in New York. What's happened between you and Catalyntie?"

"We've finally concluded what we suspected from the start. We despise each other."

It was all too sudden, too unnerving. "I don't understand. I thought we settled this," Clara said.

"Everything's been unsettled, Clara. Everything!"

He told her about his trip to Scotland, his discovery of the truth about his parentage, about Hangman Hawley and the real story of Culloden. An enormous sympathy swelled in Clara's soul. She had never seen Malcolm Stapleton as a giant. His physique was huge. Spiritually, he had always been a stunted man. Now she saw he was a crippled one.

Should she let him draw her back into his world? She resisted the idea. She had become part of the New York that swirled through Hughson's Tavern, the New York of the poor, of the forlorn, of the enslaved. No matter how unsettled he was, Malcolm could never become part of this world. He could never understand or experience the sweetness that flowed through her soul when she knelt with her face to the stars. John Ury had converted her in the deepest sense of that word. She had become a different person.

"Oh, Malcolm, I can't do it," she said. "I wish I could, for your sake. But I've pledged myself to people here, people who need me."

"Who?" he said. "That son of a bitch Caesar?"

"More than Caesar. To all of them, the slaves, the whores. I try to give them hope. I pray for them. I help them when no one else will."

He shook his head, totally uncomprehending. "I thought you loved me."

"I do. I told you I'd always love you. But not you alone, the way we once dreamed."

He began to weep. "What's to become of me, Clara? I'm not English. I'm not Scottish. I'm no one. A ghost with his head full of patriotic moonshine."

"Give me time to pray over you," Clara said.

That night, back on Maiden Lane, she told John Ury about Malcolm and asked for advice. Ury listened with mounting excitement, out of all proportion to this sad story of a man he barely knew. "His mother was a Catholic!" the priest said. "What an opportunity! You must bring him over, Clara. With him on our side, we can take and hold this city!"

"What?" Clara said dazedly.

"Take and hold this city!" Ury said. "Caesar has been organizing the slaves for a year now. It hasn't been easy. Too many fear retaliation. The Spanish Africans have been a godsend. Their anger has ignited resentment in the hearts of the wavering. But we have too few white men. Hughson, the Irish schoolteacher, a handful of others. Stapleton could stir the Jacobite spirit in hundreds."[1]

[1] _At this time, one in five New Yorkers was black. The proportion of black males was even higher—one in four._

The shy, quiet tutor, the follower in the footsteps of Jesus, the prince of peace and forgiveness, had vanished. Clara was facing a fiery insurrectionist. "Dear Clara," he said, seeing the dismay on her face. "Forgive me for shocking you. I wanted to lead you to this discovery gradually. But events seldom wait for the slow pace of the heart. If Prince Charles had won at Culloden, we might have been able to overturn this government peacefully. Now it must be a bloody struggle."

"To what end?"

"As soon as the city is seized, we plan to send couriers up the lakes to Canada to bring a French army into the game. Meanwhile, a fast sloop will sail for Havana to summon a Spanish fleet and army strong enough to hold the city against all comers."

"What then?"

"The war is a stalemate in Europe. Peace negotiations will begin soon. The French and Spanish will claim the whole colony of New York by the right of possession. The British will be forced to surrender everything north and west of Albany. We'll take our Africans and Jacobites and settle on lands up there. We'll have an English Catholic colony, where France can protect us."

Ury spoke with such assurance, Clara felt bewildered and awed. The priest emanated another kind of power now. But it was shot through with darkness. "I . . . I must pray over this," she said.

"Wait!" Ury said, seizing her arm. "I must convince you! In my years of persecution in England, hiding in holes like a runaway felon, I received a light which I think is more powerful than anything in the doctrines of the fathers of the church. It is Christ's greatest mistake, which we are destined to correct in our time. You remember, where he told the apostles, render to Caesar the things that are Caesar's and to God the things that are God's? We have learned since the rise of the Protestant heretics that without Caesar, the people of God are nothing. If Caesar becomes a Protestant, they're slaughtered like cattle, driven like sheep. Only if we wield Caesar's power can we hope to achieve the kingdom of God.''

From a figure of transcendent purity, John Ury was dwindling in Clara's eyes to a man with a soul as stunted, as haunted, as tormented, in its own way as Malcolm's—or Caesar's. ''That's a deep thought. Perhaps too deep for me,'' she said. ''I must pray on all of this.''

Upstairs, she knelt by her open window and lifted her face to the stars once more. In the street she heard a man cajoling a whore. It was Adam Duycinck. Would he have any advice to offer her? No, his soul was as stunted as his body. She would have to seek her wisdom in the voice that descended from the sky.

Clara extended her arms and prayed. *O Virgin Mother, listen to your servant, a fellow woman, torn between old love and new love, between falsehood and truth. Guide me and protect me.*

The earth seemed to heave and sigh around her. The voice whispered: *Remain true to your love, my daughter of the morning.*

Clara closed her eyes and a new vision coursed through her soul. She saw Malcolm on a cliff, gazing across a vast ocean. On either side of him stood two figures rimmed in fire, their garments glowing like molten gold. One was a woman, the other a man. Clara knew they were his mother and father. Behind them rose a forest of gigantic trees. The golden figures were pointing into the forest but Malcolm did not see them. He was lost in his torment. Both figures turned and the woman wrote on the air in flaming letters: *American.* They gazed across the distance at Clara, as if they knew she was watching them. They pointed to the word ablaze in the air and vanished. Slowly, *American* vanished too, leaving Malcolm alone, forlorn.

Clara lay awake most of the night, trying to understand the meaning of the vision—and what she should say to Malcolm about John Ury's astonishing plan. Gradually she saw that the angelic figures were trying to tell her that Malcolm must stop gazing across the ocean, thinking of himself as an Englishman or a Scotsman. He was an American. She must persuade him to transfer his dream of a nation of patriots to this side of the ocean, to this uncorrupted new world.

Ury joined her at breakfast, eager to find out if she was ready to bring Malcolm into their plot. She shook her head. "I'm sorry," she said. "It would be against his nature."

"What do you mean?"

"He can have nothing to do with your dream of an English Catholic colony, Father. It's a European idea. His destiny is American."

"American?" The word meant little to Ury. He was consumed by his struggle for English Catholicism.

"Someday it will mean more than Catholic or Protestant."

"Did your voice tell you this?" he asked with dismaying harshness.

"In a way," Clara said.

"Have you heard of Joan of Arc?"

"A little."

"She heard voices too. She died at the stake. Voices can come from Satan as well as from God."

Clara shook her head. "I know this didn't come from the Evil Brother," she said.

"We'll see," Ury said. He was deeply disappointed in her. But Clara trusted her *orenda*. She refused to seduce Malcolm. When she visited him later in the day, she realized it would be easy to do. He felt enormously guilty over his conduct in Scotland. He talked obsessively about it, while Clara held young Hugh on her lap. The boy resembled Catalyntie much more than Malcolm. He had the same thin energetic body and piercing blue eyes. He finally squirmed away and ran off, shouting for his nurse.

"Do you want Hugh to be a Scottish patriot?" she asked.

"Of course not," Malcolm growled. "That's not his fight."

"Do you want him to be a Jacobite?"

"Good God, no," Malcolm said. "That's an even more lost cause."

"Then why are you tormenting yourself about your failure to be either of these things? You're as American as he is. It's not blood that makes a man one thing or another. It's his birthplace, where and how he was raised. I wasn't born a Seneca but I'll always consider myself one because I spent the most important years of my life with them. They raised me, they gave me their gods, they taught me what to think and feel about love and honor and loyalty—fundamental things."

"A woman in Scotland—my mother's sister—told me that. But I wasn't listening," Malcolm said.

"You have a dream of a country of patriots. What do you care if there's no hope for one in England? Begin creating one here, where everything is new and possible. Give Hugh the dream. Maybe he'll see it come true in his lifetime."

"How?" Malcolm said. "As long as Walpole and the Pelhams and their fellow thieves rule the empire with their fleet and army—"

"I don't know how. I only know what I heard, what I saw, last night in my prayers."

She almost told him about her vision of his angelic guardians. But she was afraid he would think she was a madwoman. Alongside Malcolm's idealism lurked the harsh realism of the soldier. The two would always be at war in his soul.

"Perhaps the Dutch resentment of the English will spread to other parts of America. Remember our old argument about being American? When I showed you America was a hundred times bigger than England on the map?

"You're talking treason," Malcolm said, half jokingly.

"It's not treason to be a patriot in your own country."

She left him with those halfway thoughts and feelings. Malcolm could not move beyond them for the present. She could only plant seeds in his mind and heart and hope they would take root and grow. As they walked to the door, he took her hand and thanked her for good advice. Then he abruptly added: "But you'll never change what I think about Catalyntie. I'm glad you didn't try."

For a moment Clara wanted to say something on behalf of her Seneca sister. But she found no words in her heart. Essentially, her judgment on Catalyntie Van Vorst was not much different from Malcolm's.

This possible American future that Clara described swiftly receded from view as history began dragging us all down a path that was crowded with the hopes and ambitions, the fears and angers, of other men. At the tavern, Clara found John Ury talking to Sarah and John Hughson in a state of wild excitement. "Word arrived from Albany on a sloop at dawn," Ury told her. "A French and Indian army burned Saratoga. Wiped the village off the map!"

"What does it mean—beyond four or five hundred people left homeless?" Clara asked.

"It's a testing of this province's defenses. Which are nonexistent. Can't you predict what will happen? The governor will call out the militia. No one will respond. The Dutch won't fight for the English and the English won't fight for themselves."

"I think you're wrong. The Americans will fight," Clara said.

"No one recognizes that name in New York. You're

English or Dutch or Jewish or French or Irish. American is the name of a continent, not of a race,'' Ury said.

Caesar arrived, accompanied by Antonio, the leader of the Spanish Africans. Ury told him the news of Saratoga. Caesar did a war dance around the taproom. "We need more guns!" he said. "Where can we get them?"

"I'll make another trip to Yonkers tomorrow," John Hughson said. "How much money do we have?"

"I'll get more money," Caesar said. "In the meantime take it from the cash drawer."

"We can't afford a big outlay," Sarah Hughson said. "We owe Fowler a hundred pounds for last month's rum."

"We've only got fifty guns for a thousand men," Caesar said. "We need at least a hundred to take care of the independent company at the fort. The rest can use axes and knives to kill their masters and arm themselves with guns from their houses."

"Old Fowler's got two guns in his library," Antonio said.

Clara was appalled by what she was hearing. Caesar's dream of becoming king of New York had coalesced with John Ury's dream of a colony for English Catholics. They were about to breathe violent bloody life into both of them.

"Clara," Sarah Hughson said. "Can you lend us some of your money?"

Each month, the Hughsons had paid her half of their profits. Some months that amounted to nothing. But over the years, she had taken away at least two hundred pounds. She had given some of it to the poor but she had saved most of it to pay her rent and food bills when the tavern's profits shrank.

"I don't have that much," she said. "But I won't lend it to you. I think your scheme is evil! How can anything good come of murdering innocent people in their beds?"

"History is full of bloody deeds for good causes," John Ury said.

"Innocent?" Caesar said. "I don't think anybody white in this city is innocent. They're all part of the enslavement machine. They're all living off our sweat. Even if they don't own a slave, they pay money to Fowler and my master, old Vraack, for their rum and bread, sold cheap because we get no wages. They're all going to die—or become Caesar's slaves."

Clara looked into Caesar's eyes and saw nothing but hatred burning there. The breath of the Evil Brother had consumed his soul. He was a walking talking furnace of hatred. Why couldn't John Ury see it too? In the dim taproom the priest's eyes were opaque, his usually humble expression twisted into a grimace of triumph. How could her voice in the night tell her there was any hope for an America cursed by such darkness?

"Are you with us or against us, Clara?" Caesar asked.

"Neither," Clara said.

"That's impossible. If I thought you were going to betray us, I'd cut your throat, here and now."

From his hip pocket Caesar drew a razor. He pressed a button on it and the silvery blade leaped from the case.

"I'll pray for all of you," Clara said and walked out of the tavern, passing within inches of the murderous blade. On John Ury's face she saw a tremor of regret. Did he realize he was as possessed as Caesar?

Out on Pearl Street Malcolm Stapleton strode toward her, gloomy determination suffusing his big face. "You've heard about the attack on Saratoga?" he said. "The governor's asked me to raise a thousand men to defend the border. I couldn't say no."

Should she tell him the governor might soon need a thousand men here in New York? No. She could not join Caesar and John Ury. But she would not betray them. She tried to tell herself she was not part of this devouring beast called history.

In her bedroom, Clara knelt before the Virgin and pleaded for guidance. *Help me heal my divided heart.* There was a long silence. Then the voice whispered: *Prepare to weep, O daughter of the morning. Prepare to weep.*

Two

IN AMSTERDAM, I WAS SURPRISED to discover British soldiers in their bright red coats swarming in the streets. War continued to rage between Britain and France. The Dutch newspapers reported violent battles in Flanders. I took rooms at the Ster Van Oosten and sent a note to Tesselschade Hooft, hoping we could meet. There was no reply. The next day, I walked over to the great house on the Heerengracht and found it shuttered and empty.

"The Hoofts are not at home," said a familiar voice. It was the newspaperman, Vondel. He was looking seedy. His chin was in need of a razor. His breeches were stained, his coat sleeves ragged.

"What happened to them?" I asked.

"Their son Willem died of smallpox last year. Tesselschade has gone to France. Some people say she's become a Catholic and joined a convent, others that she's taken a lover. Either may be true. She no longer cares what life does to her."

"Why didn't you go with her?" I said. "She told me you were the first and only man she loved."

Vondel laughed. It was closer to a cough—even a death rattle. "She blames me for every evil thing that's happened to her."

"Where's Philip?"

"He lives at the Ster Van Oosten. A beaten man."

A man with a hundred million guilders, beaten? I could not believe it. But I soon saw it was true. I left a note for Philip Hooft with the Ster Van Oosten's room clerk. That evening before dinner, a bedraggled ghost of the stylish banker who had pursued me around Amsterdam appeared at my door.

"I saw Vondel. He told me the terrible news about your son."

"Willem was never my son," Philip said, his thick-lipped mouth a knot of anguish. "Tesselschade taught him to despise me. She reaped the bitter fruits of her scorn. Without a father, the boy was all brain and no body, no flesh, no vital connection to the world. She created an unreal monster and he atrophied. Smallpox was merely the physical agent of a spiritual death that had already occurred."

The Frog's pendulous lower lip trembled. He wept helplessly. "I'm raving. Forgive me. You saw how promising he was. I was going to take him away from her, make him my son, heart and soul, in a year or two."

Never had I been so moved. I had come to Amsterdam in a fury, prepared, even eager, to play the slut with this man in return for a loan of ten thousand pounds to pay off Malcolm's gambling debts. Dimly, even as I paced the deck of the packet boat, I had realized I wanted to use the money as a scourge, a cleanser, to wash Malcolm Stapleton out of my heart. I had even been ready to accept Vondel as a third in an orgy if Philip Hooft insisted. That would have added disgust to the scarifying solvent I sought.

Instead, I confronted this broken man asking for my sympathy. It threw me into a near panic. I did not know how to respond. I realized Malcolm Stapleton had also been groping for sympathy, but he did not believe I was capable of it.

"Oh, Philip," I cried. "What can I say? What can I do?"

Philip Hooft wiped his eyes. "I'm making a fool of myself. I should be inviting you to my rooms for dinner. Will you come, now? You're as beautiful as ever. Don't you grow old in America?"

"I'd like to dress in something better than these rags." I was wearing the same mundane traveling dress I had worn on the ship to Amsterdam.

"No. I like you as you are. You must take me the same way. I've lost my taste for ostentation, my appetite for glory."

"No wonder Vondel looks so poor."

"I've abandoned him, the bank, everything but my grief. I've made a kind of child out of it. I go to Willem's grave every day with fresh flowers."

We went to his rooms and he ordered dinner sent up, along with a bottle of champagne. I told him about my visit to England. I described Malcolm's exploits at Culloden and our dinner at the Old Lodge—omitting my husband's near assault on Walpole and Pelham.

Philip Hooft was enthralled. "What have they done for you?" he said. "If even half the story's true, they should have bought him a regiment. Or made him governor of one of the West Indies sugar islands, where a clever fellow can steal fifty thousand pounds a year."

The question struck me like a blow in the face. I was suddenly forced to confront my own grief—my abandonment by Malcolm, his hateful attempt to destroy me in the name of his lost patriotism.

"Nothing," I said. "They gave us nothing."

Suddenly I was weeping almost as bitterly as Philip had wept for his lost son. Was I mourning the death of my heart's desire?

"Catalyntie—what's wrong? What did I say?"

I shook my head. "Nothing. You only forced me to face certain things," I said. "But I came here to borrow money, not to plead for sympathy. I deserve none from you. I know exactly how much I tormented you on my first visit.''

''Now you must tell me everything,'' Philip said, moving his chair close enough to take my hand.

Somehow it seemed easier to tell the truth in my mother tongue. Perhaps speaking Dutch stirred the limitless love I felt for my grandfather and my lost father. I poured out the story of Malcolm's insult to Walpole and Pelham and my husband's repudiation of me, his drunken lunge to destruction at the London gaming tables.

''What a miserable job I'm doing—of cheering you,'' I said, wiping my eyes.

''I'm not sure I can help you,'' Philip said. ''No one's ever asked me for anything but money. And now I have none.''

I barely managed to conceal my amazement. Had he truly abandoned the Hooft bank, his hundred million guilders? To my further amazement, I told myself it did not matter. I would offer this man the affection he craved—and ask him for the sympathy I needed almost as badly. I would prove to myself, if no one else, that money was not my god.

The dinner arrived: roast duck, codfish, a galaxy of side dishes and wines. We only sampled the feast. Our hearts were already crowded with intimations of love. The whole thing seemed miraculous, incomprehensible. The Frog was just as ugly. But he was no longer a figure to be mocked in my cold heart and colder mind.

''Do you know what I love about you most?'' Philip said.

I shook my head. It had been a long time since I had heard a man say he loved me. Malcolm had never used the word. In Robert Nicolls's mouth the words had turned out to be meaningless. It seemed to come naturally to this man's tongue and it stirred a response in my soul.

"You don't seem to know how beautiful you are."

"Am I? No one's told me that in years."

"Not even your husband?"

"He hinted at it once—but he's not a loving man—"

Not loving? Clara hissed in my mind. *Maybe not for you. But I forbid you to slander him. Haven't you wounded him enough?*

"Perhaps that's my fault. I'm not—I must warn you—a loving woman."

"I don't believe there is such a creature," Philip said. "Every woman is born with love in her heart—but so many fail to meet a man who knows how to find it. I used to think a woman's heart was a small narrow place. Now I think of it as a vast mansion, in which love lurks in a single secret room."

"What are in the other rooms?"

"On the lower floor, politeness, kindness, perhaps compassion. On the upper floors, far more unexpected things: contempt, scorn, hatred, rage. The man who wanders into any of these rooms may be scarred for life—like the victim of a fire. The man who tries to live in one of them may soon welcome the flames of hell as a pleasant surcease to his sorrows."

"You make us sound like terrible creatures."

"You are. Most men don't think about women very much. But Tesselschade has made me think about you a great deal."

"Where is this secret room where love resides?"

"Some say it's on the top floor, in a room full of sunlight and visions. Others say it's hidden in the cellar, amid earth and odors and desire."

"Perhaps love resides in both places, if a man is nimble enough to enter both in the same visit."

"I've tried. But I've never managed it."

He took my hand and led me into the bedroom. It was a summer night in Amsterdam. A soft wind off the sea stirred the curtains. "How do Indian princesses make love?" he said. "Without their clothes, like the Italians? Or bundled in sheets and nightgowns, like the English and the Dutch?"

"Like the Italians," I said.

He brought more than desire to our bed, he brought his imagination, his humanity, his humor—all the gifts of the spirit that had been concealed, congealed, by Tesselschade's scorn. He told me he wanted to lead my love out of that mythical mansion, where it would always be surrounded by the tenants of the other rooms, into the forest, where it would live in a simple cottage beneath the branches of a great flowering tree.

"There are dangers in the forest too," I said. "Blizzards, fires. Warriors with hatchets who can inflict mortal wounds."

"We'll defend our cottage against all comers," Philip said. "We'll use magic and prayers and dreams. We'll outwit fate and laugh at destiny."

What I remembered afterward was his tenderness, his joy. My own joy came later. That first night it refused to leave the secret room of love; it stayed crouched in a dark corner, a prisoner of the Evil Brother, refusing to believe there was any hope for it, even when love began to call for it to join Philip in the forest.

As we drifted down into sleep, I asked Philip a question that had long puzzled me. "Did you know Vondel had been Tesselschade's lover?"

"Of course. Everyone knew it."

"Why did you befriend him?"

"To show her I forgave her—and I suppose to demonstrate my superiority to envy or revenge. There was also the satisfaction of making him my employee."

"Still she scorned you?"

"She was very beautiful. I was ugly. Scorning me was her way of saying her love was not for sale."

"I wonder if almost the same thing has happened to me."

I told him how I had acquired Malcolm as a husband. I even confessed my pact with the Evil Brother. "He'll be another enemy to keep at bay," Philip said.

For a moment, my throat was clotted with dread. No one could keep the Evil Brother at bay. He was offended by those who mocked him. The thought only made me cling with new fierceness to this unlikely lover, this frog whom sorrow and loss had changed into a prince in my heart.

The next day, Philip explained what he meant by abandoning the Hooft bank. He had sold it to a competitor and turned most of the money over to Tesselschade. He kept only enough to support himself in very modest style. But he still had enough influence on the Dam to borrow fifty thousand guilders to pay off Malcolm's gambling debt. I refused to accept it. "It must be a loan in my name at the regular rate of interest," I said. "What I gave you last night must not be tainted by money."

"You're right," he said. We went to the Bank of Amsterdam on the Dam and ordered the papers drawn for a loan. My heart swelled with gratitude. This would protect my credit in London and New York. I could forget I was a married woman for a while. I would make myself forget it. I would live with Philip in that imaginary cottage in the forest and see what happened to my heart. Perhaps I would become a different woman—a creature full of tenderness and compassion—a woman the Evil Brother would not recognize.

The next day, we traveled on a comfortable *schuit* down a series of canals to a country house in the village of Brock, where Philip had a cottage surrounded by pebbled walks and a flowering garden. There I discovered he was an ardent amateur painter. Tesselschade had dismissed his efforts and refused to let them into the mansion on the Heerengracht. With numerous apologies in advance, he led me into his studio to examine his work.

He made no attempt to match the brooding depth of Rembrandt, the greatest Dutch painter of the preceding century. Philip preferred the simpler Flemish painters of the previous century, above all, Gerard David, the first Dutchman (he was from Utrecht) to make landscapes come alive. He also loved David's realism. He had copied his painting of the Virgin stirring a pot of milk soup, while the infant Jesus sat on her lap. It was a remarkable combination of holiness and everyday life. The Virgin's eyes were lowered, suggesting sanctity—or a concern for the quality of the soup. The little boy, about three, had a spoon in his hand and a tiny smile on his face, as if he could not wait to get into the soup and make a mess.

"Isn't that life?" Philip said. "A muddle of the miraculous and the mundane. These old masters knew what they were doing. I want to paint you the same way, mixing the simplicity of American love with my humdrum European worldliness."

First he painted me as an Indian princess. We found some leather in the village and had a tailor fashion it into leggings and an overdress. I streaked my face with blue and yellow daubs in the style of a Seneca maiden at an Eagle Dance and braided my blond hair until I resembled the girl who had lived beside Lake Ontario so many years ago. Philip imagined me beneath a giant tree in a sunny forest, with deer and foxes and hares in the distance.

The effect was totally unreal. My eyes, cast shyly down, distorted my true character. The make-believe sunshine and happy animals had no resemblance to the sullen gloom of the forest I had known. Compared to the *Virgin with the Milk Soup*, the painting was an utter failure. I tried to praise it but Philip knew it was a botch. After a night of love, he strode into the studio and slashed it to ribbons.

"I can't believe in you as an American. Will you be Eve in our private paradise?"

He had no difficulty persuading me to pose naked. I still had no shame about such things. He gave me an apple to hold and posed me beneath the same tree, in the same American forest. But this time he captured my bold stare, my Seneca sensuality. I bit a chunk out of the apple, emphasizing my readiness to enjoy forbidden fruit.

Where was Adam? Philip had painted himself, peering uneasily from behind a nearby smaller tree, wondering who or what this new creature was. This was a real painting. "That's me—and you—perhaps it's all men and women," I said.

For a while we lived in a Dutch version of Eden, making love by moonlight and sometimes by sunlight, wandering the countryside until Philip found a meadow he wanted to paint; almost always it was guarded by one or two huge white windmills, turning slowly in the summer breeze off the Zuider Zee. In the studio Philip painted me in a magnificent hooped gown of Chinese silk, with patterns of the moon and stars woven through it. He called it *The Woman of the World*. It was another failure. He tried to infuse my eyes, my mouth, with a happiness that was still beyond my reach.

Why was that? One night, after another sweet round of love, I descended to the studio and studied Philip's copy of the *Virgin with the Milk Soup*. The Virgin's face was in perfect repose—her mouth was a calm gentle line, her hair was scarcely brushed, her clothing was a simple black dress. What did this woman possess that eluded me? The answer came to me in Clara's voice. She was *fulfilled*. The truth fell on my heart with crushing weight. I could never be fulfilled here, with Philip

Hooft. We were living in an unreal Eden. Only in the real world was fulfillment possible.

That playful child who sat on the Virgin's knee was also part of her fulfillment. Suddenly Willem Hooft's sad fate filled my heart with dread. What would I do if Hugh died that way while I was playing romantic games in the Netherlands? The wish, the need, to hold my son in my arms swelled in my throat.

Suddenly I was in the grip of an overwhelming nausea. I fled into the garden and vomited most of my supper. I collapsed on a bench, oozing sweat. What was wrong with me? I never had an upset stomach, not even on shipboard in the roughest seas. There was only one other time when I could not keep food on my stomach: when I was pregnant with Hugh.

It could only mean one thing. I was carrying Philip Hooft's child. During the months we had spent in London, Malcolm had scarcely touched me. Well over three months had elapsed since we parted.

I had scrupulously followed Adam Duycinck's instructions to prevent conception: inserting an oil-soaked patch of cloth before making love, removing it to soak it with more oil. Years of success had given me a false sense of assurance. Now I remembered Adam's final warning: there was no such thing as one hundred percent prevention.

What should I do? This invasion of nature—or God— into my Dutch Eden forced me to confront my identity in a new, more radical way. Should I stay here in Holland and bear Philip's child? Become his wife in all but name? I would have a life of comfort and ease, of splendor, if I wanted it. I was sure I could persuade him to return to banking. There would also be a rich dividend of happiness. I no longer had any doubt of my ability to please this man—or his eagerness to please me. I knew how much he would treasure our son.

But it would mean forever abandoning my firstborn

son. I returned to the studio and studied the painting of the Virgin and child. This time I saw something else. Through a window a country village was visible—houses, barns, hedges, and gardens. Was the painter saying this too was part of a woman's fulfillment—this sense of belonging to a place? Was New York the only place where I could find fulfillment? Was Malcolm Stapleton part of that fulfillment, in spite of the way we had wounded each other?

Upstairs, I slipped into a troubled shallow sleep. Suddenly I was in a dream crowded with angry white and black faces. Smoke and flames swirled around me. I was in New York and the town was on fire! I saw Clara fleeing the flames. I saw Malcolm clutching Hugh, running in another direction. I saw a figure in a black robe, pointing at Clara, shouting: "This woman will burn!" Philip Hooft peered anxiously from a window, wailing: "Catalyntieeeee!"

I awoke with a violent start. "Catalyntie!" Philip was calling to me from downstairs. A weary clerk from the Bank of Amsterdam was with him. The fellow had been traveling half the night. "We must return to Amsterdam immediately!" Philip said. "The country is in turmoil. The French have won a tremendous victory at Laufeldt. The Dutch army ran away, abandoning the English on the field."

I heard more as we hastened back to Amsterdam in the carriage that had brought the clerk to the house. "The government has promised to put seventy thousand troops in the field. Every bank in Amsterdam is being pressed for loans. It will require new taxes—which I fear will cause an uproar. The banking community wants me to serve as head of a committee to levy the taxes. They hope to trade on the people's memory of my father as a popular burgomaster—"

Uproar was exactly what we found in Amsterdam. The inns were jammed with wounded Dutch and British officers. When these overflowed, the rich were asked to open their houses. Philip Hooft could hardly say no. I found myself installed in the house on the Heerengracht, supervising the care of a half dozen British officers by Dutch servants who spoke no English.

Two ensigns, no more than boys, died in awful agony after a surgeon amputated their infected legs. Another man had been shot in the head and blinded. He raved and cursed the Dutch. An emaciated young major with a wide mouth and receding chin asked my name. When I told him he exclaimed: "Malcolm Stapleton's wife?" He was James Wolfe, the man who had saved Malcolm from Hangman Hawley's noose in Scotland. I soon learned from the conversations of the other officers that the major had been the hero of the day at Laufeldt. Ignoring a cruel wound in his stomach, he had rallied his regiment and held off half the French army after the Dutch fled.

We talked about America. Wolfe was fascinated by it. "England's future is in your land. Only there can we breed up a race numerous enough to fight Europe," he said. "From my talks with your husband, I think you may produce a better government than our old rotten system. He made me feel patriotism was still possible."[1]

This tribute to Malcolm shook me far more than Wolfe could possibly realize. Events in Amsterdam troubled me even more. When Philip Hooft's committee raised taxes to pay for the vastly expanded army, mobs swirled out of the back streets to loot and burn the houses of the rich. Only a cordon of British troops around the Hooft mansion spared it from destruction. From the mob flew insults that forever changed my vision of Amsterdam as a peaceful city.

---

[1] Wolfe later wrote several "prophetic" letters to friends in the army in which he predicted American greatness.

"Where's Hooft? Let's string him up with the rest of the rich pigs who pick our pockets."

"He looks like a pig."

"Where's Hooft the pig? Oink oink. Come on out, Hooft, and take your punishment."

On the Dam, Dutch troops fought a bloody battle with the mob when they tried to loot the Bank of Amsterdam. In the courtyard of one of the inns, a group of self-appointed politicians, called the Doelists, after the name of the inn, began meeting to set up a new government. The Prince of Orange, the theoretical leader of Holland, hurried to Amsterdam and dispersed them but the specter of a revolution was not so easily forgotten. Wolfe and the other wounded British officers looked on the Dutch with contempt. Their hodgepodge confederation of cities and districts was hopelessly weak and corrupt.

"With an ally like this, we don't need enemies," Wolfe told me. "All they have is money. One of these days we'll take that away from them."

During the weeks of turmoil, I had barely seen Philip. He had been embroiled in endless conferences with the city's burgomasters and assorted emissaries from the Prince of Orange and the Doelists. All traces of the Eden we had created at Brock vanished. Amsterdam and its mob would always hover at the edge of our imaginations now.

When Philip suggested another retreat to Brock at the end of that turbulent summer, I shook my head. "I think it's time for me to go back to America, Philip," she said.

"What will I do without you?" he wailed.

"Go to Paris and talk to Tesselschade," I said. "Perhaps she's changed as much as you've changed. Perhaps you can discover a new love, different and wiser than your first one."

"She'll scorn me again," he said, dwindling in front of my eyes.

"How do you know?"

"She'll have a French lover."

"How do you know? At least write her a letter, asking if she'll see you."

He halfheartedly agreed. That night we made tender love one more time in a bedroom at the rear of the mansion on the Heerengracht, far from the groans and sighs of the wounded British officers. Asleep, I was revisited by the violent dream that had frightened me in Brock— New York afire, Clara threatened with death, riot and confusion everywhere. It made me acutely anxious to begin my voyage.

The child in my womb was another reason to hasten home. I wanted Malcolm to believe it belonged to him. That meant I would have to try to restore our marriage as soon as I arrived. Would it be possible? I did not know. Perhaps I would never find the peaceful fulfillment of the *Virgin with the Milk Soup*. Perhaps I was fated to spend my life struggling for it. But I would sail with the knowledge that I could inspire love in a man. I knew there was love in my heart—if a man could find the secret room in which it was concealed.

Not until I was aboard ship with Philip a week later did I tell him about the child. "I'll name him after you. I'll love him in memory of you," I said.

For a moment he seemed to consider persuading me to stay, to give birth to the child in Amsterdam—and perhaps leave the baby there. But he realized that was impossible. "If it's a boy and he shows any sign of being a painter, send him to me," Philip said. "I'll make sure he gets the best training in Europe."

There was also another reason for letting me go. "I've heard from Tesselschade," he said. "She seems more than willing to see me in Paris."

"Give her my love," I said.

We both realized the double meaning of that word. My love was part of Philip's heart now, as his love was part of my heart. "Take Tesselschade to Brock and paint her portrait in that Chinese silk gown. Find her secret room," I said.

"I'll try," Philip said.

Down the Amstel the ship glided on the tide. In the Zuider Zee, I stayed at the railing until the roofs and towers and masts of Amsterdam slipped beneath the horizon. For a moment I was swept by regret. Some part of my Dutch blood resisted this final separation. I told myself I should be glad to say farewell to a Europe torn by perpetual war and upheaval. Then I remembered my dream and wondered if I would find worse turmoil in America.

THREE

I HAD BOOKED PASSAGE ON an English ship, *Monmouth*, bound for New York. Stumpy, pipe-smoking Captain Henry Swain had warned me the trip could be dangerous. If we encountered a French privateer, he intended to fight to defend his cargo of expensive china from the Dutch city of Delft. He had an extra twenty men aboard, and a dozen cannon lashed to the main deck, their ugly black snouts protruding through the gunports.

I was more concerned about keeping food in my stomach. I was repeatedly seized by bouts of nausea which sent me fleeing to the rail or the common toilet. Being aboard ship at least made this continual distress easy to explain as a kind of permanent seasickness. The captain was very understanding and kept offering me Madeira, rum punch, and other spirits to settle my stomach.

Midway through the third week of the voyage, as we

cruised briskly past the Canary Islands, the cry of "Sail!" brought everyone on deck. We soon bore down on a square rigger that was obviously in distress. Only half her sails were raised and she seemed closer to drifting than sailing before the wind. Captain Swain said she was English-made. But she was not sailing like an Englishman was in command.

"What ship is that?" he roared through his brass trumpet when we were about a quarter of a mile apart.

"Captain," said the first mate, who was studying the ship through a spyglass. "The crew is all Africans. The name on the stern is *Golden Mermaid*, out of Liverpool."

"What ship is that?" the captain repeated, as we drew closer.

The response was a volley of musketry from a half dozen men along the rail. "She's a slaver," Captain Swain said. "They've mutinied and captured her."

He whirled to his cabin boy. "Go below and fetch my sword! Gunners, stand by your guns! First Mate, arm twenty men for a boarding party. Mrs. Stapleton, you'd best go to your cabin."

"Give me a gun first," I said. "I know how to use one."

The captain nodded grimly to the first mate, who handed me a pistol. He was admitting this could be a bloody battle and they might lose. I was tempted to ask the captain if it would be simpler—and safer—to let *Golden Mermaid* go. But Swain was a typical pugnacious English seadog. Mutiny on the high seas had to be punished.

There was another reason to attack, which Captain Swain stated to the first mate with relish. "There's likely a hundred or maybe even two hundred prime Africans aboard her. She'll make a pretty bonus for us all in New York."

I stayed in the doorway of my cabin while *Monmouth*

came abeam *Golden Mermaid*. The Africans on the rail
only had three muskets. They fired about a half dozen
shots which hit no one before *Monmouth* blasted a
broadside into her. Half the guns used grapeshot. *Golden
Mermaid*'s decks were instantly littered with dead and
dying. It was hardly a fair fight.

"Grapple her now, lads," roared Captain Swain. In
the bow and stern, sailors flung clawlike hooks into
Golden Mermaid and hauled on the lines until the two
ships were less than a foot apart.

"Follow me now, lads, for a bit of gold and glory!"
roared Swain and sprang onto *Golden Mermaid*'s bloody
decks, sword in hand. Out of the cabin amidships leaped
an African who aimed a musket at Swain at point-blank
range. The gun boomed and the captain slumped against
the rail, clutching his chest.

"Show them no quarter, lads!" roared the first mate.
He leaped aboard *Golden Mermaid*, seized Swain's
sword, and impaled the man with the musket before he
could reload. The twenty-man boarding party followed
the mate and obeyed his savage orders. They fired round
after round into the cabin where some Africans had
taken refuge until there was no one alive in there.

"Load again and see what's belowdecks," the first
mate said.

A dozen men vanished down a hatch. There were
muffled sounds of more shots. One of the sailors came
flying back on deck. "There's two hundred of them
down there, all out of their coffles, ready to fight with
their hands, their feet, their teeth," he cried.

"Kill a half dozen. That will show the rest," the first
mate said.

After another round of muffled shots, the Africans belowdecks surrendered. The first mate, whose name was
Thompson, briskly ordered his men to throw the dead
overboard and clamp the Africans back in their chains.
They carried Captain Swain's body back to *Monmouth*.

The second mate and ten men were placed in charge of the slave ship. After a hasty prayer over Swain's body, they consigned him to the deep and resumed the voyage to New York with *Golden Mermaid* close astern.

That night at dinner in the captain's cabin, the first mate and I dined on fresh chicken cooked in Madeira wine by the beaming cook. There were one hundred and eighty-two live Africans aboard *Golden Mermaid*. They were worth at least fifty pounds each. Add that to the value of the ship, which was now *Monmouth*'s property as well under the law of salvage, and Captain Swain's promise of a bonus was more than handsomely fulfilled. It was difficult to grieve too deeply for the captain when he had left them such a handsome legacy.

"What happened to the captain and crew of the *Golden Mermaid*?" I asked.

"Slaughtered to a man, as far as we can learn from the mumbo jumbo of the black devils," Thompson said. "It's a dangerous business, the trade. I was in it myself for a while. You got to be on guard every second aboard one of them ships. Not to mention the fevers and vomits a man's likely to catch from your cargo. On one voyage we lost every third sailor."

"Why does anyone go into it?"

"The money's good. If we quit it, the French or the Dutch or the Portuguese'd take the business in a second and leave many a good Englishman without work."

That night, I dreamed of Clara again. She was in some sort of prison, reproaching me. "Your children will suffer for this to the uttermost generation," she cried. Was she talking about the attack on *Golden Mermaid*? Suddenly the prison was on fire and Malcolm was trying to tear loose the bars to help Clara escape.

I awoke and thought of the Africans in their coffles aboard *Golden Mermaid*. What can one person do to change the way the world worked? *Monmouth*'s crew had no remorse for recapturing these people. Yet Clara was unquestionably right about slavery. It was a creation of the Evil Brother. Was my cool tolerance of it proof of how inevitably I was in his grasp?

The thought of this old ally made me begin to dread what I was likely to find in New York. The more I pondered my nightmares, the more convinced I became that Malcolm had gone back to Clara—this time for good. There would be no way to disguise Philip Hooft's child.

My dread became acute when we finally glided past Sandy Hook with a brisk wind and made our way down New York's great harbor. We had to anchor off Fort George at the tip of Manhattan and wait for the tide in the East River to turn. It was late afternoon by the time we tied up *Monmouth* and *Golden Mermaid* at the Roosevelt wharf off Pearl Street.

There was a great stir on the wharf when one of *Monmouth*'s crew shouted the news of *Golden Mermaid*'s capture. She had been bound for New York; Captain Swain was well known in the city. In the hubbub, I could find no one to help me with my trunk. I left it on board and rushed past the familiar storefronts to our house on Depeyster Street. New York was as muddy, as noisy, as smelly as ever. Several friends greeted me on the street. But I was too anxious to feel any warmth in their friendly welcomes.

"Mama!" cried Hugh. He was in the hall as I opened the door. I fell to my knees and embraced him. He was as red-cheeked as a winter apple and had grown at least six inches. A moment later, a smiling Clara was kissing me. She had come by with some sweets for Hugh.

Where was Malcolm? "Playing soldier again. He's ringing the frontier with forts," Clara said. "He appointed me assistant mother until you came home. How are you? How was Holland?"

"Pleasant enough," I said. Did Clara instantly divine this was a half truth, at best? Why did I always find it difficult to lie to her?

"Your timing couldn't be better," Clara said. "Malcolm is expected in a day or two."

"He told you about Culloden?"

"We read about it in the newspapers."

"That's all he told you?"

Clara hesitated. "Yes," she said.

Now we were both lying, I thought. "It's all right. I expected him to tell you the rest. Did you console him in your usual fashion?"

Clara seemed to struggle for a moment with a strange emotion. Was it sadness? "I've been hoping—even praying—that you'd change. I see you haven't."

"I've changed more than you can possibly imagine. The question is—have you—has he—changed?"

"I think Malcolm has changed a great deal," Clara said. "I've changed too—in ways you'd never understand."

"Mama?" little Hugh said. "Why are you and Aunt Clara fighting?"

"We're not fighting. We're very old friends. We're just arguing a bit."

"Tell me about your ship, Mama. Did you have storms? We had a big storm on our ship."

"I'll tell you all about it, darling, as soon as I finish talking to Clara. Go inside and tell Peter to fix us both a cup of tea."

Hugh ran off. Clara gazed coldly at me. "I could have taken him away from you again. But I chose not to—for Hugh's sake—and for his sake."

"Not for my sake?"

"For your sake too," Clara said wearily. "But you're much more difficult to love—"

I struggled against a rush of tears that was part relief, part remorse for Clara's condemnation. Whatever my dreams meant, they were not about losing Malcolm to her. "I've had terrible dreams, Clara, all the way across the Atlantic. I've read them wrong. Forgive me."

"Tell me about them."

When Clara heard my dream of New York ablaze, she was enormously disturbed. But she made no attempt to explain her agitation to her Seneca sister. She soothed me with some empty phrases and declined an invitation to stay for tea. She rushed through the twilit streets to Hughson's Tavern, not certain what she was going to do or say. There she found Caesar and a dozen fellow Africans in a state of wild excitement. The news of the uprising aboard *Golden Mermaid* had swept the city— along with the tale of Captain Swain's death in the attack that had recaptured the slave ship. Behind the bar, John Hughson towered over the crowd, serving ale and rum that only fueled everyone's delirium.

"They say one of those Africans—a fellow who probably never used a gun before in his life—shot Swain down like a dog as he stepped aboard the ship," Caesar said. "The others killed a half dozen of his men before they ran out of ammunition. If ignorant fellows from the bush can do such things—imagine what we can do here in New York."

Clara listened with rising dread. Her voice was stifled by her promise of silence to Caesar.

"We got to find some of those Africans when they're sold tomorrow," Caesar said. "We got to trace where all of them go. They'll be prime fightin' men. I want to hear how they took over *Golden Mermaid*."

"Yeah," chortled Cuffee, Caesar's helper. "They must've got loose, one or two maybe, and slit the whites' throats in the night."

"Startin' with the captain," Caesar said. "There's a lesson for us. We've got to start with the principal people. The governor and his toadies like Stapleton."

He gazed mockingly at Clara. "Will you help us slit Big Malcolm's throat, Clara?"

Clara shook her head, still bound by her vow of silence but desperate to break it. "I've been hearing about dreams—terrible dreams."

Caesar laughed and nudged Cuffee until he started laughing too. "Listen to her, still half an Indian. Africans, Clara—African men—ain't afraid of dreams."

Beside Caesar stood Antonio, the handsome leader of the Spanish slaves. He was growing impatient with the slow pace of the revolt. "Damn dreams and damn all this talk," he said. "I say it's time to fight—with or without these Africans."

Voices on the edge of the crowd called: "Here's Father Ury. Here's the priest." Ury was ushered to a place of honor beside Caesar at the bar. He was unbothered by the use of his potentially deadly title. When one of these meetings was in session, Hughson's doors were closed and only members of the conspiracy were admitted.

"What do you think of the news, Father?" Caesar said.

He was always deferential to the priest in public. Behind his back, Caesar considered him a pious fool. But he found Ury useful because his offer to forgive sins had helped to recruit a number of slaves who were uneasy about killing their masters.

Clara knew that Ury was using Caesar to realize his vision of a colony for English Catholics under French protection. He had convinced himself that God was guiding him to this glorious destiny. "I think it's a sign. God is sending us reinforcements at just the right moment," Ury said. "These men from *Golden Mermaid* are battle-tested warriors."

"Just what I said!" Caesar cried, slapping him on the back. "We should track them down and recruit them. You can help us, Father. Ain't one of your pupils the son of old Cruger?" John Cruger was the city's chief trader in slaves.

Caesar had no interest whatsoever in Ury's Catholic

colony. He had disdained Ury's attempts to convert him. Once he became king of New York, Caesar planned to discard Ury and the handful of white Catholics who had joined the conspiracy. He was sure he could persuade the French and Spanish to reward him with an escort of warships for the fleet he would assemble from the merchant ships at the docks. The grateful allies would convoy them back to Africa, where they would establish an independent country, ready and willing to trade for profit with everyone except the English.

Listening to both men—Ury in her house on Maiden Lane, Caesar at the tavern—Clara felt more and more like she was a spectator at an oncoming catastrophe. All she could do was pray each night for a sudden end of the war, which would remove the crucial element in the plan—the early arrival of French and Spanish aid. Neither God nor the Blessed Virgin seemed to be listening to her. Watching the impact of the news of the uprising aboard *Golden Mermaid*, she began to feel the whole city was in the grip of the Evil Brother. For some reason she did not understand, the Master of Life had turned his face away from New York.

"You still ain't got enough guns," John Hughson said scornfully. He saw himself as a realist who remained skeptical of the whole scheme—while insisting he was ready to join them if they followed his cautionary advice.

"We got more guns than you bought for us, and better ones," Caesar said. "Them old bird guns you got us from Yonkers was a waste of money."

"You should have a gun for every second or third man. Pikes for the rest," Hughson said.

"We got knives for the rest. All kinds of knives," Caesar said. "They're better than pikes for close work. We got a plan to take care of the governor, too. We'll get more guns soon enough. Cuffee and me's plannin' a couple of big grabs."

Caesar and Cuffee had intimidated or persuaded house servants throughout the city to help them steal everything from silver to cash from their masters' homes. The newspapers were full of stories about an "epidemic" of thievery. The Common Council had voted extra money to bolster the Night Watch. But Caesar was confident he could outwit these haphazard guardians of the law. Caesar's stolen goods were the real motive for Hughson's participation. He was making a lot of money reselling them.

Back on Maiden Lane later that night, Clara knelt at her window to pray. But no voice spoke from beyond the stars. Nor did her prayers travel there. All she could see was the circle of African faces in Hughson's, their eyes aglow with Caesar's talk about freedom and power. Why didn't she denounce him as a fool and a fake? Why didn't she tell the Hughsons and Ury what Caesar really had in mind? Why did she listen and say nothing, night after night? She was free—free to leave New York, go to another city, to a farm on Long Island or in Westchester County. But she could not speak, she could not act. Those African faces were like a mad river, sweeping her into a wilderness of doubt and dread. The memory of her night with Caesar, listening to him rhapsodize about the lost Africa of his boyhood, was like a hand at her throat. No wonder her prayers were stillborn.

The next day Clara went down to the Roosevelt wharf to watch the sale of newly arrived slaves. About a dozen merchants and traders climbed aboard *Golden Mermaid* and the Africans were led out on the deck in small groups and carefully examined by the bidders. A crowd of whites and blacks assembled on the dock to see the men who had killed at least thirty white sailors. Around her Clara heard several whites saying *Golden Mermaid*'s cargo should all be shipped to the West Indies.

"They're a pack of murderers," one man said.

"We've got enough to do, trackin' the ones we've

got,'' his friend agreed. Clara recognized them. They were both members of the Night Watch.

On board the ship, there was a great deal of agitated argument between the first and second mates of the *Monmouth* and John Cruger, the city's cadaverous chief slave trader. ''What's up?'' a spectator called to one of the *Monmouth*'s sailors, who had angrily stalked away from the argument. From the whistle around his neck, he was the ship's boatswain's mate.

''You damned Americans are tryin' to cheat us, as usual,'' the boatswain said. ''That walkin' corpse there claims the niggers is only worth half the goin' price because they've got blood on their hands. Says no one here will buy'm.''

''I hope he's right,'' said one of the Night Watch.

Clara suddenly lost interest in this argument. Catalyntie Stapleton was going up the gangplank to *Golden Mermaid*'s deck. No one else in the crowd paid any attention to her. She was greeted warmly by *Monmouth*'s first mate, now the acting captain of both that ship and *Golden Mermaid*. Clara reminded herself that they had just spent six or eight weeks on the Atlantic together. But the sight of her Seneca sister hobnobbing with men who had deprived almost two hundred Africans of their freedom after they had miraculously regained it stirred a sullen disapproval in her soul.

After more argument, the sellers and buyers agreed to turn the auction into a ''scramble.'' The same per capita price was set for all the Africans. At a squeal of the boatswain's whistle, the buyers rushed on deck and grabbed as many of the blacks as they wanted. Some wound ropes or chains around a half dozen. Others grabbed one or two and dragged them off the ship. Quarrels erupted over the biggest and healthiest looking prospects. Anger mingled with greed on more than one white face. John Cruger was busiest. With the help of several assistants, he soon had more than fifty Africans on the dock, coffled and manacled. As they passed through the crowd on the way to Cruger's warehouse, a number of whites cursed them. One man spit on them.

As the last of the Africans vanished down Pearl Street, the first mate walked to the rail and called: "We are now takin' bids on *Golden Mermaid*. A conference with His Majesty's Judge of the Admiralty, the Honorable Daniel Horsmanden, has assured us of our ownership and he stands ready to approve a transfer to the highest bidder.

"Four thousand pounds, New York money," called George Fowler.

"Four thousand five hundred," said Johannes Van Vorst.

"Five thousand," Fowler said.

"Six thousand," said Johannes Van Vorst.

There were no other bids. After calling once, twice, three times for another round, the first mate declared *Golden Mermaid* "sold to Mr. Van Vorst." A murmur of admiration swept through the crowd. It was a vivid demonstration of Johannes Van Vorst's wealth. All Clara could see was six thousand pounds in the hands of sailors who had massacred and subdued those forlorn Africans as they struggled to sail their captured ship to freedom.

As Clara stood there consumed by this desolating thought, Catalyntie poured a shower of Spanish gold dollars into the hands of the acting captain. She was paying for her passage. Two sailors lugged her trunk down the gangplank. Clara began to see everything through a penumbra of darkness. As she walked back to Maiden Lane, the darkness slowly changed to another color. She realized it was red, the color of blood.

Suddenly Caesar was there, speaking to her through the red haze. He had a sack of flour on his shoulder. "Did you go to the scramble?"

"Yes."

"Who bought most of them? Cruger?"

"I think so."

"Good. We've got friends inside Cruger's warehouse. His foreman, Little Richard, is with us."

"How can you do this without guns?"

"We'll get guns."

"How much money do you need?"

"I don't know. Maybe a hundred pounds."

"Come with me," Clara said.

She still saw Caesar through the red haze, although it was a bright fall afternoon. Blood drooled down his forehead over his cheeks as if someone was pouring red paint from the sky.

He followed her down Maiden Lane to her house. All was cool and silent inside. She led him upstairs to her bedroom and dragged a trunk from under her bed. At its bottom was a metal strongbox. She handed it to him.

Caesar put it on the bed and opened it. At least two hundred gold Spanish dollars clustered there. "Jesus," he said.

"He has nothing to do with this," Clara said.

Caesar began laughing. It began as a basso bellow and rose at the end to a shrill near contralto. He picked up the box and poured it on the bed. "I want to take you now, on top of the money."

"No," Clara said.

The red haze was in the room, heaving and bulging against the walls, as if they were underwater. "Yes," Caesar said. "I want to make it mean something. I want it to be more than money. I want to make it holy."

"No!" Clara said.

His mocking use of *holy* horrified her. She saw the Evil Brother beneath his skin, grinning at her.

"Then I don't want your fuckin' money, Clara. Do you understand? I don't want it without you."

"You've got me. But I can't do that."

"Why? Because Malcolm Stapleton owns that part of

you? You're African down there, Clara, just like everywhere else.''

''I hate him,'' Clara said. ''I hate his wife. I hate them all!''

''So do I. Why won't you do it with me?''

Clara stared past Caesar at the statue of the Virgin. She could not tell Caesar the truth about himself. He would laugh at the idea of being possessed by the Evil Brother. Caesar followed her gaze and picked up the statue.

''Who's this? One of Ury's gods?'' Caesar said. ''There's no god mixed up in this, Clara. Except maybe that fellow they call Satan.''

''Take the money, please!''

Caesar shook his head. ''I can steal that much in a month. Watch me.''

He swaggered out of the house. Clara flung herself facedown on the golden coins and wept and wept and wept. Eventually it was twilight and John Ury was standing over her.

''Clara—what's wrong?''

''Father, stop them. Don't let them go any further. Stop Caesar!''

''I can't. Even if I wanted to, I couldn't do it.''

''The Watch knows something. They're going to catch him.''

Ury sat down beside her on the bed and stroked her dark hair. ''Clara, Clara, have faith. Whatever our destiny, Jesus will be with us, even as he stood beside the blessed martyrs of a thousand years ago in ancient Rome.''

She saw how hopeless it was, how ready he was to welcome failure, if he could embrace it like a Christian hero. He was a spent man, hunted across England to this raw continent, yearning to defy his Protestant foes one more time—even if his defiance was hurled from the gallows. His indifference to her body, to all forms of pleasure, was a kind of despair. He was in the grip of the Evil Brother, just as much as she was. Who had let this prince of darkness into their lives? What was at the root of those Africans in their chains, of Caesar's rage, of the Hughsons' frantic trafficking in stolen goods?

Money. The love of it, the perpetual hunger for it. Who personified this cold insatiable lust? Catalyntie Van Vorst Stapleton—the woman who had purchased the name, the allegiance, of the only man she had ever loved. If she and her kind lived to rule America, this would be a continent drenched in blood. Perhaps these money worshippers had to die now, to prevent that destiny. Perhaps a lesson had to be cried from the rooftops of this tormented city. Perhaps that meant more than love, more than the sisterhood of the Senecas. But the vision of Catalyntie, of Malcolm, of little Hugh, murdered in their beds or in the streets, horrified her.

"I feel destruction descending on us, Father," Clara said. "Not salvation. Destruction!"

Father Ury continued to stroke her hair. "When I'm with you, Clara, I feel the beat of angels' wings."

FOUR

ANXIETY CLUTCHED MY THROAT WHEN I heard the front door slam and little Hugh cry: "Papa!" I struggled for self-control and walked to the door of the room I had fitted out as my office. In the dim hall Malcolm looked even bigger than usual. Hugh, clinging to his neck, seemed like some elfin creature.

"Hello, Husband," I said.

"Hello, Wife," he said in a wary uncertain voice.

I went down the hall and kissed him briefly on the lips. Remembering the insults we had exchanged when we parted in London, I thought it best to make the first move. He seemed surprised—and moderately pleased. Slinging Hugh over one shoulder, he followed me into our Queen Anne parlor. Cornelius Van Vorst's portrait smiled from the wall. *Bow down, bow down,* he whispered.

"How did things go in Holland?" Malcolm asked. "When you didn't write, I feared the worst. Did you get the money?"

"Yes," I said. "But I had to borrow it in my own name from the Bank of Amsterdam. My friend Hooft has quit the banking business—"

"Why did you stay four months?"

The question flustered me badly. Had he heard something? "I . . . I thought it was best if we parted for a while."

Malcolm sat down and perched Hugh on his knee. "That may have been a good idea."

"We both said extreme things in London. I'm ready to forgive and forget, if you are."

"You've got more to forgive, I'm afraid. I acted like a madman."

"There was tremendous provocation. I understand that now. I did a great deal of thinking about us in Holland."

You're doing beautifully, you haven't said a word of truth yet. It was the Evil Brother, mocking me as usual. I glanced up at Cornelius's portrait and suddenly prayed: *Help me, wherever you are.*

"What did you conclude?"

"We're well matched, in spite of our bad beginning. In spite—"

I hesitated because of Hugh. But the little boy was not listening. Malcolm was tickling him. He was giggling and squirming, trying to escape his father's grip.

"In spite of Clara."

Malcolm nodded. The name did not seem to stir him. "I've thought about us too, up there in the woods," he said. "A kind of destiny or fate or whatever you call it seems to have brought us together. When I think of the odd chances that played a part. I wasn't planning to go to that Indian peace council where we met. Nicolls talked me into it at the last minute. So many other things—"

Was he thinking of the Eagle Dance? I felt a rush of desire. What better way to start again? "At Elizabeth White's wedding breakfast, I sat next to the most ribald old lady—her aunt. She had racy stories about all the great folks. She told me when the Duke of Marlborough came home from one of his campaigns in Flanders, he used to pleasure Lady Sarah on their bed without even taking off his boots."

A slow smile spread across Malcolm's mouth. Had he been thinking similar thoughts? "What about this young fellow?" he said.

"Peter can take him down to see the ships. They can both use the exercise."

"I want you to come too, Papa," Hugh said. He did not understand what was passing over his head but Peter was a frequent companion on his outings.

"We'll go tomorrow. We'll see every ship in the harbor," Malcolm said.

Mollified, Hugh permitted his mother and his nurse to put on his walking shoes and a jacket. He and Peter were soon out the door. I led Malcolm up the narrow stairs to our bedroom. Fall sunshine spangled the blue damask curtains and the sky blue hangings of the big canopy bed. As we undressed, I almost could not believe the ease with which I was achieving my goal. The raging man I had known in London seemed to have vanished. Had I learned some sort of magic in Philip Hooft's arms? It was hard to give myself credit for the transformation.

"My God, you're as beautiful as ever," he murmured, cupping his hands over my breasts.

I ran my hands down his massive arms and back. He stirred the same rampant desire. It was radically different from the elegiac sweetness I had felt for Philip Hooft. I was loving more than a man here. Malcolm evoked the wilderness of my girlhood, the raw vitality of rushing rivers and forested earth. I felt the throb of the seasons, the power of the wind, the beat of the rain in his arms. I had been right to come home. This man was my life as well as my love.

"Take me, take me," I whispered. "I'll never stop wanting you."

What followed was a mixture of tenderness and savagery. Affection—it was too soon to call it love—mingled with desire. There did not seem to be any lingering anger on either side. The coming was deep and mutual, not as wild as I remembered it, but I felt a need for a certain restraint because of the child in my womb. Malcolm seemed more than satisfied; he cradled me in his arms and called me "Cat" and kissed my pulsing throat.

It was done. I was safe from public disgrace—and I had managed it without humiliation. As Malcolm caressed me with surprising tenderness, I juggled numbers and dates in my head. The baby would be born in seven months, if I remembered correctly when I stopped menstruating.

Not high romance—and it had its negative effect. I had to learn again and again that souls mingle in the bedroom and the smallest alteration in feeling was detectable. Malcolm sensed a kind of withdrawal that made him wary. Was the old devious Catalyntie returning, now that he had satisfied her? I struggled to reassure him that my new sweetness was real. I told myself it *was* real. I had learned it in Philip Hooft's arms and I would use it here.

"Husband," I murmured. "How dear that word has become to me. I want to make *wife* mean the same thing to you."

"I want that," Malcolm said. "I want us to reach a new understanding, a new sympathy. I want to share with you my new thoughts about myself—and our country."

He recapitulated his turmoil, his near despair over his political discoveries in England. The extreme rottenness and savagery of their system of plundering the nation without regard for the feelings or welfare of the common people. How could a soldier, motivated by patriotism, serve such a gang of pirates? Only when he returned to New York did he realize that there was still a source of hope in his life.

"It was here, in the sight of America itself, in contemplating it on the map—the immensity of it—the reach of the continent that awaits our sons and grandsons—that I realized there was still a place that patriotism could serve," Malcolm said. "We can resist the English spirit of plunder, we can make a fresh start in a virgin land—and perhaps eventually rescue the mother country itself from her rottenness."

I thought this was the most arrant moonshine I had ever heard. I saw little or no difference in the rapacity of New York merchants and London merchants—or Amsterdam merchants, for that matter. The same animosity toward the rich permeated the lower classes. My visit to England had produced a very different view of the future. As soon as possible, the Americans must separate from the British or be devoured by them—reduced to the status of conquered provinces, like Ireland or Scotland.

But I said nothing to contradict my visionary husband. Instead, I told him the similar prophecies Major James

Wolfe had made about America's future while I was nursing his wounds in Amsterdam. "This gives me a purpose too," I said. "The stronger we become in a business way, the better we can stand up to them."

"Yes, but you must promise me an absolute end to such tricks as smuggling and bribing customs officers. I want us to raise a standard to which every honest man can repair."

"Of course I'll promise. With a merchant like Chesley White behind me in London, I have no need to stoop to such things."

There followed an uneasy silence. Were we both recognizing that we were talking more like the officers of a corporation than lovers? Ruefully, I began to see the impersonality of Malcolm's new view of me. I was his American wife, his political and business partner. Love, personal love, had very little to do with our new arrangement. That emotion was still reserved for Clara. Could I bear it? I wondered. Even more ruefully, I realized I had little choice.

We went back to talking business. I asked him about the New Jersey lands. Had he taken possession of them?

"Yes. But we'll have to borrow a devil of a lot of money to restore them. My stepmother did nothing but suck cash out of the farms through an overseer. The poor Africans are half starved, the big house a ruin. The barn roof fell in and they've used the ballroom as a granary."

"This only makes it all the more imperative for me to get down to business at the store," I said. "We have a huge debt to pay off."

The next morning, I hurried to the Universal Store. Adam Duycinck was on hand to display the books, which made unhappy reading. The goods I had shipped from Chesley White's London warehouses were not selling well. Before they arrived, Adam and Sophia Cuyler had done little but sell off the merchandise on the shelves. When they ran out of an item, they were afraid to sign bills of exchange to restock it—so fearful had I made them with my laments about imminent bankruptcy before we sailed to England. As a result we had lost dozens of our best customers who would not be easily regained.

A few minutes after I finished examining the books, we were interrupted by two agitated visitors. Rebecca Hogg was a short stout woman with a round fat face and haughty manner. She ran a small general store on the corner of Broad and South William Street. With her was a tall, long-nosed, more agreeable woman named Anne Kannady who sold candles not far away. "I'm here to report a burglary," Rebecca Hogg said. "The useless constables we pay with our tax money are doing nothing to catch the thieves."

Mrs. Hogg's shop had been broken into sometime last night. It was the tenth burglary she had heard about— she suspected the authorities were concealing the real number. She had lost over forty Spanish dollars, silver, linen, and assorted goods worth another ten pounds. "Some of the Spanish money was peculiar. Square pieces of eight. I hope you'll keep a lookout for it," she said.

"Of course we will," I said. I was being polite—and sympathetic. It seemed unlikely that any of our goods would be paid for in that kind of small change. Most of our sales were to the wealthy and charged to their accounts. Bills were sent to the buyers' husbands each month.

"We think it's the Africans," Anne Kannady said. "It's time we banished them from the city. They do nothing but make more money for the rich. Or help them live in ease."

"There are some free Africans as honest and respectable as you or I am," I responded with not a little warmth. "My friend Clara Flowers, for instance."

"Doesn't she run Hughson's Tavern?" Rebecca Hogg

said. "How can you call her respectable? Half the customers are whores and the rest are the very people we're talking about. Slaves that are breaking the curfew laws and like as not plotting their next heist."

"I don't think you have any right to say such things, Mrs. Hogg. I resent them—in Clara's name."

"She's running that place with your money, from what I hear. Some people will do anything to make themselves rich," Mrs. Hogg said.

The usually good-natured Anne Kannady grew alarmed. "Mind your temper, Rebecca. Mrs. Stapleton is one of my best customers." She smiled nervously at me. "She's very upset over her losses. It's a great deal of money to her."

"I'm upset over the way some supposedly respectable people are ready to defend thieves and blackguards," Rebecca Hogg said.

She stormed out of the store, leaving me speechless. Adam Duycinck looked haggard. I suddenly remembered what he had told me about the Hughsons' dealing in stolen goods. "Do you know anything about this?" I said.

"Not a thing!" Adam said, almost jumping out of his skin.

"Have we lost anything to these burglars?"

Sophia Cuyler shook her head. "I ordered double padlocks for our doors. Mrs. Hogg is right about the number of break-ins. It's well over twenty. My husband tells me there's been even bigger thefts out of the warehouses. Someone stole sixty firkins of butter from John Vergereau's a month ago."

"Sixty firkins! That's three thousand pounds!" I said. "What could burglars do with that much butter?"

"Sell it to some enterprising ship captain in the dark of the night," Adam said. "They'd clear two hundred pounds at least."

"Let's put three padlocks on our doors," I said. "These fellows are serious."

At Hughson's, Clara was supervising Mary Burton in a thorough cleaning of the taproom. Mary was supposed to mop the place after they closed each night. But she often begged off in her whining way, claiming she was too tired. In the morning, she would sleep late and escape the chore. Two days of this and the floor would be a mess of crusts and broken glass and burnt tobacco. Mary was whining as usual, claiming her back was sprained, her elbows practically broken from carrying heavy trays.

Through the door burst Rebecca Hogg and Anne Kannady. With them was Anne's husband, James, one of the members of the Night Watch whom Clara had overheard yesterday on Roosevelt Wharf, talking about Africans as criminals. His thickset friend, Robert Hogg, Rebecca's husband, was with him.

"Where's your master?" Rebecca Hogg said to Clara.

"My master? I have no master," Clara said. "You know that as well as I do, Mrs. Hogg."

"A likely story," Rebecca Hogg snarled. "Don't you pay him a share of what you make for your fucking?"

"I'm half owner of this tavern, Mrs. Hogg. I don't fuck sailors," Clara said.

"John Hughson!" Rebecca Hogg said. "Come down here."

Hughson soon appeared, pulling on his coat. He looked frightened, even though he towered over Mrs. Hogg and her friends.

"We have evidence that some of the square pieces of eight robbed from my store last night were passed here for drinks. Do you know anything about it?" Mrs. Hogg said.

"Not a thing," Hughson said.

"Our witness told us it was Vraack's Caesar who passed it. A known thief."

"I saw no square pieces of eight," Hughson said.

"We've got a warrant to search your premises," Constable Kannady said.

"Search away," Hughson said.

The two men stamped upstairs. Clara watched, dread consuming her. Was it the beginning of their destruction? In twenty minutes, the constables returned, looking glum. "There's nothing to be found," Kannady admitted.

Anne Kannady turned to Mary Burton. "Do you know anything about this, child?" she said in a kindly voice.

Mary shook her head.

"I've heard you complain about this man when he sent you to me for candles," Mrs. Kannady said, gesturing to John Hughson. "If you proved him a thief, I'm sure the judge would free you of your indenture."

Clara shuddered at the hungry light in Mary's eyes as she considered this offer. The girl's gaze flicked to John Hughson's bulk. Did she notice his hands opening and closing? "I know nothing of thievery," Mary said.

The constables and their wives departed, Rebecca Hogg loudly urging them to summon a magistrate and at least arrest Caesar on the basis of the witness who saw him with the money. Hughson glared at Mary. "If you ever say a word," he said. "You'll be in the river next morning."

"I won't—I won't ever!" Mary wailed. She was terrified, as well she should be. Hughson could break her neck with a single blow. "Don't let him hit me, Clara," she begged.

In the Indian part of her soul, Clara knew it would be wise to kill Mary Burton then and there. But the Christian part of her soul could not tolerate such a crime.

"Finish the floor," she said. "We'll be opening in ten minutes."

Hughson asked Clara to find John Ury. It looked as if Caesar was about to be arrested. What if he talked? "He'll deny everything," Clara said. "Passing a square piece of eight proves nothing. But those constables may come back. You better get that stuff from Hogg's shop out of here."

"Why?" Hughson said. "It's tucked away under the stairs. They didn't come close to finding it."

It was hard to deal with a man who was both stupid and arrogant. Clara went looking for John Ury. He was tutoring Adolphus Philipse's son. She knocked on the door of the family's redbrick mansion on Broad Street. A plump young woman answered the door. "Go around the back," she said.

"I'm here to see Professor Ury," Clara said.

"Go around the *back*!" the obnoxious creature said and slammed the door in Clara's face.

Clara trudged down the alley to the back door. A black cook led her up a rear stairs to the second floor and pointed down the hall. She found Ury reading French to a fat boy of twelve who looked like a male version of the young woman who had answered the front door. "Mr. Ury?" Clara said.

He closed the boy's door and they conferred in the hall. Ury paled when he heard about Caesar. "He's essential to our plan. No one else can lead the Africans," he said.

"Hughson wants to see you. He's very upset."

"I'll come within the hour."

Back at the tavern, Clara found Sarah and John Hughson in an anxious conference upstairs. "Caesar's been arrested," Sarah said. "We just heard the news from Cuffee. He's in a panic, thinking he'll be next."

"I'll try to hire a lawyer," Clara said. "If Caesar holds his tongue there's nothing to worry about."

"There isn't a lawyer in the city who'll take his case," Hughson said.

He was right about that. John Ury arrived an hour later. He had talked to a lawyer he trusted, who told him to forget the idea. Only if Caesar's master, old John Vraack, pleaded for him, as he had often done in the past, was there any chance of an early release.

The Hughsons' oldest daughter, also named Sarah, rushed into the room. She was a tall pretty girl of about twenty, with her mother's looks and father's lack of brains. "The constables came and took Mary away!" she said.

John Ury decided to leave immediately. "There's nothing to be gained if I'm arrested too," he said.

Later in the afternoon, Rebecca Hogg and her constable husband returned with Undersheriff John Mills. He was the same slovenly man who had run the city jail when Clara spent a night there with Caesar. Mrs. Hogg was bristling with triumphant exultation. "Mary Burton has told us a great deal," she said. "She's sure my stolen property's hidden in this house. She said my husband trod upon it but wasn't cute enough to see it."[1]

"She's a damn liar. I'll give her the whipping of her life when she gets back here," John Hughson roared.

"You'll do no such thing. She's been remanded to the protection of the sheriff until this matter is settled. If her word proves true, you'll see no more of her as an indentured slavey. She's told us how you've all but worked her to death."

"The girl is a liar and a whore!" Sarah Hughson said.

"Tell us where the goods are, John," Undersheriff Mills said. "You may get out of this with your whole skin if you play an honest part."

Hughson's small brain churned. Clara could almost

---

[1] *Cute meant clever in the eighteenth century.*

hear the machinery grinding. "Maybe I know where some things is hid. I'll bring them to you," he said.

Sarah Hughson could only stare in horror. Clara began seeing everything through the red haze. Hughson went upstairs and returned with a bundle of linens and a silver candlestick. Rebecca Hogg snatched them away. "You goddamned thief. You'll hang for this. You and your wife and your black whore!"

"You all better come along to City Hall," Undersheriff Mills said.

"I had nothing to do with this," Clara said.

"You own half this tavern, don't you?"

"Yes."

"Come along then. Or get dragged."

In City Hall, a constable was sent to the house of Judge Daniel Horsmanden. Mary Burton was brought in by another constable. Caesar appeared, shackled hand and foot. Mary testified that she had seen the Hughsons accepting stolen goods from him.

"But not her," she said, pointing to Clara. "She was always tellin' Caesar to change his ways."

"But she knew about his thefts?" Judge Horsmanden asked.

"Everybody in the place knew about them," Mary said.

"Did you ever traffic with this woman?" Horsmanden asked Caesar.

He shook his head. He was looking forlorn. "She's an honest woman, Your Honor. I should've listened to her."

"If she were honest, she would have notified the proper authorities of your thievery," Horsmanden said. "I hereby order all these people arrested as accessories to the crime of theft, committed by the slave, Caesar."

The doors of the courtroom swung open. Old John Vraack hobbled in, presumably to make his usual plea for Caesar's services. Horsmanden did not even let him open his mouth. "You're too late, Mr. Vraack. Caesar is through baking bread in this city."

"And well he should be," Vraack said.

Clara noticed he was carrying a bundle in his hand. He dropped it on the floor and it made an ominous clank. "Here's a parcel of linen and silver plate I found under my kitchen floor this morning. No doubt it belongs to Mrs. Hogg."

"Are you going to set bail for the others, Your Honor?" Undersheriff Mills asked.

"Ten pounds each," Horsmanden growled.

The Hughsons looked dismayed. As usual they were living on the edge of bankruptcy. "I'll pay it, Your Honor," Clara said.

"Where did you get that kind of money?" Horsmanden said.

"I earned it with hard work six days and nights a week at our tavern," she said.

"Undersheriff, go directly and collect the money before you discharge one of them," Horsmanden said.

They all trudged to Clara's house on Maiden Lane, where she pulled her chest of Spanish silver dollars from beneath the bed and counted one hundred fifty of them into Mills's grimy hand. They parted company and the Hughsons and Clara returned to the tavern. Their daughter, Sarah, had opened the taproom. It was filling with the usual mixture of whores, blacks, sailors, and soldiers. Everyone talked of Caesar's bad luck. Many of the soldiers had helped him dispose of his loot in the past. They were mostly Irish and had little regard for English laws or army regulations.

When Ury arrived around ten o'clock, Clara and the Hughsons beckoned him upstairs. He had been consulting with lawyers on their behalf. "Most of them tell me Caesar won't be hanged. He'll be banished to the West Indies. You may get a similar sentence. You'll have to move to some other colony. The goods aren't worth that much money and there's no evidence to connect you to reselling them.''

"What about me?" Clara asked.

"If Caesar and everyone else maintain your innocence, you'll get little more than a warning."

They went back downstairs in a somewhat better frame of mind. Ury seemed to have talked to level-headed, respectable men. Caesar looked like he would be the biggest loser in their bad luck. Clara found herself thinking perhaps the Master of Life had heard her prayers and was removing Caesar from the city. It would instantly deflate the larger plot. Ury seemed to accept this. "We must try to understand God's mysterious will in such things," he said to Clara as they walked into the taproom.

By now it was very late. Cuffee and a half dozen other Africans, including the leader of the Spanish Africans, Antonio, were at the bar. Sailors were propositioning whores in the corners of the room. Clara replaced Sarah Hughson behind the bar. The Africans were drinking hard. They were paying in square Spanish pieces of eight—a reckless, even an insane thing to do.

"Caesar told me where he stashed the Hogg money," Cuffee said. "I went out the back door of Vraack's place as the constables came in the front."

"We may have seen the last of Caesar," Hughson said. "Unless we fancy a trip to the West Indies."

"The hell you say," Cuffee snarled. "They ain't goin' to get rid of him that easy. He gave me an order as I ran. We're goin' to obey it, like true soldiers."

"What order?"

"Fire the town. When it's burnin' bright, and the whites are in the streets, start shootin', cuttin', slashin'. When Caesar comes out of that jail, he'll be king of New York."

Clara shuddered. There was destruction in every word of that rant.

"We're going to free those Africans from the *Golden Mermaid* and give them all swords," Antonio said. "They're Ashantis. I've learned the one word they need to know. It means kill."

The red haze descended once more, shot through with streaks of darkness. Clara saw blood drooling down their faces. The Evil Brother still ruled New York.

FIVE

"I DON'T UNDERSTAND WHAT YOU'RE trying to tell me," I said.

"How can I make myself clearer?" Clara said. "There's going to be terrible trouble here in New York. You'll be much safer in New Jersey."

"What kind of trouble?"

"I've had your dream—the whole city in flames."

"You think the French or the Spanish are going to attack us?"

"What else could it mean? Take Hugh and go to New Jersey tomorrow. I was talking to Malcolm today. He said it might be a good idea. You're feeling poorly."

"I'm not feeling that bad," I said. "The New Jersey house is a wreck—"

Had Clara changed her mind about Malcolm? Was she trying to exile me to New Jersey while she enjoyed him in New York? I could think of no other reason for this urgent suggestion—sad evidence of how little progress I had made spiritually, in spite of my resolutions to change during my sojourn in Holland. My growing pregnancy contributed to my Moon-Womanish feelings.

"I have no designs on your husband's marvelous body," Clara said.

That only sharpened my suspicions. "I want to testify at your trial," I said.

Clara almost groaned with exasperation—or despair. Or both. Caesar's plan for burning New York called for setting fire to Fort George on the first night that a strong west wind began to blow. That could happen tomorrow.

"Malcolm's going to testify," Clara reminded me. "So will many others. Peter Van Ness is a good lawyer—"

Malcolm had hired our former London lawyer-poet to defend Clara. Van Ness too had returned to New York disillusioned with our British overlords.

"I want to defend my reputation," I said. "That judge, Daniel Horsmanden, is my uncle's closest friend. They're going to try to slander both of us. If I run off to New Jersey it will look like I have something to hide."

Clara gave up and retreated to Hughson's. A month had passed since Caesar's arrest. He would be going on trial in another three weeks, when the Supreme Court began its next session. Cuffee and Antonio were trying to rally the city's slaves but it was much more difficult without Caesar. Their organization had been haphazard, at best. Now, the Night Watch had been doubled and their orders included a strict enforcement of the ban on slaves in taverns—especially in Hughson's. It was difficult and frequently impossible for any of them to move freely around the city without arousing the anger and perhaps the suspicion of their masters.

Did Clara want them to succeed in spite of these obstacles? She only knew she was still not prepared to betray them. She could do that in a five-minute talk with Malcolm Stapleton. She was even more unsure why she wanted Catalyntie, of all people, to survive, since her Seneca sister was a walking talking paradigm of white vices, from arrogance to greed to vindictiveness. But she remembered the woman who had rescued her from oblivion at Hampden Hall, the woman who had freed her without a moment's hesitation as soon as she had the power.

Why wasn't she more concerned about Malcolm? He would be a prime target of the uprising. Clara had long since decided every warrior had his individual *ondinnonk*. Nothing could kill one of them until he reached that predestined fate and nothing could save him from it once the deadly moment arrived. She also remembered her dream of Malcolm, flanked by those angelic figures.

At Hughson's, everyone lived in mute terror, unable to decide whether the Africans' plan would rescue or destroy them. John Hughson had burnt the book in which he had listed all the slaves who had agreed to join Caesar's army. But he could do nothing about the passionate hope and even more passionate anger Caesar had stirred in their hearts. The only man who might have done something was John Ury. But he remained passive, equally divided between a different hope and their common fear.

So things drifted until March 17, the day on which the Irish in New York celebrated the birthday of their patron saint, Patrick. Hughson's was jammed with Irish soldiers from Fort George that night. They were joined by dozens of Celts among the sailors in the harbor. More often than not, the toast was "A free country." Dozens of times, Clara had heard the soldiers bemoan the oppressive vise that the English had clamped on Ireland. It confirmed Caesar's contention that the plotters had little to fear from the garrison. An appeal to their Irish blood would persuade most of them to switch sides if they thought they had even a fair chance of survival.

Toward midnight, John Hughson muttered in Clara's ear. "Be prepared for trouble. Take the cash out of the drawer and hide it in the closet under the stairs."

"Why?"

"Little Quaco is going to fire the fort tonight. Can't you hear the wind? It's blowing thirty knots from the west."

For the first time, Clara noticed the March wind was beating against the windows and roof and howling in the alleys. She had willed the fateful sound out of her mind. Quaco, one of Eugenia Fowler's footmen, was the logical African to burn the fort. The abuse he had endured from his mistress for half his life had bred a violent hatred of whites in his heart. His wife was the governor's cook and Quaco was a regular visitor to the governor's mansion inside the fort's grounds. For the next hour, Clara, heart pounding, waited for the upheaval to begin. She concocted a mad scheme of rushing to the Stapleton house and offering herself as protector against the knife and ax wielders who would soon be swarming in the streets.

Two, then three more hours passed without the dreaded cry that would send everyone fleeing from their houses to meet assassins on their doorsteps. Eventually, the last drinkers stumbled off to their beds and Hughson could only mutter: "Something's gone wrong. I hope they didn't catch Quaco. He's got a loose tongue."

As they were bolting the doors and shutters, three figures emerged from the night: Antonio, the leader of the Spanish slaves, Caesar's partner, Cuffee, and Quaco. "What happened?" Hughson said.

"The devil I know," Quaco said.

"He put the coals under the eaves of the house exactly as Caesar told him to," Cuffee said. "But they didn't catch."

"I'll do it again tomorrow," Quaco said. "I want to get even with His Excellency, the son of a bitch. He don't let me see my wife."

He was drunk. No wonder the coals had not caught. They parted with Quaco reiterating his vow if the wind held. Clara hoped he would drink himself unconscious and forget about it.

The next day, around one o'clock, as Clara left her house on Maiden Lane for the trip across town to Hughson's, she noticed the wind was still blowing hard from the west. She had barely closed the front door when a cry of ''Fire!'' rang through the streets.

Men burst from houses and shops. ''Where? Where's the fire?'' they cried. In this city of shingled roofs and mostly wooden houses, no word carried more terror.

''The fort. Fort George is ablaze!''

Clara followed the running men to the tip of the island. By the time she reached the Bowling Green, flames were roaring above the walls of the fort. Someone inside was frantically clanging the bell of the chapel as a superfluous fire alarm. The hundred-man garrison was milling around outside the walls, shouting for buckets, for the town's fire engines. These soon arrived from their storage place in City Hall. But they made little headway against the flames. The stiff wind blew the water back in the hosemen's faces when they lifted their nozzles to reach the burning roof. A bucket brigade organized by Malcolm Stapleton did no better. The heat scorched them off their ladders.

The soldiers, finally taken in charge by their officers, rushed into the governor's house and carried out official records and furniture and some of their guns and ammunition from the barracks. But the rampaging flames quickly put an end to this activity. Soon it became evident that all the buildings in the fort were beyond redemption. The fire spread from the governor's house to the chapel to the barracks.

With the fort's whole interior ablaze, many of the bucketmen and hosemen retreated, fearful that the gunpowder would explode. Malcolm Stapleton conferred with the governor, who assured him that was very unlikely. The powder was stored deep underground to prevent such combustion. But most of the firemen were unconvinced and they clustered haplessly around their engines, letting the fort burn.

Glowing embers began drifting uptown on the wind to land on roofs of nearby houses. The dry shingles began smoldering. The weary firemen rushed to prevent these new fires, spraying water on dozens of roofs while panicky residents dragged furniture and other valuables into the street. Word of roofs burning farther uptown increased the general panic. More and more firemen abandoned their posts and raced to rescue wives and children and valuables from their own houses. As twilight descended, it began to look as if the entire city would be ablaze by midnight.

Clara saw Antonio and Quaco and Cuffee once or twice on the edge of the crowd, exultance on their faces. John Hughson rushed up to her, panting from passing buckets to fight the flames, and whispered hoarsely: "It's coming, it's coming, by God. Tonight will be the night. Keep the cash hidden."

Clara fled to her house on Maiden Lane. Upstairs in her room she knelt before the statue of the Virgin that John Ury had given her.

Oh Holy Mother, tell me what I should do.
Silence.
What is happening? I want to understand it.
Silence.
I want to help those I love!
Silence.
I know I'm not worthy. My heart is full of hate.
Silence.
Give me a sign, Holy Mother. My faith is so weak.
Silence.

Then Clara heard it drumming on the roof. Rain. She saw it sluicing down the windowpane. *Rain.* She flung herself facedown, arms outstretched.

O Holy Mother, I will never doubt again.

A few blocks away, Malcolm Stapleton stood among the exhausted, soot-blackened firefighters, his big head tilted toward the sky. Rain! An hour before, the sky had been clear—not a trace of a cloud. Beside him his friends Peter Van Ness and Guert Cuyler, equally grimy, were just as dazed. The rain pelted down, soaking roofs they could not reach, dousing the still-formidable fire inside the fort.

"The wind—it's dropped to nothing," Guert Cuyler said.

"Someone must be praying for us, somewhere," Malcolm said.[1]

Rushing downtown again through the rain, Clara found Malcolm in front of the Universal Store on Pearl Street. Adam Duycinck and Sophia Cuyler had thrown most of the goods into the street, anticipating the destruction of the shop. Malcolm and several other firemen were helping them return the stuff to the shelves. Catalyntie stood in the doorway, watching.

"I must speak with you," Clara said to Malcolm.

They walked a few feet down the block. The rain had dwindled to a drizzle. "You should patrol the streets with your militia tonight, guns in hand," Clara said.

"Why?"

Clara glanced toward Catalyntie. She was staring at them. "This fire was a signal. Even though it's been extinguished, there may be trouble."

"From whom?"

"I'm not an informer. Just do as I say! You should have no difficulty turning out enough men. With a war in your favor."

She left him there, staring after her. "What did Clara tell you?" I asked.

---

[1] *Historians confirm the appearance of this sudden rain shower which saved most of New York from the flames. No one, of course, has previously suggested what appears here as an explanation for it.*

"She thinks we should turn out some militia tonight."

"Why?"

"She won't tell me."

Malcolm decided to take Clara's warning seriously. He conferred with the governor, who agreed to call out a company of militia—about seventy-five men—to night duty. He also ordered the Night Watch to be alert for trouble. At Hughson's, Clara said nothing while Sarah and John Hughson discussed with John Ury the mysterious way the fire had been extinguished.

"I fear it's a sign," Ury said. "But it's written in a language I can't understand."

"The Africans would've come out, fire or no fire, if Stapleton didn't spring his damned militia on them," John Hughson said. "With the Night Watch, he's put a hundred armed men in the street. I think someone ratted."

"Who could it be?" Ury said. "Do you have any idea, Clara?"

Clara shook her head, her heart choked with pain. Was there another word for what she had done, besides betrayal? Yes, she told herself. The militiamen guaranteed a peace that would preserve everyone's life—perhaps even Caesar's. But she did not reckon with the fury in the hearts of the slaves. Was it because she was free? Was that brutal fact responsible for the gulf that opened between them?

For a week an uneasy peace prevailed in New York. But there was no peace at Hughson's. Antonio and Cuffee visited after midnight on Monday to denounce the Hughsons and Ury as traitors. Nothing could convince them that the trio had not switched sides and advised Malcolm Stapleton to turn out his militia on the night of March 18.

"Every African was ready that night, with his gun or his knife at hand," Cuffee said.

The sight of the armed men had discouraged many

members of their army. But they vowed to burn the city anyway, hoping in the chaos they could rescue Caesar and flee. A week after the fire at the fort, they struck again, using the same technique—burning coals thrust under the eaves of a targeted house. Out of touch with the plotters, Clara was reduced to the status of a horrified spectator.

"Fire!" The cry crashed through her open window around noon on that cold March Wednesday. She followed the crowd downtown and found flames leaping from the Broad Street house of royal navy captain S. Peter Warren. With no wind and a prompt discovery, the fire engines and the bucket brigades managed to soak the roof and walls and contain the blaze in less than fifteen minutes.

A week later, the dreaded cry rang out again, around the same time of day. This time the blaze was in a big warehouse full of hay, fir, and pinewood, on the East River. There was no hope of saving the building. The flames were leaping a hundred feet above the roof when the firemen got there. Instead they worked frantically to douse the roofs and walls of all the buildings in the vicinity. Being close to the river helped. In an hour, the warehouse was a heap of guttering embers, but none of the nearby buildings caught fire.

This time, Malcolm Stapleton paid Clara a visit. "That fire in Van Zant's warehouse was set by someone," he said. "It started in the roof, just like the one at the governor's mansion and Warren's house. "Do you know who's doing it?"

"No," Clara said. It was technically true. She had no idea exactly who was setting the blazes. It was probably a different slave each time—someone who had access to the various premises.

"Do you have any idea? From what you said to me when the fort burned, you're in touch with some people who want to cause serious trouble. My bet is on some of the slaves who drink at Hughson's. Who are they, beside Caesar?''

''I won't inform! I won't have that on my conscience.''

''Clara—''

''Get out of my house.''

Upstairs, she fell on her knees before the Virgin's statue. *Tell me what to do, Holy Mother.*

Silence. Was the Virgin telling her that her heart was still clotted with hate?

Three days later, another fire erupted in a cow shed at the foot of Maiden Lane. The frantic mooing of the cows alerted passersby and the blaze was extinguished in a few minutes. But there was evidence of someone hoping for a bigger conflagration. Hay had been piled almost to the ceiling and set on fire.

A half hour later, another fire burst from the upper windows of a private house only a few steps away from the cow shed. This too was quickly extinguished and the firefighters found unmistakable evidence of arson. Someone had put a hot coal beneath a straw mattress in the room, which was the sleeping quarters for the family's slave. He denied knowing anything about it. But for the first time, people began to wonder if the fires were being set by Africans. Memories of the 1712 uprising swirled to the surface of many minds.

A week later, the arsonists struck four times in one day. First a house, then a shop, then a stable, and finally another big warehouse on the East River burst into flames. The warehouse burned to the ground, but once more the surrounding buildings were saved, thanks to energetic use of the East River's water. This time a man who had climbed to the roof of a nearby warehouse saw an African run out a back door of the burning warehouse and disappear down the street. He recognized him as Cuffee Philipse.

A crowd rushed to the Philipse house and dragged

Cuffee to the City Hall jail, where he joined Caesar. The fear of a Negro plot now ran rampant through the city. All the Spanish Africans were dragged to jail by excited mobs. Almost any slave who happened to be on the street was liable to find himself behind bars. Soon there were over a hundred in the crowded cells and the undersheriff insisted he could not handle any more.

Day after day, Clara prayed before the statue of the Virgin. The voice remained silent. Instead, the word *destruction* whined in her mind, mingling with the March wind that wailed outside in the streets.

Malcolm visited her again. "Catalyntie's given me an idea that could stop these fires," he said. "She thinks the governor should issue a proclamation, offering a hundred pounds to anyone who'll come forward with information about the conspiracy."

"That's just like her. Convinced that money can solve everything and anything."

"I think it might work."

"Why are you telling me this?"

"I want you to speak first, Clara. Before it becomes profitable. It's your chance to prove your loyalty, your honesty. To show the whole city that your race is trustworthy—even if some of them are guilty."

"How little you know me," Clara said.

"I'm trying to protect you, Clara!"

"Protect me—by destroying me? By leaving me an empty box of a human being? Can't you see what you're asking me to do?"

"I'm asking you to be an American. Not an African or a Seneca. But an American. We can't be one people, Clara, if we divide ourselves and plan to cut each other's throats in the night."

"As long as there's one African in slavery, we'll never be one people. Don't you understand that?"

"They'll never win freedom by destroying every white person's trust in them. Prove to the people of this city that a free African woman can denounce treachery and murder.''

''What you call treachery, they call war,'' Clara said.

For a moment Clara thought Malcolm was going to weep. ''I'm doing this because I love you!''

''No you don't. You love your fame, your glorious military reputation more than you love me—or anyone else. You want to be the man who uncovered this terrible conspiracy. You want the credit for it.''

She did not believe those cruel words. She saw how much they wounded him. But she did not care. She was adrift between his vision of America and those African faces in the midnight gloom of Hughson's taproom, when the candles guttered low and they blended into a black current that swept her toward some underground sea. She had lost touch with the voice that had consoled and guided her. What had happened to the woman who had sworn she would never doubt again?

Malcolm stalked out. A few days later, the governor published a proclamation offering a reward of a hundred pounds to anyone who provided information that led to the conviction of those who were guilty of starting the fires. It was a huge sum of money to an average working man or woman—five years' wages, at least. Any slave who came forward was offered less money—twenty pounds—but he or she would be freed.

On the following Monday, Caesar, the Hughsons, and Clara went before the grand jury, in the matter of the theft of Rebecca Hogg's goods. Peter Van Ness had agreed to defend them, along with an older and more distinguished attorney, James Alexander. The courtroom was jammed with spectators. Rumor had already connected Caesar to the fires through his friend Cuffee.

The seventeen-man grand jury was a cross section of merchants and shop owners and ship captains and clerks. Among them was Malcolm's friend Guert Cuyler, who was chosen as foreman. The first witness was Mary

Burton. The moment Clara saw her, she sensed disaster. Mary was wearing her best outfit, a garish array of bright greens and blues and yellows. She obviously expected to play a starring role in this drama.

At first Mary pretended to be timid. She said she was afraid to testify about anything. The grand jurors assured her that she would be protected. Mary curled her lip, apparently unconvinced, and said: "I'll acquaint you with what I know about the goods stolen from the Hoggs'. But I'll say nothing about the fires."

This remark caused consternation among the grand jurors and the spectators. Most of them had little or no interest in the Hogg burglary. It was a routine case, at best. But the fires had threatened all of them with destruction. They insisted on Mary telling them everything she knew. One of them warned her that if she concealed evidence, she would be guilty of a serious crime.

Mary sat up straight in the witness box, satisfied that she had put herself in a sympathetic light. "Caesar, and Mr. Philipse's Negro man, Cuffee, used to meet at my master's tavern and I heard them talk frequently of burning the fort and the whole town," she said. "My master and my mistress were there too, and the man they called Father, the priest whose name is Ury. He sometimes baptized the Negroes that Caesar brought there and my master, John Hughson, wrote their names in a book. They said the city would burn and they would kill the white people who weren't baptized and the Spanish would send a fleet to take the place and make Caesar king and Ury the pope of the colony."

"What about the Negro woman known as Clara Flowers? Was she involved with this plot to destroy us?" Guert Cuyler asked.

Mary stared at Clara for a long moment, no doubt balancing her many kindnesses against her frequent insistence on Mary doing her job. "No," she said. "I never heard her say a word about it."

"But she knew about the Hoggs' thefts and other thefts?"

"Maybe she knew of them but said nothing for fear of her life, like I did," Mary said. "My master has a wicked temper and often threatened to kill me in front of her and others."

"She's been seen in Caesar's company. A neighbor told me she invited him to her house only a few days before he was arrested," another grand juryman said.

"She served him liquor like any other customer," Mary said. "That's all I ever saw of her knowing him."

They put Caesar on the stand and asked him if he ever shared his loot with Clara. "I'm an innocent man," Caesar said. "I've never stolen anything. How could I share it with anybody?"

The grand jury deliberated less than ten minutes and returned with indictments against the Hughsons and Caesar for theft and conspiracy to destroy New York. They also directed a constable to arrest John Ury on the latter charge. As for Clara Flowers, they found the evidence against her "too weak to form an indictment," Guert Cuyler said.

A growl of disappointment rumbled through the spectators. On the bench, Judge Daniel Horsmanden called for order in his courtroom. "Far be it from me to attempt to interfere with the rights and duties of grand jurymen," he said. "But I fear you may have made a mistake here. I've heard from numerous sources that this African creature was at the very heart of the conspiracy."

"Not by any evidence brought here, Your Honor," Guert Cuyler said.

Clara was free but it was all too clear that she was far from safe. As the courtroom emptied, Johannes Van Vorst and his wife rushed to the bench to confer with Judge Horsmanden. A dozen of their friends followed them.

On Maiden Lane, Clara knelt before the image of the Virgin. *What should I do, Holy Mother?*

Silence. The statue's graven face seemed to mock her. Was it all a bizarre series of coincidences? Why was rain sent to rescue white New York—while the Africans were abandoned in their torment? Did it mean that God's power—the Virgin's power—was tethered by laws beyond human comprehension?

Clara flung herself facedown on the floor. *Send me light, please!*

Silence.

Adam Duycinck knocked on the door. "Catalyntie's downstairs," he said.

Her Seneca sister was in a state of violent agitation. "I'm risking a great deal even to see you this way," she said. "Malcolm's heard from Guert Cuyler that half the grand jury was inclined to indict you. But Guert persuaded them to be satisfied with finding the others."

"What's your point?"

"I think you should leave New York, now."

"Where would you have me go?"

"Philadelphia. Boston. Anyplace else. Perhaps Jamaica or one of the other sugar islands."

"I've done nothing. I won't go," Clara said.

"That's exactly what's wrong. You knew all about it and you did nothing."

"If I'd done *nothing*, you'd probably be dead now. My prayers have saved you and a thousand others from slaughter. Now I wish I'd let you die. In some way I've sinned against my God! She won't speak to me!"

That was how Catalyntie Van Vorst Stapleton learned New York had been saved by a species of being as different from her as the eagle is to the fly. Her Seneca sister Clara Flowers had become a saint.

Six

DOWN WALL STREET TO THE Broadway the cart rumbled, hauled by two plodding oxen. On its swaying floor stood Caesar and Cuffee, shackled hand and foot. Around them marched a guard of twelve musket-bearing militiamen under the command of Malcolm Stapleton. They were preceded by a drummer boy in a red coat. He was thumping his drum in the funereal rhythm of the dead march. At the Broadway, where Clara waited, the cart turned north. Hundreds of people lined the street and clustered at the intersection, shouting insults.

"You're going to find out what fire feels like, Negars," one man shouted.

"Scorch them good," screamed a woman. "Roast them fine!"

"Baste them!" cried a boy.

Up the Broadway the grim procession went to the open fields known as the Common.[1] There, a crowd of at least a thousand people had gathered. Clara was the only African in the throng. Why had she come? she wondered. To offer Caesar a hint of solace? To contemplate the fate that awaited her? To face what God in his darkness permitted in this uncompleted world, where the Evil Brother wielded so much power? Yes, all three reasons.

Around two tall stakes were piled fagots to the depth of four or five feet. Caesar and Cuffee were dragged from the cart and hustled up to the stakes. A blacksmith

---

[1] Roughly the site of present-day City Hall Park.

quickly wrapped their shackles around the stakes and fastened them so they stood back to back while the crowd whooped and howled. Two constables piled the fagots around them while a bailiff stood ready, a burning torch in his hand.

On the testimony of Mary Burton, a jury had convicted both men of theft and conspiracy to burn the city. Either charge carried the death penalty but the second one had persuaded Judge Daniel Horsmanden to order this form of execution "to set terror an example by greater terror."

In court, the judge had exhorted them to confess but they had remained silent. Now Horsmanden waded through the fagots to give them one more chance. "Will you tell us the names of your fellow conspirators?" he cried. "A thorough confession can still save your lives!"

Caesar stared at the sea of white faces and said nothing. Cuffee was trembling so violently his chains rattled. Sweat poured from his cheeks and chin. "I'll tell," he said. "I'll admit everything. We burned the fort and my master's warehouse and all the other buildings. It was Caesar's plan. Caesar and Hughson and Ury."

"Who else?" Horsmanden said. Beside him a court secretary was scribbling down every word.

"Quaco and Prince and Sawney and Peter—"

He reeled off a list of almost twenty fellow Africans. Horsmanden thrashed through the fagots to face Caesar. "Is this true? Do you also admit your guilt and the guilt of these others?"

Caesar said nothing. "Speak!" Horsmanden said. "Is Cuffee telling the truth?"

"He's a damned liar."

Horsmanden thrashed back through the fagots to Cuffee. "What about the woman Clara Flowers? Was she in the conspiracy as well?"

"Yes! Yes!" Cuffee said. "She knew all. She advised us with her book of maps how to bring a Spanish fleet from Cuba! Antonio and the other Spanish fellows told us they'd come.''

"He's a goddamned liar,'' Caesar said.

Horsmanden climbed out of the fagots and told the court secretary to hurry to the home of John Murray on lower Broadway, where the governor was living, and ask him for a stay of execution for Cuffee. The secretary, a fat Dutchman, went puffing off on this errand. The crowd grew impatient. They surged almost to the edge of the fagots shouting: "Burn them, damn you. Are you going to let them go to tell more lies?''

Malcolm and his militiamen, assisted by a few constables with truncheons, shoved the crowd back. But Sheriff Jeremiah Tompkins was not happy. He began berating Judge Horsmanden. "Do you want to get us all killed?'' he said. "These people mean to have a show or else. If you reprieve either one of these fellows, we'll have a riot.''

"Light the fire!'' roared the crowd. "Torch the Negars!''

"You won't get him back to jail without a guard of two hundred men,'' the sheriff said. "And where the devil do you expect us to find them?''

"Torch them!'' screamed the crowd.

Horsmanden sighed. "Oh very well. Let the business begin. We've got a good list of names from him.''

The sheriff gestured to the bailiff with the torch. He threw it into the pile of fagots and the flames leaped around Caesar and Cuffee. "No, no, I'll tell you more!'' Cuffee screamed. "I'll tell you all the names!''

Judge Horsmanden did not even turn his head. The crowd howled its approval. The flames swirled around Caesar until his hair burned like crepe paper. He never made a sound. Cuffee made enough noise for both of them. His screams rose above the mob's howl for at least ten minutes. Abruptly the cries vanished and through the air drifted the stench of burned flesh.

Clara retreated to Maiden Lane, trembling and nauseated. Seizing a hammer, she rushed upstairs and flung the statue of the Virgin on the hardwood floor. With three savage strokes she smashed it into a hundred pieces. An hour later, constables were at her door to arrest her. She and all the slaves Cuffee had named swiftly joined the Hughsons and John Ury in the foul cells under the City Hall.

After a night of misery, she was led to Daniel Horsmanden's chambers for questioning. The judge was in an exultant mood. He told Clara he remembered the day he freed her. "I said then you'd cause nothing but trouble and I was right. You have only one hope of saving yourself. Name all the others, especially the white people in this vicious conspiracy. It's beyond the capacity of you Africans."

Poor Caesar, Clara thought. Deprived of even the credit for creating the plot. "In fact, Your Honor," she said. "Caesar first broached the plan to me ten years ago, when I had the misfortune to spend a night in one of the cells downstairs with him."

"Why did he tell you? Was he hoping to involve the Indians in it?"

"He never mentioned them. He thought he and his fellow slaves could do it all themselves."

"We think you and your friend Catalyntie Stapleton have never surrendered your loyalty to the Senecas. Tell us how she gave you the money to run Hughson's as the headquarters for the plot. If you name her, I guarantee I can get you a pardon."

"The same kind that you guaranteed Cuffee?" Clara said.

Malcolm visited Clara in her cell that afternoon. "Peter Van Ness has resigned from your case. There isn't a lawyer in the city who'll defend you or any of these people. They say their reputations will be ruined forever. They'll never be able to make another shilling here."

"Forget me. I'm going to die," Clara said. "I'm perfectly resigned."

"You're not going to die," Malcolm said. "We'll find a lawyer for you in another colony—Pennsylvania, New Jersey."

The Hughsons went on trial first. They were convicted and Clara spent nightmarish days and nights listening to their sobs and groans as their execution day approached. John Hughson discovered prayer and one night he had a vision of an angel descending to rescue them from the hangman's cart. Perhaps it was God's way of sustaining him. If so, his wife Sarah was not convinced. She cursed God and John Ury, blaming the priest for their fate.

Ury spent his time preparing a speech he planned to give from the gallows. He had no hope of evading death—though he intended to try. He said God expected everyone to do his utmost to sustain life. At his trial, the jury debated less than ten minutes before bringing in a guilty verdict.

That night, Ury rehearsed his speech for Clara. Like the Hughsons, he repeatedly insisted he was innocent of any connection with the plot—a strange avoidance of the truth. Only one line in the speech rang true: "This is one of the dark providences of the Great God in his wise, just and good government of this lower earth."

The more Clara thought of the Great God, the darker and more impenetrable He became. He was certainly not the Master of Life, the benevolent creator of the forests and the rivers and the lakes of her girlhood. He was also not the Evil Brother, who so easily triumphed over the Master of Life when they contested for supremacy in the wilderness of the human heart. The Great God transcended both these beings in a gloomy immensity shot through with only glimpses of light and hope.

First the Hughsons and then Ury went to the gallows on the edge of the Common. Among the Africans, a steady stream went to the same place; others such as

Antonio and several of his fellow Spanish slaves went to the stake. Judge Horsmanden sentenced almost all those accused by Cuffee or by Mary Burton of having an active part in the conspiracy to that fiery fate. Each prisoner received a jury trial but it was little more than a formality. Jurors barely left the box before they were back with guilty verdicts.

Three times, while this grisly process ground out death, Clara was brought to Judge Horsmanden's chambers for another interrogation. Each time she was guaranteed a reprieve if she would name Catalyntie Stapleton as a conspirator. The hatred Catalyntie had inspired in her uncle, Johannes Van Vorst, was bearing terrible fruit. Of course Clara remained silent each time, in spite of being threatened with death at the stake.

One night in July, almost five months after the fire in Fort George, Mary Burton visited me and Malcolm. She was a celebrity, feasted and petted by Johannes Van Vorst and Judge Horsmanden and their friends. But they declined to pay her the hundred pounds she thought was due her for revealing the conspirators. They accused her of sheltering Clara and me—"the Indians"—as many people in New York now called us.

Mary plaintively described how hard she was resisting their pressure. But they had the power to refuse her the hundred pounds if Horsmanden, in his capacity as trial judge and chief investigator of the conspiracy, ruled that she was not completely "forthcoming." Never in her life would she be so close to that much money. What was a poor girl to do? Mary sobbed.

"Tell the truth," Malcolm said.

"How much do you want?" I said.

"To save your friend—the least I can expect is a hundred and fifty pounds," Mary said. "If I save her I'll save you too."

Mary was a slattern but she was not a fool. Malcolm

Stapleton paced the floor in agony. Finally he made up his mind—and said what I feared he would say.

"Get out of here. We've got a good lawyer coming from Pennsylvania to defend Clara. I'll testify in court that you tried to solicit a bribe. That will prove your word is worth nothing."

"Nothing is what your word will be worth—against mine," Mary said and flounced out of the house.

I struggled for calm. There was no point in berating Malcolm. "I think we should give her the money," I said.

"No!"

"What does it matter, whether she lies for us or the other side? It's all lies. When are you going to quit your dream of an honest government? It doesn't exist and never will—in America or England or anywhere else."

"It will," Malcolm said. "Clara gave me that dream. I won't let you dirty it again."

The next day, Judge Horsmanden announced that Clara's trial was set for the following day. Malcolm asked for a week's delay to bring their attorney from Philadelphia. Horsmanden blandly denied the request. "There are plenty of good lawyers in this province you can hire in an hour," the judge said.

When Malcolm told him he had tried in vain to hire one of these good lawyers, Horsmanden said the refusal spoke for itself. No one in New York had any doubt of Clara's guilt. Besides Cuffee, a dozen other Africans, in desperate attempts to save their lives, had named her as a conspirator at Hughson's.

That night, without consulting Malcolm, I sent Adam Duycinck to the Fighting Cock, the inn where Mary Burton was living. I armed him with a hundred and fifty pounds and the promise of another fifty pounds when and if Mary left New York to take up permanent residence elsewhere. The next day in court, she astounded

Horsmanden by again denying that Clara was a conspirator.

But the judge was not so easily defeated. He paraded a dozen men to the witness box, some of them the court secretaries who had taken confessions from Cuffee and other Africans, others prisoners from the cells below the courtroom, ready to say anything to save their lives. Clara made no attempt to challenge any of this testimony.

The jury found her guilty. A delighted Horsmanden declared they had convicted the ''secret chief'' of the conspiracy. It only remained to root out her white confederate. ''It is patently impossible for anyone of African blood to have conceived so clever a scheme,'' he declared. ''We have already rooted out the white papist side of the conspiracy. Only the white Indian side remains.''

He sentenced Clara to be burned at the stake the following day. The crowded courtroom cheered. When Malcolm and I left City Hall, we were pelted with insults. Back in our house on Depeyster Street, Malcolm slumped disconsolately in a chair. I paced the floor.

''We have to save her, no matter what it costs us,'' I said.

''How?'' Malcolm said.

''I don't know,'' I said. ''Bribe the governor?''

''He wouldn't dare reprieve her. There'd be a mob in the streets yelling for his scalp.''

Malcolm rose to his feet. For a moment he seemed to fill the room. ''There's only one way,'' he said. ''She told me when I tried to persuade her to speak out early on that I cared more for my reputation than I did for her. I'll have to prove she's wrong.''

''You'll be an outlaw!'' I said.

''So be it.''

Not for the first but perhaps for the last time I had to face the bitter truth that Malcolm loved Clara more than he loved me. I could have used Hugh against him—and the child that was swelling in my belly. I was now at least eight months pregnant. But I also faced the melancholy truth that I loved Clara too and was ready to sacrifice everything I had struggled to build here in New York—my store, my business reputation, my dream of establishing the Stapletons as one of the city's first families.

"Tell Duycinck to have a boat at the foot of Nassau Street at eleven o'clock with my gun and fifty rounds of powder and ball," Malcolm said. "Give me half of all the cash you've got. We'll go up the Hudson until dawn and then strike out across country for the Delaware. We'll go up that to the Susquehanna. Will the Senecas take her back?"

"Yes. If her grandmother is alive, without question. I think they'll take her anyway. But what will you do?"

"I don't know."

"I don't think I can bear never seeing you again!"

Malcolm kissed me with surprising tenderness. "I'll value those words, no matter what happens," he said.

He slid a pistol under his coat. He put a smaller one in his boot. "You better be prepared to go to New Jersey as soon as possible," he said. "I don't think you'll be any more popular than I'll be."

"I'll survive. They won't abuse a pregnant woman," I said.

"I'm not so sure," Malcolm said. He kissed me hard and vanished into the night.

I sent Peter for Duycinck. When I told him what Malcolm had in mind, his eyes bulged with terror. "We'll all get hanged," he said.

"Perhaps. But we owe Clara the risk. You as much as anyone. Perhaps more."

That shut him up. He took Malcolm's gun apart and put it into a sack with the powder and balls. Finding a boat along the river would be no problem. There were plenty of them tied up at the piers, often with their oars in the thwarts. But to be on the safe side, Adam thought it might be a good idea if he headed for New Jersey afterward.

"You know I'm no hero," he said.

"You'll do until one comes along," I said and kissed him on his balding head.

An hour later, Malcolm strode into City Hall and descended to the basement, beyond the jail cells. He found Undersheriff Mills finishing supper at his desk. He was halfway through a bottle of brandy.

"I want to see Clara Flowers," he said. "I think I've found some evidence that could save her."

"What the devil would that be?" Mills said.

"This," Malcolm said and put a pistol to his head. He relieved him of his gun and keys and prodded him down the dank corridor to Clara's cell.

"They'll hang you, General Stapleton," Mills said.

"They'll have to catch me first," Malcolm said.

The cells were mostly empty. Only a few more slaves remained to be tried. Clara was kneeling in her cell, praying, her arms outstretched. "I knew she was a bloody witch," Mills said.

"What are you doing?" Clara said.

"What does it look like?" Malcolm said.

Malcolm manacled Mills's hands and feet and gagged him to guarantee them several hours' headstart. Locking him in the cell, he led Clara into the office, where he hauled a set of men's clothes out of a sack. "Put these on," he said. "Fast."

"Does Catalyntie know you're doing this?"

"Of course."

"I'm not worth it."

"Yes, you are. Hurry up. Get into those breeches and that shirt."

She struggled into the clothes and Malcolm handed her a big cocked hat. She shoved her hair under it and he lowered it on her brow. "Perfect," he said.

As they strolled out of City Hall, Malcolm threw his arm around Clara, as if they were a bit drunk. No one paid any attention to them. The streets were largely deserted. They only had one close call. On the Broadway, they passed two members of the Night Watch.

"Good evening, General Stapleton," one said.

"Good evening," Malcolm said.

In five minutes they were at the Hudson on Nassau Street. Adam stepped out of the shadows by the wharf. "The boat's below," he said. "It's got a sail. You'll have the wind and tide with you. By morning you should be well north of Judge Horsmanden's clutches."

"You're a true friend, Adam," Clara said.

"Maybe now you'll forgive me for what I did to you out of cowardice that day in Hampden Hall," Adam said.

"I forgave you long ago."

Out on the river, Clara was silent until the lights of the city slipped behind them. "I'm still not worth it," she said. "You're ruining your life—and Catalyntie's life—"

"Our lives would have been ruined if you died at that stake."

"I don't love you anymore," Clara said. "Do you realize that?"

"I can understand why."

"I don't think I love God, either."

Malcolm answered her out of his own pain. "It's ended my illusions about America. Patriotism here will be just as hard to realize—maybe harder—than in England. It will be a long struggle—maybe a losing one."

"I'm afraid you may be right."

"I wish I believed in your God. I don't understand His purposes."

"Neither do I. I can only testify to His presence."

They slid into the night on those anguished words.

Back in New York the next morning, I prepared for trouble. I sent Hugh and old Peter and his wife Shirley across the Hudson with money to proceed by hired wagon to Hampden Hall. An hour later, about 9:00 A.M., a fist pounded on my door.

I opened it to face a livid Undersheriff Miller and Sheriff Tompkins. "Where is your husband?" the sheriff roared.

"I don't know. He went out about ten o'clock last night and didn't return," I said.

"The hell you don't know. We're searching this house."

They stormed through the rooms, hurling clothes out of wardrobes, peering under beds, scouring the cellar and the backyard.

"What's wrong? What's he done?" I said.

"You really don't know?" the sheriff growled.

When he told me, I burst into tears, putting to good use my ability to cry on demand. "You'll protect me, won't you?" I said. "I'm afraid I'll be mobbed."

"I don't see why or how we can do that," the sheriff said.

The two lawmen stalked out. About a half hour later, I heard the roar of the mob. The news of Malcolm's escape with Clara had swirled through the city and the people were about to take their revenge. They ripped open the door and crowded into the house, shouting curses in my face.

"If you weren't with child we'd have burning fagots at your feet by noon," Rebecca Hogg screamed.

"It proves all Judge Horsmanden's said about you in private," shouted her husband.

"Your own aunt says you're possessed by the devil," cried a woman.

"Can't you have pity on a wife who's been abandoned by her husband?" I said. "Traduced and abandoned?"

"Abandoned, hell," snarled an older man. "He's never done a thing you haven't thought for him first!"

Many of the mob were Night Watchmen and constables, carrying their clubs. They methodically smashed every window in the house. Then they began pitching everything—silver, dishes, clothing, out the windows into the street. What would not fit out the windows, they flung out doors, including beds (dismantled), chairs, tables, and rugs. In a furious hour, the house was a stripped shattered shell. In the street, people pawed through the wreckage, taking what they pleased as if it were the spoils of war.

"On to the Universal Store!" shouted one of the constables.

I would bear it, I told myself. I would bear it for Clara's sake. But it was hard. The thought of them looting the store brought real tears down my cheeks. Between my losses in the house and at the store, the day would cost me five thousand pounds. I would never sell another item in New York again. I had no idea how I could be a businesswoman in rural New Jersey. The biggest town was Newark, with a grand total of six hundred souls.

My next visitors were Judge Daniel Horsmanden and Governor Clarke. Horsmanden was apoplectic. "I have conferred with His Excellency here on the advisability of confining you in the city jail until your husband returns with Clara Flowers and faces the justice they both so richly deserve. But he has decided for your own safety and the good order of this city, it would be best if you immediately departed this province."

"I don't have much choice," I said. "Unless I want to sleep on the floor."

"How could your husband throw away his good name this way?" the governor said.

"He's a patriot, Your Excellency," I said. "He'd rather disgrace himself than see his country commit an injustice."

The governor goggled. "He doesn't love her? It's all patriotic moonshine?"

"Oh, he loves her too. He loves her more than me or this damned stupid country."

This time my tears were beyond real. They were eternal.

BOOK

SIX

IN THE CRUDE FARMHOUSE I had built from the stones and timber of Hampden Hall, I faced myself in the bedroom mirror. Was that creature with the streeling hair, the soiled dress, the same woman who never ventured out of her New York house without her hair crimped and permanented, her hat, shoes, dress, and cloak in the latest, most expensive style? I was growing ugly and coarse. Was that what happened to a loveless woman?

For the hundredth time I told myself I was not loveless. Never had I felt so much love in my heart. Joining Malcolm in his decision to rescue Clara had united me with him on a level we had never before attained. I felt that I had won his love and respect for the first time.

No, I was not loveless. I was merely deprived of immediate love, the love that was created by touch, by words, gestures, presence. But another kind of love was in my heart—a love that often seemed stronger than immediate love.

At other times, this spiritual love seemed so much vapor, a compound of moonshine and wish. My furious heart, my aching belly, wanted Malcolm with a violence that frightened me. I found myself drifting back to hating Clara, even hating the color of her skin, the fate of her race—all the things that compounded pity and desire into love in Malcolm's warrior soul.

Two years had passed since Malcolm and Clara fled north to the Iroquois country. I had heard nothing from them. But no news meant they were still free. Their capture would have been trumpeted in the *New York Ga-*

zette, to which I stubbornly subscribed, even though reading it made me melancholy for hours each week.

I did not expect a letter. They would have had to entrust it to a stranger. No one could be relied on to resist the two-hundred-pound reward that Judge Daniel Horsmanden had persuaded the City of New York to offer for their capture. That offer still stood, but opinion in New York about Malcolm's exploit had been undergoing a slow change. The war with France and Spain had ended in a negotiated peace. With the threat of invasion and rapine removed, many people began to regard the Great Conspiracy in a calmer light. In particular, they accumulated grave doubts about Mary Burton as a witness— and Daniel Horsmanden as a judge.

Mary had taken her hundred-pound reward from the city and combined it with my one-hundred-fifty-pound bribe to live in luxurious style in Clara's house on Maiden Lane. As her funds dwindled, she had turned to her original trade, prostitution, to replenish her purse. The neighbors were soon complaining that she was running a bawdy house. The city fathers had arrested her and offered her a choice of the stocks or a one-way passage to the West Indies. Mary was last seen boarding a ship to Barbados.

Around the same time, people began assailing Horsmanden in public and private for the reckless way he had stampeded juries to guilty verdicts against every person indicted by the grand jury. Many New Yorkers began to mutter that most of the Africans who died at the stake or on the gallows had been innocent. The judge grew so defensive, he published a "Narrative" of the trials which made him sound like the savior of the city— but convinced no one.

I had been encouraged enough to hire a well-known Philadelphia lawyer to appeal Clara's conviction on the ground that she had been denied counsel by Judge Horsmanden's rush to judgment. The case was now before New York's Supreme Court. I vowed to appeal it to the highest court in England, if necessary. If Clara's guilty verdict were voided, Malcolm's so-called crime would be transformed into an act of courage.

Meanwhile, I had been struggling to survive. I had found the great house, Hampden Hall, unlivable. It was virtually impossible to heat. The roof leaked; half the windows were broken. I decided to tear the grandiose structure down and build a more sensible house with the materials. Adam Duycinck borrowed a book of architectural drawings from a neighbor and designed a two-story slope-roofed farmhouse with wings to which more rooms could be added if necessary. We used the labor force from the farm to build it during the summer months, with some help from carpenters and stonemasons imported from New York and Hackensack.

With the mansion a heap of rubble, I decided the place should no longer be named after a long-forgotten English general. I renamed it Great Rock Farm, after a big grey boulder that lay in a field about a quarter of a mile from the house. "It's an American name," I said, remembering the way the Senecas named places and persons after the world around them.

Adam heartily agreed. He had taken on the job of overseeing the farm. One of the Africans, Luther, had long been working as foreman and handled the discipline and settled disputes about housing and other matters among the workforce. Adam handled the business end, keeping the books, buying seeds and tools. The twenty-five Africans working the farm were all slaves. I decided to promise them their freedom—but not immediately. I did not have the money to post the required two-hundred-pound bonds for each of them—and I pointed out there was no way for any of them to earn a living in rural New Jersey. To prove I meant my promise, I

gave Luther and his wife, Bertha, the cook, their freedom and hired them for ten pounds a year wages.

The result of this small act of generosity—which I
made in Clara's name—was remarkable. The productiv-
ity of the farm doubled. Our wheat and corn and rye
crops were twice as big as the previous year, under the
miserly supposedly businesslike rule of a hired overseer.
Granted, we had enjoyed better weather, but it was still
a startling development. It showed the amazing power
of that word *freedom,* the way it energized people's
souls.

There was a dark side to this inspiring story. As I
studied Adam's books, I saw it would be impossible to
free the rest of the slaves, even on a gradual basis, and
pay them decent wages if they all chose to stay—and
show a profit. Wheat from New York and New Jersey
was being undersold by newcomers from Europe who
were swarming into western Pennsylvania and Maryland. The price was dropping steadily—and like the fur
trade, the market was controlled by London merchants
who resold at whacking profits what they bought from
the hapless Americans.

Another problem was my slave-owning neighbors.
Some of them ran huge farms, with as many as fifty
field hands. On Sundays, Great Rock's Africans visited
other farms and the news of my attitude toward slavery
soon became common knowledge. I began receiving un-
signed letters such as this one:

*If you want your house burned around your ears
one night soon, free another of your Africans. We
know the story of the part you played in trying to
burn New York and would consider it simple rec-
ompense for the losses suffered by friends and relatives in that city. We will tolerate no talk of
freedom for these ignorant creatures here in New*

Jersey. It will be answered as it was in New
York—with the gun and torch.

If Malcolm were only here, I would dare them
to try mobbing me. But the only man I had in the house
was Adam, who begged me to cease all talk of freeing
another African. I could only ruefully consent. But it
buttressed my conviction that Malcolm's dream of a
morally pure America was patriotic moonshine.

In another month, I had not even Adam to protect me.
The little fellow sickened and died of the great pox[1] with
lamentable swiftness. He bore it like the philosopher that
he was, saying it was the price a man with a hump on
his back must be prepared to pay for his pleasure. At
the end he held my hand and again voiced his regret at
destroying Clara's child. I told him he was forgiven by
her and any god worthy of our worship.

I had other worries. One was my new son, Paul. I
gave birth to him a month after I arrived at the farm;
Bertha, Luther's wife, served as midwife. My first look
at the child was unnerving. I had feared he would look
like Philip Hooft. Instead, he was almost unnaturally
beautiful, with features as perfectly formed as the Infant
Jesus in a sacred painting and a head of black hair and
dark brown eyes that could never be explained by any
Dutch or Scottish genealogy. I was almost glad Malcolm
was not present to ask me bluntly if the baby was his
child. I abandoned my plan to name him Philip (Malcolm had heard a good deal about Philip Hooft) and
called him Paul.

Paul's brother Hugh was bounding into manhood. I
had to think of giving him an education worthy of the
great merchant I wanted him to become. I took him with
me in our buggy to Hackensack, the nearest town, in
search of a tutor. I discovered the minister of the Dutch

[1]*Syphilis.*

Reformed Church was none other than Harman Bogardus, the teacher Cornelius Van Vorst had hired to civi-
lize me and Clara. He was still a teacher at heart and for
a modest fee offered to board Hugh in his house five
days a week and instruct him in arithmetic and spelling
and grammar.

At first Bogardus and I discussed the upheaval that
had brought me to New Jersey in neutral terms. I remarked disconsolately that everyone in both provinces
seemed to know the story. Bogardus abandoned his reserved pedagogic manner and revealed his true Dutch
feelings. "I've told everyone I'm sure the charges
against Clara were false and denounce as atrocious lies
everything that's rumored about you. Only an English
judge like Daniel Horsmanden, with his barbaric ideas
of justice, would have committed such atrocities against
innocent Africans."

I decided it would be best not to mention that some
of the Africans were guilty—or that my Dutch uncle
Johannes was Judge Horsmanden's enthusiastic collaborator. Instead I lamented the loss of my business and
talked plaintively about my financial problems at Great
Rock Farm.

"Why don't you open a store here in Hackensack?"
Bogardus said. "Good-sized ships come up the river
with no difficulty. From Hackensack to the New York
border you have the most prosperous farmers in America—and almost every one of them is Dutch. The only
store in town is run by an Englishman—who charges
double New York's prices and has nothing but cheap
goods."

For a moment I could not breathe. I was sure Cornelius Van Vorst was speaking to me in the voice of this
man of God. It was, of course, exactly what I had been
hoping Bogardus would say. I was familiar with the
depth of the Hackensack River—I had seen oceangoing
ships as large as Killian Van Oorst's *The Orange Prince*

at the town's wharfs. I had also reconnoitered the Englishman's store and was sure I could outsell him.

Back at the farm, I got the shock of my life. Drinking tea in my parlor was Robert Foster Nicolls. He gazed disdainfully at the oversized chairs and tables and sofa from baronial Hampden Hall and told me Chesley White had died six months ago. Thanks to his marriage to Elizabeth White, Robert was now the head of the firm. He had decided to expand the business by opening stores in all the major port cities in America and had come over in pursuit of this object. He was also determined to collect the numerous debts which the kindhearted White had allowed various American merchants to pile up. One of the biggest was two thousand pounds to a certain Catalyntie Van Vorst Stapleton, former proprietor of the Universal Store on Pearl Street in New York.

"I've heard all about Malcolm's fit of madness—and its predictable effect on your business," Robert said. "How in God's name did you let him do such a thing?"

"It was my idea as much as his," I said. "We both love—and esteem—Clara. We couldn't let her die on trumped-up charges extorted from witnesses threatened with the stake."

Robert smirked at the way I stumbled on the word *love*. "You might have given some thought to people like my father-in-law, who'd trusted you to behave like an intelligent businesswoman. Two thousand pounds' worth of goods thrown into Pearl Street! I can assure you, no one in London will ever do business with you again."

"How is your wife? Has she come to New York with you?"

"Elizabeth's in London saying her prayers. That's all she's good for," Robert said.

His patent unhappiness was a small but empty satisfaction. I could almost hear Malcolm warning me not to betray an innocent young woman like Elizabeth White into the hands of a scoundrel. It was dismaying to discover that honesty and honor might have some value in this confusing world. Or, to put it another way, just desserts had a way of turning up at the most unexpected moments.

"I can't pay you the money now," I said. "But I plan to open a store in Hackensack soon. I'll put you at the head of my creditors."

Robert shook his head. He saw no reason to have mercy on me, remembering the coldness I had displayed toward him in London. If there is anything more heartless than sworn enemies, it is former lovers. "You would have been wiser to pack your baby on your back like a squaw and follow your husband north. I'm sure Clara has been warming his wigwam all winter."

Robert finished his tea and smiled in a wry humorless way. He had grown less attractive with age. Some men acquire flesh as they grow older; others grow lean. Was it a commentary on the state of their souls? I was sure this was the case with Robert. His dry lips, his rheumy eyes, his sallow complexion, suggested some sort of withering process was at work.

"I've always rather fancied this estate," he said. "Perhaps it's got something to do with the scenes of my youth. I'm thinking of staying in New York for a while. Every gentleman needs a country house. I rather hold it against you, tearing down Hampden Hall."

"You wouldn't—you couldn't—turn out Malcolm's sons. No matter what you think of me."

"Think of you? I think you're still a rather attractive woman. Perhaps it comes down to what you might be willing to do to persuade me to extend this debit."

"Get out of here."

He sauntered to the door. "I'm staying at the Fighting Cock on the Broadway. You know where it is, I'm sure."

"I'll get a lawyer. No judge will turn me out."

He laughed at this idea. "Jonathan Belcher, the new royal governor of New Jersey, is an old friend of my father's. He's here to repair a damaged fortune, I might add. It would be cheaper to pay me than bribe him."

He mounted his horse and rode off. Should I give myself to him? It was more than mere desire. He wanted to savor the triumph of forcing me to submit—to do anything and everything to please him for money. Having loved and abandoned me for money, he was eager to flaunt me around New York as his whore, proving him right about my character from the start.

In the morning, Bertha appeared with little Paul. She had become tremendously fond of the child. "He wants his momma. No one else will do," she said, and lifted the boy into the bed, where he surprised me by curling up with a contented sigh and falling asleep. It was the first time he had exhibited an iota of affection for me.

The sight of his innocent face recalled my sense of loving purpose, the reason why I was in New Jersey. I would not turn my back on that memory now, no matter what Robert Nicolls threatened to do. I climbed into my buggy and returned to Hackensack for another conference with Harman Bogardus. When I told him about Robert's threat, his Dutch blood virtually simmered with indignation.

"Come next week to a meeting of the Board of Elders," he said. "I'll have them ready to consider your plight as their Christian duty—not to mention their honor as Dutchmen!"

A week later I was back in Hackensack in Bogardus's dining room, which was so full of tobacco smoke I could barely breathe. Dutch farmers never went anywhere without their pipes. Around the big mahogany table sat the half dozen elders of the Dutch Reformed Church, listening to Bogardus tell them to open their purses and persuade their friends to do likewise to help this good woman in distress.

The fattest of them, Arent Schuyler, who owned the largest farm in Bergen County, looked enough like Cornelius Van Vorst to be a younger brother. "We live in New Jersey," Schuyler said. "Why should we worry about a judgment for debt from New York courts? Everything depends on the attitude of our royal governor. I understand he's badly in need of money—and the assembly has declined to raise his salary. In my grandfather's day, when a governor found himself in such a fix, he solicited donations from the citizens. We had something called 'the blind tax' which wise men paid— because it guaranteed them the governor's friendship. I suggest a new blind tax on behalf of Mrs. Stapleton— which I'll take to Perth Amboy for a little talk with the governor."

Each of the elders promptly subscribed ten pounds to the blind tax and recommended that all the members of the church be exhorted to contribute at least a pound. In two weeks, Bogardus reported they had collected four hundred pounds. The spirit of Dutch independence was alive and well in Bergen County! Once more I felt the sheltering presence of Cornelius Van Vorst's spirit.

Arent Schuyler, puffing cheerfully on his pipe, soon appeared at Great Rock Farm to report on his trip to Perth Amboy. "His Excellency greatly appreciated the concern of the citizens of Bergen County for his welfare," he said with a straight face—though the glint in his blue eyes left no doubt that he appreciated his own wry humor. "After much talk about crops and the late war, I mentioned your problems as of great concern to us. He assured me he would speak to the chief justice of the province about the matter and that henceforth you should not have the slightest concern about losing your land. Now you can get to work on your store in Hackensack."

"I haven't a cent to buy goods. No one will honor my credit, with Nicolls's judgment against me."

"You go to New York and buy whatever you need and draw the bill on me," Schuyler said. "Once, many years ago, when I was a very young farmer, my wheat crop rotted. I didn't have enough money to pay for new seeds. I had just married and my wife had expensive tastes. I had many bills to pay. I went to New York and a merchant named Cornelius Van Vorst, a fat old fellow like I am today, loaned me two hundred pounds on my good name. He didn't even ask me to sign for it. He said he knew an honest Dutchman when he saw one."

"I fear I'll run up a good deal more than two hundred pounds—"

"I know, I know. But I bet you'll make it back before the snow flies. The *vrouws* of Bergen County know how to spend their husbands' money, believe me."

I rushed to New York and spent a thousand pounds to launch another Universal Store, with the emphasis on quality. I bought nothing but the finest silks, lustring, satins, and velvets and persuaded one of New York's best seamstresses to move to Hackensack to make dresses and negligees and nightgowns on the spot— guaranteeing a perfect fit. I bargained furiously to get the goods at close to wholesale prices—not difficult because the end of the war with France and Spain had created a worldwide slack in business.

Back in New Jersey, Arent Schuyler invited me to his spacious house on the Hackensack River above the town and from there we rode out each day to visit farmhouses throughout Bergen County. Again and again, he introduced me as Catalyntie *Van Vorst* Stapleton, leaning on my Dutch name so hard the English name was barely pronounced. He told everyone about my new store and allowed me to do the rest of the talking about my goods. The old man closed the conversation by remarking that Mrs. Schuyler expected to buy all her clothes at this remarkable new emporium.

Customers flowed through my doors. My English

competitor soon closed his second-rate shop in disgust, leaving all the business in the county to me. In three months, I was able to repay half of Schuyler's loan. But the effort this took was virtually all-consuming. I barely saw little Paul at Great Rock Farm. Many nights I slept on a cot in the rear of the store. When I went back to the farm, I seldom arrived before dark and left the next day at dawn. I saw as little of Hugh at school in Hackensack.

One Sunday I arrived at the farm in midafternoon. "Paul. Where are you, Paulie?" I called as soon as I came in the door. I had a wooden gunboat I had bought on a shopping trip to New York.

There was no response to my call. Finally his brother Hugh said: "He's in his room. He's angry at you."

"Why in the world?"

"He says his tummy hurt all night and you didn't come when he cried."

In his room, I found Paul sitting on the floor with a red crayon in his hand, drawing great broad strokes on a piece of paper. "Look at the boat I brought for you, Paul," I said.

"No like boats."

"Aren't you going to give me a kiss?"

He shook his head. "No like you. Bad!"

Bertha confirmed his stomachache. "He's the strangest child. I think he understands more than most his age," she said. "He cried and cried for you. When I told him you weren't here, he suddenly stopped crying, even though his stomach still hurt. He rubbed it and rubbed it but he wouldn't shed another tear."

I wooed Paul for the rest of the day but he barely relented his condemnation of me. At supper, when I made an exasperated remark about his stubborness, Bertha could no longer restrain her disapproval of my child rearing. "The poor little boy has no father—and now no mother. Can you blame him for being troubled?"

But I can't take any time from the store now, with the business on the brink of doubling in size. I was about to hurl this rationalization at Bertha when Paul leaped up and ran to her, crying: "I love *you*, Bertha!" I forced myself to face the vacuum at the center of my life. My sons had no father—and I had no husband. The new store was a sorry substitute for a living, loving man in my house.

Where was Malcolm? What was he doing? Did he have any desire to return to me? Or had he become Clara's lover again, as Robert Nicolls nastily assumed? Could the bribe to New Jersey's governor be extended to include both the safety of our land and the safety of my husband? Could he return here without fear of prosecution from New York? It was time to find out.

TWO

FOUR HUNDRED MILES AWAY, ON the shore of Lake Ontario, Clara stood in the doorway of the longhouse of the Bear Clan, watching Malcolm Stapleton stain his white flesh dark brown with berry juice. Next, he painted streaks of bright blue and yellow and red down his face. He wore only a warrior's breechclout that displayed his massive thighs and huge torso. Against the wall rested his oiled, gleaming rifle. From his waist belt dangled a hatchet and a scalping knife. Clara's heart swelled with instinctive pride as she gazed at him—but her soul was afflicted with doubt. Malcolm had become a Seneca chief in an undeclared war Clara feared and opposed.

She remembered their arrival in the village two years ago, the excitement they had stirred, as Malcolm told their story to the assembled sachems and chiefs and the matrons of the clans, asking them for refuge in Clara's name. Clara had translated his words and added her own witness to the fate she had narrowly escaped in New York. Her father, Hanging Belt, had died, but her mother was now the matron of the Bear Clan. She embraced her daughter and urged the acceptance of both fugitives. No one spoke against her. Malcolm's daring rescue of Clara aroused everyone's admiration. Many stories in the Seneca past celebrated famous warriors abducting women they loved from hostile clans or villages.

Shining Creek's sachems voted unanimously to grant refuge to both fugitives. But some people wondered if a white man could live happily in an Indian village. Wouldn't he yearn for his lost luxuries? Wouldn't the warriors regard him with contempt, as he hoed corn with the women?

When Clara translated this, Malcolm had pointed to the sky, where a full moon was shining, and replied: "If I don't prove myself a warrior worthy of adoption by the Seneca before the next moon—I'll return to New York and the hangman's noose."

The next day, he was invited to join some warriors in a hunting party. They came back three days later laden with game, most of which Malcolm had killed at amazing distances with his rifled gun. Next a round of lacrosse was suggested. Malcolm was given the long stick with the basket at the end and the rules were explained to him. The young warriors did not bother to mention the battering they planned to give him as they raced up and down the village street. They swiftly discovered that Malcolm shrugged off their most ferocious blows and returned them with devastating whacks that sent more than one brave reeling out of the game. Malcolm's team won, five to nothing, with Malcolm scoring three of the goals. In challenge games with nearby villages, they were soon winning valuable prizes—bear robes, wampum belts, English muskets—thanks to his prowess.

With Clara's help, he learned the Seneca's language and spent long hours with one of their oldest sachems, listening to tales of their valor in wars against the Hurons and other tribes. He went into the woods with some of the youngest warriors and spent three days without food purifying his body and soul, chanting prayers to the Master of Life. He submitted to a ritual baptism in the frigid waters of Lake Ontario. Finally, he allowed Clara and her mother to pluck out the hairs of his head until he had nothing left but a Seneca scalp lock.

As the moon began rising with ever brighter, more golden light, the sachems declared Malcolm was ready to receive his name and become a member of the Senecas. Clara was told to choose the name. She spent a day and night fasting and praying to the Master of Life before she let the words speak in her mind. Great Heart would be his family name. Standing Bear would be his warrior name.

As the sachems and Clara's mother, now the matron of the Bear Clan, were about to give their approval, an angry voice shouted from the door of the longhouse: "How dare you allow filthy white blood to soil the purity of the Senecas?"

It was Grey Owl—once Clara's lover, when his name was Bold Antelope. Someone in the village had sent for him. He had followers in almost all the villages of the Six Nations. Year after year he traveled throughout the Iroquois country, preaching his hatred of the white man, urging the Great Council that met each year at Onondaga to drive out white traders and force white farmers to leave the Mohawk country and other places where they had purchased land on the borders of the Six Nations.

Grey Owl strode to the center of the longhouse and delivered a tirade against white men in general and Malcolm Stapleton in particular. He was a criminal, wanted for attempting to burn New York—there was a price on his head. Why not deliver him to the white men and collect the reward of two hundred pounds? They could buy many guns with the money. He had seen Malcolm at Oswego, cheating Indians out of their furs. An even bigger cheat was his wife, the Moon Woman, whom the Senecas had raised from infancy and cherished as a daughter. This was how she repaid their generosity.

The sachems and even Clara's mother had been stunned and intimidated by Grey Owl. He had won enough followers to make him formidable. Were they bringing dissension into their village by adopting this white man? Clara saw no one else could answer Grey Owl's slanders. She rose to her feet and confronted her former lover.

"You claim to be inspired by the Master of Life," she said. "But when I look into your eyes, Grey Owl, I see nothing but the low cunning of the Evil Brother! I was there at Oswego when the man we have just named Standing Bear and the Seneca daughter we call She-Is-Alert traded for furs. I was their partner and friend! I shared in their profits! We dealt honestly with every warrior, even when other white men got them drunk! Do you dare to accuse me, a daughter of the Bear Clan, of cheating my brothers? Do you wish me to return to New York and die at the stake? That will be my fate, because where this man goes, I must go too. I have loved him all my life. The Evil Brother prevented us from becoming man and wife. But that hard fate has never altered my love."

Grey Owl was struck dumb by this torrent of words. Everyone present recognized in their force the terrific power of Clara's *orenda*. "Speak, Grey Owl," Clara's mother said. "Do you have any response to this testimony of Nothing-But-Flowers?"

"Only this," Grey Owl said. "She—and all of you—will live to see the folly of trusting white men."

For a terrible moment, Clara saw in Grey Owl's eyes the pain of Bold Antelope's humiliation on that April morning long ago. A moment later, his face turned into Caesar's African features—and his hair blazed in the dim light of the longhouse's candles. She sensed a horrendous truth at the center of those words. Yet they did not alter the love she had just declared for Malcolm Stapleton.

"What matters, Grey Owl, is not the color of a man's skin," Clara said. "It is the strength and purity of his soul that a Seneca judges as worthy or unworthy. I have brown skin. But my mother considers me a daughter and I regard her as my mother with all the love and loyalty we would owe each other if I came from her body. To say all white men are bad is as foolish as it is to say all Indians are good or all Africans are bad. The Senecas—and the Great Council of the Six Nations to which they belong—do not judge whole peoples in that way. Even when we make war on them, we adopt their captives into our tribe. We make peace with them and exchange promises of good behavior."

"You speak with a tongue that is twisted, Nothing-But-Flowers. Twisted by the desire you feel for this man," Grey Owl said, pointing at Malcolm. "We shall see which of us speaks with the wisdom of one who has seen the future! The Manitou has opened my eyes to the Indians' fate. Whether my words come from the Master of Life or the Evil Brother does not matter. They are true!"

Grey Owl retreated into the night. The sachems declared that Malcolm was worthy of adoption into the Senecas and would henceforth be known as Standing Bear. After a feast and a dance of welcome around the fires outside the longhouses, Clara led Malcolm into the cool darkness of the September woods.

"Did you understand what I said to Grey Owl?"

"Yes."

"Watching you over these months has been like being reborn. The love I felt for you that first time has returned in a new wonderful way. But how can I act on it? How can I betray Catalyntie?"

He was silent. "Only if we see it as something that must end—that will end when you return to her," Clara said.

He was still silent. "Do you understand?" she said.

"I feel the guilt of it too," he said. "Maybe it will end—too soon. But—"

Her mouth sealed his lips. The years fell away and they were back in the New Jersey woods beside their secret lake. The sweetness was redoubled by their mutual confession of guilt and inevitable separation. Never had Malcolm seemed more desirable. Gratitude was part of Clara's passion as well as pride. She had created the soul of this magnificent warrior who had sacrificed his white future for her. The Seneca and the African side of her nature fused in a tremendous burst of joy.

A few days later, a hunting party was attacked by Ottawas from Fort Niagara—a not infrequent occurrence because the boundaries between the hunting grounds of the Seneca and these French-allied Indians were vague. Often these encounters, in which shots were exchanged and men wounded or killed, were more or less ignored. This time, a young Seneca warrior named Red Hawk was badly wounded. When he died the following day, Malcolm took the lead in urging instant retaliation. He stripped to the skin, painted himself in red and yellow war colors and appeared before the village's sachems with a hatchet in his hand. He told them that their honor as Senecas depended on avenging the insult by pursuing the Ottawas—and killing as many of them as possible. It was time to teach them and the French respect for the Senecas—respect rooted in fear.

Clara was filled with dismay. Her mother was even more dismayed and exerted all her influence inside the

Bear Clan to prevent the expedition. She persuaded the sachems to propose a compromise. Malcolm and Clara and the parents of Red Hawk would journey to Fort Niagara and demand compensation for his death. Malcolm argued that only a war party would impress the French but he accepted the decision of the village council.

It was not a happy trip. Red Hawk was an only son and both his parents were haggard with grief over his loss. His father, Little Beaver, wept and cursed the Evil Brother every night with a violence that chilled Clara. She saw no point in antagonizing this powerful being. His wife was equally disconsolate but more silent. On the third evening of their journey, she suddenly cried: "Grey Owl is right. This white man has brought a curse on our village. They're all in the service of the Evil Brother."

Clara assured her this was not true. But it was another ominous sign of Grey Owl's influence on many people. At last they reached the sprawling stone fort at the junction of the Niagara River and Lake Ontario. A white giant dressed as a Seneca brave in deerskin leggings and moccasins virtually guaranteed a sensation. Malcolm had no difficulty locating a Frenchman who spoke passable English and they were soon introduced to the commander of the fort, an affable young French captain named Armand Pouchot.

Malcolm made a vigorous speech, describing Red Hawk's death and his parents' grief. Instead of demanding compensation, however, he threatened the Frenchman with retaliation. The Senecas, he said, were prepared to take a French scalp because they knew the Ottawas were armed by France and sent out to assert the French claim to this side of the lake. Fort Niagara, he coolly declared, was a violation of the territory of the province of New York and if the French wanted to avoid a war, they should abandon it immediately.

Captain Pouchot was more than a little astonished by this aggressive stance. Although New Yorkers had protested Fort Niagara when it was built, no one had challenged it for two decades. More important, Malcolm was the first Englishman he had seen wearing Indian dress, claiming the right to speak for a tribe. The French had made a habit of sending men to live with their Indians in Canada and they prided themselves on the loyalty this policy had created. If the English were about to launch a similar policy, it could easily affect the delicate balance of power in North America.

Captain Pouchot invited Malcolm to stay at Fort Niagara while he consulted his superiors in Montreal about how to reply to his challenge. This gave Malcolm and Clara time to spend a day going down the Niagara River to see the great falls. It was a stupendous spectacle—but for Clara it recalled the chilling memory of her dream of oblivion.

"Remember when we talked of coming to see this wonder?" Malcolm asked.

She remembered all too well—and it reminded her of how temporary their life together was now. How hopeless, really. But they spent the night within earshot of the falls, wrapped in each other's arms, pretending to regain that long-ago rapture. Were they both pretending, Clara wondered, as Malcolm filled her with sweetness that her soul both welcomed and denied?

Back at Fort Niagara, they waited impatiently for several more days before Captain Pouchot summoned them to his quarters again. "We've made inquiries about you, my friend," the Frenchman said. "We've discovered you're a fellow with nerves of brass. You're wanted for murder and kidnapping in New York—and there are other stories that connect you to a vicious attack on one of our ships on this lake."

Red Hawk's mother had obviously talked freely. During his initiation into the Senecas, Clara had urged Malcolm to tell vivid stories in the Indian style to bolster his claim to the status of a warrior. He had described the Battle of the Bracken and the encounter with the French sloop and made a great impression.

"We could easily hang you and your African squaw," Pouchot said. "But a fellow like you is clever enough to be useful to us. Here is my offer. A thousand livres a year if you switch sides and do your utmost to make the Senecas our allies in the next war."

"Will there be another war?" Malcolm said. "I thought the last one ended to your satisfaction."

"Not over here," Pouchot said. "We've decided it's time to draw a line down the rivers and through the forests and say to the English—no farther. We have all the western tribes on our side. If we could bring the Senecas and some other Iroquois over, we would have a force ready to strike at their rear if the English tried to attack us."

"Where will you build these forts?" Malcolm said.

Pouchot unrolled a map across his desk and invited Malcolm and Clara to follow his finger as he traced the French plan. "First we'll take Oswego. Then we'll move down the Lake of the Sacrament[1] to the juncture with Lake George and build a strong fort there. Meanwhile, we'll send an expedition from Detroit to build another fort where the Ohio River meets the Monongahela in western Pennsylvania.[2] There will be intermediate posts elsewhere—with the goal a ring of steel around the English colonies—from which we'll launch attacks that will drive them out of the Mohawk Valley and the western parts of Virginia and Pennsylvania."

"Fascinating," Malcolm said. "Will you have the men to manage this?"

"We've been guaranteed sixteen first-class regiments.

[1] *Lake Champlain.*
[2] *The site of Pittsburgh.*

We've thoroughly defeated the English in Europe. They won't dare challenge us there again—so we have a comfortable surplus of troops.''

"I'm deeply impressed, Captain," Malcolm said. "Will you give me time to consider your offer?"

"Of course. We'll begin by making this mission a success. We're prepared to pay handsomely in guns and wampum and cloth to compensate Red Hawk's parents. We want them—and you—to return to your village praising Onontio.''[3]

"As well we should. I have no reason to be loyal to a government that persecutes me and the woman I love. But I must calculate a few things, Captain. A man can easily lose his head in this business."

Clara listened to this with astonishment. She was even more astonished by what Malcolm said when they walked into the woods outside the fort to discuss the captain's offer.

"You're not seriously thinking of joining him, are you?" she asked.

"I'm thinking of pretending to join him. He's already told me enough to set the burghers of Albany and even the smug sophisticates of New York City trembling with fear. Sixteen regiments! Do you realize what they can do with that many trained men? We don't have one British regiment in the entire thirteen colonies. This is information that can change the course of history, Clara. I've got to get it to the governor of New York as soon as possible. Meanwhile, we've got to do everything in our power to hold the Senecas to our side in this war—''

Our side. The words came naturally to Malcolm. They made Clara realize the dimension of the danger into which they were plunging. She suddenly felt as if she were on a raft, whirling down the Niagara River toward

[3]*The Indian name for the French governor of Canada.*

the great falls. "What do you mean by our side?" she said.

"The Senecas—the Iroquois—have been England's allies for a long time."

"But they may not choose to be this time. I've been listening to my mother and to the sachems in the long-house. They see no point to another war with the French in which we lose men and gain nothing. They think the right path for the Senecas—and the whole Iroquois league—is to remain neutral."

"That's impossible. And disgraceful!"

"Is it? You're talking like a white man, Malcolm. I'm talking—and thinking—like a Seneca."

"I'm talking—and thinking—like an American. This time the French are throwing down a gauntlet. They're saying only one of us will rule this continent. If we can drive out the French, the Americans will be in a position to deal with the English. To insist on taking charge of this continent as their own country. That will mean a better life for everyone here, including the Iroquois."

It was a magnificent vision. But did she believe it? Would the traders at Fort Oswego stop selling rum and cheating the Indians? Would idealists like Malcolm have the power to pass laws against them?

"It could also mean the end of slavery—freeing every African and giving them a province of their own, like the Iroquois. It may not happen right away—but eventually Americans will realize that this continent stands for liberty. Slavery has no place in it."

Would the people who screamed "Roast the Negar!" as Caesar went to the stake agree to free their Africans, because Malcolm Stapleton and a few other idealists urged it? Again, Clara wavered between loving this man for his vision—and the realities she had seen in New York and New Jersey. Above all she clung to the im-mediate reality that war meant death and desolation. For the Senecas—the northernmost tribe of the Iroquois, face to face with the French on the lakes—it meant possible destruction.

"I still think the Senecas should stay neutral."

Clara sensed that something profound occurred in Malcolm's soul when he heard these words. He separated from her in a new way. Marriage to Catalyntie had separated him. But that had been a barrier which desire and circumstances had repeatedly dissolved. Now she saw a man who regarded her as a mere woman—the equivalent of a child. She realized how deeply paternity was woven into Malcolm's mind and heart. He could accept—or discard—advice from a woman with equanimity. He would never be a true Seneca, a man trained from birth to heed a woman because everything in the longhouse—rank and wealth and power—flowed from women.

"I'm going to do my best to change that opinion," he said.

Suddenly Clara could hear in the distance the roar of the great falls—that image of oblivion. "It's not just my opinion!" Clara said.

"I'll change everyone's mind before I'm through," Malcolm said.

Back at Fort Niagara, Malcolm told Captain Pouchot that he was ready to work with him. He received an immediate down payment of two hundred livres,[4] with more forthcoming if he performed well as a secret agent. Red Hawk's parents received a shiny new musket, a half dozen yards of cloth, and a white wampum belt that was almost three feet long. They were well satisfied with Onontio's generosity and praised the French repeatedly on their journey back up the lake to Shining Creek.

Malcolm said nothing until they reached the village. That night, around a fire, he gathered the younger warriors and told them about Captain Pouchot's bribe. "I

---

[4]Roughly eight pounds.

took the Frenchman's gold," he said, holding the gleaming livres in his big hand. "But now I throw it in the dirt. Those who wish to pick it up may do so. I would prefer to die before selling my honor for gold."

He flung the money on the ground, summoned Red Hawk's parents and pointed to the coins. "Take this from Onontio. It will further compensate you for the loss of your son, Red Hawk, whom I was proud to call my friend. But I hope it won't buy your heart, which should still demand vengeance for his death, vengeance repeated a hundred times, as the only way to recoup such a loss."

Red Hawk's mother picked up the money and stared at it. "Standing Bear speaks with a powerful voice," Little Beaver, Red Hawk's father, said. "I am ready to raise my hatchet whenever he raises his to avenge my son."

Watching from the door of the Bear Clan's longhouse, Clara's mother said to her: "I think you have brought a dangerous man into our village. A man only you can command."

She was telling her to get Malcolm under control. But this proved impossible. Clara could not heal that separation she had sensed in the woods outside Fort Niagara. Instead, Malcolm became more and more reckless. He persuaded the village's younger warriors to accept him as their leader. He sent one of them to New York City with a message for the governor, asking him to send a trusted subordinate to the village.

In four weeks the young warrior returned with Malcolm's friend, Guert Cuyler. He was predictably stunned by France's plan for a renewed war and promised to get the news to the governor, who would send it to London as soon as possible. Clara could only watch helplessly as Malcolm told Guert what he thought the Americans and the British should do. "Let's attack them first, before these regiments get here. I'll have the Senecas ready to fight in six months' time—''

Malcolm accompanied Cuyler back to Oswego in a canoe. When he returned he told Clara that he had broached the possibility of a pardon for both of them for discovering France's plans—and preparing the Senecas for war.

"A pardon? I didn't commit a crime. Why do I need a pardon?" Clara said.

"It would be just a formality. A way of voiding the sentence."

"It doesn't matter to me. I have no intention of returning."

"Never?" Malcolm said.

"I'm at peace here. I can never be at peace where I see Africans as slaves. I hope to keep the Senecas at peace with me."

"Clara—"

"If you want me to love you, it's time you listened to me. My mother and leaders of the other clans don't want this war you're bringing to us."

"I'm not bringing it. I'm helping you survive it. Do you think the French will ever treat the Senecas with respect? The Ottawas, the Chippewas, the western tribes beyond the lakes are their people. You'll be shoved out of these lands as soon as they win the war. They're making promises to those tribes right now."

He might be right. But what did it prove? Only that both sides in this white man's war cared nothing for the Indians. Was Grey Owl right? Clara groped for a place between disagreement and hatred. "All the more reason to remain neutral."

"No one respects a neutral. Your warriors will be called old women."

"You're making me hate you!" Clara cried.

Malcolm stood there, pain on his face. "I hope not," he said.

When he tried to kiss her, she shoved him away. "I mean it, Malcolm," she said.

He went stubbornly ahead, preparing the village for war. He traveled to other villages where young warriors, bored with peace, were thrilled by his oratory. They gleefully joined in his tactics, which called for elaborate rehearsals so they would be ready to attack the moment the war began.

This trip across the lake to Frontenac was one of these expeditions. They would not strike a blow at the French fort, but they would see how easy it would be to sweep into the harbor and burn the sloops of war and plunder the warehouses before the fort's garrison could react.

Malcolm continued to visit Fort Niagara, where he convinced the befuddled Captain Pouchot that his elaborate rehearsals were preparing the Seneca for war on France's side. He handed over the bribes he received to Clara's mother, to buy whatever the village needed at Oswego. He even seduced the village shaman into predicting glorious victories. The more successful he became, the more Clara withdrew from him in her heart.

Outside the longhouse, war drums were throbbing. There would be hours of feasting and dancing and boasting before they set out. Clara could not bear the sight of Malcolm hefting his hatchet and telling how many French scalps would soon decorate the walls of the Bear Clan's longhouse. How could he ignore her this way? Didn't he see how he was reducing her to nothing in her mother's eyes?

She fled into the woods and tried to pray. But no voice descended from the stars. She knew why. She had sinned against Catalyntie by becoming Malcolm's Seneca wife. She was cut off from the world of the spirit—and she had lost Malcolm too. He did not understand—or care.

She returned to the deserted village and the half-empty longhouse. Her mother's voice found her in the dark. "I have had a terrible dream," she said. "I saw you and Standing Bear on a small island above the great falls. The river was slowly wearing it away. I was on the shore, trying to persuade someone to paddle a canoe out to rescue you. But no one would do it, because the river was so swift. I stood and watched while the island slowly disappeared and you were both swept over the falls. Below, in the rapids, only he emerged and clung to a rock. You had vanished forever.''

"I think that's what is happening to me. I'm vanishing little by little. He won't listen to me. I'm useless to you and to myself. I can't bear children. What can I give the Senecas to make me worthy of my heritage?''

"I don't know,'' her mother said. "You can only wait for what the Manitou reveals. I still believe he has a special purpose for you. Your grandmother believed it from the day she saw you. She dreamed of you the first night you came here as a yellow sunflower, blooming in the snow.''

Clara slipped into a shallow restless sleep. When she awoke, summer sunshine was pouring through the door of the longhouse. There was a great racket outside, voices shouting, dogs barking. Had the warriors returned from Frontenac? They were not expected back for another day. Into the longhouse darted the woman, Big Claws. She was still as lean and nasty as she had been as a girl.

"Nothing-But-Flowers,'' she said. "Wake up. You have a visitor. Your friend She-Is-Alert has journeyed all the way from New York. She has her two sons with her.''

Clara flung aside her deerskin robe and rushed into the street. There I stood, escorted by Guert Cuyler and Peter Van Ness. In my arms was Paul, who kicked and squirmed until I lowered him to the ground. His brother Hugh seized him by the arm and stopped him from careening into a nearby cooking fire.

"Hello, Clara,'' I said.

She kissed me and Hugh and little Paul. She seemed enormously pleased to see us. There was not a scintilla of a sign of regret or embarrassment. On our long journey up the Mohawk to Oswego and down Lake Ontario to the village, I had wrestled with my Moon Woman self. A hundred times I had vowed I did not care if Clara and Malcolm had become lovers again. I wanted to preserve that moment on the night of Clara's rescue when Malcolm and I had discovered love in our souls, thanks to our mutual love for Clara. I vowed I would not desecrate that moment with envy and recrimination.

"I've come with wonderful news," I said. "The governor of New York has pardoned you and Malcolm. You can come home."

Clara's heart soared. The Manitou had answered her prayers at last. Malcolm could not turn his back on his wife and sons. He would return home with them—and she and her mother would regain control of the Senecas and cool their war fever.

"We have other news that's not so wonderful," Guert Cuyler said. "The war with the French has begun."

"Where—how?" Clara asked, horrified.

"In Virginia. A colonel of their militia named George Washington and about four hundred men were on their way to the forks of the Ohio to stop the French from building a fort there. They were attacked in the woods by a party of French and Indians. There were a good many killed and wounded on both sides."

Her Seneca mother's dream leaped like a panther in Clara's mind. Tears poured down her cheeks. "Is there no place on earth where I can find peace?" she cried.

THREE

"IT WAS A ROUT. AN utter total rout," Malcolm said, his voice a croak, his eyes blank with exhaustion.

He was telling me about the latest fiasco in the war with France—the brainless frontal assault on the French fort at the carrying place between Lake George and the Lake of the Sacrament.[1] Almost two thousand British soldiers had been killed or wounded. The British general, James Abercromby, had never come within five miles of the battlefield. Malcolm and his American rangers had been attacked in the woods by hundreds of Canadian Indians, inflamed by the French victory. Scarcely one man in five had survived.

He was back at Great Rock Farm from another campaign in this pitiless struggle with France. Year after year, the war had been a series of sickening defeats, beginning with the slaughter of two British regiments in western Pennsylvania and a thousand Americans who marched with them, confident of victory. In the north, along the border with Canada, it had been more of the same. Oswego fell with a crash that shook New York to its foundations. The French ruled the lakes and rivers to within a few miles of Albany.

In the valleys of the Mohawk and the Susquehanna and even in the northern hills of New Jersey, Indian war parties from Frontenac and Fort Niagara swept down to burn and loot and scalp. Another holocaust sprang from the fort at the forks of the Ohio, with Shawnees and

[1] *Now known as Fort Ticonderoga.*

other western tribes spreading torture and destruction across western Pennsylvania and Maryland and Virginia. People died within sixty miles of Philadelphia.

The ineptitude, the corruption, of the British government under the dithering heir of Walpole, the Duke of Newcastle, was unbelievable.[2] Their favoritism-ridden army, led by generals and colonels without talent or brains, was soon a continental-length joke. Malcolm Stapleton was one of many Americans who decided the colonies would have to rescue themselves. At a congress in Albany, he supported men such as Benjamin Franklin of Pennsylvania and Stephen Hopkins of Rhode Island who argued urgently for an American confederation— in vain. The British opposed it because it smacked of independence and there was too much jealousy and suspicion between the thirteen very different, often quarreling provinces. They could not even agree on whom to deputize to negotiate a new alliance with the Iroquois.

As a result, the sachems of the Six Nations went home from Albany disgusted and Malcolm's dream of a Seneca spearhead, backed by the full weight of the Iroquois confederation, splintered into disillusion and demoralization. When Oswego fell, many Iroquois decided the French were sure winners and abandoned all pretense of neutrality. The French soon had emissaries in the Seneca villages along Lake Ontario, offering gifts of guns and gunpowder and luring the young warriors south with promises of plunder against the inept, treacherous English.

The few villages that followed Malcolm's leadership and tried to remain neutral while waiting for renewed negotiations for an alliance with England were threatened with destruction. Last year, to prove their grim intentions, the French and their Canadian Indian allies

---

[2]Newcastle's brother, Henry Pelham, Walpole's immediate successor, died after an overeating binge in 1754. Walpole died in 1745.

attacked Shining Creek with an overwhelming force. Malcolm and his comparative handful of warriors were compelled to flee into the woods with the women and children, leaving behind many old and infirm people. The attackers torched the village and laid waste the cornfields and fruit orchards, reducing the survivors to pathetic refugees, begging for food and shelter among the Mohawks, the Oneidas, and other tribes of the Six Nations. Only the Mohawks, whose country was closest to the Americans and who remained sympathetic to King George's subjects, showed them some mercy.

Each year, Malcolm spent all but the worst months of the winter in the northern woods, either fighting or planning the war. He helped build and garrison a series of forts along New Jersey's northern border. He conferred repeatedly with the governors of New Jersey and New York on how to raise men, how to coordinate some sort of defense with New England's contentious Yankees. Our sons were growing to manhood with a stranger for a father, a visitor who appeared and vanished like a creature in a myth, who was better known in the newspapers than he was in the flesh.

I was not much better as a parent. The flood of British troops into New York produced a fantastic prosperity among the farmers of New Jersey, who sold their wheat and rye and sheep and bullocks at vastly inflated prices. This meant the *vrouws* of Bergen County had unprecedented amounts of money to spend at the new Universal Store in Hackensack. I had long since paid off my loan from Arent Schuyler and my debt to Robert Foster Nicolls—and sent Jamey Stapleton his half share of the value of Great Rock Farm. I used the rest of my surplus cash to outfit a privateer. Guert Cuyler had taken command of it and was soon on his way to piling up prize money from a string of spectacular captures. I used my share of the profits to open a forge in New Jersey's northern hills, which was soon producing a ton of iron a month. The stuff sold for fantastic profits in London, where the war-driven demand for metal was voracious.

But these business triumphs seemed hollow, the cash overflowing my account books meant little, while the war raged on. More and more, I began to think it was Clara for whom Malcolm was fighting, not his wife and children, comfortable and safe in New Jersey. I began to suspect he secretly hoped for death in some forest ambuscade to prove to himself and Clara that it was she and she alone that he loved. Again and again I reproached myself for this egotistical view of a war between two great empires. I said nothing to Malcolm. Each year, I struggled to welcome him as a wife, to be grateful for the few months he spent with me.

This year, Malcolm had barely recovered from his exhaustion and melancholy when he announced he was planning to leave for the frontier once more. I lost what little self-control I had left. "I can't stand the thought of you going back to Clara," I sobbed. "I've tried to accept it but—"

"How many times do I have to tell you—she won't let me touch her," Malcolm said.

"Whether that's true or not, you go back there for her sake. You want to die for her sake—instead of living for my sake—for your sons' sakes."

"I'm going back to help Clara's people. Your people. They're refugees. Maybe with some help from the British we can get them back to Shining Creek."

We were in our bedroom at Great Rock Farm—the room in which we performed the ritual of married love with a dogged persistence that was a tribute to nothing but my need for him and his guilty wish to love me in spite of Clara. I knew he had become Clara's lover again. But how could I reproach him when I had deceived him about Philip Hooft? I even recognized the tormented love for me that prompted Malcolm to lacerate his conscience and lie about Clara so stubbornly.

"I'm sorry. I'm a fool. It's easy to see why you don't love me," I wailed.

Malcolm seized me by the shoulders. "Don't love you? If I didn't love you, I wouldn't lie with you in that bed. I love you as a wife, as loyal a wife as any man has on this continent. I know your crosspatches. I know I've put some of them there and God or destiny or the Evil Brother has put others. But they don't diminish the love I have for you."

It was useless. He was talking to the mirror across the room, desperately trying to convince himself that he was telling the truth. While waiting for him beyond Albany was the woman who exalted his soul. I let him have the benefit of my perpetual doubts—and kissed him good-bye with tearful fervor.

At Albany, where the British army was camped for the winter, Malcolm discovered a modicum of hope. Chagrined by repeated defeats, the British Parliament had ousted the Duke of Newcastle and installed a new prime minister, William Pitt, who had in turn sent new generals to America. One of them was Malcolm's friend James Wolfe, finally promoted after years of neglect. Malcolm thought he detected a new spirit of patriotism replacing the quarrelsome self-interest that had prevailed in the royal army—along with an obnoxious anti-Americanism. Pitt had a new slogan, which he had given his generals to pass on to the army: "In America, England and Europe are to be fought for." He saw, with a prescience few other Britons possessed, that the control of this vast continent was the key to world power in the future.

Malcolm soon located William Johnson, the Irishman who had first rented and then bought our Mohawk River lands. Johnson had a letter from Clara, whom he had met at Onaquaqua, the Indian town on the Susquehannah, where the Irishman kept a store. The letter told Malcolm she had gone north to the Seneca country. Her mother had died and she had become matron of the Bear Clan. Johnson had told her about the all-out military effort the British were about to make. With the French on the defensive, she hoped to reconstitute their village on Shining Creek. She begged Malcolm to bring seeds for a corn crop and for apple and pear and peach trees. The men needed gunpowder and bullets, the women blankets and warm wool cloth against next winter's snows.

Malcolm asked Johnson, who had become superintendent of Indian affairs, to issue these supplies as gifts from the British government. At first Johnson demurred at giving presents to the Senecas. Too many of them had joined the French in previous campaigns. But Malcolm described the price Clara's people had paid for their loyalty and persuaded him to relent.

As the supplies were being packed and loaded on horses, Johnson asked Malcolm if he was interested in leading an expedition into the heart of Canada to cripple France's Indian allies. The target was a large Indian town on the St. Francis River, not far from Montreal. From there had come many devastating war parties. General Jeffrey Amherst, the new British commander, wanted to strike a blow that would warn Canada's Indians that they could not slaughter Americans with impunity.

"I told Amherst you were the perfect man to lead a raid like that," Johnson said. "He wants an answer from you the day before yesterday. Time is at a premium. Any day your friend General Wolfe will arrive by sea with an army to attack Quebec and Amherst wants to draw as many French and Indians as possible out of his way."

How could Malcolm say no? Especially when he learned that his brother Jamey's regiment was in Wolfe's army. It was the sort of mission that stirred the recklessness in his soldier's soul. Best of all, he would take the warriors from Shining Creek with him for the assault. They would be ideal scouts for his force of rangers—and their good conduct would resolve Johnson's doubts about the Senecas, making them candidates for more generous present-giving.

Within an hour, Johnson was introducing him to General Amherst. At the general's side was a familiar, if unexpected, face—Robert Foster Nicolls. Thanks to his father's political pull and his own familiarity with America, Robert had become Amherst's commissary, in charge of feeding his huge army. William Johnson enviously muttered to Malcolm that Nicolls was making a fortune at the job. He got eight percent of all the money he spent.

Nicolls heartily seconded Johnson's recommendation of Malcolm. "I've seen him attack Indians unarmed and chase them into the woods," he said, recalling the fateful morning Clara and I had met him and Malcolm.

General Amherst was impressed by Malcolm's promise to recruit fifty Senecas. No one in the English or the American wing of the British army had been able to persuade more than a handful of Indians to serve with them. A handshake sealed the bargain. Malcolm would deliver the Senecas and General Amherst would find the volunteers in a month's time.

Malcolm journeyed to Shining Creek with the gifts of seeds and goods and found her presiding over a new longhouse with the symbol of the Bear Clan over the door. The other clans had also built new longhouses; most of the warriors, their wives, and children had returned. Clara greeted Malcolm gratefully. The bags of seeds, the bundles of blankets, and barrels of salt meat and gunpowder on the packhorses he had hired from William Johnson were proof that he still cared about her and her people.

But Clara's gratitude dwindled when Malcolm assembled the warriors and told them about the expedition to Canada. Once more his oratory mesmerized them. Here was a chance for revenge against their ancient enemies, who had burned their village and caused the deaths of many of their grandparents and parents. Clara was even more dismayed when she studied Malcolm's route into Canada on his map. They would have to pass no less than four French forts. They might manage this with reasonable stealth on their way to the attack—but once the assault became known, the exit route would be patrolled by French troops and Indian allies hungry for vengeance.

"You're leading these men to almost certain death!"she told Malcolm.

He stiffly disagreed. It was no more dangerous than any other war party. They would have the advantage of surprise. It was an opportunity for Americans—he was sure most of his volunteers would be Americans—to distinguish themselves in a war where the British regulars were now doing most of the fighting. "This is our kind of warfare, Clara, one the British can't fight," he said. "They can't go anywhere without artillery, supply wagons, all the abracadabra of a regular army."

He was still trying to create an American presence, an American consciousness. But he stubbornly refused to see that it was irrelevant as far as the Indians were concerned. The war was a quarrel between white men. "What does it have to do with us?" Clara said. "We only want to live in peace, to grow our corn and hunt our game on our ancestral lands."

"The British—and a lot of Americans—are angry at the Iroquois—at all Indians. At least ten thousand people have died on the frontier in the last five years. This raid could change their minds about the Iroquois. It could win better treatment for your people after the war."

"If you win."

"We're going to win, Clara. The British have poured in men. They've got twenty-five thousand regulars in America now. They've pinned down a big chunk of the French army by fighting them in Europe. It's a worldwide war, Clara. They're fighting the French in India, in Africa, in the Caribbean—and winning most of the battles.''

Clara capitulated and allowed the warriors to go off with Malcolm. It would have been difficult for her to oppose them. She lacked the authority her mother and grandmother had wielded over the Bear Clan's sachems and war chiefs. They would have to be wooed patiently over many years before they granted her the power which she possessed in theory now.

That night, as the warriors feasted and danced and boasted of the scalps and booty they were going to collect, Clara remembered her mother's dream of her and Malcolm on the dwindling island above the great falls. Was this part of the current that was slowly destroying their fragile foothold? If this expedition ended in disaster, she would be blamed. She might become a pariah, driven out of the village, possibly killed. Grey Owl's followers had grown more numerous during their years as refugees. Red Hawk's mother was one of the leaders, constantly preaching hatred of all whites.

Clara could not explain any of this to Malcolm as he took her hand and led her into the woods. They were still lovers. She could not deny the desire she felt for him whenever they met.

''Does Catalyntie know?'' Clara asked, as the familiar sweetness gathered in her flesh.

''I lie to her,'' Malcolm said. ''I tell her you won't let me touch you.''

''That's probably better than telling her the truth,'' Clara said.

''I'll tell her someday—when the war ends and we say good-bye, once and for all.''

''No. I'll tell her. I'll take all the blame. I deserve all the blame.''

''I can't imagine life without you, Clara. Or without her and the boys—''

"If you're right about the war ending soon—"

The thought of an imminent farewell made their mutual coming sweeter, deeper, darker. Clara wept as he held her against him. She was as divided, as tormented by guilt as he was. "Let me go with you on this raid," she said. "I want to protect the women and children in the villages you're attacking."

"I'll do my best to save them," Malcolm said. "But it's become a very dirty war."

In every imaginable way, history, personal and public, stained and disfigured their love. Why did it survive? For a moment Clara almost hated it—as if it were a grotesque abortion to which she had given birth. She could not deny its reality. But she could not see its purpose.

FOUR

WHEN CLARA AWOKE, MALCOLM AND the warriors were gone. They hurried east down the lakes and rivers to Albany, where Malcolm found his two hundred volunteers waiting for him. Most of them had served as rangers in earlier campaigns. Almost all were Americans and they welcomed the Indians as valuable companions-in-arms. A month later they were on their way up the Lake of the Sacrament by night, hugging the shore to avoid the French warships that patrolled the center of this narrow 140-mile stretch of water.

At the head of the lake, they hauled their canoes into the woods and left two Indians to guard them and the extra parched corn and dried beef and bread that they would need on their return journey. Into Canada they slogged for two days. As they made camp for the second night, a commotion in the rear guard spread swiftly through the ranks.

The two Senecas they had left with the boats stumbled up to Malcolm, gasping for breath. They babbled dismaying news. A force of four hundred French troops had found the canoes and burned them. They were now on the trail of the invaders. Malcolm called a council of war with his chief officers, and the leader of the Senecas, Little Beaver. Some favored an immediate retreat, but Little Beaver supported Malcolm's argument that a forced march would put enough distance between them and their pursuers. On the way back they would take another route to the east of the lake.

For the next week, they marched all day and half the night, struggling through swamps that often soaked them to the waist in freezing water. There were no fires to dry their clothes. For beds they laced together spruce boughs in the branches of standing trees. Meals were cold nibblings of dried beef, sausage, corn meal. Some men had eaten too much from their dwindling packs and for the last three days many were starving.

Finally, Malcolm saw grey swirls of smoke rising above the trees. He halted the column and with two of his officers crept forward to reconnoiter the village. It was huge—at least a thousand Indians were living there. As they watched, darkness fell and fires blazed. Soon a major feast was in progress, with dancing, singing, and the whirring of pebble-filled turtleshell rattles. Liquor was consumed in large quantities by the men, who whirled drunkenly around the fire until they collapsed and were dragged into one of the many bark cabins.

Malcolm waited until the last of the revelers reeled off to bed. He and his officers crept back to the men and ordered them to stack their packs and load their guns. Bayonets slid softly over the muzzles and locked with a murderous click. Tomahawks and knives were loosened.

Malcolm gave a brief speech, in which he urged them to spare the women and children. He sensed no one paid much attention to him. Too many of these men had lost sisters, brothers, wives to raiding Indians. That was why they had volunteered for this dangerous job.

In a column of twos, they advanced on the village through a thick chilling mist. At a half hour before dawn, Malcolm raised his hand and roared: "Now!"

Into the village they charged, the rangers howling as wildly as the Senecas. Most of the French Indians were still on their pallets when doors crashed open and bayonets pinned them to the earth or the butt end of a musket smashed their skulls. Those who stumbled into the street were shot or bayoneted before they could find a weapon. In the semidarkness, little discrimination was made between women and men.

Many ran for the nearby St. Francis River. Malcolm had detailed forty men to cut off this line of retreat. Muskets roared from the shore and bodies toppled into the dark water. Those who tried to launch canoes were easy targets. Soon dozens of corpses were drifting downstream.

In the village, one of Malcolm's men shouted: "Look at the scalps!" On poles in the center of the street were literally hundreds of scalps, many of them with long soft strands of hair—obviously from women. This sight redoubled the rangers' blood lust. For a while, they showed mercy to no one. Malcolm tried to control them but he soon abandoned his efforts as hopeless. "It's our turn!" one man screamed as he hacked the corpses of a woman and her child.

A few St. Francis Indians found guns and fired back from doorways or windows. Torches flung on their roofs soon turned their cabins into funeral pyres. They could be heard inside, quavering death chants. Others ran out, aflame from head to foot, to be bayoneted or tomahawked. Only as the carnage subsided did the Senecas prevail on the rangers to spare about twenty women and children, whom they herded around the scalping poles. They intended to take them back to their village to replace their recent losses.

Cowering in one hut the Senecas found a Jesuit missionary. They dragged him out and the rangers decided he would be given a trial. In twenty seconds the priest was found guilty of 302 murders—the number of scalps one enterprising ranger had counted on the poles. The murderous man of God was dragged to the nearest tree and hanged.

One of the Senecas emerged from the Jesuit's hut with a silver statue of the Blessed Virgin. "Is this worth money, Standing Bear?" he asked Malcolm.

"If it's real silver, yes," Malcolm said. "Put it in your pack."

In three huts they found baskets of corn. Malcolm ordered everyone to load his pack with as much of the precious stuff as could be crammed into it. This would have to sustain them on the long march home. By 9:00 A.M. they had begun their trek south along the shore of the St. Francis River. The region was a wilderness, badly mapped. On their heels came enraged French and Indian pursuers. The rear guard fought a number of bloody skirmishes in which a dozen men died.

In a week, they had eaten most of their corn and were still far from safety. By now it was mid-October and the Canadian winter was coming on. Game fled before their numbers. Malcolm decided they should split into small parties, hoping it would enable them to find food. The Senecas decided to travel west above the head of the Lake of the Sacrament as the most direct route home.

It proved to be a trail of tears. They were attacked a dozen times by the French or enemy Indians, losing men each time. They stumbled into Shining Creek, half-starved skeletons. Only five of the captured children survived the journey. The village was filled with wails of mourning and songs for the dead. Hardly a family had not lost a son or nephew. The surviving warriors had nothing to show for their travails but the silver statue of the Virgin Mary.

When Clara saw that serene face, she felt doom gather around her. The Virgin had not forgotten the blasphemy she had committed after Caesar's death. She had returned to remind her of the lost sweetness of her celestial voice. Clara took the statue into the longhouse of the Bear Clan and put it in a dim corner. That night, while everyone slept, she knelt before it and begged the Virgin to forgive her, to guide her once more. There was no answer.

At British headquarters in Albany, Malcolm was being feted as a hero. His exploit was extolled in every newspaper in America. General Amherst praised him and his men in his orders of the day and in an official dispatch to London. All but forty of the rangers had survived the return trip.

They were soon involved in a much larger celebration. Down the lakes came a messenger to report that General James Wolfe had captured Quebec. He had paid for the triumph with his life—but it meant the war was over. It was only a matter of time before the scattered demoralized French capitulated. A hundred cannon roared a victory salute and everyone from General Amherst to the lowliest private got gloriously drunk. No one drank more joyously than Malcolm—his brother Jamey had survived the battle with only a minor wound.

At the victory banquet at Amherst's headquarters, Malcolm found the conversation disturbing. After the toasts to Wolfe and other heroes, including a nice compliment to "our American brothers-in-arms" from the general, the aides and colonels began discussing how much money the war had cost—and how they could economize to pay off the staggering debt the British government had run up.

"The first thing we should do is get a grip on the money we spend on these bloody Indians," one aide declared.

Robert Foster Nicolls emphatically agreed with him. "We've poured ten thousand pounds a year into presents for those Iroquois for the better part of a century," he said. "What did we get for it in this war? The scalping knife and the torch. From now on, it should be cash on the barrelhead for anything they get from us."

"After the Indians, we've got to get these bloody Americans up to the line," rumbled a colonel. "Do you realize how few taxes the bastards pay?"

Malcolm ignored the last remark but he protested vehemently against the proposal to cut off presents to the Iroquois. Presents were needed more than ever now, because the Six Nations were their best spokesmen with the western and Canadian Indians. William Johnson, speaking as Indian superintendent, wholeheartedly agreed with Malcolm. They tried to explain to these foreigners (what the British really were) that Indians did not see presents as bribes, but as proof of a continuing friendship. An abrupt end of presents would be seen as an insult—a virtual declaration of war.

Robert Foster Nicolls, playing the American expert, disagreed. He said it was time to teach the savages how civilization worked. "I don't use that last word lightly," Robert sneered. "The lazy bastards should learn to do something besides hunt and screw."

Malcolm and William Johnson angrily refuted this slander. They described the harsh life of the warriors who spent winters in the woods trapping beaver, muskrat, and other animals. The Seneca and the rest of the Iroquois had almost hunted them to extinction in their own lands, which made it more and more difficult for them to earn money.

General Amherst listened to the argument without

committing himself. Malcolm hoped that with Johnson's backing, he had scotched a very bad idea.

A month later, the snow lay deep on the ground as Malcolm slogged into Clara's village on snowshoes. Ice floes drifted on the lake, driven by a freezing wind from the north. On two packhorses were bushels of corn and barrels of salt meat. The calls of children and warriors drew Clara to the door of the longhouse. There was no smile of greeting on her face.

"Do you think you're welcome here because you bring gifts?" she said. "Do you think these can replace the lives of twenty-five warriors?"

Malcolm was stunned by the Senecas' losses. "I begged them to follow me down the east bank of the lake to Albany," he said. "But they were too eager to get home."

"Everyone here says you abandoned them. You gave them no food. You kept it for your white men."

"That's a lie," Malcolm said. "None of us had any food."

Grey Owl's people had been busy refashioning the story of the raid into a parable of white treachery. As the horses were unloaded, Clara told him she had lost all semblance of authority as the matron of the Bear Clan. "You can't stay here, even for a night," she said. "I can't protect you."

"I'm a warrior of the Seneca nation. I can protect myself," Malcolm growled.

Out of the longhouse of the Wolf Clan hurtled Red Hawk's mother. Her husband, Little Beaver, had been killed on the way home from the raid. "Look at him," she screamed. "This is the Evil Brother in the flesh. Look at the man who betrayed the Senecas to starvation and death."

In the doorway of the Wolf Clan longhouse stood Grey Owl, his tattered prophet's blanket around his shoulders, a sneer on his lips. "Here is the messenger of death, returned to seek more souls," he said. "Does anyone doubt that the Manitou speaks through me, now?"

"The Evil Brother has possessed your soul, Grey Owl," Malcolm said. "Ever since you proved yourself a coward in your combat with me, and preferred surrender and flight to honorable death."

"I am no longer a warrior," Grey Owl said. "I cannot make you die for those words. But I have followers who are eager to undertake the task."

"I welcome the attempt," Malcolm said. "I have no doubt I'll prove them as cowardly as you."

In the Bear Clan longhouse, a frantic Clara dragged Malcolm to the dim rear of the building and pointed to the silver statue of the Blessed Virgin. It gleamed like a small ghost on the shelf in the corner. "You brought her back to me. All she does is reproach me for what I've become—what I've let us both become."

"I don't understand."

"I love you too much. I can't stop you even though I see you leading my people to destruction."

"I'm trying to save them—"

"You can't. You're white. You don't understand them—or me. Go now, before Grey Owl sends to the next village where he has a hundred warriors ready to kill you. He can't find a murderer here. Our warriors still adore you. But all the women have turned against you. They'll tie you to the stake and torture you for days. They'll force me to watch!"

"I'll go if you come with me," Malcolm said.

"I've told you. I can't go back."

"Neither can I—until I know you're safe."

Malcolm went into the woods and with his usual uncanny combination of luck and marksmanship killed a huge buck with a single shot. He carried the carcass back to the village and proclaimed a great feast to celebrate the English victory over the French. The warriors were

astonished and delighted by the news. He told them that
he would do everything in his power to make sure their
contribution to the victory was remembered by their father, King George.

Grey Owl receded into the shadows, overwhelmed
once more by this giant with his confident prophecies of
future power and contentment. The Senecas would be
the king's spokesmen with the Canadian and western
Indians. All the gifts, the peace councils, the distribution
of hunting grounds and the control of the fur trade would
flow through their hands. It was a dazzling vision. There
was only one thing wrong with it. Malcolm had no authority to say such things. He was talking for Clara's
sake, to insure her safety and happiness. He was ignoring those ominous words he had heard from Robert Foster Nicolls and others at General Amherst's victory
banquet.

FIVE

IN NEW JERSEY, TWO MONTHS later, I received a letter
that was so obviously full of lies, it drove me half mad.

> *Dear Wife:*
>
> *I have decided to remain here on the lake with
> the Senecas for the winter. The war is won, thank
> God, but the political situation between the En-
> glish and the Indians is very unstable. There is talk
> of discontinuing the presents to the Iroquois and
> treating the tribes who formerly dealt with the
> French in the same harsh way. "We are conquer-
> ors and they are conquered," some people around*

General Amherst are saying. "We owe them nothing." A worse understanding of the Iroquois and the Indians in general cannot be conceived. I have been to Albany a number of times where with William Johnson and others we are doing our best to prevent such a policy from being put into execution. If it is attempted, more blood may flow on the frontiers and even in places as settled as North Jersey than we saw during the worst of the war with the French.

I know you want to see me at home and no one wishes it more fervently than I do. If all seems well, I may manage it in the early spring, the end of April, perhaps.

Clara sends her love.
Your affectionate husband,
Malcolm

Clara sends her love. I raged up and down the bedroom for an hour, letting those words burn a furrow in my brain. The war was over, he was a hero once more, acclaimed on all sides—but he could not bear to part with Clara. I easily convinced myself that the stuff about the British not giving presents to the Indians was so much drivel. He was using wild rumors to delay his departure from Clara's arms.

In the northern woods, Malcolm spent much of the winter far from Clara's arms. He traveled throughout the Iroquois country, conferring with sachems and chiefs and clan leaders, compiling a dossier of warnings against abandoning the traditional policy of annual gifts of cloth and blankets and gunpowder and wampum to the Iroquois. The ruling sachems of the Six Nations received him at the council fire in Onondaga and urged him to issue a solemn exhortation to King George to convene a council as soon as possible to resolve these rumors

that were endangering the great chain of friendship between the two peoples.

In the spring, when the ice thawed, General Amherst
deputized Malcolm to cross the great lakes and accept
the surrender of the French forts at Detroit and Michilimackinac. Robert Foster Nicolls persuaded the general
to let him go along. Robert was eager to explore the
prospects for profits at these posts. With Amherst's
backing, Robert saw himself becoming the king of the
fur trade in America.

At these distant forts, Malcolm saw even more ominous portents of trouble. Around these places dwelt
about twenty-five hundred French Canadians, tough
frontiersmen who had spent their lives in intimate con-
tact with the western Indians. They had no enthusiasm
for accepting English rule because a French army had
lost a battle in distant Quebec. Malcolm rushed back to
Albany to tell Amherst that astute diplomacy—and
thousands of pounds' worth of presents—were going to
be needed to keep these people from influencing the
western Indians.

Nicolls told Amherst the precise opposite. Back him
with a regiment at each fort and he guaranteed he could
turn Detroit and Michilimackinac into immensely profitable entrepôts for British goods. In that polite but arrogant style that is a British trademark, Amherst ignored
Malcolm. He also ignored his own Indian superintendent, William Johnson, who backed Malcolm with growing desperation.

To some extent, General Amherst was only obeying
orders. His superiors in London were determined to reduce the expenses of running this vast empire they had
acquired and the Indian departments offered an irresistible opportunity to cut and slash. Soon from British
army headquarters came the announcement that, henceforth, if any Indian wanted a musket or a blanket or cloth
for his wife, he would have to pay for it by exchanging

furs of the proper value—or coin of the realm. Robert Foster Nicolls backed by two British regiments announced the policy at Detroit and Michilimackinac.

A profoundly anxious Malcolm returned to Clara's village with a cargo of guns, gunpowder, more blankets and cloth, and a box of jewelry which he purchased on his own account, sending the bill to me. He was trying to create an island of loyalty on which Clara could live in safety.

It was not to be. Clara and her people at Shining Creek were grateful for Malcolm's generosity and they welcomed him back into their midst as an adopted member of their tribe. But the impact of England's mean-spirited policy flooded into their village from all sides. First came war belts of red wampum from the Senecas closer to Niagara. They had often been loyal to the French. The messengers carrying the belts told how the British had declared the end of presents and brotherhood and mutual respect. The Indians were to be reduced to mere buyers and sellers—and eventually to beggars.

The Niagara Senecas said a great chief had arisen among the Ottawas at Detroit, named Pontiac. He was calling on all the Indians to form a union against the white man. Then came messengers from the Shawnees and other tribes who lived in the Ohio country, telling of a terrible drought and the failure of their crops. When starving Indians had sought food and medicine at the fort on the forks of the Ohio River, the British commander had turned them away.

"You knew about this policy?" Clara asked Malcolm, in the rear of the Bear Clan longhouse that night.

"I . . . I feared it. I heard something about it."

"You *knew*?" Clara said, insisting on the truth.

"Yes. But this village has nothing to fear. You'll never be in want. Catalyntie has plenty of money. We'll supply you with everything you need."

He was thinking like a white man again. "This village

doesn't exist on the moon,'' Clara said. ''We're blood relations of all the Senecas. Do you think Grey Owl's supporters aren't talking to their brothers and sisters and sons and nephews in the longhouses, telling them he was right from the start—that you're a liar and a seducer? Do you think they've forgotten those twenty-five dead warriors who went with you to the St. Francis River and never came back? Their ghosts are still calling for your scalp.''

She was right, of course. Malcolm was dismayed to see how many warriors shunned him in the next few days. Others listened to his assurances of perpetual support and turned away. One said: ''Do you think we're women, to be bought and sold? Have you forgotten what we taught you when you became a Seneca? All the Senecas, in their different villages, are one people, descendants of the same parents long long ago.''

A week later Grey Owl arrived, accompanied by a prophet from the Ohio country, Neolin. He was a tall gaunt old man, a Shawnee chief who said he had received a vision from the Manitou. The Indians must change their ways. They must abandon the white man's guns and kettles and cloth. They should wear skins and furs of their animal brothers once more and rely on their bows and arrows to hunt them. They must cease killing so many animals for furs and take only those they needed to sustain life. They must drink no more of the white man's rum, which made them kill each other in drunken frenzies. If they obeyed these commands from the Manitou, they would regain their ancient strength and pride and drive the white men out of their country forever.

Neolin preached this message with tremendous authority around a council fire in the village street. Grey Owl added words of approval. ''This man is a greater prophet than I am. He has seen into the heart of the

Manitou. He has taken my message and transformed it into a vision of glory!''

Malcolm stepped out of the group of sitting warriors and responded to Neolin and Grey Owl. ''I speak as an adopted Seneca warrior, a title I consider the proudest I shall ever wear. I do not claim to have a vision of the Manitou. But I have a heart full of love for the Seneca people. Time is like a swift river. You cannot paddle against the current. Even the Manitou cannot make the river flow backward. The white men have settled many leagues of this land. The Seneca and the other Indians must learn to live with them. We must be strong and patient and firm and force the English to treat with us. My own people, the Americans, must learn to do the same thing.''

Grey Owl leaped up and whispered in Neolin's ear. ''Grey Owl asks me to look in this man's eyes and tell you what I see,'' Neolin said.

He stared at Malcolm for a long solemn moment. ''I see the face of the Evil One,'' he said. ''He has taken this man's form to lead you to destruction. He has already cost you many warriors. Why do you listen to him? Drive him from your midst. If he does not go, kill him.''

A murmur of angry assent rose from many throats. Red Hawk's mother strode to the edge of the fire. ''He destroyed my son and my husband with his magic. Why don't we kill him now?'' she cried.

Clara rose to her feet. ''If you kill him, you'll have to kill me too,'' she said.

''She lies,'' Grey Owl said. ''The white men have pardoned her for her services. She has opened her cunt to hundreds of them. They want her back for a thousand more of her wonderful fucks.''

At another time or place, Malcolm would have killed Grey Owl for saying that. But in a Seneca council, everyone was free to speak without fear of retaliation.

Malcolm had to content himself with saying: "Grey Owl's tongue is rotten with lies."

"No, white man," Neolin said. "It is your tongue that is rotten. Your stench sickens my belly." He turned to other villagers. "All along the Ohio and the lakes, the war drums are beating. Your brothers, the Senecas of Niagara, have responded with red war belts. Will the people of Shining Creek be known as the old women, the cowards, of the Seneca nation? I hope not."

The prophet stalked into the forest, followed by Grey Owl and his escort of two dozen warriors. The village council exploded into discord. Dozens of people rose to urge the banishment of Standing Bear. Red Hawk's mother reiterated her demand that Malcolm be seized and tortured at the stake. She was in a minority but the voices in favor of banishment were clearly in the majority.

Clara said nothing. She was in her mother's dream again, watching the island dwindle to a spit of mud, while the falls roared their message of oblivion in her ears. Neolin was another Caesar, lost in a fantasy of impossible hope, preaching hatred as a nostrum. Evil could fester in the forest as readily as in the cities. Malcolm was right, of course, time could not be reversed, but he refused to see what time was doing to the Indians, with its relentless flow.

In the longhouse of the Bear Clan, Clara fled to the rear corner and dropped on her knees before the statue of the Virgin. Again, she begged her to speak, to tell her what she should say or do to alter the doom that was descending on them. Malcolm stayed outside, arguing stubbornly with a half dozen warriors who were urging him to go in peace. She could hear his angry voice, refusing to leave, daring them to kill him.

Suddenly the Virgin began to speak in Clara's soul.

You are bathed in my tears, O daughter of the morning. I do not understand any more than my son the inner

darkness of the Manitou, the great god, whom we call
Father. Be consoled by this promise. Your love will
never die. It is in your beloved's heart forever. It will
pass down the generations through his sons and their
sons and daughters like a river winding slowly to a vast
sea where love and hate, sorrow and joy, hope and de-
spair will be reconciled at last.

Clara stretched her arms in the form of a cross. She
felt waves of warmth beating against her body. The Virgin's face was aglow with light from beyond the stars.
Clara did not know how long she knelt there, suspended
between heaven and earth, filled with a sweetness that
transcended anything she had ever known in Malcolm's
arms.

Suddenly a Seneca woman's voice was whispering
anxiously behind her. "They've sent me to tell you. Do
not sleep in the longhouse beside Standing Bear tonight.
He refuses to leave the village. They are coming to kill
him with knives and hatchets."

The roar of the great falls filled Clara's soul. She
thanked the woman and told her she would try to persuade Standing Bear to leave the village. In a few
minutes she heard Malcolm's heavy footsteps. Clara lit
a candle and gestured him down beside her. "You must
go. They'll do nothing to me. You must go back to Catalyntie before this war starts. No white man will be safe
anywhere beyond the Mohawk."

"I won't go without you," he said.

"I won't go *with* you. How many times must I say
it?"

"Clara—"

"Hold me. Hold me and listen to what I'm saying.
You must go now for the sake of your sons. Bring our
love to them as your gift. Bring it to Catalyntie as a
reward for the love, bitter but no less true, she's offered
both of us."

"I can't do it."

"Yes you can. It will come slowly, painfully out of your heart, as the memory of our love ripens in your mind, as you remember its hopes and dreams, its joy and sorrow. If you do it well, it will never die. It will flow through the years, a great growing river. I promise you it will happen exactly as I say."

"I have no faith in such a thing," he said. "If I go, I'll spend the rest of my life condemning myself as a coward."

Clara saw how hopeless it was to reconcile his warrior soul and the voice of the woman who spoke within her. The Virgin spoke for a god of peace, for the Master of Life, who flowered once in the body of her son. Malcolm only understood a god of war. With a sigh she abandoned the struggle. The great falls thundered in her soul. She knew what she must do.

She said nothing to him about the assassins who would soon invade the longhouse of the Bear Clan. Instead, she kissed him and they made sad tender love one more time. When he finally slept beside her, with deep mournful breaths, she rose and knelt before the Virgin for a long time, worshipping silently, not seeking a voice, simply rejoicing in the words she had heard.

She lay down again beside Malcolm and waited. At last she heard small noises as the assassins crept past others who were pretending to sleep. A moment later they loomed in the darkness—at least three of them. With wild yells they sprang forward. Clara flung herself on top of Malcolm as the knives descended. Into her flesh the blades plunged, with amazingly little pain. But she screamed as if she were in agony, throwing them into confusion.

Malcolm flung Clara aside and seized a lacrosse stick off the longhouse wall. With a half dozen ferocious swings, he demolished the demoralized would-be killers. They fled with broken arms and jaws and noses, while uproar consumed the longhouse.

"A light. A candle," Malcolm cried.

A woman offered one with a trembling hand. He looked down on Clara's blood-soaked body. She was bleeding from a half-dozen wounds. "No!" Malcolm cried, sinking to his knees beside her.

"Don't weep. And don't seek revenge," Clara said. "Go home to Catalyntie. You belong to her now."

"No!" Malcolm cried again.

"Promise me—"

A tremendous roaring filled Clara's body and mind. The great falls opened its billowing arms to embrace her. She slipped away from Malcolm's grasp into the mist of eternity.

Two weeks later, when Malcolm appeared at Great Rock Farm, I saw calamity on his haggard face. I thought it was caused by the upheaval that was shaking America's frontiers. From Detroit to the forks of the Ohio, the Indians had risen to massacre British garrisons and white settlers in a blazing swath a thousand miles long. Among the dead was Robert Foster Nicolls. Ottawa and Seneca warriors had dragged him from his trading house outside the fort at Detroit and burned him at the stake.

"Thank God you're alive," I said.

Malcolm stumbled past me into the parlor, where our son Hugh was reading a New York newspaper that denounced the British and the Indians with equal fervor. Malcolm patted him listlessly on the shoulder and treated little Paul no better when he ran to him. Hugh asked Malcolm if he was going to recruit a regiment and march against the Indians. Malcolm shook his head. "I can't fight my own people," he said.

I sent the boys to their rooms and brought Malcolm a cup of strong tea. He waved it aside and told me what had happened in the longhouse of the Bear Clan. My heart dwindled to a speck of dust. I could never match Clara's love now. I was sure Malcolm loathed the sight of me. If I had not been at Great Rock Farm demanding my due as a wife, Clara might have been willing to leave Shining Creek.

Words sprang to my lips, words I had never dared to speak before. I realized as I spoke them that they also belonged to Clara. "Remember the morning we met, how beautiful it was? The sun on the green meadow and the trees in bud? I loved you then with my whole heart. But I didn't speak because I was afraid Clara would claim you first. Let's go back to that morning and begin again, the two of us, let's love each other without fear or doubt for the years we have left—"

Malcolm stared numbly at me. I might have been speaking Dutch or German or Chinese. Then something marvelous—perhaps even miraculous—began to happen. Within my voice, blended like the diapasons of a hymn, Malcolm heard Clara's voice. He saw Clara's love in my eyes. Tears streaked his hollow cheeks. He opened his arms to me.

A few months later, the great Indian uprising ended in an armed truce. Prophets like Grey Owl and Neolin, war chiefs like Pontiac, died in the fighting or lost face when it became apparent that the white men were too numerous to defeat and the Indians could not survive without white trade goods. The chastened British promised to restore the annual presents to the Iroquois and other tribes—and secretly vowed to get the money out of the Americans' pockets.

Since those days of tears and sorrow, Malcolm and I have struggled to love each other without blame or regret, anger or reproach. We have failed at times, as too such different hearts must. Those close to us, including our sons, saw little change in our everyday selves. But we knew love had conquered our hearts in Clara's name and would never leave us.

As I write the final words of this story of America's morning that memory has compelled me to tell, I feel Clara's hand on my pen, her lips against my cheek. The story is her testament and mine, proof—I hope—that love can transcend history's agony and endure within the recesses of the heart.

AFTERWORD

THIS IS THE SIXTH IN a series of narratives from the archives of the Stapleton family. The earlier volumes are *Liberty Tavern* and *Dreams of Glory*, which tell the story of the Stapletons in the era of the American Revolution, *The Spoils of War*, which describes their odyssey in the era of the Civil War, and *Rulers of the City* and *Promises to Keep*, which concern the modern Stapletons. Although all these books have dealt frankly with the past, *Remember the Morning* is by far the most controversial. Some members of the Stapleton family objected to its publication. But they were persuaded by other members that it was too important to omit from the series.

Apparently, Catalyntie Van Vorst Stapleton gave the finished manuscript to Harman Bogardus, pastor of the Dutch Reformed Church in Hackensack, with orders that it be held in the church's archives until she and her husband and their two sons died. Thereafter it was to be handed over to their descendants, who were at liberty to do whatever they chose with it. These grandchildren placed it in the vault of a local bank and forgot about it. There is little evidence that anyone ever read it. Future-minded like most Americans, each generation of Stapletons has tended to regard their predecessors as quaint relics of an irrelevant past.

The research and editing required to prepare this and

the other manuscripts for publication have been funded by the Principia Foundation, set up by the late Paul Stapleton to deepen the historical consciousness of his descendants—and other Americans who share with them the voyage of the American nation into the uncertain future.

James Kilpatrick
President
The Principia Foundation

AND LOOK FOR

THE WAGES OF FAME

NOW AVAILABLE IN HARDOVER

TWELVE

AMERICANS WANT TO BE POWERFUL—AND good. Only a few of us understand we can't be both things. Caroline lay in the canopied bed where she had expected to embrace a triumphant George Stapleton, listening to Aaron Burr's mordant wisdom. In the morning, without even five minutes of sleep, she arose and faced a haggard husband at the breakfast table. If there was any comfort in their joint insomnia, it was as cold as the weather outside. The rain had turned to sleet overnight, coating trees and buildings with an icy glaze.

"There's no hope of changing your mind about Mexico?"

George's face froze into a mask of antagonism. He shook his big head. She shoved aside her coffee cup and told Mercy to order the chaise brought to the front door.

"Where are you going?"

"To the White House."

She dressed in black, as if she were in mourning. In a way, she was. She was mourning the death of her dream of fame—and the death of her dream of love for her husband. Would she also have to face the death of another love? What should she tell Sarah Polk about George's revolt?

Rolling through the empty ice-glazed streets, Caroline almost hoped the skittish mare that Judson Diggs had chosen for the chaise would stumble or run wild. A fatal accident would be the simplest solution to her dilemma. She composed an obituary in her head: *Mrs. Stapleton's salon at her 3600 Pennsylvania Avenue home has been one of the adornments of Washington . . .*

''Mornin', Miz Stapleton.''

She was at the South Portico of the White House. The smiling Negro porter, Ezekiel, was calming the jumpy horse. The ice glistening on surrounding trees made the place look like a mansion in a fairy tale—or a Gothic horror novel.

Upstairs, a maid said Mrs. Polk was in her study. Sarah was also in black. She was performing her daily ritual of reading the latest newspapers from New York, Boston, Chicago, and other cities, crowded with the usual sneers against President James Knox Polk.

They exchanged a kiss and Sarah sank into her chair again. ''Wait until you hear the latest news from Mexico,'' she said. ''General Scott has court-martialed General Worth and General Pillow. The president and I were up until three A.M. drafting a letter that reprimands everyone.''

How could she tell this exhausted woman more bad news? But it had to be done. ''George arrived from Mexico last night. He intends to take his seat in the Senate and support the treaty without reservations.''

''Is that all you have to tell me?''

Caroline struggled fiercely to suppress her tears. Today if ever she must not, she could not, be weak. But the tears remorselessly trickled down her cheeks. ''I don't want to burden you with my—my pain.''

''When two people love each other, the word *burden* loses its meaning.''

"If I told you everything, you—might despise me. It would be the end of our love."

"Try me."

"It concerns an immoral act, a sin—"

Caroline stopped in utter confusion, unable to believe that she had said that last word. Sins were only committed by believers in God. Was she trying to anticipate what Sarah would call it?

"Dearest, we're all sinners in God's eyes. Surely you must know that every day I've spent in this house, I've faced my sin—my domineering pride—which has destroyed a good man's love and may yet destroy his life."

There were tears on Sarah's face now. She wiped them away with the back of her hand, a gesture that somehow underscored her fierce determination to persevere in spite of the way her dream of fame had become a nightmare.

A wild hope that love would understand, that love would forgive, seized Caroline's soul. Wordlessly, she took Jeremy Biddle's letter from her purse and handed it to Sarah Childress Polk.

Caroline watched disbelief, then dismay, then revulsion, play across Sarah's face. She slumped in her chair as if someone had struck her a savage blow. "It makes me wish that there was no such thing as a woman."

"But there is," Caroline said. "There always will be."

"There isn't a word of truth in what he says about you and Sladen—since?"

"None," Caroline said.

"Has Sladen behaved honorably toward you?"

"Not always. But I've tried to forgive him. Men are tormented by dreams of mythical desire. Men like him, at any rate. With souls full of rage."

Sarah nodded. How much they had learned since they walked down Pennsylvania Avenue on that summer morning in 1827, twenty-one years ago. "Should we abandon All-Mexico?" Sarah asked.

"By no means. What George said to me last night has severed all and every bond of love, of loyalty between us. In a curious way, I feel desolated—but free."

"I know what you mean," Sarah said in a low, musing voice.

She was confessing what she had hinted more than once—that her marriage with James Polk was as dead as Caroline's with George Stapleton. Had James snarled atrocious insults at her between midnight and dawn when he faced the truth about his floundering presidency?

"We should proceed with our plan," Caroline said. "The treaty should go to the Senate with a noncommittal message from the president. Senator Sladen and his friends will understand that they have your permission to destroy it."

Sarah nodded. It was still a good plan.

"This will become very ugly before it's over," Caroline said. "There's another woman involved."

She told her about George's affair with Maria Pena de Vega. "John Sladen will use it to vilify George in the newspapers. You may want to use it yourself."

"I'm not sure I could go even that far." .

"You must be prepared to do the *worst*. Don't allow sympathy for me to influence you. I'm prepared to be despised if George sees fit to defend himself with this abominable letter."

"I've never been more certain of our course," Sarah said. "Everything I read in the mail and in the newspapers from the South convinces me that All-Mexico is the only alternative to the collapse of the Union. The abolitionists have unhinged every politician south of Virginia."

"George seems to think he can find a middle ground where Democrats can rally. I told him he's dreaming."

They were like priestesses in a secret religion, chanting exhortations to each other. For a soaring moment Caroline felt a thrill of pride, even of exultation. They were no longer mere acolytes in the Temple of Fame. They were mistresses of the establishment.

"I'll go see Sladen now," Caroline said.

Out on Pennsylvania Avenue, the bitter wind pummeled Caroline's face. Tree limbs were down everywhere. Slaves, many of them wearing nothing but thin cotton shirts, were hauling the debris to the curbs.

Soon she was knocking on the front door of John Sladen's rooming house. It opened to emit a redhaired woman who had slattern written all over her. She shivered in the icy blast whirling down the street and clutched a shawl around her.

"Seen any hacks?"

"No," Caroline said.

Inside, a fat Negro maid said Senator Sladen had not come down to breakfast. Caroline climbed a stairway that reeked of whiskey and cigars and knocked on the senator's door. He admitted her, pulling a soiled blue bathrobe around his spare frame.

"I'm here on a political errand," Caroline said.

She told him about the peace treaty and George's support of it—in spite of the president's opposition. She described Jeremy Biddle's letter, but she did not show it to him. Her voice was as matter-of-fact and empty as her heart.

"I'm going to shoot that son of a bitch!" John raged.

"Stop acting like a Southern idiot and start thinking like the intelligent man I hope you still are," Caroline said. You've got the president's backing to destroy this treaty. That will leave us with All-Mexico as the only alternative. With proper handling, it will revive the party and guarantee that the next president will be a Democrat."

"But that Democrat won't be George?"

"No."

"Will you continue to live with him?"

"I suppose so. Our house is big enough to avoid each other most of the time."

"What if I became the Democratic candidate for president?"

"I'd vote for you."

"Is that all you'd do?"

She gazed into Senator Sladen's unshaven face. The man's soul had been shrinking before her eyes all these years, but she had never realized it so graphically until this moment.

"That is all I'd do, John."

"I may still try for it."

"Good luck. The president will wait for word from you before sending in the treaty."

"I understand."

"Rise to the occasion, John. Restrain your impulse to be snide. Speak like a statesman—an American statesman."

"You don't really think I'm one, do you."

You can take the boy out of the gutter, but you can't take the gutter out of the boy. She almost said those appalling words. She drove them from her tongue by an act of the will.

"I want you to be one—perhaps for my sake. I'll love that part of you."

"It will be your creation. Like all the rest of me."

He lunged toward her in a blundering attempt at a kiss. She blocked him with her forearm and sent him stumbling back. "No, John. *No.*"

Down the fetid stairs to the freezing street Caroline went. She welcomed the savage cold. It could not begin to match the winter in her heart. But the icy gale was a tolerable companion. Summer would be the really difficult time. What would she do when the earth opened its warm mouth to the winds of June?

She would worry about that in June. Now, in the midst of winter, she had a country to save. The future of Caroline Kemble Stapleton's soul was irrelevant.